Irish author **Abby Green** ended a very glamorous career in film and TV—which really consisted of a lot of standing in the rain outside actors' trailers—to pursue her love of romance. After she'd bombarded Mills & Boon with manuscripts they kindly accepted one, and an author was born. She lives in Dublin, Ireland, and loves any excuse for distraction. Visit abby-green.com or email abbygreenauthor@gmail.com.

Canadian **Dani Collins** knew in high school that she wanted to write romance for a living. Twenty-five years later, after marrying her high school sweetheart, having two kids with him, working at several generic office jobs and submitting countless manuscripts, she got The Call. Her first Mills & Boon novel won the Reviewers' Choice Award for Best First in Series from *RT Book Reviews*. She now works in her own office, writing romance.

THE GREEK'S UNKNOWN BRIDE

ABBY GREEN

A HIDDEN HEIR TO REDEEM HIM

DANI COLLINS

MIX
Paper from
responsible sources

FSC

FSC C007454

This book is produced from independently certified FSC
to ensure responsible forest management
For more information visit www.harpercollins.co.uk/green

Printed and bound in Spain

MILLS & BOON

First Published in Great Britain 2020
by Mills & Boon, an imprint of HarperCollins*Publishers*
1 London Bridge Street, London, SE1 9GF

The Greek's Unknown Bride © 2020 by Abby Green

A Hidden Heir to Redeem Him © 2020 by Dani Collins

ISBN: 978-0-263-27815-6

paper

en.

THE GREEK'S UNKNOWN BRIDE

ABBY GREEN

This is for Orwell, my fluffy little shadow,
who enriches my life and provides vital moral support
when I'm banging my head off the keyboard.
Even if he is on his back, paws in the air,
snoring softly.

CHAPTER ONE

APOLLO VASILIS STARED out of the window at the ornamental lake set in lush grounds. Athens lay under a hazy smog in the distance, and the sea was a barely perceptible line on the horizon. But he noticed none of that. His arms were folded tightly across his chest and tension wound like a vice inside his body. A tension he'd been feeling for months now. Three months, to be precise.

There was a faint rhythmic *beep-beep* coming from behind him and suddenly it changed. Skipped a beat, and became slightly faster. Heart rate increasing. *She was waking up.* Finally.

He turned around. A woman lay on a raised bed. She was as pale as the sheets underneath her. Rose-gold hair spread around her head. There was a gauze dressing on her forehead, over her right eye.

There were bandages around one arm. A scratch down her left cheek. All in all, minor cuts and bruises. A miracle, considering the car that she'd been driving was at the bottom of a narrow ravine about one hundred metres deep, a charred mass of black twisted metal.

He moved closer to the bed. Her almost blonde lashes were so long they cast faint shadows on her cheeks. Her brows were darker, finely etched. He frowned. Her face looked...thinner. The bones of her cheeks were standing out more prominently than he seemed to remember.

But then...looking at this woman in any kind of forensic detail was not something he'd done lately.

Not since he'd looked at her as if he'd never seen a
woman before. Four months ago, when they'd first met.
When her naked body had filled his vision and made his
blood roar so loudly it had deafened him.

He could still see her body now as if the image had
been burned onto his brain. The small but perfectly formed
breasts. Flat belly, gently curved hips. The cluster of tight
reddish curls at the apex of her legs. Slender limbs. She'd
looked so delicate and yet when he'd joined his body to
hers, he'd felt the innate steely strength of her and it had
been the most erotic experience of his life.

To Apollo's surprise and consternation, a heat he hadn't
felt in months flooded his veins. He rejected it utterly. This
woman had deceived him in the worst way possible.

He despised her.

At that same moment that her eyelids fluttered, the door
opened and the doctor and a couple of nurses entered. The
female doctor looked at Apollo. 'I need to remind you not
to expect too much at first. The extent of the injury to her
head can only really be ascertained once she regains consciousness.'

Apollo nodded curtly, and watched as they tended to
the machines around the bed. The doctor sat down beside
the woman and took her hand. 'My dear, can you hear me?
Can you open your eyes for me?'

Apollo could see movement behind the delicate eyelids. For a second he found himself holding his breath as
her eyelids fluttered again. As if, for a moment, he'd forgotten, and a small part of him actually *cared* if his wife
woke up or not.

She could hear the voice coming from far away. It was like
a buzzing bee, distracting her, tugging her away from the
lovely cloak of darkness surrounding her in blissful silence and peace.

A pressure, on her hand. The voice. Louder now. She couldn't make out words, just intonation. *Mmm. Mmm!*

She tried to swat away the pressure but it only got stronger. A brightness was pricking at her eyes, pushing away the darkness. Her head felt so thick…fuzzy. Heavy.

And then, as if a curtain had been pulled back, very clearly she heard a sharp voice. 'Mrs Vasilis, it's time to wake up.'

For a second she lamented leaving the peaceful darkness behind but she knew she had no choice but to follow the voice. She understood the words but they didn't make much sense to her… *Mrs…?*

She opened her eyes and light exploded onto her retinas, making her shut them tightly again. She became aware that she was lying in a bed. She could sense the flurry of activity around her. And also, disturbingly, the fact that in that split second she'd noticed a tall dark shape looming at the end of the bed.

A shape that was familiar and made her heart pound for no reason she could understand.

'Mrs Vasilis, can you try opening your eyes again? We've lowered the blinds to make it easier.'

Experimentally, she cracked her eyes open again and this time it didn't hurt so much. The face of a woman she didn't know came into focus. There were a couple of other women, also strangers. They all had dark hair and dark eyes. There was a humming noise and rhythmic beeping of machines. White everywhere. Antiseptic smell.

A word popped into her mind: *hospital.*

There was movement in her peripheral vision and she looked towards the end of the bed. The tall dark shape was a man. She knew him. 'A-A…' Her voice cracked like rust. She tried again. 'Apollo?'

'That's good.'

She barely noticed the relief evident in the doctor's voice

as she took in the man at the end of the bed. He wore a dark long-sleeved top. Round neck. Soft material. Broad shoulders and chest. Powerful. But not overly muscular. Lean.

Short dark hair. Strong masculine features. Deep-set eyes. *Green eyes.* She knew this, even though she couldn't see their colour properly from here. Strong jaw. Stubble. Firm mouth. *Hot, on hers.* A shiver went through her. She'd been kissed by this man.

She felt her hand being pressed. The doctor's voice. 'You know who this man is?'

It was hard for her to tear her gaze away from him, as if she was afraid he might disappear. She nodded. 'Yes…we just met, the other night. At a function.' He frowned slightly, but she barely noticed as heat crept into her cheeks, remembering seeing him for the first time. How he'd stopped her in her tracks with his breath-taking beauty and charisma, wearing a tuxedo that had been moulded to his powerful body like a second skin.

He'd looked bored. People had hovered around him but at a distance as if too intimidated to get close.

And then their eyes had met and… *Bam!* Her heart had somersaulted in her chest and she'd never been the same since…

Slowly it was sinking in that she was in a hospital. But what was she doing here? With a man she barely knew?

But you do know him. Intimately.

She felt it in her bones, like a deep knowing. But *how* did she know this if she'd only just met him? She tried to latch onto the question to find the answer but it skittered out of her grasp.

Confusion clouded her brain and for the first time she had a sense that something was very wrong. A tendril of fear…or panic…coiled in her belly. She looked at the doctor. 'What's happening? Why am I here?'

As she said the word *I*, she stopped. *I.* Nothing. Blank.

A void. The fear grew. 'Wait... I don't know...who I am... Who am I?'

Then something popped into her head. The doctor had called her... 'You said Mrs Vasilis...'

The doctor looked at her with an expression that was hard to decipher. 'Because you are Mrs Vasilis. Sasha Vasilis.'

Sasha. It felt wrong. Not her. 'I don't think that's my name.'

'What is your name?'

Blank. Nothing. Frustration.

The doctor spoke again. Soothingly. 'Sasha. Your name is Sasha and you are married to this man, Apollo Vasilis.'

She looked at the man again. He was definitely frowning now and he didn't look particularly happy to be married to her. She shook her head briefly but it caused a sharp pain over her eye. She stopped. 'But that can't be possible, we just met.'

So, if you just met, how can you know him intimately? How can you be married?

A headache was forming, right between her eyes. A dull throb. As if sensing this, the doctor said briskly, 'That's enough for now, she needs to rest. We can come back later.'

A nurse stepped forward and did something to a drip beside the bed. Soon that comforting blackness was enveloping her in its warm embrace again and she eagerly shut out the growing panic and fear, and disturbing questions. And *him*, the most disturbing thing of all, and she wasn't even sure why.

Two days later

'We think your memory loss came from the traumatic experience of the crash. There's no perceptible or obvious injury to your brain that we can see after the scans we did, but you can only remember meeting your husband for the first time and nothing else. Nothing from before or after. Sometimes the brain does this as a form of protection when an event occurs. We've no reason not to believe that in time your memory will return. It could come in small pieces, like a jigsaw coming together, or it could happen all at once.'

Or it might not happen at all?

She was too scared to voice that out loud.

'Which is why...' here the doctor looked expressively at Apollo Vasilis, who was a forbidding presence as he stood by the window with his arms folded '...you need to be monitored closely while you recuperate.'

The doctor looked back at Sasha, who still didn't feel like a *Sasha*. 'Don't worry too much about trying to make your memory come back. You need to focus on recovering from your injuries. I'm sure everything will return to full functionality.'

Sasha wondered what her brain was protecting her from.

The doctor stood up. 'You can go home now. We'll keep in touch to monitor your progress and let us know as soon as you start to remember anything.'

That felt like a very dim and distant possibility. Her brain still felt as if it was just a dense mass of grey fog. Impossible to penetrate. And where was *home*? The doctor had told her she was English, so presumably she'd been born and brought up there.

When she'd enquired about family, her husband had told her that her parents were dead and she had no siblings. Just like that. Stark and unvarnished. She'd felt an ache in her chest near her heart but when she couldn't put names or faces to her parents it was hard to feel profound grief.

The doctor left now and Sasha looked at Apollo Vasilis. Her husband. He looked as grim as he had when she'd regained consciousness. Wasn't he pleased she'd survived the accident? He wore a three-piece suit today, steel grey, with a tie. He oozed urbane sophistication but Sasha sensed the tightly wound energy in his body. As if he was ready to cast off the trappings of civility to reveal a much more elemental man underneath.

Ironically, the one memory she did have, of the night they'd met, she remembered him smiling. Laughing even. His face transformed from breath-taking to devastatingly gorgeous. She remembered his voice. Deep and accented.

Except she'd been told that that night had been four months ago. And since then they'd been married. And she'd apparently moved to Greece from England. It was all too huge to absorb and Sasha found herself avoiding thinking about it too much.

'Are you ready? The car is waiting outside.'

Was she ready? To leave here with a man who was little more than a stranger to her? In a foreign land she had no memory of coming to? But she nodded once, briefly, and stood up, her limbs still feeling a little weak.

Apollo picked up a bag. He'd brought her clothes to change into and they only compounded her sense of disorientation because she couldn't imagine choosing clothes like this. Flared cream-coloured silk trousers with slits up each side, a matching silk singlet top and a cropped blazer jacket. Spindly high-heel sandals that made her feel even more wobbly.

He opened the door and stood back. Sasha locked her limbs and walked out of the room with as much grace as she could muster.

Apollo walked down the corridor beside his wife. She was walking slowly, as if she'd never worn high heels before, with all the grace of a spindly-legged foal. Which was bizarre because the only time he could recall ever seeing her in flat shoes had been when they'd met that first night.

She stumbled a little and he took her elbow to steady her. She glanced up at him, her cheeks a little pink. 'Thank you.'

Her hair was down around her shoulders in soft natural waves that he knew she usually preferred to be straightened.

'It's nothing.' He gritted his jaw at his body's reaction to the feel of her arm under his hand, her slender body brushing against his ever so slightly. She wasn't wearing the scent she usually did. He'd watched her take it out of the bag earlier and she'd tested it on her wrist, immediately scrunching up her nose. She'd looked at him. 'This is my perfume?'

He'd nodded. Privately he'd always had the same reaction when he'd smelled it. To recoil. It was too overpowering. Sickly sweet. She'd put it back without spraying any.

But now all he could smell was *her*. Soap and something uniquely and mysteriously feminine. Her scent reminded him uncomfortably *again* of meeting her for the first time when he'd been blown away by her fresh-faced beauty. Her impact on him had been like a punch to his solar plexus, driving the breath out of his lungs.

And to this day he couldn't figure it out. He'd seen plenty of women who were more beautiful than Sasha. Slept with them too. But something about her, from the moment he'd laid eyes on her, had got to him. Captivating him. As much as he hated to admit it.

She'd seduced him with her wide-eyed act of innocence, and had then trapped him with the oldest trick in the book. The burn of that transgression and the burn of his momentary weakness for her was like permanent bile in his gut.

His desire for her had dissipated as quickly as it had blown up, and he'd welcomed it, in light of her betrayal, but now it was back, as if to mock him for ever believing he'd had it under his control.

She was playing him all over again but this time he wouldn't stand for it.

Sasha winced as Apollo's fingers tightened almost painfully on her arm. She tried to pull away and he looked at her. 'I'm okay now, you can let go.'

Instantly his expression blanked and he took his hand away, saying smoothly, 'My car is here, just outside the door.'

Sasha saw a sleek silver SUV waiting for them, with a driver holding the open back door. It reinforced her sense of being in an alternate dimension where nothing made much sense.

She stepped out of the hospital and gulped in fresh air, hoping that might make her feel more grounded. The Greek sun was warm but the early summer air wasn't too humid yet.

Sasha climbed into the car. Her shoes were pinching painfully after only walking a few feet. She couldn't believe that she wore this kind of shoe on a regular basis.

Or... She slid a look at Apollo, as he got into the back of the car on the other side, *maybe Apollo liked them and she wore them to please him?*

That thought sent another shiver through her. The thought of pleasing him. Except, if the frosty vibes were anything to go by, he wasn't pleased and she had no idea why.

The car pulled away from the hospital and Apollo exchanged a few words in Greek with the driver, who then put up the privacy partition. Sasha was so aware of him it was as if an outer layer of skin had been removed.

A hand rested on one thigh. Square, masculine. Long fingers. Blunt nails. His suit looked as if it had been made specifically to hug his muscles and emphasise his powerful physique. He looked at her and she didn't have time to pretend she wasn't ogling him.

'Okay?'

She nodded. It was a civil question but the tension was

palpable. Instead of asking a question she wasn't sure she wanted the answer to, she asked, 'Where are we going now?'

'The villa. It's not far from here.'

'Have I lived there long?'

'For the past three months, since we married.'

'Where did we marry?' It suddenly struck Sasha at that moment that, if not for the fact that this man had turned up to claim her after the accident, when apparently she'd been found wandering by the road in a disorientated state a day and night after being reported missing, he could be anyone.

He looked at her for such a long and assessing moment that she could feel heat creeping back into her cheeks but then he plucked a small sleek phone out of his pocket and tapped the screen and handed it to her. 'We married in Athens in a civil ceremony.'

She looked at the screen of the phone. On it was a link to an official press release announcing their marriage with an accompanying picture. Sasha enlarged it. It was her. But it didn't feel like her. She wore a knee-length floaty silk sleeveless dress, cut on the bias and slashed almost to the navel. Eye-wateringly high heels. Her hair was teased into big curls and she seemed to be wearing a lot of make-up. Gold jewellery. An enormous-looking diamond ring. She felt a rush of exposure and embarrassment when she looked at the picture. And then she looked down at her bare fingers. 'Did I have rings?'

'Yes. The doctors said you must have lost them in the accident.'

She looked at Apollo. 'I hope they weren't too valuable.'

He gave her a funny look. 'Don't worry, they were insured.'

Sasha looked back at the picture on the phone. She was clutching Apollo's arm and beaming; however, her new husband looked anything but happy in the picture. The memory she had of him smiling had to be a figment of her imagination. A conjured-up image.

She skimmed the press release.

Apollo Vasilis, Greek construction tycoon, weds his English girlfriend Sasha Miller in a private civil ceremony.

The bare minimum of information. Sasha handed the phone back, feeling even more disorientated. A million questions buzzed in her head but she could feel a headache starting and the doctor had told her not to overdo things.

She looked out the window and saw glimpses of huge houses set in verdant grounds behind tall wrought-iron gates or massive walls. Clearly this was a wealthy area.

Before long the car turned in towards a massive pair of wrought-iron gates. They opened mechanically and a man in little security hut outside waved them in after a few words with the driver.

Sasha stared out the window in awe as lush grounds opened up around them. The driveway led up to a massive courtyard and a two-storey villa-style house with steps leading up to the front door where a woman in a uniform was waiting.

Apollo got out when the car had stopped at the bottom of the steps and before Sasha could figure out where the handle was, the door was being opened and she saw his large hand extending towards her.

She had no choice but to put her hand in his and her skin prickled with a kind of foreboding, as if her body knew it would react in a certain way and she had no idea what to expect.

Yes, you do.

Her hand touched his and an electric jolt went right through her. Reflexively her fingers curled around his.

Face flaming at her reaction, she let him help her from the car and as soon as she could, she snatched her hand back.

Her reaction to him on top of the fog in her brain was too much. She resolved not to touch him again if she could help it and then that little voice reminded her that they were married.

She stopped at the bottom of the steps at the thought that they must be sharing a room. *A bed.* Her heart seemed to triple its rate. Apollo was almost at the top of the steps. He turned around and she saw a look of something almost like impatience cross his face.

'Sasha?'

She thought furiously as she climbed the steps, taking care in the impractical shoes. Maybe she could suggest they sleep separately until her memory returned? Surely he wouldn't expect her to share his bed when she felt as if she hardly knew him? No matter what her body might be telling her.

At the top of the steps was the older woman in the uniform. She was a stranger to Sasha. And she didn't look welcoming. Dark hair pulled back and a matronly bosom. She seemed to be eyeing Sasha warily, as if waiting for her to do something unexpected.

Sasha stepped forward and held out a hand. 'Hello.' The woman flinched minutely and then she glanced at Apollo and seemed to get some kind of sign because she looked back at Sasha and took her hand, saying in heavily accented Greek, 'Welcome home, Kyria Vasilis.'

Sasha felt a light touch on her back that distracted her from the woman's odd reaction. 'You don't remember Rhea?'

She shook her head, 'I'm so sorry, but no.'

The women let her hand go, eyes widening. Apollo said, 'I'll show my wife around the villa. We'll eat something light in a couple of hours, Rhea. On the smaller terrace.'

The woman nodded and disappeared into the villa. Sasha looked into the massive circular reception area. She felt absolutely sure, at that moment, that she'd never seen these marble floors or set foot in this place before.

Which was wrong. She'd been living here. She obviously couldn't trust her own instincts.

She stepped over the threshold warily, and followed Apollo as he led her into the first of a dizzying array of rooms leading off the circular hall. There was a formal reception room, informal reception room. Formal dining room, informal dining room.

The rooms were all furnished with sumptuous but elegant furniture. Muted colours in varying but complementary shades in each room. It was modern but felt classic. Huge canvases adorned the walls and antiques nestled among more modern artefacts.

Each room had huge French doors that led out to a terrace that ran the length of the house, overlooking the impressive garden. Even more impressive was the view of Athens in the distance.

Sasha walked out of the formal dining room onto the terrace. They were far above the teeming ancient city, the air heavy with the scent of the flowers that climbed the wall of the terrace in colourful profusion. She tried desperately to conjure up a memory of having looked at this view from here before, but her mind stayed blank. Apollo came and stood beside her on the terrace and her skin prickled. Sasha asked, 'Is this an old house?'

'No, I built it on this site.'

Sasha looked at him. '*You* built it?'

His jaw tightened. 'Not me personally. My construction company.'

Sasha turned to face him. 'So…you own a construction company?'

He looked at her and nodded. 'Vasilis Construction.'

Sasha frowned. 'Is it a family business—do you have family?'

An expression flashed across his face so fast she couldn't decipher it but it had looked for a second like pain. 'My family are dead. A long time ago. My father was in construction but he worked for someone else so, no, it's not a family business.'

'I'm sorry to hear your family are gone.' Both their families were dead. 'What happened?'

For a long moment she thought he wouldn't answer and then he said, 'A series of unfortunate events.'

He stepped back. 'Let me show you the rest of the villa.'

Sasha pushed aside her curiosity about *'a series of unfortunate events'* and followed the broad shoulders of her husband as he led her back into the hall and up a majestic flight of stairs. *Villa* seemed like an ineffectual word for what was, clearly, a luxurious mansion.

She wondered what it must have been like to come here with her new husband for the first time. A small voice pointed out that she was getting to relive that experience right now. Except, she wondered, had he been any warmer the first time round?

The villa retained that modern but classic feel throughout. Little touches of period features to give it a sense of timelessness.

In the basement there was a state-of-the-art gym and media room, which could convert into a home cinema. On the same level there was a lap pool and steam and sauna room. Not to mention the extra rooms for massage and treatments that opened out onto a lower-level garden with a couple of sun loungers and a hammock hung between two trees.

Apollo waved a hand towards the gardens, 'There's also an outdoor pool and changing area.'

He showed her his study on the first floor. A very masculine room with walls lined with shelves and books. Across the hall he opened another door and said, 'This is your office.'

She couldn't contain her surprise. 'I had an office?'

He put out a hand and she went in, not sure why she suddenly felt reluctant. The room was pretty but overdone. A plush white carpet and a white desk were the simplest things in the room. There was an expensive-looking computer on the desk.

The walls were covered with flowery chintzy wallpaper and there were framed prints of the covers of glossy magazines on the wall. Lots of shelves that were mainly empty. A handful of books.

A pink velvet chair and matching footstool. It looked as if it hadn't been touched.

'What did I use this for?'

Apollo was leaning against the doorframe, arms folded across his chest, a look of almost disdain on his face. 'You said you wanted to set up a PR business.'

Sasha looked at him. 'Is that what I did? PR?'

He shrugged. 'When we met you were serving drinks at a reception. I don't think your knowledge of PR extended beyond the service end of the industry.'

There was a tone to his voice that Sasha chose to try and figure out later. She followed him up to the second level where the bedrooms were situated. He led her past several guest rooms to the end of the corridor, opening a door. 'This is your room.'

She went in and stopped, turning around. '*My* room?'

'Your room.'

Apollo filled the doorway easily. Sasha's mouth felt dry. She was aware of her feet hurting from the high sandals. And a dull ache at the front of her head.

'We weren't sharing a room?'

Slowly he shook his head. 'No.'

Sasha desperately wanted to know why and he looked as if he expected her to ask that question but for reasons she couldn't understand she didn't want to know. Just yet.

Because this would also, surely, explain his cool and aloof manner. Why the housekeeper had looked at her so warily.

She had a very tenuous grip on reality as it was, and she didn't know if she was prepared to hear more revelations about herself.

So she said nothing and walked into the room. It was luxurious, as she'd come to expect in a very short space of time. Carpet so plush her heels sank right into it. Instinctively, she slipped off the sandals, relishing the relief and the sensation of the soft covering underfoot.

She was aware of the massive bed dressed in cool and pristine-looking linens to her left-hand side but ignored it, not liking the way she was so aware of it.

She carried the sandals in her hand over to where French doors opened out onto a balcony that was big enough to hold a sun lounger and table and chairs. From here she could see that the villa had another wing, one storey high, with a smaller terrace covered over with trellis. The outdoor pool was just beyond this area, surrounded by bougainvillea. There were loungers and a changing area.

The grounds sloped away from here, down the hill, leaving the vista open to Athens and the sea beyond.

The full extent of this sheer luxury sank in. It was overwhelming.

She turned back into the room, blinded for a moment by the sun. When her eyes adjusted again she realised that Apollo was a lot closer than she'd expected.

Immediately her pulse quickened and her skin seemed to get tight and hot all over. The bed loomed large behind him. He looked at her with a strange expression, as if fixated, for a moment. She noticed that he had undone his tie and it hung loose now. His top button was open, revealing the strong column of his throat.

He blinked, and the moment was gone. He stepped back and went to a door in the wall, opening it. 'This is your walk-in closet and the bathroom.'

Sasha followed him, feeling light-headed and a little jittery. But those disturbing sensations and the way he'd just looked at her fled her mind when the space revealed itself and she looked upon more clothes than she could have ever possibly seen in her life. And shoes. And jewellery, in a special glass cabinet.

The clothes—dresses, skirts, trousers, shirts, jeans, leisure-wear—were stacked, hanging and folded in a room the size of a small boutique. There was every colour of the rainbow.

Without even realising she'd moved, Sasha found herself reaching out and touching a glittering lamé dress in dark blue. It slid between her fingers. It looked hardly capable of staying on a body.

She dropped it and looked around, half-horrified as much as fascinated. 'These are all…mine?'

Apollo was still trying to get his body back under control. For a moment when Sasha had turned from the balcony back into the bedroom, she'd been backlit by the sun, turning her hair into a blazing strawberry-blonde halo around her head.

Her flimsy silk top had clung lovingly to her breasts, the lace of her bra just visible under the delicate material. And he'd had an almost uncontrollable urge to stride forward and take her by the arms and demand to know what she was playing at with this wide-eyed act of innocence. She'd played that card before.

But that urge had fled, to be replaced by a far more dangerous one when she'd looked at him as if he was a wolf about to gobble her up. Instead, all he'd wanted to do was crush that temptingly lush mouth under his and punish her for reawakening this desire, which had lain mercifully dormant for the past three months, in spite of her best efforts to seduce him.

But not any more. It was awake and ravenous. And she was playing him with this little game. After all, feigning amnesia would be child's play to a woman who had feigned a lot worse.

He'd had enough of the charade. His anger burned bright and hot and he told himself it was *that*, and not desire that he was feeling.

He said in a low voice that barely contained his anger, 'You know damn well these are all your clothes because you spent many vacuous hours shopping for them with my credit card. You might have fooled the doctors and nurses at the hospital but there's no one here but you and me now, so who are you trying to fool with this act, Sasha? What the hell are you up to?'

CHAPTER TWO

'WHAT THE HELL are you up to?'

Sasha looked at Apollo and it took a few seconds for his words to sink in, they were so unexpected. But then there was almost a strange sense of relief to have the tension bubble over into words so that she could find out why he'd been acting so coolly with her.

She felt his anger but it didn't scare her. It perplexed her. 'What are you talking about?'

He waved a hand, bristling all over. 'This…farce. Pretending to have lost your memory.'

Sasha felt confused. 'But I'm not. Don't you think I want to know who I am, or what's going on?'

She shook her head. 'Why would I do such a thing?' But just then a pain lanced through the building dull ache in her head. She winced and put a hand to her forehead, feeling light-headed all of a sudden.

Apollo's voice was sharp. 'What is it?'

Sasha was about to shake her head again but she stopped for fear of making it worse. 'It's just a headache, the doctor said that they might be frequent for a few days. If I do too much.'

The recent outburst hung between them, the atmosphere charged, but after a few moments Apollo stepped back and said tightly, 'You should rest for a bit. I can have Rhea bring some food up in a couple of hours.'

Sasha remembered the way the woman had flinched earlier. 'No, I'll come down. I'm sure I'll be feeling better.'

Apollo walked out of the closet space, leaving Sasha with the throbbing pain in her head and feeling utterly bewildered. *He thought she was lying?*

She heard a noise in the main bedroom and went back out to see a young girl she hadn't met placing her hospital bag on the bed. The girl looked at her but didn't smile. She backed away, staring at Sasha as if she might jump at her, and said in halting English, 'Your bag, Kyria Vasilis.'

She left and Sasha stared after her for a long moment. After Apollo's outburst just now, it was patently evident that their marriage was not a harmonious one, and that people didn't seem to like her very much.

Her head throbbed even more, and Sasha went over to the bag that had just been delivered and pulled out the box of painkillers she'd been prescribed. She saw a tray on a table with water and glasses, and took two of the tablets.

She explored further, into the bathroom, which was almost as big as the bedroom. A massive bath and walk-in shower. Two sinks. Cream tiles and gold fittings that looked classy, not tacky.

She caught sight of her reflection in the mirror and sucked in a breath. She was deathly pale. No wonder Apollo had asked if she was okay. She looked a wreck. Shadows under her eyes. The scratch on her cheek. The yellowing of the bruise on her forehead where she'd bumped her head.

She felt disconnected from herself, which she supposed was only to be expected. But she felt as though didn't belong here, in this hushed rarefied place. Where people looked at her as if she'd done something to them. Where her husband accused her of lying.

Why would he think she'd do such a thing?

She pushed that to one side for the moment, it was too much to absorb and think about.

'Sasha…' She said the word out loud. It still didn't feel

right. 'Hello, my name is Sasha Vasilis.' Nothing but a faint echo.

She didn't need to have bruises and scrapes to know that she was very far out of this man's league. But a memory flashed into her head at that moment of feeling effervescent. Of him, smiling at her indulgently.

She'd been so happy.

If anything, that memory only made her feel more disorientated. She spied the bath behind her and suddenly wanted to wash away this confusing chain of events. If such a thing was possible.

She ran the bath and stripped off, stepping into the luxuriously scented silky water a few minutes later. It soothed her bruised and injured body, but it couldn't soothe the turmoil in her belly or clear the pervasive fog in her head.

Apollo stood looking at the woman on the bed. She was in a towelling robe that dwarfed her body, her hair spread around her like a rose-gold halo. One arm was on her chest, the other flung above her head.

One slim pale leg was visible through the gap in the robe and Apollo could see the smattering of freckles across her knee. And it made his blood run hot.

Damn her.

Damn her to hell and back.

He'd met her four months ago and he hadn't had a full night's sleep since then. First of all because he'd been unable to get her out of his head and then because she had shown him who she really was. A manipulative, conniving, mercenary—

She moved on the bed and made a small sound.

Those pale eyelids flickered open and he was looking down into two bright pools of blue. So blue that the first time he'd seen her huge eyes he'd been instantly reminded of the skies of his childhood, before things had grown much darker.

She blinked and Apollo came out of his trance, suddenly feeling exposed. He took a step back. 'I knocked on the door but there was no answer.'

Sasha sat up. He caught a scent of something like crushed roses. And clean skin. He gritted his jaw before saying, 'Dinner is ready. I can have the food delivered to your room.'

She shook her head and that bright hair slipped over one shoulder. He was rewarded with a memory of wrapping it around his hand as he'd tugged her head back so that he could press kisses down along the column of her throat, and then lower to the pouting provocation of her tight pink nipples.

'No, it's fine. I'll come down. My headache is much better.'

Sasha was still somewhere between waking and sleeping. She hadn't expected to conk out like that when she'd lain down for a short nap after her bath, but now she could see the dusky sky outside. It had also taken a minute to realise she wasn't dreaming when she'd opened her eyes to see Apollo standing by the bed. It had been the fierce expression on his face that had woken her properly.

It reminded her of his angry words. *What the hell are you up to?*

He'd changed into dark trousers and a dark shirt, open at the neck. Sleeves rolled up as if he'd been working at his desk. In this position, looking up at him, it felt intimate. An echo of a previous moment teased at her memory, as if she'd sat in this very position looking up at him like this, but in a very different situation.

'I'll just change and come down,' she said quickly.

Apollo took another step back and Sasha could breathe

a little easier. He said, 'Very well. I'll send Kara to show you down in a few minutes.'

Sasha had the distinct impression that he would have preferred it if she'd said she'd eat alone in her room and in a way it would have been easier for her too. But she also had a strong instinct to try and do her utmost to regain her memory and if that meant interacting with her antagonistic husband then so be it.

'Just through here, Kyria Vasilis.'

Sasha smiled at the same young woman who had brought up her bag earlier. Kara. The girl didn't smile back.

After Apollo had left, Sasha had washed her face and gone into the walk-in closet to find some clothes. She'd finally pulled out the plainest and most modest clothes she could find. A pair of slim-fitting Capri pants and a cropped sleeveless shirt. The shirt was white but the trousers were yellow. Apparently she didn't really do muted colours.

And, thankfully, she'd found some flattish shoes. Wedge espadrilles. Unworn, still in the box.

She walked through a less formal lounge on the ground floor that she hadn't seen earlier and through open French doors to another smaller terrace. The one she'd seen from her balcony earlier, covered by a trellis and surrounded by a profusion of flowers. The view here was of the gently sloping grounds down to the outdoor pool.

The scent of the flowers permeated the air when she stepped outside. The air was warm and still. Peaceful. It soothed her fraying edges and foggy mind a little. Apollo looked up from where he'd been staring broodily into the distance, long fingers around the stem of a glass of wine.

He stood up immediately and something about that small automatic gesture gave her a tiny spurt of reassurance. He pulled out a chair and she sat down, his scent easily eclipsing the sweeter scent of the flowers to infuse the air with something far more potent.

She felt the tension between them. Not surprising after his words earlier but there was also another kind of tension, deep in the core of her body. A hungry kind of tension, as if she knew what it felt like to have that tension released.

He sat down opposite her and picked up a bottle of Greek white wine. 'Would you like a glass?'

Sasha wasn't sure. Did she like wine? Might it help take the edge off the unbearable tension she was feeling? She nodded. 'Just a little, please.'

When he'd poured the wine, she lifted her glass and took a sip, finding it light and sharp. She did like it. The housekeeper Rhea appeared then with appetiser plates of dips and flatbreads. Apollo must have noticed her looking at the food because he pushed a bowl towards her. 'This is tzatziki with mint, and the other one is hummus.'

She dipped some bread in each, savouring the tart taste of the tzatziki and the creamier hummus.

Apollo seemed to have directed his brooding stare onto her and to try and deflect his attention she said, 'Your home is lovely.' It didn't feel like her home, even if she had been living here for a few months. 'You must be very successful.'

Apollo took a sip of wine. She thought she saw a quirk of his mouth but it was gone when he lowered his glass. 'You could say that.'

She had the feeling he was laughing at her. Before she could respond, Rhea appeared again to clear the starters and then Kara brought the main courses. Chicken breasts with salad and baby potatoes. Sasha blushed when her stomach rumbled loudly. She took a bite and almost groaned at the lemon-zesty flavour of the chicken. She felt as if it had been an age since she'd eaten anything so flavoursome.

When her plate was clean she looked up to find Apollo putting down his own fork and knife and staring at her.

'What?' She wiped her mouth with her napkin, suddenly aware that she'd fallen on the food like a starving person.

'Apparently you've discovered an appetite,' was Apollo's dry response.

Rhea appeared again and gathered up the plates. Sasha said automatically, 'That was lovely, thank you.'

Rhea stopped and looked at her as if she had two heads before just nodding abruptly and leaving. Not wanting to ask but feeling as if she had no choice, Sasha said, 'What do you mean about the food, and why does she look at me like that? And Kara too…as if they're scared of me.'

'Because they probably are. You didn't exactly treat them with much respect. And before, you treated any food you were served as if it was an enemy to be feared.'

Sasha could feel the onset of that faint throbbing, signalling a headache again as she absorbed his answer. 'You really don't believe that I have amnesia?'

Apollo was expressionless. 'Let's just say that your past behaviour wouldn't give me confidence in your ability to tell the truth.'

What happened?

The words trembled on Sasha's lips but like a coward she swerved away from inviting an answer she wasn't ready to hear yet. Especially if what he'd just told her was true. Apollo was looking at her with that disdainful expression that was fast becoming far too familiar, and painful.

'I'm not lying. I promise. I wish I could make the fog in my brain clear but I can't. Believe me, there's nothing more frightening that not knowing anything about yourself, your past, your future. All I have to trust is that you *are* my husband and that I do live here with you, when it feels like I've never been here before.'

She added, 'I don't know what I did but if your attitude and Rhea's and Kara's are anything to go by it wasn't good. But how can I apologise for something I can't even remember doing?'

Shocked at the surge of emotion catching her unawares and making her chest tight, Sasha stood up and went to the edge of the terrace, arms folded tight across her breasts. To her horror, tears pricked at her eyes and she blinked furiously to keep them at bay.

Apollo's whole body was so rigid with tension he had to force himself to breathe in and relax. He looked at Sasha's tense body. The curve of her naked waist was visible where the cropped shirt rode above the waistline of her trousers. Her skin was pale. Her hair glinted more red in the light of the setting sun, like a flame against the white of her shirt.

She seemed genuinely upset. Agitated. Apollo didn't trust her for an instant but for whatever reason—maybe she was buying time to figure out a way to convince him to stay married—she was insisting on this charade.

For the past three months she'd been playing every trick in the book to try and entice him into her bed, but not wanting her had made it easy to resist. Now, though…he couldn't be sure he would be able to resist and if she knew that…

He stood up and noticed how she tensed even more. He went over and stood beside her. She didn't look at him. Her jaw was tight. Mouth pursed. He was about to look away but did a double-take when he saw the glistening drop of moisture on the lower lashes of her eye. *She'd been crying?* To his shock and consternation, instead of feeling disgust, Apollo felt his conscience prick.

In all her machinations up to now she hadn't ever manufactured actual tears. She'd looked close to tears when she'd turned up at his London office three months ago but she hadn't cried.

Maybe she's telling the truth.

He'd be a fool to trust her after everything that had happened, but he knew who she was now, so she couldn't surprise him again. 'Look,' he said, turning to face her. 'You've been through an ordeal and you need to recuperate. We can talk about whether I believe you or not when you're stronger.'

For the week following Apollo's pronouncement Sasha existed in a kind of numb fog. She was still bruised and battered enough not to fuss when Kara or Rhea insisted on bringing food to her room, or when they appeared as she sat on the terrace to put a light rug over her legs in the early evening, in spite of the Greek heat.

Sasha noticed that as the days dawned and faded into dusk, the women grew less wary around her. Although she still caught them looking at her suspiciously and whispering in corners when they thought she wasn't looking.

Of Apollo, there was no sign. He seemed to go to work as dawn broke—she usually woke when she heard the powerful throttle of an engine as it disappeared down the drive—and she was asleep before she heard it return.

In fact, she realised now, if it wasn't for hearing the engine each morning, she couldn't even be sure that he came home at all. A man with a house like this would surely have other properties. An apartment in Athens?

A mistress?

That thought caught at her gut as she sat in the dusk on Friday evening on the smaller terrace. The end of the working week. The start of the weekend. If they weren't sharing a bedroom then obviously this marriage was not a functioning one. And yet the thought of Apollo with another woman made her feel…nauseous.

She barely knew the man beyond some very hazy memories. And yet…she felt a sense of possessiveness now that shocked her because it was so strong. And also a sense of injury, as if something had been done to her.

'Good evening.'

Sasha nearly jumped out of her skin. She looked around to see the object of her circling thoughts standing just a few feet away. A jolt of electric awareness zinged into her belly. Disconcerting, but also familiar.

He wore dark trousers and the top button of his shirt was open. His hair was slightly dishevelled, as if he'd run a hand through it. His jaw was stubbled.

'I didn't hear you come back, I never do.' She blushed when she said that, aware of how it must sound. 'I mean, I usually hear your car in the mornings, not in the evenings. I wasn't sure if you were staying somewhere else. Do you have a property in the city?' Aware she was babbling now, she clamped her mouth shut.

He walked in sat down on a seat at a right angle to hers. His shirt pulled taut across his chest and she had to drag her eyes away. What was wrong with her? All week she'd been existing in this numbness but now she felt alive, fizzing.

'I can't account for why you don't hear the car in the evening, as I've been returning to the villa every night. But, yes, I do have an apartment in Athens. It's the penthouse at the top of my office building.'

'You have a building.' Not just an office. A whole building.

He nodded. 'And another one in London. And offices in New York, Paris and Rome. I'm finalising plans to open an office in Tokyo next year.'

Sasha couldn't help but be impressed. 'That's a lot of offices. You must have worked very hard.'

He looked utterly relaxed but she could sense the tension in his form. He said, 'For as long as I can remember.'

'Did you study for it?'

He nodded. 'Yes, but I worked on sites at the same time, so I got my diploma while I was working my way up the ranks. I didn't want to waste any time going to college full time.'

Apollo went still. He hadn't come here to *chat* with his treacherous wife who may or may not be feigning amnesia, but if she was faking it then he had to hand it to her for stamina. She hadn't let her mask slip all week.

Rhea and Kara had told him that she'd been as civil and polite as much as she'd been selfish and rude in the recent past. There seemed to be no glimmer of that earlier incarnation of his wife this evening. Just those huge blue eyes looking at him guilelessly.

He wanted to get up and walk away. So he did get up. But instead of walking away he went over to the low terrace wall and sat on that.

She'd turned in the seat to look at him. She was wearing a white shirt-dress with a gold belt. The dress was buttoned up to a modest height.

Previously, Sasha would have had a dress like this buttoned so low that her underwear would have been visible. Then it had aroused nothing more than irritation. Now, though, all he could see were those little buttons and think about how easy it would be to undo them, baring her breasts to his gaze.

He could see her pale legs. Long and slender. Together and slanted to the side, ladylike.

He would have laughed if he'd been able to muster up a sense of humour. Not too long ago she'd been involved in activities very unbecoming to a lady.

He diverted his mind away from her dress, her legs. Abruptly he found himself saying, 'My father used to be a foreman for one of Greece's biggest construction companies. He got injured on the job, and became paralysed from the waist down.'

Sasha put a hand to her mouth, visibly shocked.

A familiar sense of rage that hadn't been dulled by time settled in Apollo's belly. 'He never really recovered. All he knew was how to manage a construction site. He could have done that in an office, in a wheelchair but everyone turned him down. His own employer refused to give him any compensation. His pride was in tatters. He couldn't support his wife and two sons.'

She frowned, 'You have a brother?'

Apollo ignored that. He felt ruthless as he told her the rest, watching her reaction carefully. 'My father killed himself when I was eleven and my brother was thirteen. My mother got cancer not long afterwards and died within a couple of years. My brother and I were sent to into foster care. My brother got involved with a drugs and gang crime. He was stabbed to death when he was sixteen.'

Apollo's eyes were glowing with intensity. Like dark green jewels. Sasha felt pinned to the spot by them. By his words. She couldn't speak. Anything she thought of saying felt too trite. Ineffectual.

Apollo continued. 'I made it my life's mission to go after the man who had employed my father and cast him aside like a piece of unwanted trash. And I succeeded. It didn't take much to dismantle his business because he was corrupt to the core. As soon as he went down, hundreds of disgruntled ex-employees came out of the woodwork looking for compensation and that's what ruined him in the end.'

He was looking at her now as if he expected her to be shocked. And she was. 'I'm sorry,' she said huskily. 'I can't imagine what it must have been like to lose so many when you were so young. I don't know about my family…when my parents died.'

Apollo was reeling that he'd let all of that tumble from his mouth. A bare handful of people knew about his past, and yet he'd just told Sasha everything. The one person in the world that he should trust the least. He waited for the mask to slip, for her to take advantage of sharing his sad story. But it didn't.

She'd gone pale. And her eyes were huge. And she was

frowning now. 'You said my parents are dead, and I've no siblings?'

He nodded. 'You told me that your mother was a single parent. Your father left when you were small. You looked for him but found out that he'd died some years ago and then your mother died a couple of years ago.'

'Oh…it's so strange not to be able to remember my mother. Or looking for my father.'

She seemed to be genuinely tortured. Biting her lip. Apollo had a sudden flashback to kissing her for the first time, feeling the cushiony softness of her mouth opening under his, allowing him to delve deeper…all the way… His hands curled tight around the lip of the wall in a bid to douse the growing inferno in his blood.

He stood up. 'I have some work calls to make. Goodnight, Sasha.'

She looked distracted. 'Goodnight.'

He was walking out but he couldn't get those huge bruised-looking eyes out of his head. He stopped at the door and looked back. She cut a curiously vulnerable figure on the large couch.

'I'm sorry about your parents.'

She turned around and some of that vivid gold and red hair slipped over her shoulder. 'Thank you.'

Desire squeezed Apollo like a vice. He wanted to go back over there and pull apart that flimsy dress material and spread it wide so he could see her pale beauty. He wanted to force her to admit that she was just acting. Messing with his head again. He wouldn't make love to her. He'd have her begging for it and then he'd leave her there, panting and admitting who she really was.

'Goodnight, Sasha.'

Apollo walked out before he followed his base instincts and did something stupid because that way lay madness. The same madness that had made him want her with a primal need he'd never felt before, the first time he'd looked at her.

He got to his study and poured himself a drink and sat down, unable to excise the image of those huge blue eyes out of his brain. Or the impact they'd had on him the first time he'd seen her.

That night, in that anonymous function room in London, had been the first time that anyone had managed to slip past Apollo's defences so skilfully, and without even trying. By just looking at him. Something wild and untamed had crackled to life inside him and he'd realised that he'd never truly felt desire before. He'd taken many lovers but had never allowed them to get close. Satisfying his physical urges only.

After his experiences—seeing his father humiliated and belittled and ultimately destroyed; after seeing his mother wither and fade from their lives, a sad broken woman; and after watching his brother self-destruct—Apollo had vowed never to let anyone close enough to make him care when they would inevitably leave. He'd been left behind too many times.

But for the first time, with Sasha, satisfying his physical urges had taken on a whole new level of need. He'd had to have her. And so he'd followed his base instincts and indulged.

He'd lost himself in her before he'd come back to his senses. And remembered who he was. And what he was. And what he was was empty inside.

Revenge had filled that space for a long time. He'd only been coming to terms with the fact that it hadn't felt more cathartic to have achieved his goals when he'd met Sasha. He'd put her effect on him down to that curious space he'd been in. Anticlimactic. Restless. Dissatisfied, when he should have been satisfied. At peace.

There was a knock on his door and he tensed. 'Come in.'

* * *

Sasha took a deep breath outside Apollo's study door. She knew he'd said he was taking or making calls but she hadn't heard his voice when she'd diverted to his office en route to her bedroom, so she'd acted on impulse.

She opened the door and he was sitting behind his desk, a brooding expression on his face. He frowned. 'Is everything okay?'

She nodded, but immediately regretted her decision when that awareness of him coiled tight, down low in her belly. 'Fine. I just…' She stopped. She shouldn't have come here now. The way he made her feel just by looking at her was so…disturbing. She wanted to run but also stay rooted to the spot.

He frowned. 'Sasha—'

She spoke in a rush. 'I know you're busy, but I want to know why our marriage is…like this. Separate bedrooms. Tense. You don't like me very much.'

At all, whispered a little voice.

Apollo put down the glass in his hand. He stood up and came around to sit on the edge of his desk. Arms folded across his chest, which only drew attention to his muscles. Heat washed up through her body and she couldn't stop it.

Had she always been so aware of men?

Maybe it's just him, whispered a voice.

Somehow, she couldn't deny that it was entirely possible she only reacted like this to him.

Apollo saw the twin flags of colour in Sasha's cheeks. He was almost disappointed that she was showing her true colours again so soon. She'd nearly had him convinced. But coming here like this now…she must have seen his desire for her. And now she was taking advantage of it.

He was tempted to just confront her right now, but something in him counselled against acting too hastily. 'Our marriage had some…issues, but I don't think now is the time to go into them.'

He watched her carefully, which only made him more aware of her. Aware that he wanted her.

Witch.

She looked at him. 'I don't know why but I feel I need to apologise, as if I've done something wrong and that's why you hate me and Rhea and Kara look at me as if I'm about to do something unexpected.'

Apollo fought the pull to believe her. To trust in this image of innocence she was putting forward. She'd done it before. He straightened up from the desk. He told himself he was moving closer to test her, just to see if she would show her true colours. Not because he wanted to.

Her eyes got big and round and the pink in her cheeks deepened as she looked up at him as if he were a big bad wolf. Something snapped inside Apollo, some control he'd been exerting since she'd woken in the hospital bed and looked at him with those blue eyes, re-igniting his desire.

He reached out and caught a lock of her hair, winding it around his finger. It felt like silk. It reminded him of how it had felt when her hair had trailed over his naked chest the night they'd made love.

'I prefer it like this, loose and wild. You preferred it straightened.'

'I did?' Sasha's chest constricted. Why couldn't she seem to breathe? The air was thick and full of something that felt alive. The awareness she felt turned into a pulse in her blood. Heavy and persistent.

Almost as if he was talking to himself, Apollo said, 'It was like this the night we met.'

'I don't… I don't remember. I mean, I remember bits of that night but not details…'

Apollo stood in front of her, eyes roving her face. 'Are

you sure, Sasha? Really? Or is this just an elaborate stunt to gain my trust? To get back into my bed?'

His words acted like cold water in her blood. She pulled back, dislodging his hand from her hair. *'No. I wouldn't do that.'*

He moved closer again and put his hand under her chin, tipping her face up. So much for his words dousing the heat. It sizzled back at his touch, just as potent.

'Wouldn't you? It's no less than you've already done, but I have to admit, if you are acting, your skills are exemplary.'

For the first time since she'd woken up in the hospital something more than confusion and bewilderment rushed through her, distracting her. Sasha took his hand to pull it down. 'Maybe that's because I'm not acting.'

But instead of pushing his hand away to break all contact with him and his cynical words, she couldn't seem to let go. Electricity hummed through her, mixing with the high emotion to create a volatile mix.

For a crazy second she almost thought he was going to kiss her. But then he broke contact and stepped back. His eyes were so dark in the dim light they looked black. Sasha felt a little dizzy, as if they *had* kissed.

He said curtly, 'You should go to bed, Sasha. It's late.' He went to the door and held it open.

Sasha couldn't understand what had just come over her. The depth of the need to have him kiss her still left her shaken.

Dear God, had she actually asked...?

She all but ran out of his office before she could read the disgust on his face or, worse, let him see the awful surge of humiliation climbing up from her gut.

Apollo waited until Sasha had disappeared before closing his door. He went back to his desk and downed his drink in one, as if that might burn away how close he'd come to taking what she was offering, lifting that lush mouth towards him, begging with those huge eyes to kiss her.

One minute he'd been wondering how she'd managed to sneak under his guard again, and the next he'd been on the verge of hauling her closer to relive that night they'd shared—which was exactly what she'd been angling for since they'd married.

His hand tightened around the crystal glass so much he had to relax for fear of breaking it.

Sexual frustration bit sharply into his gut. He'd spent the last three months without so much as a flicker of arousal when he'd looked at his wife. And now it wasn't a flicker. It was an inferno.

He couldn't understand what was happening. But he knew that, no matter how intense it got, he would not be weak. He'd been weak for her once before and she'd up-ended his life. It wouldn't happen again.

CHAPTER THREE

SASHA WENT UPSTAIRS to her bedroom, feeling dazed. She stood in the middle of the room and put her fingers to her mouth, almost as if to test that they hadn't kissed, it had felt so real, so inevitable. But, no, her mouth was the same. Not swollen. Throbbing with sensation.

Because she knew what that felt like.

It hit her then, like a sledgehammer. She'd wanted it so badly because she knew what it felt like to be kissed by him. That's why her body had literally ached…from the memory of knowing his touch. Wanting it again.

She sat down on the end of her bed, going cold inside. Thank God he'd pulled back before she'd have been able to articulate her need any more than she already had, silently. She cringed to think of how he'd put his hands on her arms, literally pushing her away.

She realised something else. Maybe she'd craved it so badly because it had felt familiar to her body to be kissed by him. And since everything else around her was so unfamiliar she'd gravitated towards that. A natural response of her body to seek anything familiar?

And exciting, whispered a little voice.

It didn't give her much relief to put it into this context. A flimsy justification for what had nearly happened.

And with a man who resented her presence and had told her to her face that he didn't trust her. What kind of a masochist was she?

* * *

When Sasha made her way down to breakfast the next morning she felt ragged. She'd woken at dawn, sweaty, tangled in her sheets. Dissatisfied. She'd slept fitfully and her dreams had been full of X-rated images. Images that she couldn't be sure now *were* just from her dreams. They'd felt like memories…

When she walked onto the small terrace where she'd eaten breakfast alone all week, she wasn't prepared to see Apollo. She hadn't heard his car that morning but she'd still been hoping she might have missed it. But then she realised it was a Saturday so he must be off work.

He looked up at her as he lifted a coffee cup to his mouth, but immediately put it down again and stood up. There was no discernible expression on his face.

She avoided his eye, hating the way her body prickled all over with the same heat she'd felt last night. She almost resented his presence, which was ridiculous when it was his house.

Their house.

But it didn't feel like her house. 'Good morning.'

'Kalimera.'

Sasha sat down and Rhea appeared with coffee, which she poured into a cup for Sasha.

Sasha smiled tentatively at her and said carefully, *'Ef-haristo.'*

Rhea nodded her head and smiled. When she was gone Apollo said, 'You've been learning Greek?'

Sasha picked up a pastry, anything to avoid looking at Apollo and reliving that moment last night when she'd all but begged him to kiss her. 'Just a few everyday words. Kara helps me.'

'You didn't seem inclined to want to pick it up before.'

Sasha's knife stilled. She looked at Apollo. 'Can we agree that perhaps things might be different now? You keep telling me things I did, or the way I was, and I can't remember any of it. Can we just…go forward from here?'

He looked at her for a long moment. So long that she felt her face get hot. Eventually he inclined his head. 'Very well. That's fair.'

Sasha breathed out.

'How are you feeling now? Physically?'

She took a gulp of coffee, composing herself. 'I'm fine… much better. Physically.' She made a face. 'Mentally…the fogginess has gone but now it's just a great big blank.'

And the way you make me feel like I'm plugged into some hot electrical force.

She clamped her mouth shut in case the words fell out.

Apollo wiped his mouth with a napkin. 'I've arranged for the doctor to come this morning to check you over.'

Sasha's gut clenched. Was he trying to get rid of her? What would happen once she was well enough? Why did she feel sick at the prospect when he obviously resented her presence? Impulsively she asked, 'Was it ever good? Between us?'

Apollo put his hand on the table, face unreadable. 'Briefly.'

The thought of him wanting her as much as she'd wanted him last night was too overwhelming to contemplate for a moment. She struggled to understand. 'But…then why—?'

'Didn't it work?' His voice was harsh.

Sasha nodded. Just at that moment Rhea appeared and Sasha cursed the interruption.

Rhea said, 'The doctor is here to see Kyria Vasilis.'

Apollo looked at Rhea and smiled. A proper smile. The first smile Sasha had seen on his face. Her heart flip-flopped. It transformed him from merely gorgeous to devastating.

But then he looked back at her and it faded. Sasha felt a chill breeze up her spine. He really hated her. For whatever she had done. And a moment ago she'd been ready to hear it but now she was glad of the interruption.

'Physically you've made a remarkable recovery, Mrs Vasilis. Emotionally, how are you doing?'

Sasha tucked her shirt back into her trousers. The doctor had seen her in her bedroom. The same kind female doctor who had attended to her in the hospital after the accident.

She sat down on a chair by the writing desk, aware of the doctor's keen dark eyes on her. 'I'm… I guess I'm okay. Getting used to my life.'

And the husband who doesn't want me here.

The doctor nodded. 'I can imagine it'll take some adjustment. And your memory…anything coming back yet?'

Sasha shook her head. 'Not really. It's just all blank. But I had dreams last night.' She stopped, blushing.

The doctor said, 'Go on, my dear.'

Embarrassed to have mentioned this, Sasha said, 'It's just that they felt like memories more than a dream. Of me and my husband.'

The doctor nodded. 'That could very well be the case. I'd advise you to keep a notebook by the bed, write down your dreams and that could help jog something. But don't put too much pressure on yourself, our minds work in mysterious ways.'

The doctor stood up and Sasha stood too. 'There was something else.'

'Oh?' The doctor was putting things back into her bag. She stopped.

'I just… My husband tells me that I'm behaving differently from how I was before. Would that be normal?'

The doctor considered this and then said slowly, 'It has been known…for head trauma injuries to cause some kind of personality change but we saw no indication of such trauma in your brain scan. You just got a very hard knock to the head. It's just going to take time to readjust to your life, Mrs Vasilis. Don't worry, and let me know as soon as there are any developments with your memory.'

By the time Sasha had waved the doctor off, it was late morning. She turned around to see Kara adjusting a vase of exotic blooms on the table in the middle of the hall. Sasha walked over, 'Have you seen Apo—my husband?'

Kara nodded, 'He left a little while ago for the office. He said to tell you he'd be home later this afternoon.'

'Oh.' Silly to feel so disappointed. She wasn't even sure what she would have done if he had been here.

Feeling her way, she said, 'He seems to work a lot.'

Kara looked at her and rolled her eyes. 'Always he is working. Morning, noon and night, except before we thought it was because—'

Suddenly she stopped and Sasha felt a burn of humiliation rise up inside her.

To get away from her?

She swallowed it down. 'Thank you, Kara. The truth is I'm not sure what to do with myself. What did I normally do?'

Kara avoided her eye, clearly embarrassed. 'You liked shopping, a lot.' Sasha's heart sank at the thought of shopping. What could she possibly need?

'Was there anything else?'

The young girl's face brightened. 'You could go and lie by the pool, you like that.'

'I do?'

Apollo walked into the gardens towards the pool, where he'd been told Sasha had been all afternoon. Maybe she'd finally cracked and was showing her true colours again. He'd found her by the pool countless times before, surrounded by the detritus of afternoon snacks and sugary drinks. Dog-eared magazines.

Once he'd questioned whether it was good for her, but that had been before he'd found out about— He came to an abrupt standstill as he rounded the bush that artfully hid the pool from prying eyes.

Apollo lifted his sunglasses onto his head. Sasha lay on a sun bed under an umbrella. At first he thought she was naked and his blood rushed straight to his groin. It wouldn't be the first time. She'd habitually sunbathed topless, scandalising Rhea. Trying to tempt him. Not that it had worked.

But, no, he realised she wasn't naked. She wasn't far from it though, in a flesh-coloured one-piece, which was low-cut enough to reveal the plump pale flesh of her breasts. He could already imagine what it might look like if she stepped out of the pool, her red hair slicked back like a wet flame down her back. The clingy material would leave nothing to the imagination. The way her nipples would have gone hard in the water, pressing against the—

Christos.

Disgusted at his lack of control, Apollo tore his gaze off his wife's body. There was no detritus around her. Just a book. And a glass of water.

He could still recall how close he'd come to hauling her against his body last night, crushing that rosebud mouth under his. He could try to convince himself that he'd just been testing her, but he knew his motivations went much deeper and darker than that.

He wanted her again.

When his assistant in London had told him that she was waiting to see him three months ago, a month had passed since their night together. She'd been on his mind constantly, especially at night, when he'd got used to waking from erotic dreams, aching with frustration.

He'd taken more cold showers in that period than he'd ever taken in his whole life.

And he hadn't been able to stem the tide of something that had felt a lot like…relief. That she'd been the one to make the move. To expose herself for wanting more.

But then as soon as she'd walked into his office that day, he'd felt…nothing. Less than nothing. Not a blip of response. Even though she'd looked exactly the same. Fresh face. Hair loose around her shoulders. Innocent. Tremulous.

He hated to admit it now but relief his desire for her had waned hadn't been the overriding sentiment. It had been a sense of disappointment. Because it was proof that she wasn't different from any other woman he'd slept with. And that what they'd shared that night couldn't have possibly been as amazing as he'd remembered it. Amazing enough to make him regret telling her—

Suddenly her body jerked on the bed and a sound came out of her mouth, like a cry. Indistinct words. Something like, *'No, please don't stop!'*

Before Apollo knew what he was doing he'd come down beside the bed, two hands on Sasha's bare arms. They felt impossibly slender. Her body was tense all over, he could see a slight sheen of perspiration on her skin. His insides clenched with an emotion he didn't want to name.

'Sasha…wake up.'

Apollo's hands were on her skin. Burning. She ached all over with a hunger she'd felt only once before. It was so clear now. She needed him to assuage that hunger…to make her come alive—

'Sasha!'

Sasha opened her eyes and all she could see were the deepest pools of green. A kind of green that made her think of mysterious oceans. Vast. Impenetrable.

'You were dreaming.'

Apollo's voice. Hard. Unyielding. Suddenly Sasha's

consciousness snapped back. She was on the lounger. She'd fallen asleep. But Apollo still had his hands on her. She could smell his scent. See the stubble on his jaw. She wanted to reach out and see how it felt. She imagined it would prickle against her skin.

She remembered how that felt.

Dreams and the present moment were meshing disturbingly and she felt disorientated.

She sat up abruptly, dislodging his hands. He stood up. She reached for the robe, pulling it on awkwardly, very conscious of the revealing swimsuit. It had been the only one-piece she could find in a sea of brightly coloured string bikinis.

'Apollo, I didn't hear you. What time is it?'

Sasha looked deliciously tousled, cheeks flushed, eyes sleepy. Apollo gritted his jaw as his eyes tracked her movements, her small breasts high and firm under the stretchy material. She was so pale her skin was almost translucent. He frowned. She'd been more tanned before. But, of course, it must have been fake. A welcome reminder of who he was dealing with. Memory loss or no memory loss.

The lingering tendrils of concern for her distress made his voice harsh. 'You should watch yourself in the sun,' he said. 'You can burn even in the shade.'

Sasha flinched inwardly at his abrupt tone, belting the robe tightly around her. The robe chafed against her tingling skin. She could still feel the imprint of his hands on her arms. Defensively she said, 'I found sun block in the bathroom, of course I put some on. I may have lost my memory but I'm not clueless about the dangers of the sun.'

She risked looking up at Apollo now that she was covered up again, diverting her mind from the vividly disturbing dream. He was wearing a short-sleeved polo shirt and cargo shorts. Unexpectedly casual and effortlessly sexy.

He said, 'I just came to tell you that I'm going out this evening.'

'Oh.' It was strange but for the first time she was aware she hadn't left the confines of this estate since her return from the hospital. She had a sense of claustrophobia. 'Where are you going?'

'It's a charity ball, in aid of research into cancer.'

For some reason that struck a chord with Sasha and for a moment something hovered on the edge of her mind but then it was gone.

She stood up. 'Should I come with you?'

He shook his head. 'No need. I'm just letting you know I won't be here for dinner.'

It wasn't as if they'd been having cosy dinners all week but Apollo was the only constant familiar thing in her world right now and she was determined to try and improve relations. What else could she do? She couldn't continue to exist in this limbo where they circled each other like suspicious foes.

She still didn't know exactly what had happened between them and she wasn't even sure if she wanted to know what she'd done to lead to this impasse, but she could work with what she had. She wanted to at least try to mend bridges.

'Didn't I go to events with you? As your wife?'

Apollo searched for any hint of a crack in her facade but she looked utterly guileless. Did she really not remember saying to him, 'Why not use me? Surely it's better for you to be seen with a wife than not? It'll help your business to be seen as more settled.'

When they'd married, he hadn't had any intention of involving her in his life more than he'd had to, but he'd had to admit that on some level she was right. And so he'd taken her to a couple of events.

Sasha was looking at him now. 'What is it? Why are you looking at me like that?'

'You don't remember?'

She went pale. 'No. What did I do?'

'Let's just say that you ruffled some feathers.'

'How?'

'You were rude to staff and visibly bored when you realised that the social and corporate events I attend aren't generally designed for entertainment purposes.'

Sasha felt queasy. Was there anything she had done right? 'I can't keep apologising for things I can't remember. But maybe this is an opportunity to make it up to you. No matter what I did, won't your friends and colleagues be wondering where your wife is?'

He didn't refute her question so she asked, 'What time do you have to leave? It won't take me long to get ready.'

He arched a brow. 'I'll believe that when I see it.' He put his sunglasses back over his eyes and without that laser-like gaze stripping her bare she breathed easier.

'I have to leave in an hour. If you're coming, be downstairs waiting for me, or I go alone. I won't wait, Sasha.'

Less than an hour later, Sasha waited nervously downstairs in the main hall for Apollo. After his ultimatum she'd panicked. She had no idea how on earth to get ready for such an event. She'd found Kara in the kitchen and had begged the young woman to come with her to help her. Initially she had been reluctant but then she'd relented, telling Sasha that Apollo had asked for his tuxedo to be ready for him so at least they knew it was black-tie.

They'd managed to find a dress that was suitable and not too revealing, and Kara had helped with her hair and make-up. And now Sasha stood here, wondering what on earth she'd been doing, saying she'd go along to an event— she had no idea if she would be able to handle herself in such a milieu. She'd been serving drinks when she'd met him, not drinking them!

She would make a fool of herself and any hope she had of redeeming herself in Apollo's eyes would be gone. And what deeper impulse was whispering to her to look for redemption? Then what? Did she want him to like her again?

Want her again?

Panic gripped her. She couldn't do this. She turned to flee back to her room before Apollo saw her—he'd obviously not expected her to be ready anyway. But it was too late. He was at the top of the stairs and staring at her as if she were a total stranger. Her own eyes widened and her chest constricted as the air rushed out.

He was wearing a classic black tuxedo. White shirt, black bow-tie. She was not prepared for his impact on her. And yet she'd seen him like this before, the first night they'd met. A vivid flashback assailed her before she knew what was happening—Apollo had been helping her with her heavy tray of drinks and she'd been laughing and getting hot with embarrassment. 'Honestly, I'm fine. If my boss sees you helping me, I'll get into trouble.'

He'd kept hold of the tray, 'I'm not letting go unless you agree to come for a drink with me afterwards.'

She'd seen her boss then, across the room, clocking her. Terrified she'd lose the job, she'd said, 'Okay, fine! Now, please…let me go.'

That memory faded but, as easily as if it had been there all the time, just hiding behind a curtain, she now remembered that evening, and fragmented images from another evening, a date…going for dinner with him in a beautiful restaurant in a tall glittering building with London laid out before them, a sea of twinkling lights… She'd been so excited. Nervous. Incredulous.

Happy…

* * *

Apollo couldn't believe what he was seeing. Sasha, waiting for him. Ready. And looking presentable. More than presentable.

Beautiful.

She was wearing a black silk one-shouldered dress, with ornate silk flowers trailing over one shoulder. Cut on the bias, the dress fell in soft billowing folds to the floor.

A braid framed one side of her face and her hair was pulled back into a low bun. It was all at once pretty and youthful but also elegant. Discreet diamonds shone in her ears. Her hands and throat were bare. Her make-up was minimal.

The starkness of the black dress only served to highlight her delicate fair colouring. Those vivid blue eyes. It was a far cry from her usual style, which was showing as much skin as possible, with lots of make-up, jewellery and big hair.

Desire pulled taut like a drum inside him. He had to force himself to move down the stairs. When he got close, her eyes were huge, on him, as if she'd never seen him before. She looked pale and he could see that her fingers were holding her clutch bag so tight her knuckles were white.

'What is it? Are you okay?'

She swallowed and nodded jerkily. She sounded a bit breathless. 'I just… I just remembered London. More about that night we met. And another night?'

He nodded slowly. 'I took you out the following evening for dinner.'

'We were in a building…it looked like a piece of broken glass.'

'The Shard?'

She nodded. 'Yes. I still don't remember much else beyond that building, the view…but it's a start.'

Something uneasy moved through Apollo. If she *was*

acting then she'd gone beyond a point that most people could keep up a pretence. He said carefully, 'That's good.'

A little colour came back into her cheeks and now she looked nervous. She gestured to the dress. 'Is this okay? I wasn't sure... Kara helped me.'

'Kara?'

She nodded and then looked worried. 'Is that a problem? Shouldn't I have asked her?'

Apollo, for the first time, had to bite back a smile. 'On the contrary, she tried to help you before but you insisted on getting in a professional stylist.'

Sasha looked tortured. 'I had no idea. I should apologise.' She made to go towards the kitchen but Apollo caught her hand, aware of how small it felt in his.

'It's not that big a deal, you can tell her another time.' But he couldn't seem to let her hand go. His gaze swept up and down, taking in the way the swells of her breasts pushed against the thin fabric of the dress. He wondered if she was wearing a bra—imagined cupping one firm weight in his hand, feeling the stab of her nipple— He shut down his rogue imagination and let her hand go. 'We should leave, or we'll be late.'

He took her by the arm and led her out of the villa and into the passenger seat of his car.

Sasha took in the view of Athens as they came down from the hills and entered the ancient city. The view was helping to distract her from the proximity of Apollo's all too masculine presence beside her.

The city was bustling, full of young people out on the streets, enjoying the weekend, laughing and enjoying life. She could see the Acropolis standing majestically over the city, like a sentinel. 'Have I been to the Acropolis?' she asked, as the thought occurred to her.

Apollo glanced at her, slowing to a stop at a set of lights. 'No, you didn't express an interest in seeing it.'

Sasha frowned. It was so disconcerting that someone else knew more about her than she did. Before long, they were driving into a wide leafy street with tall exclusive townhouses, and then through huge wrought-iron gates manned by serious-looking security men. They pulled up outside what could only be described as a neo-classical mansion.

Lots of people were milling around outside, then slowly making their way inside. Women dressed in long glittering dresses, men dressed like Apollo, in tuxedoes.

Nerves erupted like butterflies in her belly. Again, she regretted ever saying anything about coming. But the car had stopped and Apollo was uncoiling his tall body out of the car and handing the keys to a young man.

Then he was opening her door and holding out a hand. She took a deep breath and let him help her out. Not even her awareness of him was able to eclipse her nerves. Her palms were clammy. She didn't belong in a place like this and she didn't need to regain her memory to know that.

CHAPTER FOUR

APOLLO'S HAND WAS on Sasha's elbow, guiding her through the throng. He noticed the looks from his peers. The widening eyes as they registered his wife by his side. He gritted his jaw. He'd never asked for this—to be married—but he'd been surprised at what a difference it had made. Much as he hated to admit it, Sasha had been right in her estimation of the worth of having a wife by your side.

It made his married colleagues less nervous. It kept predatory women at bay. And it had lent a more stable veneer to his business. A couple of business associates he'd been trying to meet with for years had finally agreed to meetings and Apollo had realised that it had been because they were family men and they hadn't totally trusted him when he'd been a bachelor. He'd been seen as a rogue operator.

He looked down at Sasha to check how she was reacting and saw her expression. Genuinely awed, as if she'd never been in this kind of environment before. Certainly not how she'd reacted the first time he'd brought her to an event. Then she'd looked as entitled as everyone else here. Or, at least, she'd tried to.

Now she wore the kind of expression that one would never see in a place like this because everyone was too used to this level of luxury, or wouldn't be caught dead admitting to being impressed. Or too cynical.

To his surprise, her reaction reminded him of how he'd

felt when he'd first started being invited along to high society events: out of his depth and as if he didn't belong.

He quickly quashed the sense of empathy. Sasha had
led him a merry dance for months now, and she owed him.
She seemed determined to act the part of his wife again
and he'd be an idiot not to take advantage of that. After all,
they wouldn't be married for much longer—as soon as she
had fully recuperated—

She interrupted his thoughts, asking, 'What *is* this
place?'

'It's the French Ambassador's residence. He's hosting
this evening. His wife died of cancer some years ago and
now he and his family host this ball every year.'

'Oh, that's sad.'

Apollo looked at her suspiciously. But she seemed genuinely concerned. A little frown between her eyes. Mouth
turned down.

Sasha was unaware of the speculative look from her husband. She was too consumed and awed by her surround-
ings. She'd never seen such glittering opulence. The ceilings
had elaborate frescoes and the walls seemed to be made
out of gold.

Hundreds of candles and sparkling chandeliers imbued
everything with a golden glow. It truly was another world.
She was sure she'd never seen so many beautiful people in
one place. Or maybe she had, if she'd been serving them
drinks. But not like this…not as one of them.

Frustration bit at her insides. She hated this…*not knowing.* Being at the mercy of her mind choosing to reveal
memories totally at random. When *it* chose to. Like when
she'd seen Apollo in the tuxedo.

To distract herself, Sasha tried to tune into the conversation Apollo was having with some men, but she gave up as
it was in Greek, or other languages she didn't understand.

Waiters came around offering champagne and canapés.

Sasha was too afraid to eat in case she ruined her dress. Then they were led into another large and impressive room with round tables set around a small stage. They sat down and a charity auction took place. The items up for auction included cars, date nights with famous celebrities and even a small island off the coast of Ireland.

Sasha gasped when that lot was announced. 'That's outrageous!'

Apollo looked at her and his mouth twisted slightly. 'That's the super-rich.'

Then a lot came up for a luxury yacht. To her shock and surprise, Apollo started bidding on it. Within a few short minutes people were clapping him on the back and cheering. He'd paid an extortionate amount of money for it.

Sasha was in shock. 'You just bought a yacht.'

He looked at her. 'Well, I already have an island and an island isn't much use without a yacht.'

He said that without any discernible sense of awe that he owned such fantastical things. In fact, he almost sounded… bored.

'You don't seem very excited to own such things.'

Apollo felt something hitch in his chest at Sasha's comment and the way her blue eyes seemed to be looking right inside him, to the place where a sense of novelty had become something else. Something *less* novel. When had that happened?

He shrugged nonchalantly when he felt tight inside, not relaxed, 'Like I said, an island needs a yacht.'

'But will you use it?'

Apollo was surprised at the hollow feeling that seemed to spread outwards from his centre. He hadn't even consciously bought the yacht with a view to using it. More as a reflex to do what was expected of him. But now he couldn't help imagining the vessel bobbing in azure waters under a clear sky, and this woman laid out in all her slender, pale glory...red hair spread around her head—

The crowd seemed to stand en masse as the auction came to an end and Apollo seized the opportunity to divert Sasha's attention. Since when had his wife had the ability to probe so insightfully and deeply with just a casual question?

He stood up and reached for her hand. 'It's time to move on.'

Sasha had a very keen sense that Apollo hadn't appreciated her innocent questions. Clearly she'd hit on a nerve and maybe she was being spectacularly naive: in this world, islands and yachts were mere luxury trinkets to be added to a portfolio of even more luxury items.

There was just something about his lack of enthusiasm that struck at the heart of her, making her feel a little...sad.

The crowd was moving into yet another glorious room, even bigger. A ballroom. There was an orchestra and a singer singing sultry jazz songs. The lighting was dim and intimate. French doors were open, leading out to a terrace lined with flaming lanterns. Dusk was falling and the sky was a deep lavender colour. It was like a scene from a fairytale or a movie.

Her hand was still in Apollo's and she was very conscious of his long fingers wrapped around hers, so much so that she didn't even notice that he was leading her onto the dance floor. When she realised where they were, it was too late. He was drawing her in front of him and wrapping one arm across her back.

She went rigid in his arms from the impact of his body against hers as much because of where they were; in the middle of a dance floor. Around them, couples were moving sinuously to the music. Graceful and elegant. At ease.

Apollo started to move, taking Sasha with him, and she hissed, 'I don't even know if I can dance.'

'Just follow my lead.'

After a few robotic moments, Apollo pulled her even closer to his body. Sasha couldn't fight the force it took to remain rigid and so she softened against him.

She was surrounded by him, his steely strength. They were so close she could smell the sharp tang of his aftershave. Her heels put her even closer to his jaw and mouth. She wanted to press her lips there, taste his skin. Immediately she tensed again and he lowered his head, saying in her ear, 'Relax. Just let me lead.'

After a few torturous seconds she allowed herself to soften again. She realised they were moving around the floor with relative grace. She looked up, avoiding looking at his jaw and the faint line of stubble.

'Where did you learn to dance?'

She felt the tension come into his body. 'My mother. She loved to dance, she used to dance with my father all the time.'

'That's romantic.'

He looked down at her, his expression anything but romantic. 'It was, until he had the accident and couldn't dance any more.'

Sasha thought of what he'd told her about getting revenge for his father's death. She shivered slightly, thinking of how ruthless he must have been. Single-minded. But she remembered him being like that with her—until she'd agreed to go for a drink with him.

She wondered how on earth she'd caught his eye in London when they'd been surrounded by women as beautiful as the ones here tonight, in their peacock dresses and glittering jewels. Even though she was dressed like them now, she felt dowdy and colourless in comparison.

She noticed one dark brunette pass by in the arms of her partner, her voluptuous body poured into a silver sheath dress. She also noticed how she looked at Apollo, and then at Sasha, dismissing her with a flick of her hair. No competition.

The song came to an end and Sasha seized the opportunity to escape for a moment, hating this feeling of insecurity. Especially when she thought of how close she'd come last night to showing Apollo how much he affected her. When he clearly felt nothing similar. She pulled back from Apollo's arms. 'Excuse me, I just need to go to the bathroom.'

Apollo watched Sasha hurry from the dance floor. Her face had been the colour of milk. He couldn't stop the spike of concern. Was she feeling ill? Was it her memory? Was she remembering more?

He cursed and made his way over to the bar. Concern for his wife was a novel and unwelcome sentiment. Also unwelcome was the raging arousal still lingering in his blood after that dance. Holding her so close, smelling her scent. The thin fabric of her dress doing little to hide how her slender curves had felt against his body…no other woman had ever had such an effect on him.

He took women he desired to bed. He told them up front that he wasn't looking for anything permanent. Except *her*. Everything about his experience with her had been so novel, and that's why he'd let his guard down momentarily. A moment she'd exploited when she'd come to him in London a month after their night together with her shock announcement.

But all of that was in danger of being forgotten with the rush of hot desire in his blood. Clouding his judgement. Blunting his control. Changing things. He should never have agreed to let her join him tonight. They weren't a couple.

They never would have married if it hadn't been for—

Apollo saw Sasha return to the room. Her head was turning left and right, clearly searching for him.

She looked vulnerable. Out of place. He saw more than one man look at her twice, caught by her fresh-faced beauty. She stood out in a crowd of rich and jaded cynics. And that's why she'd appealed to him that very first night.

But it had all been a mirage. Her memory loss might very well be real, but underneath it lay the true Sasha Miller. A liar and a mercenary bitch. It wouldn't be long before she showed her true colours again. At that moment, as if hearing his thoughts, she saw him and their eyes locked across the room. Apollo vowed not to forget who she really was.

The journey winding back up the hills to Apollo's villa was taken in silence. Sasha was engrossed in her own thoughts. The questions buzzing in her brain were growing increasingly loud and hard to ignore. Especially after tonight when she'd gone out in public, pretending to the world that she was this man's wife. When reality couldn't be further from that truth.

Apollo parked the car at the foot of the steps leading up to the front door of the villa. Sasha turned to him in the gloom of the car. 'Why did you let me come with you tonight?'

Apollo put his hands on the wheel. 'Primarily because I didn't expect you to be ready on time. You never were before.'

'So that would have been your excuse for leaving me behind.'

He looked at her and shrugged minutely, unapologetic.

Sasha shook her head. 'What happened, Apollo? Why are we like this? You liked me in London. You pursued me…asked me for a drink. Took me for dinner.'

Took me to bed?

She couldn't remember those details but she sensed *yes*, because her body was attuned to his on a level that she couldn't deny. And would a man like Apollo have married her without sleeping with her? He didn't strike her as the traditional type.

Was she? Had she been a virgin?

'You really want to get into this now?'

Once again she wasn't sure. Did she want to know everything? But she heard herself say, 'Yes.'

'Are you sure you're ready?'

Sasha swallowed the rising fear. 'I need to know. I feel like I'm the only one left out of a secret.'

'Very well. But not here—inside.'

A feeling of panic eclipsed the fear as Sasha followed Apollo inside the villa. Was she really ready for this? *No.* But she knew she couldn't continue not knowing either.

It was quiet. The staff had gone home or were in bed. He led the way into one of the less formal drawing rooms, flicking on low lights.

He went over to a drinks cabinet, tugging at the bow-tie around his neck. He looked back at her, 'Would you like a drink?'

'Will I need one?' Sasha joked, but it felt hollow.

He arched a brow and she said, 'A small brandy, please.' She wasn't even sure if she'd ever had brandy before but felt like it might be necessary.

Apollo poured a drink for himself and brought her over a small tumbler. She took a sniff and wrinkled her nose at the strong smell. She took a tentative sip and the liquid slid down her throat and into her stomach, leaving a trail of fire and a lingering afterglow of heat. It wasn't unpleasant.

Apollo shrugged off his jacket and Sasha wished he hadn't because now she could see the play of muscles under the thin material of his shirt. He faced her. 'What do you want to know?

Everything.

She swallowed. Where to start? 'Did we sleep together?'

'Yes. We spent one night together.'

An instant flush of heat landed in Sasha's belly that had nothing to do with the alcohol. Her instinct had been right. She'd slept with this man.

That was why her body remembered.

But she didn't.

She swallowed. 'The night we had dinner in... The Shard?'

He nodded. 'Yes, then you came back to my apartment.'

Ridiculously she almost felt like apologising for not being able to remember. Instinctively she felt that it had been memorable, and that a man like Apollo wasn't easily forgotten.

Her hand gripped the glass. 'Was I...? Was it my first time?'

His jaw clenched. 'I believed it was, yes. But since then...let's just say that I can't be sure you didn't make it seem that way.'

Sasha felt something like shame creep up inside her. 'Why would I lie about being a virgin?'

He looked at her and she couldn't escape that green gaze or the clear admonishment. 'To make yourself appear more innocent than you were. Because you thought it would appeal to me, a jaded cynic? Who knows?'

'I didn't tell you beforehand?'

He shook his head. 'You said you were afraid that if I'd known how inexperienced you were, I wouldn't want you.'

Sasha sat down on a seat behind her, her legs feeling distinctly wobbly.

'What happened then?'

Apollo drank the contents of his glass and put it down carefully. He faced her and folded his arms across his chest. He looked like a warrior, preparing for battle. All sinew and muscle. Not an inch of softness.

'After that night we went our separate ways.'

Sasha absorbed that. Had it been a mutual decision? She

shied away from asking that question now. It was enough to absorb that he'd been her first lover.

Or had he?

She felt an instinctive need to reject his claim that she might not have been innocent. But how could she defend herself when she didn't know for sure?

She took another sip of the fiery drink, her hand not quite steady. 'If we went our separate ways…then how… did we end up here, married?'

For a second her heart palpitated. Maybe he'd come after her? Maybe one night hadn't been enough?

He paused for a moment and then he said, 'Because a month after that night, you came to my offices in London and you told me that you were pregnant with my child.'

Sasha stood up slowly, there was a roaring sound in her ears and she had to shake her head to clear it. 'I'm sorry… I what?'

He spoke slowly. 'You told me that you were pregnant with my child.'

CHAPTER FIVE

THE WORD SANK into Sasha's head but didn't make sense. *Pregnant.* She put a hand to her belly but it was flat. Something occurred to her and she felt her blood drain south. The glass fell out of nerveless fingers but she barely noticed Apollo stride forward to pick it up and take her arm, pushing her gently back into the chair.

She looked up at him. 'Did I lose it?'

How could she not know if she'd lost her own baby? Was that why Apollo hated her? For losing their baby?

Both hands were on her belly now as if that could help her to remember something so huge…so cataclysmic.

But Apollo was shaking his head. 'No. You didn't lose it, because you were never pregnant in the first place. You deliberately lied about being pregnant to get me to marry you, Sasha.'

She hadn't been pregnant.

In the midst of the relief that she hadn't forgotten such a seismic event, Apollo's words sank in.

'You deliberately lied. To get me to marry you.'

Sasha's first reaction was denial. Rejection. She shook her head. 'No… I wouldn't have said that. I couldn't have done something like that…'

'But you did,' Apollo countered curtly.

She was glad she was sitting down because she was pretty sure she would have collapsed otherwise. 'I… I told you I was pregnant. But I wasn't?'

He nodded. His face was impossibly grim.

She tried to make sense of it all, and also the gut-wrenching knowledge that he *hadn't* come after her, because she'd been the one to go to him in the end. 'But why would I do such a thing?'

His mouth went thin. 'You really have to ask that question? We slept together and you saw an opportunity.'

He indicated with a hand. 'Look around you. You hungered for a better life and you were going to use me to get it.'

A moment ago Sasha had felt as if her legs wouldn't support her but now she stood again, too agitated to keep sitting. She paced back and forth. 'But that's...' She stopped. 'That's an awful thing to do.'

'Yes, it is,' he agreed.

She struggled to recall any hint of what might have led her to do such a drastic thing but her mind stayed annoyingly blank.

'Maybe I believed I was pregnant? Did we...use protection?'

His whole body bristled. 'Of course. I would never be so lax. But I will admit that I didn't check afterwards. There's always a possibility of failure and you capitalised on that, sowing the seed of doubt in my mind.'

'But how were you so sure I'd lied about the pregnancy?'

'I had my suspicions when you showed no signs of pregnancy and then after an...incident you admitted it was a lie.'

'An incident...?'

He nodded and paced away from her, turned back. 'I was in London on business and came back after a panicked call from Rhea. You were hosting a party with some new-found friends.'

The way Apollo's lip curled on *friends* told her what he'd thought of them. 'I found you snorting cocaine and drinking. When you'd sobered up you admitted it had been a lie to trap me.'

Sasha went back to the chair and sat down again. Reeling. She felt cold and wrapped her arms around herself.

She forced herself to look at Apollo. She felt deep in her bones that she wouldn't have done such heinous things— lying about being pregnant, taking drugs—*couldn't* have. And yet why would he lie? This explained his antipathy and also the way Rhea and Kara had looked at her like an unexploded bomb on her return from the hospital.

She went even colder as she absorbed the full extent of everything he'd told her. 'You didn't want to marry me.'

His jaw tightened. 'No.' Just that. *No.*

Why not? trembled on her lips but she didn't have to ask that question. He hadn't been interested in her after their night together in London. Her innocence must have been a huge turn-off.

Desperately trying to salvage something positive, she said, 'But in London you took me for dinner…to your apartment… You liked me then?' She hated how insecure she sounded.

A sense of exposure hit Apollo again. His voice was taut with self-recrimination. 'You captivated me. Briefly. You were different.'

'Different from what?'

Sasha looked so guileless. Pale. Eyes huge.

Was she really faking this amnesia? Was it too convenient that she was remembering snippets but not everything? Was she laughing at him? Forcing him to articulate why he'd wanted her?

But something uneasy in his gut told him that she couldn't be faking it. She looked too tortured.

He said, 'Different from everyone else. Other women.'

Twin flags of pink made her cheeks flush and for a moment Apollo was rewarded with a flashback to watching her face flush with pleasure as she'd moved under him, around him.

She said tightly, 'You mean I wasn't as sophisticated.'

Apollo had to use every atom of his control to counter the rush of desire. Damn her. 'You caught my eye. You were refreshingly unaffected. Open. Friendly. But it was all a lie.'

Sasha remembered feeling invisible that night. Until he'd looked directly at her, and the flash of pure heat that had gone through her body. Her tray of drinks had wobbled precariously and he'd stepped forward and steadied it. His lazy, charming smile.

'Promise to meet me for a drink and I'll give the tray back.'

She couldn't remember sleeping with him or the aftermath, but she could imagine all too easily how he would have laid it out. Telling her not to expect more. A man like this would have been used to such scenarios with women. Had she been so desperate that she'd begged for more? She felt ashamed for herself.

In a way now Sasha was glad she couldn't remember exactly what had happened. This was humiliating enough without recalling in excruciating detail how banal the experience must have been for a man of the world like him. To sleep with a virgin. She'd obviously been a novelty for a jaded billionaire and her appeal hadn't lasted long.

Her head was starting to throb faintly. 'What happens now?'

'Nothing. Until you've recovered fully. Then we can discuss the future.'

The future.

Sasha felt slightly hysterical. She couldn't recall much of the past, never mind the future.

She stood up. 'I'm getting a headache. I think I'll go to bed.'

Apollo watched as she turned and walked out. She was the colour of pale parchment. Maybe it had been too soon to tell her the unvarnished truth? No matter how much she'd insisted she wanted to know.

He felt an impulse to go after her and make sure she was okay but he told himself he was being ridiculous. The woman who had engineered a fake pregnancy to trap him into marriage was no delicate soul. Accident or no accident.

He poured himself another shot of whisky and downed it in one. It burned his throat. But he couldn't get her pale face and huge shocked eyes out of his mind. He had to admit that he was finding it hard to continue suspecting that she was faking the amnesia. Sasha would never have been able to play this far more innocent incarnation for so long without cracking.

Which meant...this news was as shocking to her now as it had been to him when he'd first heard it.

Apollo cursed and put down the glass. He went upstairs and stood outside Sasha's bedroom door for a long moment. He heard no sounds.

He knocked lightly but again there was no sound. He opened the door and went in. His eyes took a moment to adjust to the dim light. He could see no shape in the bed. And then he saw her, standing outside on the balcony.

She must have heard him because she turned around. She'd changed. She was wearing a diaphanous robe over what looked like a short negligée. From where he stood, Apollo could see the outline of her body. All slender curves and pale skin.

His blood surged, and he realised in that moment that he shouldn't have come up here. Sasha stepped into the room. 'Is something wrong?'

But instead of leaving, Apollo moved towards her as if drawn by a magnet. The moon was behind her, low in the sky. A perfect crescent. The milky glow made her look ethereal, adding a silver tinge to her rose-gold hair. It was down again, falling in soft waves over her shoulders.

He had an urge to touch her to make sure she was, in fact, real. He stopped a couple of feet away. Her scent reached him—lemon, underlain with something more tantalisingly exotic. But soft, not overpowering.

Different.

'You said you had a headache.'

She touched her head. 'It's okay now, thank you. I think it was just taking in all that information...'

Sasha wasn't sure that she wasn't hallucinating right now. Was Apollo really standing in her room, looking at her as if he'd never seen her before?

But then, at that moment, he said, 'I just wanted to check you were okay,' and then turned around as if to leave.

Sasha acted on an impulse, reaching out with her hand. 'Wait.'

He stopped. Turned around. Sasha wasn't even sure what she wanted to say. And then she did. She dropped her outstretched hand. 'I don't remember anything of what you said... It doesn't feel like something I would do but then how do I know?'

She bit her lip. 'Did you even care about the baby?'

Apollo had to school his expression in case she saw something he didn't want to reveal. The pain of losing his entire family over a period of a few years had been so acute that he'd always vowed to avoid such pain again by not having a family of his own.

But, to his surprise, after the initial shock and anger at Sasha's pregnancy news had abated, he'd found that the thought of a baby he could protect and nurture had softened something inside him. And had restored a broken sense of hope, optimism.

But then, the fact that she'd lied about it and roused those feelings had made a cruel mockery of the defences he'd built up over the years. They hadn't been strong after all. Now, though, they were ironclad. Not that he would ever reveal to her what she'd done to him. She'd revealed a weakness, and reopened a wound and he would never forgive her for that.

'I had never intended on having a relationship or becoming a father. Not after losing my entire family. But of course I would have cared for any child of mine. I'm not a monster.'

Sasha's eyes were huge. Full of emotion. Exposure prickled over his skin just as she said huskily, 'I'm sorry…for what happened. I don't know why I pretended to be pregnant but I'd like to think I had good reasons.'

He fought against the image she was projecting of someone compassionate, who *cared*. He should move back, out of her dangerous orbit, but instead he found himself moving closer. All he could see was her. Looking impossibly innocent. Impossibly because she hadn't been innocent at all. Or had she? Physically perhaps, at least.

He had an intensely erotic memory of how it had felt to thrust deep into that silken embrace. Her muscles had clamped so tightly around him he'd seen stars.

Angry at his lack of control, he asked curtly, 'Are you really sorry, though? Or is this just an elaborate showcase of your acting skills to entice me back into your bed so you can try to get pregnant for real?'

Horror at his relentless cynicism made Sasha take a step back. '*No.* How can you say such a thing?'

Apollo's mouth was a thin line. 'Very easily, because you did it before, countless times, including the memorable occasion when I came home to find you naked in my bed.'

Shock and disbelief made Sasha take another step back. She shook her head. 'No, there is no way I would have ever done such a thing.'

Apollo just arched a brow. 'Why would I lie? You have to agree it made sense. After all, you weren't pregnant so you needed to get pregnant. Fast.'

Sasha swallowed. Had that really been her? So desperate? Conniving? She struggled to defend herself when she felt as if everything inside her was crumbling. 'But it's obvious you don't want me—why would I have humiliated myself like that?'

Apollo was looking at her so intensely she could scarcely breathe.

He said something under his breath then, a word she didn't understand, and then said, almost as if to himself, 'I thought I didn't want you any more, but now it's all I can think about. What kind of sorcery is this?'

Sasha's heart slammed to a stop, and then started again in an erratic rhythm. She suddenly became very aware of her flimsy garments. The silky thigh-skimming negligée and floaty dressing gown. Garments she didn't feel particularly comfortable in, but apparently she hadn't favoured comfort over style.

She tried to speak. 'I don't… There's no sorcery.'

His gaze raked her up and down and she trembled under its force. Her breasts felt heavy, their tips tightening into hard points, pressing against the silky material. Her body remembered this man. His touch. But she didn't. Frustration coursed through her. She couldn't take her eyes off his mouth, the firm sculpted lines.

Apollo barely heard Sasha's denial. He knew this was madness. That he shouldn't have come to her bedroom. But rational thought was fast dissolving in a haze of lust. He reached out and caught a loose tendril of silky hair, winding it around his finger, tugging her gently towards him.

When he looked down he could see her breasts rising and falling with her rapid breath, pale swells framed enticingly by lace, inviting him to touch, explore. Electricity hummed between them, thick and urgent.

He tipped her chin up with his forefinger and thumb. Her eyes were huge pools of blue. He had a flashback to the first time he'd kissed her, sitting in a discreet booth of the exclusive hotel bar where he'd taken her for a drink when she'd finished work on that first night.

It had been a rare novelty, waiting for her to emerge from a staff entrance of the hotel. He could remember the sensation of something loosening inside him. He'd been so focused for so long and suddenly he'd been diverted from that single-mindedness.

She'd been endearingly self-conscious in her black skirt, white shirt and black jacket. Flat shoes. Sheer tights.

He'd wanted her then and he wanted her now. He lowered his head, anticipation prickling across his skin. He'd thought he'd never kiss her again.

Hadn't wanted to.

But he was being punished for that complacency now, because here he was, as consumed with lust as he had been the first time.

Tension was a tight coil inside Sasha as she waited for Apollo's mouth to touch hers and she told herself desperately that he'd kissed her before—more than kissed her, so it shouldn't come as a shock—but when his mouth touched hers, it was more than a shock. It was an earthquake, erupting from her solar plexus and spreading out to every nerve-ending, bringing with it thousands of volts of electricity.

She wasn't even aware of her hands going to his shirt and clinging on for dear life. His hands were in her hair, angling her head, and their mouths were on fire. She tasted the whisky he'd been drinking and she felt molten and solid all at the same time. It was intoxicating, and nothing could have prepared her for this.

His chest was a steel wall against her breasts. She arched instinctively closer, seeking closer contact. One of his hands moved down, skimming over her arm, around to her back, pressing her even closer.

His arousal pressed against her lower belly and the flood

of damp heat between her legs was almost embarrassing. She pressed her thighs together in a bid to stem the rising tide of desire but it was impossible.

But at that very moment Apollo pulled back. It was so sudden that Sasha went with him and he had to steady her, putting his hands on her arms. She opened her eyes, feeling dizzy. Stunned.

She was breathing as if she'd run a race. Her heart was hammering, and a hunger that was new and yet familiar at the same time pounded through her blood, demanding to be satisfied. She felt greedy. *Needy.*

It took a second for Apollo's face to come back into focus and when she registered his harsh expression she pulled free of his hands, even though her legs still felt jittery.

He said, 'That shouldn't have happened. It was never part of this marriage deal. Go to bed, Sasha, it's late.'

He turned and left the room and Sasha stared after the empty space for a long minute. She felt too shell-shocked to even be irritated that he'd spoken to her like a child, as if she'd walked into *his* room and kissed *him.*

Her skin felt seared alive, her heart was still racing and her whole body was crying out for a fulfilment it knew but couldn't remember. Her breasts ached and she throbbed between her legs, and that was after just a kiss.

She moved on autopilot, closing the doors to the balcony, slipping out of the robe and under the covers of the bed. She eventually fell into a fitful sleep, with thoughts and dreams full of disjointed, disturbing images.

Apollo stood under the punishing spray of a cold shower for longer than he could almost bear. Eventually he got out and hitched a towel around his waist, catching his reflection in the mirror above the sink.

He looked pained. And he knew it wasn't from the cold shower. What the hell had he been thinking—going to Sasha's room? Kissing her? He hadn't been thinking. That was the problem.

It had taken every ounce of his restraint to pull back and not rip apart those flimsy garments, spreading her back on the bed so he could relive the night they'd shared in London. So that he could consummate this marriage.

This marriage was not about consummation or sleeping together. And while he hadn't wanted her it had been all too easy to forget he had ever wanted her.

You never forgot.

He scowled at his reflection.

But now the floodgates were open. He'd tasted Sasha again and she was as potent as she had been the first time.

He wanted his wife.

But she was the last thing he should want. Especially not when she had the ability to reopen old wounds with just a look from those huge eyes. What he needed was to excise Sasha from his life once and for all.

And for that to happen she needed to regain her memory. The sooner that happened and she reverted to her duplicitous nature, the sooner Apollo could get on with his life and forget she'd ever existed.

What he needed to do now was provide every opportunity to nudge her memory in the right direction.

Sasha was trying to avoid looking at Apollo across the breakfast table on the outdoor terrace. She was still raw after that kiss and gritty-eyed after a mostly sleepless night, broken by disturbing dreams she was afraid to analyse.

The impulse to look, though, was too strong and she glanced his way to see him lifting a small coffee cup to his mouth, his gaze on the paper in his hand. To her intense irritation he looked as if nothing had happened last night. He was as cool and fresh as if he'd enjoyed the sleep of a baby.

He was clean-shaven and the memory of his stubble

against her jaw made heat rise up through her body. For a breathless panicky moment she wondered if she'd, in fact, dreamt that kiss, but then he put his paper down and looked at her and the jolt of electricity that went straight to her solar plexus told her that kiss at least hadn't been a dream. It was of little comfort.

'We're going to go to Krisakis for a few days.'

She forced her brain to function. 'Kris— Where?'

'It's the island I own. It's part of the Cyclades chain of islands. Santorini, Naxos, Paros…'

She'd forgotten that he owned an island.

'I'm constructing an eco-resort and I need to check progress and meet with some of the designers.'

'Have I been there before?'

He nodded. 'I took you there when we first came to Greece.'

Sasha tried to conjure up an image of what the island might be like but her mind stubbornly refused to provide anything.

Right at that moment, after the dreams she'd had last night, she relished the thought of a change of scenery. 'When do we leave?'

Apollo looked at his watch. 'In an hour. I've instructed Kara to pack some things for you.'

She felt prickly. 'I can pack my own bag.'

Apollo shrugged. 'As you wish. I need to make some calls before we go.' He got up and walked out of the room and Sasha's breath got stuck in her throat as she watched him go. He was wearing a polo shirt and faded jeans that lovingly hugged his buttocks and thighs.

Rhea bustled into the room and Sasha looked away quickly, mortified to have been caught ogling her husband, but also when she recalled what Apollo had told her about the party she'd hosted.

Taking drugs.

Her conscience wouldn't let her say nothing, though, and she caught Rhea's hand before she could clear the plates. The woman looked at her warily. Sasha said, 'I'm so sorry, Rhea...for what happened. For disrespecting you and this house.'

The older woman's expression softened. She patted Sasha's hand awkwardly. 'Is okay, Kyria Vasilis. Don't worry.'

She cleared the plates efficiently and left the room. Sasha still felt humiliated but a little lighter.

She stood up to leave the table and on an impulse walked down through the gardens. In spite of the sun, tentacles of those disturbing dreams from last night lingered, making her shiver a little.

The dreams had been shockingly erotic. She'd been on a bed, making love to Apollo. Their naked bodies entwined in the most intimate way possible. He'd held one of her hands over her head, capturing it, and his head had moved down, over her body, his mouth fastening over one nipple, feasting on her tender flesh. She could still feel it now, the delicious pulling, dragging sensation that had gone all the way down to between her legs where he'd pushed them apart with his thigh, opening her up to his body...

But then, abruptly, Sasha had realised that she was no longer in the body on the bed; she was standing apart, looking at him making love to another woman. Not her. But then the woman's face had been revealed and she'd smiled mockingly at Sasha and Sasha had realised that it *was* her. But it wasn't her.

She'd been separated from them by a glass wall. Able to see everything but not feel it. The woman on the bed was an imposter, pretending to be her. And Apollo didn't realise. She'd watched helplessly as he'd moved his powerful body between the woman's legs, how she'd opened up for him, and then the moment when he'd thrust deep inside.

The woman's legs were wrapped around Apollo's waist

and the whole time she'd looked at Sasha and then her mocking smile had turned to nightmarish laughter and that's when Sasha had woken, sweating and trembling from the force of it, filled with a feeling of doom and betrayal so acrid that she'd felt nauseous.

Sasha shook her head to try and dislodge the images and that horrible feeling of betrayal. But it had felt so real. And it couldn't be, obviously.

She went back inside, but on her way to the bedroom she passed by her office. She could hear the deep tones of Apollo's voice through his own office door.

On an impulse she went into the white and fluffy room, still a bit bemused at the thought that she'd insisted on having an office. There was a computer on the desk and she sat down and tapped a key experimentally. It opened automatically in an internet browser.

Wondering how it hadn't occurred to her before, she put Apollo's name into the search engine. The first items to pop up were recent deals and headlines like *Vasilis and His Midas Touch Strike Again!*

Sasha skimmed a recent profile article done for a prominent British financial newspaper where it talked about Apollo's myriad achievements and rapid rise to stratospheric success. He was also one of the first construction titans to commit to working ethically. Every worker on one of his sites had proper healthcare and insurance and if accidents occurred, workers were rehabilitated and then redeployed either back to where they'd been or to a new area more suited to them.

Consequently, his workers were among the happiest in a normally fickle industry and by holding himself to a higher standard, he was forcing the industry to change around him. He was a trailblazer.

At the end of the article it said:

When asked about his recent marriage to Sasha Miller, Vasilis was curt, saying, 'My private life is off-limits.'

Sasha felt sick. Unsurprisingly he hadn't wanted to divulge the details of his marriage of inconvenience to an interviewer.

It only made Sasha want to know more about her own past—what had happened to her to make her behave like that? To trap a man into marriage? She went back into the history of the computer and saw some social media account tabs and clicked on them. But they'd all been logged out and she couldn't remember the passwords.

For one of the main social accounts she could see a small picture of herself, smiling widely against a glamorous-looking backdrop of a marina. She was wearing more make-up. Her skin was tanned...which must have been fake because she was naturally the colour of a milk bottle. She was holding up a glass of sparkling wine. It sparkled almost as much as the massive diamond on her ring finger. It eclipsed the much plainer gold wedding band. The rings that had gone missing in the accident.

She rubbed her finger absently, imagining them being torn off somehow, but there was no mark on her finger or bruising to indicate what had happened. Something about that niggled at the edges of her memory. A sense that she had seen them somewhere...but not on her hand. But the memory refused to be pinned down. Again.

Sasha touched the picture of her face with a finger, as if that could unlock the secrets of her past.

Nothing.

Nothing except a tiny shiver down her spine. Looking at her face like this reminded her of that dream, because it was like looking at another person.

She turned off the computer, eager to put that image of

her face, and the dream, behind her. She saw a drawer in the desk and opened it, vaguely wondering if she might find some other clues to her past.

There was a thick manila envelope inside and she pulled it out. It had her name on it. For some reason, she felt superstitious about looking at the contents but the envelope was open and it was addressed to her.

She pulled out a thick sheaf of papers and read the words at the top of the first page: 'Application For Mutual Consent Divorce Proceedings Between Apollo Vasilis and Sasha Miller'.

It was dated a few days before the accident.

Sasha started to look through the pages, which weren't signed yet. They outlined the grounds for divorce. Irreconcilable differences. And non-consummation of the marriage.

They hadn't slept together.

So he really hadn't wanted her. But last night…he had. And he hadn't welcomed it.

'What are you doing?'

Sasha looked up to see Apollo standing in the doorway. She was too shocked to be embarrassed or feel like he'd caught her doing something illicit.

She held up the document. 'We were going to divorce?'

'We were always going to divorce.'

Sasha dropped the document back on the desk. 'But what about at first…when the baby…?' She trailed off, realising what she was saying.

He arched a brow, 'The baby that never existed?'

She flushed guiltily.

'When I believed you were pregnant we agreed to marry for a year, enough time to have the baby and then reassess the situation.'

Sasha frowned. 'What does that mean?'

'Custody.'

She struggled to understand. 'But presumably as the mother I would have had custody.'

Apollo shook his head. 'In the pre-nuptial agreement you signed away your right to full custody. You agreed to an arrangement where I would have full custody and I would set you up somewhere close enough for you to see the child on a regular basis.'

Sasha stood up. She shook her head. 'I can't believe I would have signed away full rights to my own baby.'

Apollo's lip curled. 'Don't forget there *was* no baby. I should have guessed something was amiss when you agreed so quickly to that, and when you were more interested in the alimony you would receive in the event of a divorce.'

Sasha remembered what he'd told her last night about how she'd tried to seduce him. To try and get pregnant. She felt sick. And even sicker when she thought of how he'd found her in such a debauched state. Taking drugs.

She forced herself to look at him. 'That's when you initiated the divorce, after the party, when you knew I wasn't pregnant.'

He nodded.

'Why didn't you just throw me out, once you knew?' She would have thrown her out. She felt angry at *herself.*

'I considered it. I wanted to. I never wanted to see you again. You disgusted me.'

Sasha felt every word like a little sharp knife to her heart. 'So why didn't you?'

'Because we are married. I couldn't trust you. I didn't know what you would do. You could have gone to the papers with some sob story and I have a reputation to maintain. The last thing I needed was adverse press attention.'

'And then I had the accident.'

He nodded. 'A few days later, you took one of the cars and disappeared for hours. When you hadn't returned by dinner-time, Rhea called me and a search was started. You eventually appeared by the side of a road not far from here, further up into the hills.'

Sasha felt cold. 'This marriage never had a chance.'

Apollo faltered for a moment when he thought of that first night he'd met Sasha. How easily she'd caught him with her fresh-faced beauty. How novel it had been to meet someone unjaded. Open. Joyful. But it hadn't been real. He forced the memory out. 'No.'

Sasha looked bewildered. 'Why did you agree to marry me at all? Why did you believe me?'

Feeling almost defensive now, he said, 'You had a note from a doctor confirming the pregnancy. And I consulted my legal team. We came to the conclusion that once you agreed to sign a pre-nuptial agreement, marrying you would offer me the best chance of custody and securing my child's future. There was a clause to say that if anything happened to the pregnancy or if the baby proved not to be mine after a DNA test, you would get nothing. Obviously you'd decided that the risk of marriage was worth it, even though you weren't pregnant. Hence your attempts to try and seduce me once we were married. Attempts that didn't work.'

Sasha winced at that. 'Why did you bring me back here after the accident? Why not just kick me out of your life for good now that you can?'

Why not indeed? mocked a little voice in Apollo's head. He could have done exactly that. He could have taken advantage of her amnesia to get her to sign the divorce papers and set her up in an apartment in Athens with a small allowance and a nurse to attend to her needs until the divorce was through.

But no matter how much he'd hated her for what she'd done, the way she'd looked after the accident—so pale and defenceless on that hospital bed—it had caught at him. And then she'd woken up and looked at him and it had been as if the previous months had fallen away and all he could re-member was that night they'd met.

Her memory loss had only complicated things further. Changing her. Reminding him of that first impression she'd made. Re-igniting his desire.

He said now, 'I'm not letting you go anywhere until we sign the divorce papers. I don't trust that you won't do something to exploit the power you have as my wife.'

He went on, 'I don't know why you took the car on the day you disappeared or where you went to…and until you regain your memory and you can tell me, you won't be going anywhere. For all I know, you took your wedding rings off because you have a lover, perhaps someone you were hoping to turn to because I hadn't fallen under your spell.'

A memory of that kiss last night blasted into Apollo's head, mocking him. He was under her spell again whether he liked it or not.

Sasha held up the sheaf of papers. She was pale. They were trembling lightly in her hand and that evidence of her emotions caught at him, making him feel an urge to pro-tect her. He rejected it.

She said, 'So why don't we just sign the papers now and be done with it?'

To his disgust, his immediate emotion wasn't one of re-lief that she was showing a willingness to put all this be-hind them and get out of his life. It was something much more ambiguous and disturbing. Reluctance to let her go.

He said, 'It's the weekend, my offices won't be open. And next Monday is a national holiday. In any case I've made plans to go and inspect the site on Krisakis. We will stick to this arrangement and sign the papers when we re-turn to Athens in a week. We'll be out of each other's lives within a month. And perhaps Krisakis will help jog your memory.'

Sasha felt winded. 'Once we sign the papers, it can happen that quickly?' The thought of never seeing Apollo again made her feel panicky. She told herself it was because he was the only familiar thing in her life, not because he'd come to mean anything to her. Clearly there had been little love lost between them.

Apollo's mouth firmed. 'Yes, it can happen that quickly. But obviously if your memory still hasn't returned by then, I'll make sure you're set up in a situation and place that feels secure and safe for you.'

Sasha wanted to curl inwards. The thought of Apollo pitying her enough to have to keep an eye on her after their marriage was over was a whole new level of humiliation.

'I'm sure that won't be necessary, but thank you.'

CHAPTER SIX

A COUPLE OF hours later, Apollo's words still reverberated in Sasha's head.

'I'll make sure you're set up in a situation and place that feels secure and safe for you.'

The perks of a rich man. Able to dissolve marriages and set up inconvenient ex-wives with a minimum of fuss.

The fact that the imminent dissolution of a marriage she'd apparently engineered into being through lies and deceit wasn't filling her with a sense of relief, only brought about more confusion.

She could remember being stunned by Apollo's interest in her when they'd first met. Intimidated but excited too. How had she gone from that to wanting to deceive him so heinously?

With a sigh, she let the landscape beneath her distract her from circling thoughts that were going nowhere and not helping.

They were in a helicopter, flying over the Aegean, and she looked down in awe at boats and islands that looked like toys beneath them.

When she'd seen the sleek black machine at the private airfield, she'd balked. Apollo had looked at her. 'You flew in this when I took you to the island the first time. You loved it.'

'Did I? Sasha had asked doubtfully. For the whole journey, in spite of her tortured thoughts and the beauty below them, her heart had been in her throat. And even more now as they started descending over an island and the helicopter tipped perilously to the left.

This must be Krisakis. Sasha forced down the fluttering panic and took in the rocky coastline where pockets of brightly coloured flowers flourished along the cliffs. The sea lapped against rocks and then they rounded a headland and an empty white sand beach appeared, like something on a postcard.

Sasha could see steps cut into the rocks, leading up to lush grounds and then up further to a white modern building—a series of buildings laid out like interconnecting cubes. Sunlight glinted off acres of glass. An infinity pool with sun loungers had never looked so inviting.

Apollo was saying into her headset, 'This is the villa, the first thing I built here. The island was hit by an earthquake about half a century ago, leaving only a small population behind. With the development I'm building on the other side of the island, it's becoming a thriving community again. People who were born here but who had to leave have returned to live out their last days, bringing their sons and daughters with them to make new lives.'

Sasha couldn't help thinking it was ironic for a man who'd professed little interest in having a family to be invested in bringing them together like this.

The helicopter was landing now on a helipad a little distance from the villa. When the pilot had touched down, Apollo got out. He opened Sasha's door and helped her out. Her legs felt like rubber and Apollo's hand tightened on hers. 'Okay?'

She locked her knees to stop them wobbling. 'Yes, fine.' She took her hand back.

Apollo stepped aside to talk to the pilot for a moment and then once the bags were unloaded he led her over to a safe spot while the helicopter lifted back up into the air before tilting to the right and heading off into the azure-blue sky.

Sasha put the sun hat she'd carried on her head, glad of Kara's thoughtfulness. Which was even more thoughtful now considering what she'd put them through. Sasha heard a faint sound and turned around to see what looked like a golf cart bouncing across the grounds towards them.

Apollo waved at the person driving who waved back enthusiastically. He said, 'That's Spiro—he's the son of my housekeeper here, helping out before he goes back to college.'

The young man jumped out when he'd come to a stop beside him, a big grin directed at Apollo as he took the bags, stowing them in the back.

Sasha couldn't help smiling at his cheerful effervescence but when he looked at her his smile faltered. Sasha's insides plummeted. Not again. Had she been rude to him too? The young man's eyes grew round and he said something to Apollo, who said something sharp back.

He held out his hand. 'Kyria Vasilis, nice to meet you again.'

Sasha forced a smile and took his hand, mentally apologising for whatever she'd done.

By the time they reached the stunning villa, she was preparing herself for the same reaction as she'd got from Kara and Rhea when she'd returned to the villa in Athens. Sure enough, Spiro's mother, Olympia, looked wary but kindly. Maybe Sasha hadn't behaved too badly on the island. After all, it didn't seem as if there was much in the way of distraction.

Apollo said something to his housekeeper and then turned to Sasha. 'Olympia will show you around, and take you to your room. I'll join you after I've made a couple of calls.'

Sasha took in the bright white spaces and minimalist furnishings as she followed the matronly woman through the villa. It oozed modernity and serenity. A contrast to the more traditional villa in Athens. Sasha liked it. She liked the starkness. The lack of fussiness. Its simplicity soothed some of her ragged edges.

Olympia led her down a long corridor and opened a door, standing back. She smiled. 'Your room, Kyria Vasilis.'

Sasha tried not to be self-conscious about the fact that she obviously had a separate room here too. She forced a polite smile, which promptly slid off her face as she walked into the vast room. Actually, it was a suite of rooms. They flowed into each other, no doors between them.

There was a vast bed with a four-poster frame and muslin drapes pulled back. The bathroom had two types of shower, one outdoor and one indoor, and a bath that was more like a private lap pool.

There was a dressing room and then a lounge, with its own soft comfy couch and media centre, with TV and a sound system. Perhaps, Sasha thought with an edge of hysteria, he was going to lock her in here, and keep her prisoner.

But then Olympia was signalling for her attention and Sasha followed her to the huge windows that were actually sliding doors leading outside to a private terrace, with sunbed and umbrella.

Olympia said in halting English, 'We will unpack your things while you take tea on the terrace. Follow me, please.'

Sasha smiled, silently trying to communicate her apologies for however she'd behaved before. Olympia led her back through the villa to the main living area again and out to a shaded terrace where a table was laid out with fruit and small cakes and pastries. Tea and coffee were in two pots, or there was sparkling water.

Everything was hushed and very exclusive. Sasha poured herself some tea and could feel herself loosening in spite of herself, as if she couldn't *not*, against this breath-taking backdrop. All she could see in the distance was the blue of the sparkling Aegean and the hazy outline of other islands on the horizon.

She didn't think she'd ever been anywhere so deeply peaceful. But apparently she had been here before, so why wasn't there even a tiny piece of recognition? Sasha fought off the feeling of frustration. She had to trust that her memory would come back to her sooner or later. It had to. And yet…with that assertion came a little shiver of foreboding.

Apollo stood in the shadows for a moment, watching Sasha where she sat on the terrace. She was wearing pale blue culottes and the white sleeveless shirt tied at the waist. She consistently seemed to choose the very opposite of what she would have gone for before.

He'd never imagined a woman in this place. There was something about the peace and tranquillity of this island that had always soothed a raw part of him and it had felt too personal to share, apart from with the islanders, of course.

He'd never brought a lover here, and he hadn't counted Sasha as a lover when he'd brought her here nearly three months ago. It had been a strategic decision.

But much as he hated to admit it, this time was very different from that first visit. She looked good here now. As if she belonged. In spite of that pale colouring. Her hair was down and it blew gently in the breeze, the rose-gold strands wavy and untamed. He could almost see her freckles from here. Freckles she'd always seemed obsessed with covering up, apart from that first couple of nights they'd met. He could still remember being fascinated by them on her naked body, the little clusters in secret spots. She'd been embarrassed…until he'd distracted her.

Heat gathered in his groin, making his muscles tight. Hard. He cursed. It was as if she'd had a personality change. He'd seen a film once about a man who had been ruthless and uncaring and who'd lost his memory in a shooting, and how, afterwards, his whole personality had changed.

Could it be something like that? Sasha looked troubled now, as if she was thinking the same thing as he was. He couldn't imagine what it must be like to know…nothing of yourself. A curious small ache formed in Apollo's chest. For a moment, he felt a sense of…pity? Concern?

She looked at him then, as if sensing him, and Apollo shoved down the fleeting moment of whatever it was. It wasn't welcome. He came out onto the terrace, shades hiding his eyes from the sun. And her.

'How do you like the villa?' he asked, sitting down.

Sasha sat up. 'It's beautiful, stunning. I feel like I've never seen anything like it, but apparently I have. And this island…it's so…'

Apollo took a sip of coffee, 'Boring?' he supplied.

She shook her head, looking away. 'No, not at all, it's so peaceful.' Apollo went still, looking at her suspiciously. Her voice was husky, as if she was genuinely moved.

She glanced at him then, her mouth taut. 'Don't tell me, I didn't like it the first time around?'

He shook his head, almost feeling slightly guilty now. 'No. You looked around and asked when we were leaving. You stayed one night.'

'Why did you bring me here the first time?'

Apollo's conscience pricked. He ignored it. 'I thought it would be somewhere you'd enjoy relaxing.'

'You mean, somewhere you could hide me away? Your inconvenient wife?'

Sasha stood up suddenly, shocked at how incensed she was. 'What about now? Is this where you're planning on hiding me away until the divorce comes through?'

She went to walk off the terrace, her sense of peace shattered, but Apollo stood up and caught her hand. Electricity sizzled up her arm, and she bit her lip against the sensation.

No. And then, grudgingly, 'Maybe, the first time. I

wasn't really thinking. I was still in shock that you were pregnant and how that was going to affect my life.'

Sasha looked at him, forgetting for a moment that she hadn't been pregnant. 'What about my life?'

She flushed and pulled her hand free, walking a few feet away. This was all so messed up.

Out of the corner of her eye she could see Apollo run a hand through his hair. 'Look,' he said, 'we're here for a few days. I've got some business to attend to with the resort they're building and I've been invited to an opening of another resort on Santorini, not far from here, later this week. You're still recuperating, so take this time to rest and it might help your memory.'

Sasha looked at Apollo. She couldn't see his eyes behind his shades. Just the hard line of his jaw. That decadent mouth. The width of his shoulders and the breadth of his chest. Her heart beat faster. 'You're not leaving me here, then?'

Apollo's jaw clenched as if her words had affected him. 'I'm not a gaoler, Sasha. When we leave here, we'll sign divorce papers and we'll be able to move on with our lives.'

'Move on with our lives.'

Whether her memory was back or not. Suddenly the thought of going back into a world she couldn't remember was beyond intimidating. At that moment she'd never felt so alone.

Sasha looked vulnerable to Apollo, with a tiny frown between her eyes. Pale face. Very slight and slender. Yet he could remember the innate strength of her body as she'd taken him in so deeply he'd seen stars. The press of her breasts against his chest, nipples like bullets.

He took a deep breath, fought for control. He heard himself saying the words before he'd really articulated them to himself. 'I told you, Sasha, I'll make sure you're in a safe and secure environment. You won't be expected to navigate a world you don't remember if your memory hasn't yet returned.'

Something flashed in her eyes, an emotion Apollo couldn't decipher. 'Thank you. I appreciate that…after everything…'

She looked away from Apollo and gestured with a hand. 'This is paradise. Thank you for bringing me here.'

Her expression had turned indecipherable. Her voice and tone as if she were a guest. For a moment Apollo had to battle the urge to take her arms and force her to look at him, force her to reveal the emotion she'd just hidden from him.

Disgust at himself made him say something curt about checking work emails and he strode off the terrace, every cell in his body crying out for another taste of the woman who had torn his life asunder.

During the days following their arrival on Krisakis, Sasha found that with the peace and tranquillity she was finally feeling totally recuperated. And also it gave her mind time to settle too, and absorb all the revelations. The fake pregnancy, the divorce. Her behaviour.

Questions kept niggling at her—what had happened between them when she'd met Apollo and had then pretended to be pregnant? Why would she have done such a thing?

She still couldn't remember sleeping with Apollo. But she suspected she was remembering in her dreams, which were becoming more and more vivid and erotic. Last night she'd dreamt of him again.

They'd both been naked and he'd been kneeling between her legs, pushing them apart. She'd felt gauche, self-conscious, but all of that had dissolved in a pool of electric heat when he'd lowered his head and pressed kisses up the inside of one thigh.

She'd been shaking, trembling with need. Body dewed with a fine sheen of perspiration. And then he'd hooked her legs over his shoulders and he'd put his mouth to her *right there*, at the centre of her being. His tongue and mouth had done such things to her—she blushed in the late afternoon heat just thinking about how his tongue had felt, thrusting inside her.

She'd woken up, her nightshirt clinging to her damp body, heart racing, inner muscles clamping around a phantom erection. Mortified, she'd dived into the shower in a bid to bring herself back to reality.

She took a deep shuddering breath and forced her mind away from disturbing dreams. She didn't know what was worse—inhabiting her body in the dream or watching herself making love to Apollo from a distance. Both were equally disturbing.

She liked this time of the day best, late in the afternoon, when the intense heat of the sun had died down and it was more bearable. She'd found books on the well-stocked shelves of the informal living room and was reading a very unchallenging thriller. What did they call them? A cosy mystery? It was perfect for her exhausted and frayed brain.

She woke late most days, and wondered if she'd always had a habit of sleeping in. She was too scared to ask Apollo when he appeared every evening for their dinners on the terrace for fear of what he'd say.

He'd been gone every day from early, much like he had in Athens—presumably tending to business on the other side of the island.

They were both careful to stick to neutral topics at dinner, but Sasha couldn't ignore the growing pull she felt towards him. The throbbing undercurrent of electricity that sprang to life as soon as he came near her.

As if on cue, the small hairs stood up on the back of her neck and she heard a movement and looked around to see Apollo walking out to where she sat on a sun lounger near the pool, under an umbrella.

She was glad of the light covering of a kaftan over her swimsuit—the only one she seemed to own—as her body reacted to seeing him. And the memory of that dream. His clothes didn't help to calm her pulse. He was wearing board shorts and a polo shirt that showcased the bulging biceps of his arms and the hard pectorals of his chest. She saw dark hair curling just above the top open button.

As he came closer she said quickly, 'I'm wearing sunscreen. Factor fifty.'

Was that the slightest twitch at the corner of his mouth? He sat down on the lounger beside her and Olympia appeared with a tray holding two tall glasses of homemade iced lemonade.

He smiled at Olympia. *'Efharisto.'*

The woman smiled back, looking ridiculously pleased with herself. Sasha couldn't blame her.

Sasha watched as his Adam's apple moved up and down as he took a gulp of the drink. Even that movement was sexy. She took such a quick gulp of her own drink to calm her ragged nerves that she coughed and spluttered. Immediately he was beside her, a hand on her back. 'Are you okay?'

Eyes watering, Sasha could only gasp and try to breathe but all she was aware of was his hand on her back and the tight musculature of his dark naked thigh near hers.

When she could, she got out, 'I'm fine…fine.'

Thankfully he moved back to his lounger. He'd pushed his glasses up on his head and Sasha spotted something in his hair. Feeling shy, she pointed to his head. He ruffled his hair, dislodging fine dust. He grimaced. 'I need to take a shower, it's dust from the site.'

'Are you actually working on the site, too?'

'Just a little here and there. I like to be hands on.'

That only made Sasha think of how it had felt to have his hands on her thighs, pushing them apart, in the dream.

Without even thinking about what she was saying, she asked, 'Could I come and see it?'

He lifted his brows in surprise. 'You want to see a construction site?'

She felt self-conscious now. 'If it's not too much trouble?'

His expression was bemused. 'Sure, if you want. I can take you with me over the next couple of days.'

Sasha smiled tentatively. 'I'd like to, as long as I won't be in your way.'

For a second something shimmered between them, a lightness. Then Apollo stood up. 'I'm going to go for a swim. Cool off.'

He downed the rest of his drink and put his glass down. Before he left he said, 'I'll see you at dinner? Unless you want to join me for a swim. I'm going to go down to the sea.'

The thought of swimming in the sea was immediately appealing but then something occurred to Sasha. 'I don't even know if I *can* swim.'

'Have you been in the water yet?

She shook her head. It had looked inviting but something had held her back. A wariness.

Apollo waited a beat and then he said, 'Okay, wait here, I'll be back in a minute.'

Sasha wasn't sure what he meant by that but it was apparent when he returned in a few minutes, carrying a towel and wearing nothing but short swim shorts. She stopped breathing. They were moulded to his hips and thighs. Their black colour only made his skin seem even darker. He was six feet plus of hard, honed male, not an ounce of spare flesh. He threw the towel down on the lounger and held out a hand.

Sasha averted her gaze from acres of honed olive-skinned flesh and looked at his hand suspiciously. 'What's going on?'

'We're going to see if you can swim.'

Suddenly reluctant, she said, 'I don't know if I want to know.'

'We'll go into the pool at the shallow end. You won't drown, I promise.'

Reluctantly, she stood up and lifted up the kaftan, very aware of the flesh-coloured swimsuit underneath. She avoided Apollo's eye, self-conscious and more nervous than she liked to admit.

He was still holding out his hand and after a moment's hesitation she took it, feeling his long fingers close around hers. His touch immediately soothed the nerves that had sprung from nowhere.

She followed him over to the steps that led down into the infinity pool. He tugged her along gently and she stepped in, the water a cold shock against her sun-heated skin.

He led her down until the water reached the tops of her thighs.

'Take my hands, keep coming.'

Sasha looked at Apollo. She took a breath and put her hands in his. He kept pulling her in until the water lapped up around her chest. She sucked in a breath.

'Now, come onto your front and just let me pull you along.'

Sasha shook her head, suddenly scared. 'I'll sink.'

'You won't. I'll be holding you. Your body is buoyant in the water. Trust me.'

Something about his voice was so...reassuring. So implacable. Sasha literally had no choice but to do as he said. She leant forward, putting her chest in the water, and suddenly her feet were off the bottom and she was floating and being pulled along, on the surface of the water, by Apollo.

When she realised she was no longer touching the bottom she panicked, her fingers tightening around his. 'Don't let me go.'

'I won't. Just keep looking at me and kick your legs.'

She kept her eyes on his, and did as he asked, tentatively kicking her legs. She could feel herself being propelled forward. Apollo leant back. 'Keep going, that's it.'

They went around and around the pool while Sasha got used to the sensation of being in the water, kicking her legs. It moved like silk along her body. No longer cold. Pleasantly warm.

After a while, Apollo stopped in the middle of the pool. He said, 'I'm going to let your hands go now. But I'll be right here. Just keep kicking your legs and use your hands and arms like this to move through the water.'

He mimed doing the doggy paddle.

Before she could protest, or say anything, Apollo was letting go and moving backwards, away from her. Sheer instinct kicked in and Sasha's arms moved of their own volition in a sloppy kind of movement, along with her legs. It was several seconds before she realised that she was following Apollo as he trod water on his back, moving away from her all the time.

She stopped and promptly started to sink once she'd stopped using her arms and legs. She couldn't touch the bottom here and her head went under the water. Immediately she felt strong hands under her arms, hauling her up before she could start panicking. She broke the surface, spluttering and coughing. 'You tricked me!'

He held her securely as her heart beat frantically. 'You were swimming, Sasha, and you didn't even notice.'

Her legs were scissoring back and forth as she took that in. Impulsively she said, 'Let me go again, I want to check something.'

'Are you sure?'

She nodded. He let her go and she moved her arms and

legs frantically. Euphoria gripped her. 'I'm not sinking!' She had to be making the most graceless fool of herself but she was elated with this tiny success.

Then Apollo smiled. And suddenly Sasha's body stopped functioning and she slipped beneath the surface again.

When Apollo pulled her up this time she was choking with embarrassment, not water. The effect of his smile had almost drowned her. He was frowning now. 'Okay?'

She nodded, just then realising that his hands were under her arms, brushing the sides of her breasts. The corded muscles of his arms were like steel under her palms.

They were very close. So close that Sasha could see the darker flecks of green in Apollo's eyes. The start of fresh stubble on his jaw. Droplets of water clung to his skin. The dark curling hair lightly dusted his chest.

The air between them became charged. And she watched as his gaze seemed to fixate on her mouth and then drop, colour flaring across his cheeks. He muttered one word: *'Theos.'*

Sasha looked down too, and saw what he was looking at. The swimsuit had turned translucent in the water and she could see the pink buds of her nipples and the pebbled areolae as clearly as if she were naked.

Her entire body flooded with heat and she became all too aware of Apollo's naked flesh. All she'd have to do was bend her head forward and press her mouth to his chest. She wanted to taste his skin.

He muttered something else in Greek and started to tug Sasha back towards the steps. Her body felt like jelly. She wasn't sure if she could ever stand again. Apollo still had his hands under her arms and he moved her so that she was sitting on the steps leading down into the water.

He loomed over her, hands either side of her body. She was half in, half out of the water.

'What are you doing to me, witch? All I can think about is having you again.'

Sasha struggled to make her brain work but it wouldn't form coherent thoughts. All she could see was him and that sculpted mouth. She wanted it on hers. She was jealous of her body because *it* knew how it had felt to make love to him. But she didn't.

'Please, Apollo.'

'What is it, little flame? What do you want?'

Little flame.

It echoed in her head. He'd called her that before. He'd been lying beside her on a bed and her hair had been in his hand and he'd said, 'It's like a living flame…'

She forced her mouth to work. 'You… I want you.'

He brought a hand to her shoulder and with excruciating slowness pulled the strap of her swimsuit down. Anticipation prickled across her skin in goosebumps.

He dragged down the top of the swimsuit, baring her breast. He looked at it for a long moment before cupping it in his hand, a thumb rubbing her nipple, making her gasp.

And then he bent his head and his mouth surrounded her nipple in hot, wet heat. The same kind of heat she could feel between her legs. She tried to push them together to stem the tide, but Apollo was between them, his mouth on her breast and his hand moving down to cup her bottom, hitching her against him.

Apollo had gone past the point of restraint. Past the point of his last shred of control. He rolled the taut bud of Sasha's nipple in his mouth, feeling it swell and harden even more against his tongue. He nipped at her flesh gently with his teeth and then laved her with his tongue again.

Her body was quivering against him, like a taut bowstring. He dragged the rest of her swimsuit down and lavished attention on her other breast. When he pulled back both peaks were pink and wet. She was lying back, panting, her hair spreading in long skeins of red-gold in the water. She was like a sea nymph. *A siren.* Luring him to his downfall. But right now he didn't care about any of that.

He was throbbing with need—seeking a fulfilment he'd thought couldn't possibly be as earth-shattering as he remembered. But tasting her skin, feeling her shudder against him in response, he knew it hadn't been a one-off.

He looked down into unfocused blue eyes. Dark with desire. Bee-stung lips. A distant sane part of his mind couldn't believe he was capitulating like this but he was only human and he couldn't resist…

'I want you, Sasha.'

Sasha looked up at Apollo. He eclipsed the sun and the sky. She'd never felt so attuned to someone else. The words he spoke resonated through her entire body.

'I want you too…'

His gaze dropped down over her body and he pulled her swimsuit up over her breasts, the wet material chafing against her sensitive breasts. She shivered slightly and he looked at her. 'Okay?'

She nodded, hands gripping his arms. 'Please… Apollo.' She wasn't even sure what she was asking for, just knew that she needed to be with this man in the most elemental way. Now.

He muttered something in Greek and gathered her into his arms, standing up from the water. But just as he was about to walk towards the villa he stopped.

Sasha was about to ask, *What is it?* when she heard the noise. The distinct *thwack-thwack* of a helicopter's blades. Apollo tensed. He cursed. Then Sasha saw it—the black spider shape of the machine, coming closer to the island.

Apollo walked over to the loungers, carrying her as easily as if she weighed no more than a bag of sugar. He put her down on her feet and she had to lock her knees to keep upright. He handed her the kaftan and said, 'Put this on.'

The sensual desperation that had been so urgent between them only moments ago now seemed like a mirage. Apollo looked grim. Sasha pulled on the kaftan, feeling the need to hide herself a little. Especially when she thought of how needy she'd just felt.

Still felt.

'What is it?'

Apollo looked at her and ran a hand through his hair. 'I forgot. The party in Santorini tonight. I arranged with the pilot to transport us to the party and back later.'

'Us?'

'Yes.' There was a burning intensity in his dark green gaze that made Sasha shiver all over again. He reached out and tipped up her chin with a finger, just as the whining roar of the helicopter's blades died down in the distance.

'You're coming with me. I know what you did and I can never forgive you for that, but, God help me, I want you, *agapi mou*. We will finish what we just started.'

Sasha jerked her chin free, his arrogant words setting something alight inside her. 'Maybe I don't want to finish what we started. Why would I allow someone who doesn't even like me to make love to me?'

She realised she was feeling hurt. And that was humiliating.

Apollo was shaking his head. 'This goes way beyond *like*. This is pure chemistry and I don't think either one of us is strong enough to resist it.'

Sasha felt conflicted. Torn between wanting to throw caution to the wind and acquiesce to his arrogant assertion that they would finish this, and wanting to pull back and defend herself against his mistrust.

There was a sound and Sasha tore her gaze from his to see Olympia appear. The woman said something in Greek to Apollo. He answered and then said to Sasha, 'Go with Olympia, she will help you to get ready.'

After a moment when she felt ridiculously like a petulant teenager wanting to stamp her foot, Sasha followed the woman back into the villa. Who was she kidding? Apollo was right. There was a force of nature between them powerful enough to make her feel awed.

She felt an awful sense of futility because she knew that even in spite of Apollo's mistrust and all that had happened, if he so much as touched her again, she wouldn't have the strength or will to deny him. *Or herself.*

CHAPTER SEVEN

APOLLO WAS WAITING for Sasha outside the villa, by the golf buggy. She wasn't late but his skin prickled all over. He'd gone beyond the point of no return earlier, and there was no way now that he could, or would, deny himself where Sasha was concerned.

However inconvenient it was, he wanted her and he would have her until she was burnt out of his system once and for all.

He heard a noise behind him and turned around but nothing could have prepared him for the vision searing itself onto his retinas.

It was a deceptively simple dress. Off-white, sleeveless, it dipped in a V between her breasts, with narrow gold straps criss-crossing across her bodice, highlighting her high firm breasts and narrow torso.

It fell from her waist in soft billowing folds to the floor. Her hair was caught up in a bun, a plain gold band holding it back from her face.

She looked like a Greek goddess. Albeit with red hair, and pale skin and freckles. She made him think of the myth of Helen of Troy. Achilles, his brother, had used to love that story.

She indicated the dress. 'Kara packed it, is it okay?'

Apollo looked at her suspiciously. She was genuinely uncertain. Did she really have no idea how stunning she was?

'You look beautiful.'

Her face went pink. 'I… Thank you.'

Apollo desperately wanted to resist this act of innocence. It *had* to be an act. But his gut told him it wasn't. No one could keep up an act like this without slipping.

He couldn't stop imagining peeling that dress off her later, revealing her breasts to his gaze. Pulling up the layers of chiffon to find the centre of her body where she would be hot and— *Enough.*

The sooner he'd had his fill of her, the better. As soon as this crazy heat dissipated between them he'd move her into an apartment in Athens for the duration of the time it took for the divorce to be finalised. He would be done with her.

They reached the resort just as the sun was dropping in the sky. The was a palpable air of anticipation among the crowd assembled, the women tanned and lithe and beautiful, and the men in their suits.

She still hadn't fully regained her breath from the view as they'd descended over Santorini with its distinctive white and blue buildings perched precariously on cliffs over the caldera—an underwater crater—which had been formed in a volcanic eruption.

Not to mention the sheer magnificence of Apollo in a dark bespoke suit and white shirt. It was open at the neck, and he oozed casual masculine elegance and a raw sex appeal that reminded her of how needy she'd felt earlier, at the pool.

A hostess greeted them and handed them glasses of champagne. 'Welcome, you're just in time to view the stunning sunset. Please, make yourselves comfortable.'

The delicate layers of chiffon in her dress whispered around Sasha's legs. She'd never felt like a princess before, but she felt like one now. Kara had somehow unearthed this dress from all the more revealing ones in Sasha's wardrobe in Athens and for once she felt as if she was in something she might have chosen for herself.

Which was a weird thought to have…who else could have chosen her clothes?

Apollo took her elbow at that moment and led her over to where a terrace jutted out over the cliff edge, nothing but a stone wall between them and certain death. Sasha took a sip of champagne to try and alleviate the nerves jumping in her belly.

She pointed to a nearby town. 'That's Oia?

'Yes. That's where everyone goes to watch the sunset… give it a few minutes, you'll see why.'

They stood in companionable silence as more and more of the guests started to join them along the terrace wall. The sun was dipping lower now, casting out an orange and pink glow into the vast sky.

Sasha could see how the sun was bathing Oia in a warm golden glow, making the white buildings look even whiter. And then the sun touched the horizon and the world was bathed in pink and orange and apricot. It seemed to fill the entire sky and Sasha could see thousands of flashes coming from cameras and phones in Oia.

'It's stunning,' she breathed, deeply touched by the natural phenomenon. And then just as quickly the sun was gone, leaving behind the faintest of pink trails and a bluish gloaming. Lights started to come on in Oia, like fairy lights in a string.

Reluctantly Sasha left the view behind to follow Apollo as they were led around the resort on a private tour. It was beautiful. Idyllic. A place for romance and decadence.

When they were seated at a series of long trestle tables, beautifully laid out with silverware and wildflower centrepieces, Apollo asked her, 'So, what do you think?'

Sasha swallowed a piece of delicious herb-infused fish. 'You want my opinion? But I don't know anything about this kind of thing.'

He shrugged. 'Still…indulge me.'

She took a drink of water and wiped her mouth with a napkin, hiding how pleased she was that Apollo cared for her opinion. 'I think this is beautiful, luxurious. I know I haven't seen your resort yet but I don't have to, to know that it'll be far quieter than here. Krisakis isn't overrun with tourists. How long would it take to get to there from here by boat?'

Apollo shrugged again. 'About two hours.'

'Krisakis could become a very exclusive day trip or couple of days' trip from here when it gets too frenetic. From what I've seen, you might not have the stunning geology of the caldera but you have peace and solitude and that counts for a lot.'

Apollo tipped his head to one side and regarded her. 'Not a bad assessment and you're right about Santorini being overrun.'

Again, Sasha was embarrassed by how Apollo's regard for her opinion made her feel. Was she so starved for praise?

When the dinner was over, the guests were led down to another level where a DJ was playing salsa music. The happy compelling beat resonated in Sasha's body. It was infectious.

Apollo pulled out a chair for her at a small table near where couples were already dancing, moving sinuously to the beat. He got her a glass of champagne. 'Excuse me for a second? There's someone I see that I need to speak to.'

Sasha feigned a nonchalance she wasn't feeling to be left on her own. 'Sure.'

She watched him walk away through the crowd, lithe and graceful, and saw how everyone he passed turn to look. Women especially. Her insides tightened low down when she thought of what he'd said. *We will finish what we just started.* He couldn't possibly want her that much. Could he?

A sense of insecurity assailed her. This party was peopled by some of the most stunning-looking women Sasha had ever seen. Women that Apollo couldn't fail to notice. What had happened earlier had been an anomaly. A heated moment.

She looked away from his departing figure and took a sip of her drink in a bid to try and pretend she was part of the wealthy crowd around her. The bubbles fizzed down her throat. That sensation, together with the uplifting music, the warm air, the scents, the vast starry sky, all conspired to make her forget her insecurity, and feel lighter than she'd done in days. Weeks.

Her toe tapped to the music.

'Come on! You look like you want to dance.'

Sasha looked up to see a young man holding out a hand. He was with another couple, and they were dancing energetically to the music. She immediately drew back, smiling, 'No, no, I'm just a spectator.'

'Don't be silly!' Before Sasha could object the man had taken her hand and was pulling her up from her seat. She spluttered a surprised laugh and put down her glass, with no choice but to give in to his exuberant invitation.

Apollo frowned as he looked over the heads of the people he was talking to. Sasha wasn't sitting at the table. Then a flash of billowing white caught his peripheral vision and his breath stopped in his throat.

Sasha was dancing—inexpertly, it had to be admitted— but all the more compelling for that because she was clearly enjoying her efforts, head back, laughing.

She was dancing with a young man who was swinging her round with more enthusiasm than skill. She stood out effortlessly and he could see people stop to look, smiling in spite of themselves at her sheer happiness.

A sense of possessiveness he'd never experienced before rose up before he could deny it.

He was jealous.

And then another emotion, less identifiable, made Apollo's chest go tight. He remembered she'd smiled like this when they'd first met. She'd captivated him like she was now captivating everyone here. And that's how she'd sneaked under his guard, by defusing a set of defences he hadn't even been aware of. A need to be controlled and on guard at all times for fear that the world would pull the rug out from under his feet at the next moment, like it had each time he'd lost a family member.

He'd believed his defences were impenetrable, vowing not to allow anyone to get too close, and certainly never entertaining thoughts of family—until she'd appeared and wreaked havoc.

You let her wreak havoc.

She'd exposed a weakness in him, a need for something he'd denied himself…and she was doing it again.

Yet even now, with this knowledge, he knew he wouldn't be able to resist her. A spurt of rebelliousness rose up from his gut. Why should he? She owed him…

Even before her dancing companion had noticed him and stopped and turned pale, Sasha was aware of Apollo's presence a nanosecond beforehand.

He snaked an arm around her waist and in the lull between one song and the next he said, '*Agapi mou*, the next dance is mine.'

Sasha might have laughed at how quickly her dance companion handed her back to Apollo, if her insides weren't coiling tight with awareness and something much sharper.

Apollo swung her expertly into his arms just as the music slowed to a more sultry beat. He was all around her and she could barely breathe because of her proximity to his tall, whipcord body.

To her relief, he didn't speak. Didn't say anything about the man she'd been dancing with, even though she hadn't missed the tightness of his jaw when he'd appeared to interrupt them. She didn't think it was for any other reason, though, than because here in public, no matter what had happened between them, she was his wife.

He pulled her close and after a moment of trying and failing to resist sinking against him, Sasha gave in, allowing her body to cleave to his. He held one hand up, and brought it in close between them. Her breasts were pressed against his chest. She stumbled for a moment when she felt the evidence of his arousal against her belly. She looked up and met that dark green gaze.

'You look surprised.'

Sasha swallowed, her previous sense of insecurity burning away in the face of this evidence. 'I thought… There are so many beautiful women here…' She stopped, feeling inarticulate.

'You thought I wouldn't want you?'

She couldn't speak or nod or move, and he stopped moving too so now people danced around them. He said, 'I won't stop wanting you till I have you again.'

He let her hand go and cupped her jaw and time was suspended as she waited for his mouth to touch hers. When it did she clutched at his jacket to stay standing. The kiss was all-consuming, and Sasha had no defence for it.

After long drugged moments Apollo broke the contact and pulled back. Sasha opened her eyes with effort, everything blurry for a moment. He was looking at her with a harsh expression on his face. 'What do you do to me?'

She had no answer because she could ask him the same question. A sense of urgency seemed to infuse the air around them. Apollo took her by the hand to lead her off the dance floor.

He stopped next to a couple of people and exchanged a few words and then they were sitting into the back of a car and being driven back to the helipad where the helicopter was waiting.

The short journey back to Krisakis felt like a dream and Sasha purposely kept her mind blank as if that could help to not think about what was to happen, because she was in no doubt where this evening would end. In the reality of Apollo's arms and bed. Not a dream of a hazy memory.

All was still and quiet at the villa when they returned. The air was heavy with the scent of night-blooming flowers. Sasha took off her three-inch-heeled sandals and relished the feel of the cool marble floor under her aching feet.

Apollo took off his jacket and draped it over a chair. He walked to the sliding door that led out to the back of the villa. His back was to her and Sasha took a moment to let her eyes linger on his tall, broad form.

He was so beautiful. Her heart gave a funny little skip.

Had she fallen for him after sleeping with him that first time?

Was that why she'd engineered a fake pregnancy? Because she'd been so desperate to cling to him by any means?

Was she in love with him now? Her heart thumped. She knew he consumed her on every level. And she wanted him with a fierce desire she didn't even really understand. The thought of him casting her out of his life made her feel breathless with pain. Not fear. So it had nothing to do with the memory loss.

Dear God, she loved him. Was that why she'd lied to him?

He wasn't moving but standing very still. For heart-stopping seconds Sasha thought he might have changed his mind. But then he turned around.

'Come here.'

It was a command. A command that Sasha could not ignore or disobey, even if she'd wanted to. The relief that he wanted her made her feel weak. She walked towards him and came to a stop in front of him. His eyes were so dark they looked black. His jaw was already darkening again with stubble.

'Take down your hair.'

Sasha complied, lifting her hands to where pins held the bun in place. She took them out and her hair fell to her shoulders. Apollo reached out and caught a strand. 'It's like golden fire…little flame.'

Sasha's nerves were tingling. Her breath came in short choppy bursts. She closed one hand around the pins and they dug into her palm. As if sensing she was hurting herself, Apollo took her hand and opened it, taking the pins and putting them on a nearby surface.

Then he caught her face in his two hands and moved closer. All she could smell was him. The scents of the island clung to him. Citrus, sea. And something infinitely more masculine and human.

She didn't need his hands to raise her face to his as she was already doing it, every cell straining to get closer, for his touch. When his mouth covered hers, she wound her arms up and around his neck, telling him with her body that she wanted him.

Sasha could have happily stood there all night just kissing Apollo, but he drew back and took her by the hand, leading her through the softly lit villa to his room. Her dress whispered around her legs, heightening her sensitivity.

His room was at the opposite end of the villa from hers, with its own suite of rooms like hers, except much grander. She hadn't been shown this part of the villa and felt a little pang of hurt now to think of how divided they'd been.

But all her thoughts fled when they entered the room. It was palatial but minimalist enough to be a monk's cell. Albeit a billionaire monk. The sky was dark outside, cocooning them.

The massive bed was the focal point in the room. It didn't have four posters like Sasha's. It had no adornment apart from pillows and sheets. Stark. Like the expression on Apollo's face now as he turned to her. Sasha locked her knees in a bid to stop her legs trembling.

She'd never been more aware of the disparity in their sizes. Everywhere he was broad she was narrow, slender. He was tall, she was short. He was hard, she was soft.

His hands were on her shoulders. He tugged her gently but inexorably towards him. He tipped up her chin and bent his head, hovering mere centimetres from her mouth for a second. Then he said, 'Do you want this, Sasha?'

There was a tiny flicker of something in her brain at the way he said her name. Like something not fitting quite right. Like when she'd had that curious sense earlier that she hadn't actually chosen her own clothes. But it was too elusive to try and analyse or pin down.

Apollo was asking her permission to make love to her, when he didn't even have to. She'd answered him in the pool earlier that day. Her answer was in every cell of her body, in the rush of blood and liquid heat between her legs.

She nodded jerkily. 'Yes, I want this.' She put her hands on his chest, the heat of his skin nearly burning her hands through the thin material of his shirt.

His mouth touched hers and Sasha melted. One arm wrapped around her back and his other hand speared through her hair, cupping her head and holding it as he plundered and demolished any last coherent thought with his mouth and tongue.

He swept inside and explored with devastating precision. It was all Sasha could do to accept him and mimic his movements. He'd told her he wouldn't let her drown earlier in the pool, but she was drowning now, her arms and hands climbing around his neck, arching her body against his in a bid to get even closer.

This felt familiar.

New, but familiar.

She was barely aware of him undoing the zip at the back

of the dress, and then peeling the straps of her dress down over her arms. The top of the dress fell down to her waist. He pulled back and looked at her and she could feel her nipples tighten under his gaze. The design of the dress had precluded her wearing a bra. She brought her arms up and crossed them over her chest, suddenly feeling embarrassed.

He stepped forward and pulled them apart. 'No, *agapi mou*, let me see you.'

There was a husky tone in his voice that made her feel less self-conscious. Feeling shy now, more than embarrassed, she said, 'I want to see you too.'

Apollo put down his hands and looked at her. Presenting himself. She reached for his buttons, undoing them one by one, little by little revealing that broad impressive chest with its smattering of dark curly hair.

When it was open he shrugged his shirt off and it fell to the floor. With efficient movements, he undid his belt, opened his trousers and pulled them down and off, taking his underwear with them.

He stood before her, naked. Sasha's eyes widened as she took in the sight of him. How could she have forgotten this? He was erect, long and thick. The head was glistening with moisture.

'If you keep looking at me like that, this will be over before we've even started.'

Sasha looked up, mortified. There was an echo of a memory now, feeling the same way, gauche. Inexperienced. Out of her depth. But before she could focus on it, Apollo was taking her by the hand again and leading her to the bed.

He sat down on the edge and pulled her in front of him. He slowly pulled the dress down over her hips, leaving her standing before him in just skimpy lace underwear.

He spanned her waist with his hands and tugged her forward, pressing kisses against her exposed skin, mouth and tongue finding a nipple and sucking it into his mouth.

Sasha gasped and clutched his head, losing all sense of reason and sanity at that delicious tugging sensation.

Her legs finally gave way and he caught her, placing her back on the bed, coming over her on two hands. His eyes were glittering.

He claimed her mouth again in a kiss that felt almost desperate. It resonated inside Sasha and she matched him, stroke for stroke, reaching for him.

Apollo's hands were on her breasts, cupping them, thumbs stroking her sensitive nipples. Tension pulled tight low inside her. She felt empty, hollow. She needed him to obliterate those disturbing dreams. To replace them with reality. To finish what they'd started earlier, exactly as he'd promised.

Ever since she'd woken in the hospital with nothing but blankness in her brain, she'd felt rudderless. Here in Apollo's arms, his mouth fused with hers, she felt anchored again.

Safe.

He pulled back and Sasha realised how fast her heart was beating.

His mouth trailed across her jaw and down to her neck. She was panting. And her breaths got even faster when his hands expertly dispensed with her underwear.

His torso lay against her belly. Her thighs were spread wide to accommodate his body. His mouth lingered on her breast, teasing. She let out a little moan of distress and he looked up at her. 'Patience, little flame, patience...'

He dipped down lower, spreading her legs even further apart and he just looked at her there. A moment ago she'd been breathing like she'd run a marathon and now she couldn't breathe at all.

When Apollo put his mouth on the centre of her body she nearly wept.

She knew this. It hadn't been a dream.

* * *

Apollo was so drunk on the taste and feel of Sasha's body under his mouth, and his hands, that he almost forgot.

Almost.

At the last second, he reached for protection in his bedside drawer, ripping it open with all the finesse of a horny teenage boy and rolling it onto his penis.

He looked down for a moment after donning protection and almost came there and then. Her breasts were rising and falling with her breath, pink after his ministrations. Her entire body was flushed with arousal.

Her lips were swollen. Her eyes were huge and blue enough to make his breath catch, as if he'd never seen them before.

Making love with women had always been a short-lived thing—he'd gone through the motions dictated by society in order to find fleeting physical satisfaction—the chase, the seduction and the consummation. Invariably the seduction and the consummation never lived up to the promise. And Apollo had always chosen women who were experienced. The kind of women who understood not to ask for more. The kind of women who were not expecting anything beyond physical fulfilment.

But with Sasha there had been none of that. They'd met and combusted. There had been very little logical thought involved.

And right now all of his logical faculties were melting in a haze of lust. He notched his erection against the centre of her body, where she was so hot, and wet.

Ready for him.

He hadn't even entered her yet but his mind was already blasting back to that night in London and the way her body had clamped so tightly around his, sending him into orbit.

Something desperate caught in his gut. It couldn't possibly have been as amazing as that—and in a bid to try and prove to himself that he'd misremembered how amazing it had been before, Apollo thrust into Sasha's body, seating himself deep.

He saw her eyes widen even more, colour race across her cheeks. Her hands went to his arms, fingers curling around his biceps.

For a second he couldn't move, because in that moment he knew that the last time hadn't been as amazing as he remembered. It had been *more*. And that this was going to eclipse everything.

Sasha's hips moved tentatively and he nearly exploded. 'Please, Apollo…make love to me.'

A thousand horses couldn't have stopped him from obeying her entreaty. He pulled out slowly, feeling her tight muscles massage his length, and then…back in.

Sasha's body was moving with his in ways that were totally instinctive. She had no control. She was his. Body and soul. It was as if they'd been made to fit exactly.

Apollo came down over her body, twining his fingers with hers and lifting one hand over her head. His other arm was around her back, lifting her into him, deepening his thrusts even more.

A tight coil of need was building inside Sasha, a need for this tension to end, to explode. Apollo's rhythm was remorseless. He had the precision of a master magician or a torturer. Bringing her to the edge, keeping her there, stoking the fire but never letting it burn itself out…

Sasha cried out brokenly, her body dewed with sweat, her mind incoherent with need. 'Please… I…'

'Look at me, Sasha, look at me.'

Something inside Sasha went very still. She forced her eyes to focus on Apollo's face. That flicker was there again, but more than a flicker… Her name. It was *wrong*.

Apollo was saying, 'What do you need, little flame?' He moved and sent fresh tremors through her body.

Her thoughts scattered, flickers forgotten. She couldn't think, she could only feel. 'You...' she said brokenly. Apollo's powerful body moved over her, into her. Stealing her breath and her sanity.

She remembered this.

Being with him like this.

The next moment Apollo touched Sasha so deep and hard that she cried out as ecstasy tore her apart. Seconds later, Apollo convulsed with pleasure and his broken cry of 'Sasha...' echoed around the room.

She went very still deep inside, even as the powerful waves of ecstasy held her in their grip. Something cataclysmic had just happened. Shockwaves slowly obliterated the effects of the intense orgasm as the knowledge sank in.

At that moment of peak union, every cell in her body had rejected his calling her by another woman's name.

Because she wasn't Sasha at all. She was someone else entirely.

She remembered now.

She remembered everything.

Apollo was barely conscious when he felt Sasha wriggle out from underneath him, every touch of her body against his sending fresh flutters of need into his blood. Again. *Theos.*

He flipped onto his back just as he saw a sliver of pale curve of skin disappear into the bathroom and out of sight.

He was stupefied in the aftermath of one of the most erotic encounters of his life. The fact that the other most erotic encounter had been with the same woman made an uneasiness prickle over his skin.

But then his whole body went still when he heard the sounds of retching coming from the bathroom. He sprang out of bed and went to the doorway. The toilet was discreetly tucked away behind a wall and something held him back from intruding. 'Sasha? Are you okay?'

Nothing. Then a weak-sounding 'I'm okay, I'll be out in a minute.'

Apollo's mind raced. Had he been so consumed with his own insatiable need that he'd assumed Sasha had been with him all the way? He went cold—had he? But no. He could remember her nails digging into his hands as she'd begged him to keep going.

Don't stop.

He pulled a pair of sweats out of a drawer and put them on. He went back over to the bathroom door. Now he could hear the shower running—also hidden from view by a glazed glass wall. He paced back and forth for what seemed like ages, and then the water finally stopped.

He gave her a few minutes to get out, dry herself. He heard nothing. Impatience and something that felt like a tendril of fear made him say, 'Sasha? Are you sure you're—?'

But then suddenly she appeared, enveloped in a white towelling robe, and Apollo sucked in a breath. She looked like a ghost. Ashen.

Her hair hung in wet tendrils over her shoulders and the red looked dark against the white robe covering her body. He stepped back so she could come into the bedroom. She scooted past him, her eyes huge. Haunted.

Apollo's hands fell to his sides. 'What is going on, Sasha?'

She'd backed away into a corner, looking at him but not really seeing him. It was eerie. And then her gaze focused on him and her saw her throat move. She said in a broken-sounding voice, 'That's just it. I'm not Sasha.'

Apollo shook his head as if that might help him understand what she was saying. 'I'm sorry, what are you talking about?'

He noticed that she was trembling violently now. He cursed and went towards her, catching her hands. They were icy. Her teeth were chattering.

He drew her down to sit in a chair and knelt before her. Concern punched him in the gut. 'Should I get a doctor?'

She shook her head. 'N-no. I don't... I think it's just sh-shock. I can remember ev-everything. My memory. It's back.'

Apollo went very still. He'd actually forgotten for a moment. A cold finger traced down his spine. He'd become so used to *this* Sasha. He forced himself to focus. 'Are you in pain? Is your head hurting?'

She shook her head, more hair slipping over her shoulder. She looked very young. She looked scared.

He stood up. 'If I leave you for a minute, will you be okay?'

She nodded jerkily. 'I think so.'

She watched Apollo leave the room. She felt numb. She didn't even feel herself trembling but she could hear her teeth. She clamped her mouth shut and tried to wrap her head around what had just happened.

It had been the way Apollo had said, *'Sasha, look at me.'*

At that moment in her head, a very clear voice had said, *But I'm not Sasha.*

And then, when he'd said *Sasha* again, everything in her had rejected it, even as a powerful climax had torn her apart.

As if she'd known all along but had just blocked it out—she now knew everything. All the pieces of the puzzle were sliding back into horrific place.

She heard a noise and looked up to see Apollo return. He was holding a bottle and two glasses.

He said, 'Brandy.' He poured her a shot and handed her a glass. When her hand shook too much he put his hand around hers and lifted it to her mouth. She drank and winced as the fiery liquid burnt down her throat into her stomach. It worked almost instantly, sending out comforting tendrils. Creating a warmth between her and the numbness that had taken hold.

The shudders started to subside slowly.

Apollo poured himself some brandy and slugged it back. He held up the bottle. 'More?'

'A tiny bit.' She didn't want to become insensible, not when her mind was actually functioning again. She took another small sip and the warmth extended from her stomach out, creating a calming effect.

Apollo sat on the edge of the bed. After a minute he said, 'So, do you want to tell me what's come back exactly? How much of your memory?'

She forced herself to look at him. What they'd just shared… She knew that would be the last time he'd ever allow intimacy between them once she had finished telling him what she had to.

'All of it. Everything.'

'Why are you saying you're not Sasha?'

She took a deep breath. 'Because I'm not. I'm Sophy. Sophy Jones. Sasha is…*was*…my twin sister.'

CHAPTER EIGHT

SOPHY COULD SEE Apollo try to absorb this. Eventually he said, 'Twins.'

She nodded. She felt sick. Again.

He stood up. 'What the hell is this...some kind of joke? Now you're trying to convince me you're someone else? Did you ever have amnesia?'

Sophy stood up, even though her legs felt like jelly. 'The accident...happened. It was real. Sasha was driving, she'd picked me up from the airport.'

'Well, if you're a twin, and she was driving, where is she now?'

She was driving manically up a winding road, speaking so fast that Sophy couldn't understand half of what she was saying. And then she turned to Sophy.

'You have to seduce him, Soph,' she said. 'He wants you, not me. Isn't that ironic? He wouldn't sleep with me—he knows the baby doesn't exist now. But if you sleep with him you can get pregnant. Then there will be a baby.'

Sophy looked at her sister, her insides caught in a vice of anxiety and confusion. 'Sash, what are you on about?'

And that was when Sasha took a bend too fast.

Sophy could see that they were too close to the unprotected edge and she called out. Sasha slammed on the brakes but it was too late.

They stopped right on the edge, the front of the car tip-

ping over. Sophy felt nothing but blood-draining terror as the ravine appeared below them, narrow, deep and dark.

She said, 'Sasha, don't move.'

She pushed through the gut-churning terror to open her door carefully and undid her seat belt. If she could inch out of the car then the weight would be redistributed...

Sasha was crying. 'Soph, I'm so sorry... I should never have done this to you. I've ruined everything.'

Sophy looked over and saw blood trickling down Sasha's forehead. She must have hit her head on the wheel.

She said, in as calm a voice as she could muster, 'Sash, don't think about that now. Just look at me, and keep looking at me—not down. I'll get you out.'

Sophy put her leg out of the car and felt for the ground. Then she eased her body so that she was perching on the seat, her feet on the edge of the cliff.

She looked back at her sister. 'Keep looking at me, Sash.'

Sophy kept her eyes on Sasha while she reached out to try and get hold of something that might anchor her if she jumped free of the car.

But at that moment a strange expression crossed her sister's face and Sasha said, 'I'm sorry, Soph, but I won't take you down with me.'

And then, before Sophy could stop her, Sasha was reaching across and pushing Sophy out of the car.

Sophy fell into space, her breath strangled in her throat, and then she landed on a hard surface, the breath knocked out of her body.

The only thing she heard before blackness consumed her was the faint sound of metal crashing far below her...

Sophy looked at Apollo.

Sasha was gone.

She tried to answer Apollo's question but her voice sounded very far away.

'She's in the car... I couldn't get her out. She's dead.'

And then, like when she'd landed on that ledge, far above the bottom of the ravine, darkness came over her again like a comforting cloak.

The next few hours passed in a blur. Sophy was aware of coming round and a concerned doctor asking her some questions. Olympia had helped her to dress and then they'd been flying over the sea with Apollo's voice in her ear.

'Are you okay? We're nearly there.'

When they reached the bright hospital in Athens where a team of doctors and nurses was waiting for them, Sophy knew that, as much as she wanted to, she couldn't hide from the painful reality waiting to be unearthed from the depths of her newly returned memory.

'It would appear that the trauma of the crash, of seeing the car disappear with her sister in it, along with the bump to her head, caused a classic case of trauma-induced amnesia. And, because her sister was in the accident, she blocked out everything about her sister, which was her whole life. Effectively.'

Apollo was silent. Taking this in. He was standing outside the private suite at the hospital with the same doctor who had treated Sasha—*Sophy*—after the accident.

Theos. Even now it was hard to get his head around it. No wonder he'd always thought of her as so pale. She'd been a different woman. He realised now that all those little anomalies he'd noticed since the accident hadn't been anomalies.

He didn't think he'd ever be able to excise the image from his mind of Sophy crumpling before him like a ragdoll and the terror he'd felt as he'd waited for the island doctor to arrive.

She'd come round at the villa but she'd retreated to some

numb place Apollo couldn't reach. Even if the doctor hadn't recommended it, Apollo would have returned to Athens as soon as possible to seek further treatment.

Through the window he could see a detective talking to Sophy now. She was still deathly pale. Any lingering doubt he might have had about whether or not she'd been lying about the amnesia was well and truly gone.

It was too huge to absorb and try and figure how he felt about this, and the fact that Sasha—his wife, however inconvenient she'd been—was now dead.

The detective stood up and came out. He stopped in front of Apollo. 'I'll have a team sent to look for the crashed car immediately. And your wife's body. We should find Ms Jones's documents in the car if they haven't been destroyed. That will help clear things up.'

'Thank you.'

When the detective had disappeared the doctor said, 'We'll keep Sophy in for the rest of the night as a precaution, but she should be okay to go home tomorrow. It's going to take her some time to adjust to having her memory back. Be gentle with her.'

Apollo's mind was instantly filled with vivid images of making love to her with a desperation that hadn't exactly been gentle. His conscience smarted. Had sex precipitated her memory's return?

The doctor was waiting for his response. He said, 'Of course.'

She walked away and Apollo went into the suite.

Sophy knew when Apollo walked in. A volt of electricity went through her blood. Steeling herself, she turned her head to look at him. She quailed inwardly. His expression was stony. She had a sense of déjà vu from when she'd regained consciousness after the accident to find him with a similar expression.

'How are you feeling?' he asked.

'Okay, I think. My head feels full again.' She put a hand to it briefly.

Apollo looked at her for a long moment. 'Can you tell me one thing?'

She nodded, tensing inwardly. There was so much she had to explain but she needed to make sense of it herself first.

He asked. 'Was it you that night? The night we met?'

Something inside her relaxed a little. That was an easy question. 'Yes, it was me.'

An expression crossed his face fleetingly. Too quick for her to decipher. She tensed again. What would he make of that information?

He took a step back from the bed. 'I'll leave you now. The doctor said you need to rest. I'll come back in the morning.'

Sophy watched as he turned to leave. She only noticed now that he was wearing sweat pants and a long-sleeved top. Hair mussed. Not his usual pristine self. The thought that he hadn't showered since they'd made love made her skin prickle with awareness. She wondered how on earth she could be feeling so carnal after what had just happened.

After what she and her sister had put him through. He was almost at the door and on an impulse she called out, 'Wait… Apollo?'

He stopped and turned around. A muscle clenched in his jaw. 'Yes?'

Her fingers plucked at the sheet nervously. 'I just wanted to say… I'm so sorry. For everything.'

Apollo nodded tersely. 'We'll talk about it when you're ready. Get some rest.'

He walked out, closing the door behind him. That was the problem. Sophy didn't think she'd ever be ready to talk about it. She sagged back against the pillows. She felt more fatigued than she'd ever felt in her life.

There was little relief in remembering everything, even though she was grateful to have her memory back. To have *herself* back.

Sasha was dead.

She knew it instinctively, if not factually yet. There was no way she could have survived that crash. Sophy was still too numb with shock to fully absorb the death of her sister who she had loved more than life itself for so long. But who had also caused her more heartache than anyone else.

To say they'd had a complicated relationship was an understatement, but Sophy would never have guessed that Sasha would go as far as she had to engineer a good life for herself.

She'd also never forget that awful last haunting image of Sasha, pushing her free of the doomed car and saying, *'I won't take you with me.'*

For all of her faults and frailties, her sister had saved her twice in her life…

Oh, Sash…what did you do?

Tears filled Sophy's eyes and she turned her head to the wall, unable to stem the rising tide of emotion that engulfed her. She realised she wasn't just crying for her sister, she was also crying because she now remembered everything that had happened the night she'd slept with Apollo.

She remembered why he hadn't pursued her after their night together.

Because he hadn't wanted to see her again. Because she'd been inexperienced, a virgin.

And now she knew why. Because he'd told her he didn't *do* relationships after losing his entire family.

So not only had she lost her sister and realised she'd been betrayed by her too, she'd also remembered that she'd fallen for Apollo all those months ago, when they'd first met.

And they'd never had a chance.

Two days later

Sophy's nerves were wound tight. She'd had a reprieve of sorts from facing Apollo and the inevitable discussion since returning to the villa because he'd had an emergency meeting to attend in London.

He'd left her in the capable hands of Kara and Rhea and the doctor had come to check on her that morning. Apollo must have explained everything to his staff because at one point Sophy had attempted to start to tell Rhea but she'd just patted her hand and shaken her head, saying, 'You don't need to tell us. We knew something was different. We're sorry for your sister.'

Sophy had been inordinately touched, especially after everything Sasha had put them through. She knew how difficult her sister could be. She'd endured a lifetime of it and had never been quite able to break away completely.

They'd been living together in London and that was how Sophy had ended up covering for Sasha that night at the function where she'd met Apollo and where she'd had to call herself Sasha. It had been a classic Sasha request: *'Cover for me, Soph, please! This other thing has cropped up—I'll lose my job!'*

She'd done it, of course. Just as she'd said yes to most of Sasha's requests. After all, she'd owed Sasha so much... If it hadn't been for her sister, Sophy might not even be—

There was a sound behind Sophy on the terrace and she looked around. It was Kara. 'Kyrie Vasilis is in his study—he'd like to see you.'

Sophy's heart thudded against her breastbone. She'd known Apollo was due back but hadn't heard him return.

She'd dug through all of Sasha's clothes to find something vaguely suitable to face him and she'd found an unworn shirt dress, blue stripes, with a black belt. Wedge sandals. It was strange, looking at Sasha's choice of clothes now and realising why they'd never felt like *her*. Because she and her sister had always had diametrically opposed taste, in everything.

Sasha had been flamboyant, into fashion and pop culture. Always ambitious for a life more glamorous than the one they'd experienced growing up in a small market town outside London.

Sophy had been bookish and studious. Into clothes that made her fade into the background. She'd been happy to let Sasha shine but for the first time in her life she found herself wondering uneasily why it had been so easy for her to let Sasha claim the limelight.

She was outside Apollo's study now and had to collect herself. She knocked on the door and there was an abrupt, 'Come in.'

She took a deep breath and steeled herself but seeing Apollo after a couple of days' absence hit her straight in the chest like a sledgehammer. He was wearing a dark grey three-piece suit. And he'd never looked more gorgeous. His physicality was overwhelming, as if she was seeing him all over again with new eyes.

He was also a million miles away from the man who had been uncharacteristically dishevelled at the hospital.

Her heart skipped a beat and she sounded breathless when she said, 'Kara told me you wanted to see me.'

Had his gaze always been so dark green and unnervingly direct? He pulled at his tie and opened the top button of his shirt. 'How are you feeling?'

Dizzy.

But Sophy knew that had nothing to do with regaining her memory and everything to do with him.

'Fine. Much better. Thank you.'

He went over to the drinks cabinet and asked if she wanted anything. She shook her head. He poured himself a shot of golden spirits.

Something inside her ached. A few days ago she'd lain in this man's arms, their bodies entwined. Her soul had sung. Now there was a gaping chasm between them. And how could she blame him?

Apollo downed the shot he'd just poured. It did little to calm his thundering heart or douse the heat in his blood. He'd hoped that a couple of days' distance from Sophy and time to absorb all the revelations would somehow miraculously defuse this intense need he had for her…but as soon as she'd walked into the room his blood had boiled over.

He'd never expected to see her again after that night in his apartment in London. He'd told himself he didn't want to see her again but the relief he'd felt when she'd turned up in his office in London had made a mockery of that.

Dealing with Sasha had been easy because she hadn't been Sophy. Now he had to deal with Sophy.

He poured himself another shot and turned around.

Sophy hoped her emotions weren't as nakedly obvious as she feared. She'd never been as adept at hiding them as her sister. She had no idea what would happen now. What to expect. What she wanted.

You still want Apollo, whispered a voice.

She pushed it down.

Apollo came over and stood with the window at his back. It cast him into shadow slightly, making him look even bigger.

'I need to tell you something.'

She swallowed. 'Okay.'

'The detective contacted me. They found the car. And they found a body… They've identified your sister by her dental records and the DNA sample you provided.'

Sophy sat down on the chair behind her, the wind knocked out of her, even though this wasn't a surprise.

'Are you sure you don't want a drink?'

She shook her head. 'No, it's okay.' She looked at him. 'Did they find anything else?'

He nodded. 'Your bag, with your passport and personal items. There was luggage in the boot but it was ruined. Your things will be returned to you once they've been catalogued. They've ruled her death as accidental.'

Sophy sucked in a sharp breath. 'Was…was there any suggestion it wasn't?'

Apollo's face was expressionless. 'They have to look at everything. You'd just arrived on a flight from London that morning. Sasha picked you up from the airport?'

Sophy nodded.

'Yes.' Her voice sounded raw.

Apollo said, 'We can do this later, or tomorrow.'

She shook her head again. 'No, I know you have questions and you deserve answers.'

She steeled herself but wasn't prepared when Apollo said, 'I'm sorry for your loss, Sophy. I know what it's like to lose a sibling. I might not have liked Sasha very much but she was your sister and you must have loved her.'

Sophy couldn't stop the tears that sprang into her eyes. She stood up and fished a handkerchief out of the pocket of the dress. She went over to the other window and gathered herself.

Apollo said from behind her, 'We really don't have to do this now.'

Sophy swallowed down her emotion and turned around when she felt more composed. 'No. It's okay. Really.'

She said, 'I know Sasha was…a difficult person. More than anyone. But I did love her. I owed her a lot…'

Apollo frowned. 'What are you talking about?'

She looked at him. 'When I was eight, I contracted leukaemia. I needed a bone-marrow transplant. Because we were identical twins, Sasha's bone marrow matched mine so she was asked to donate her marrow.'

Apollo said nothing so she went on, 'She had no choice really, and she never forgave me for having to go through the painful donor procedure without the benefit of actually being sick and getting the attention. I think, unconsciously, I spent my life making it up to her.'

Sophy had never really analysed that before now but something clicked into place inside her as if finally she was acknowledging the role she'd given her sister out of a misplaced sense of guilt.

Apollo said, 'That must have been traumatic. The illness.'

Sophy made a face. 'A lot of it has faded with time. In a way, Sasha's constant demand for attention helped to distract from the memories...

'She was never content with what she had. She lied about our parents to people, friends in school. They were too boring for her. Our father was a postman and our mother was a part-time secretary for the local doctor's office. We had a perfectly happy home life, albeit modest. The worst thing that happened was that they both died within a year of each other, when we'd just left school. My father had a heart attack and then my mother contracted breast cancer.

'After they died, Sasha wanted to move up to London to make her mark. She'd never been happy in our little town. I went with her because the truth is I felt lost without her. She'd been the dominant one for so long.'

Sophy looked away from Apollo as she admitted that. She'd *let* Sasha dominate her, a dynamic they'd played out since they were children, exacerbated by her illness.

Apollo asked, 'Why is your name different from hers if you're sisters? Her name is Miller on her passport and papers.'

Sophy forced herself to look at him again. He was frowning. 'Sasha took our mother's maiden name, changed it legally—she thought it sounded more interesting than

Jones. She did it when she was going through a phase of wanting to be an actress.'

Apollo paced away and back, and then stood at the window for a moment with his back to Sophy. It all made sense in a sick kind of way. He'd met Sasha. He could attest to her ruthless deviousness. If anything, he suspected that Sophy hadn't really acknowledged half of what her sister had been capable of. The woman had tried to seduce him so she could try and get pregnant for real.

Her childhood illness... It tugged on him deep inside. Imagining a small girl with huge blue eyes and light red hair losing that hair because of chemotherapy. Being subjected to all manner of invasive procedures.

To counteract the sense of sympathy he felt, Apollo turned around again. Sophy's chin was tipped up, as if she was mentally preparing for the next onslaught. He pushed down the surge of something more than sympathy. He needed to know.

'That night in London. Why did you pretend to be your sister?'

Sophy's insides clenched with guilt. 'Because I wasn't meant to be there. I work—worked—as a receptionist in a solicitor's office. Sasha asked me to cover for her. She was double-jobbing at another event. It wasn't unheard of for me to cover for her like that. I didn't tell you my real name afterwards because I was afraid she'd get into trouble and lose her job with the event company.'

He frowned. 'Why didn't you tell me the following night when I took you for dinner? When we slept together?'

How could she explain how overwhelming it had been for a man like Apollo to show interest in her? Mousy Sophy. She lifted a hand and let it drop. 'I should have told you... but I couldn't believe that you wanted *me*. Sasha was the one who was confident. Glamorous. Not me.'

She shrugged minutely. 'Somehow it felt more appropriate to be her...not me.'

She winced inwardly, knowing how ridiculous that sounded. Apollo shook his head. 'I wanted you, not your sister. I think we've established that pretty comprehensively.'

A wave of heat, uncontrollable, moved up inside Sophy's body. She clamped down on her response, terrified he'd see the effect of his words. His gaze was too direct, too incisive. She felt as if she was being sliced open and all her vulnerabilities and frailties being laid bare for inspection.

She put her arms around herself and walked over to the window again, staring out unseeingly. Maybe if she didn't look at him as she tried to explain, it would be easier?

'The truth is that I felt out of my depth with you. Really out of my depth. You were suave and cultured. Way out of my league. Sasha was more experienced than me—'

Apollo cut in, 'You mean she wasn't a virgin? Unlike you.'

Sophy's face burned at that reminder. Her arms were so tight around herself now she was in danger of cutting off her air supply. 'I thought you wouldn't notice.'

'Well, I did.'

Yes, he had.

And Sophy could now remember his reaction in full glorious Technicolor. She remembered being so caught up in the moment that when he'd thrust into her and it had hurt, she'd tensed all over.

He'd looked down at her. 'Sasha? Are you—?'

Terrified he'd stop, she'd put her hands on his buttocks and said, 'Please, don't stop.'

For a torturous moment he hadn't moved. She'd felt impaled, stunned at the feeling of being so invaded, but then he'd started to move and the pressure and pain had eased.

What had followed had been nothing short of life-changing. Earth-shattering. She'd still been lying in a sated stupor when she'd felt him leave the bed and heard the shower come on in his bathroom.

A few minutes later, he'd emerged with a towel around his lean hips, his face rigid with anger.

'What the *hell*? You were a virgin.'

Sophy had reached for the sheet to cover herself, suddenly feeling very small and exposed. 'I thought you wouldn't notice.'

He'd emitted a curt, unamused laugh. 'Notice? How could I not? Why didn't you tell me?'

He'd spoken before she could formulate a response. 'I seduced you because I thought you were experienced... that you knew.'

'Knew what?'

He'd run a hand through his damp hair, muscles rippling, making Sophy's tender inner muscles clench again in reaction.

'Knew how these things go. Knew not to expect anything more.'

'More than what?' She'd known she'd sounded like a parrot but had been unable to stop herself.

'More than one night.' He'd folded his arms. 'I don't sleep with virgins, Sasha. If I'd known, I wouldn't have touched you.'

The thought that she might not have made love with this man had been a physical pain. 'But...why?'

A scarily blank expression had come over his face. He was like a statue. 'Because virgins are innocent and have expectations. The kind of expectations I can't, and don't want to, meet.'

'What do you mean?'

He'd emitted something that had sounded like a curse and his green eyes had narrowed on her face. 'Can you deny that you'd thought this was something more? That this wasn't just about sex?'

Mortified heat had flooded up her body and into her face. She *had* thought there was something between them. Romantic. Unique.

He'd seen it instantly. 'That's what I'm talking about. An expectation of something *more*. I don't do relationships, Sasha. I have no desire for a girlfriend. I have short-term relationships with women who know better than to attach emotion to the proceedings. This is just sex for me.'

She'd winced at that.

He'd said icily, 'This ends here now. Take a shower and get dressed. When you're ready I'll have my driver take you home.'

Sophy's focus came back to the present. It wasn't much comfort that she had more context now for why Apollo would have found seducing a virgin so unappealing. He was averse to relationships after losing his family. And she knew what that loss felt like. Ironic that they had so much in common.

She turned to face him, steeling herself not to show him how the memory of that night flayed her.

Apollo tried to resist the image of intense vulnerability Sophy displayed when she faced him again. Arms wrapped around herself. Her cheeks had two bright pink spots but the rest of her face was pale.

It didn't help that images of that first night they'd spent together kept intruding on his thoughts. The way her hair had spread out around her head like a halo of fire.

Little flame.

He gritted his jaw and bit out, 'We really don't have to continue this now if you're not up to it.'

She looked at him. 'No, I want to do this now. Maybe I will have a small drink, though.'

Apollo went over and poured her a measure of brandy.

He brought it over and said gruffly, 'Sit down, before you fall down.'

She sat down again in the chair and he handed her the drink. He let her take a sip, and sat back on the edge of his desk. 'Were you and your sister in on the act together? Was she sent to me a month later because you didn't have the nerve?'

Sophy sat up straighter, a look of shock and horror crossing her face. 'That's... *No*, it wasn't like that. I had no idea.'

Apollo forced himself to resist trusting his first impression of her innocence. 'You weren't working together?'

'Not at all. How can you think that?'

'How did she end up in my office then? Telling me she was pregnant, if you weren't working together? How did she know if you hadn't told her?'

He saw the slim pale column of her throat work as she swallowed. She avoided his eye, as if ashamed. 'Sasha and I lived together. She knew something had happened...she eventually got me to confide in her. I told her your name. I know Sasha had her faults, but I never in a million years thought that she would use that private information. She looked you up, kept going on about how I should contact you, try to go out with you again...but I wouldn't.'

She looked at him again. 'After all, you'd left me in no doubt as to how you felt about seeing me again.'

His conscience smarted. Yes, he'd told her that but he also hadn't been able to get her out of his mind in the following days, weeks. Making a total mockery of his words to her.

Sophy continued, 'It was around the time of our birthday and Sasha said she was concerned about me, so she bought me a return flight to one of the Canary Islands for a holiday. I didn't want to go but she insisted.'

Apollo said. 'Go on.'

'By the time I got back she was gone. She'd left a note

saying something about securing our future. Then I saw it in the papers. Your marriage.'

Apollo remembered the feeling of claustrophobia that day. 'If you weren't working together, when you heard about the marriage, why didn't you contact me to tell me who she was, who *you* were? That she was tricking me?'

Sophy looked sheepish. 'I didn't know about the pregnancy. It wasn't inconceivable to me that you'd met Sasha and had been more attracted to her. That you'd wanted something *more* with her.'

Apollo felt a surge of anger mixed with frustration rise up inside him. Before he could say anything Sophy cut in, 'I know it sounds pathetic. But in a weird way it made sense. I'd been innocent and you hadn't wanted to see me again. Sasha was experienced…the experienced version of me. I felt like you'd seen something in her that I hadn't been able to give you, and that had made you fall for her. I know how convincing Sasha could be.'

Apollo grimaced at that. The fact that he'd fallen for her act negated his anger a little. Sasha had managed to dupe them both.

He stood up again, paced back and forth. 'Why did you come to Athens?'

Sophy fought not to squirm under that exacting gaze. 'Sasha rang me, she was hysterical. Incoherent. It must have been when you found out she wasn't pregnant. When you'd shown her the divorce papers. She begged me to come as soon as I could… I arrived the next morning.'

She went on. 'I couldn't even understand half of what she was saying when she picked me up at the airport. She was gabbling about you not wanting her, and that I needed to go and pretend to be her so I could seduce you…'

Apollo went very still. 'She was hoping that if you switched places, I'd suddenly want you and in spite of everything sleep with you and get you pregnant?'

Sophy avoided his eye. 'Something like that, I think.'

Apollo cursed. And then he said, 'The truth is that she wasn't that far off the mark. As soon as I saw you again I wanted you.'

Sophy's face got hot again. She risked a glance at Apollo, who looked grim. He might be admitting he hadn't stopped wanting her but it didn't feel like a compliment. More an accusation.

'And if this crazy plan of hers had worked and you'd managed to seduce me and get pregnant, then what?'

Sophy felt sick. 'I don't know. I don't think she'd thought it through… I certainly had no idea what she'd planned. It sounded like gibberish to me.'

Apollo hated to admit that *if* Sophy had returned to the villa in Athens in the place of Sasha, and he'd wanted her as much as he wanted her now, she could very well have seduced him.

It was a bitter pill to swallow. He wanted her now. He was acutely aware of the buttons on the shirt-dress—how easily they would come undone, baring her to his eyes and touch.

No make-up. No adornment but her exceptional natural beauty. How could she have ever thought she was less attractive than her sister? The minute Sasha had turned up in his office in London he'd had an adverse reaction to her. Much to his relief.

At first you were disappointed.

He ignored that unwelcome reminder.

Sophy looked at him and he noticed the shadows under her eyes. He felt wrung out. He could only imagine how she felt.

'What happens now? I expect you want me to leave as soon as possible.'

Apollo couldn't stem the visceral rejection he had to that suggestion. He told himself it was incredulity that she could think she could walk away so easily, not the pulsing ever-present desire in his blood.

He shook his head. 'I'm afraid that's not possible.'

Sophy hated the little jump in her pulse when he said that. He must despise her after everything. She wasn't even sure if he believed her. 'Why?'

'For one thing, we have a situation on our hands. Obviously we won't need to divorce now. But I've been seen out in public with a woman who is not my wife. A wife who has been deceased for some weeks.'

'We'll have to announce the accident and her death and the press attention will be intense. You'll be hounded when they find out she had a twin sister and that you were also in the car, but we can try to delay that until her death has been announced and the press moves on to the next story.'

Sophy frowned. 'How can you do that?'

'By taking you back to the island for a couple of weeks when the news is announced tomorrow. It'll keep you insulated from the press and it'll take about that long to process the repatriation of your sister's body. By then, the press should have moved on. Also, it'll give the authorities time to return your personal items.'

CHAPTER NINE

AND THEN WHAT? That was the question that had been re-verberating around Sophy's head for the past twenty-four hours since they'd landed back on Krisakis. Olympia had shown her back into her bedroom, separate from Apollo's. Sophy chastised herself. What had she expected? For them to blithely continue where they'd left off before her memory had returned?

Yes.

Her conscience stung. How could she be so selfish when her sister was dead?

Because it was your sister who was selfish in the first place, betraying your trust, going behind your back to try and seduce Apollo to further her own ends. Lying to trap him.

Sophy sighed deeply and hugged her knees tighter to her body. Yes, she could blame Sasha for so much, but also it had been *her* who had set this chain of events in motion by not revealing her true self because it had been easier to hide behind her sister, rather than believe that someone like Apollo could possibly be interested in her.

The waves lapped up gently onto the shore near her feet. It was soothing. It was also very quiet here on the beach in the late afternoon. The heat was less intense now.

Since they'd arrived on the island, Apollo had been busy, either in his study in the villa or when he went to visit the construction site. They hadn't talked about anything since that last conversation.

Sophy knew she should be feeling some sort of cathartic weight lift off her shoulders, with her memory returned and full knowledge of what had happened, no matter how painful it was to face.

But she felt more tangled up than ever. Aware that her feelings for Apollo ran far deeper than she liked to admit. And she hated the sense that she was now a burden for him to deal with until the press attention died down.

Because surely he was just waiting for the earliest opportunity to let her go? Get on with his life? Say good riddance to her, and Sasha?

He couldn't want her any more. Surely his desire was well and truly eclipsed by disgust for what her sister, and she, however unwittingly, had done to him?

Sophy shut down her circling thoughts. Torturing herself like this was getting her nowhere. Apollo was keeping her here to protect himself as much as her from the adverse press attention.

The water was lapping at her feet now, refreshingly cool. She was about to move back but she was too slow as another wave on the incoming tide rushed in faster, soaking her bottom. She jumped up with a little squeal.

She was about to step back out of the way but another wave broke over her bare feet. Suddenly she was filled with a sense of longing to feel the water on her body. Even though the thought of walking into the sea terrified her. She remembered now why she couldn't swim and with a kind of sickening predictability it came back to Sasha.

They'd been very little and she and Sasha had been playing in a pool while on holiday. When their parents had been momentarily diverted, Sasha had taken the opportunity to dunk Sophy's head under the water, holding it there until Sophy had panicked and taken in a lungful of water, nearly drowning.

She'd been too terrified to swim after that, refusing

to take lessons. Until Apollo had taken her into the pool that day.

Something defiant rose up inside Sophy. Anger and an impotent sense of rage at her sister—for all that she had done, for all that Sophy had allowed her to do, and for dying, before Sophy had got to tell her that she loved her one more time.

Tears were sliding down Sophy's cheeks before she could stop them, emotions overflowing. Obeying an urge she couldn't ignore, she stripped down to her underwear, pulling the sundress she was wearing over her head.

She wanted to feel a wave breaking over her head, as much to prove to herself that she wasn't scared as to cleanse something inside herself. Something she couldn't even really articulate.

At the last moment she looked around. The beach was entirely empty and private. Not another soul.

She could almost hear her sister's voice in her head. *'Go on, Soph, don't be such a scaredy-cat.'* It spurred her on.

She stripped off her knickers and bra and threw all her clothes to a safe distance from the incoming tide and took a step into the water.

It felt glorious—the cool water on her sun-warmed skin. She took another step and the waves crashed around her knees. Another step. She gasped as the water reached her hips and lower belly.

Another wave was approaching, bigger, and taking a deep breath, heart pounding, she ducked down, letting it break over her head. Instantly she sprang back up, sucking in deep breaths, skin tingling all over from the cold and exhilaration, and the decadence of being naked in the water.

Another wave was coming, and she ducked down for that one too, spluttering a little as she came back up, but suddenly she realised she was in deeper water that came almost up to her breasts and another wave was coming, breaking over her head. When she emerged again there was another wave almost immediately and suddenly she couldn't get her breath.

Before panic could set in, a strong pair of hands was under her arms, lifting her out of the oncoming wave. She blinked and spluttered, hands going out and landing on a wall of muscle.

'What do you think you're doing, you little fool? You don't know how to swim, you're not ready for the sea yet. You could drown out here.'

Apollo.

Waves were breaking around them now. Apollo's hair was slicked back from the sea. His face stark. He looked down and she saw his cheeks flush. 'You're naked.'

Sophy was gasping. 'I...didn't bring a swimsuit... I wasn't going to get into the water...but I just...wanted to feel it against my skin.'

Her teeth started chattering, as much in reaction to Apollo as because the water was cold.

Apollo was grim. 'There's a storm coming, this tide is coming in fast.'

He swung her effortlessly into his arms and carried her out of the water. It was only then she realised how far in she'd wandered. Her arms were around Apollo's neck, her bare breasts pressing against his chest.

She burned with mortification but also something stronger.

When they reached the shallows she said, 'You can put me down, I'm okay now.'

He ignored her, long legs striding back up the beach. She could see a towel on the ground, near her discarded clothes. Apollo put her down and picked up the towel, wrapping it around her shoulders. He caught the ends and pulled her towards him.

She was very aware that he was naked too, apart from

swimming shorts that hugged his body, leaving little to the imagination.

'What were you thinking? You could have drowned.'

Sophy blinked up at him. 'I wasn't thinking... I didn't expect it to get rough so quickly.'

She didn't even realise she was still trembling until Apollo cursed and started rubbing her skin with the towel. She wanted to say she wasn't cold—it was his effect on her. His eyes dropped and his hands stopped moving. She didn't have to follow his gaze to feel its effect on her breasts, nipples tight and sensitive after brushing against his chest.

She wanted him with a desperation she'd never experienced before. That recklessness that had sent her into the water rose up again and for a heady moment Sophy wondered if this was the real essence of herself that she'd repressed for so long, while she'd hidden in Sasha's shadow?

She dislodged his hands and the towel fell off her shoulders. There was something very elemental about being naked in front of him like this. Apollo's eyes flared bright green. His jaw clenched. 'What are you doing?'

Sophy also realised in that moment that she desperately needed Apollo to make love to *her*. To Sophy. To know who he was making love to this time. To call out *her* name. Exorcise Sasha from their past.

She opened her mouth but then she went cold inside. She'd just imagined seeing his reaction to her. He didn't want her any more. How could he after everything that had transpired? All her bravado leached away and she crossed her arms over her chest, looked for the towel. 'I'm sorry... I know you can't still want—' She spied the towel and bent down to retrieve it but when she straightened up Apollo took it out of her hands and pulled them apart, baring her to his gaze again.

'I can't still want *what*?'

'Me.'

'*Theos*. If only I didn't want you, my life would be infinitely simpler.'

He tugged her towards him and she stumbled slightly, landing against him, a sense of relief rising inside her. He took his hands off hers and cupped her face, tilting it up to his. Then he bent his head and covered her mouth with his in a kiss that was so explicit and carnal that Sophy lost all sense of time and place.

When he pulled back she felt dizzy, plastered against his body. She could feel the bulge of his arousal through the thin material of his shorts and put her hand down there, exploring tentatively.

He put his hand on hers. His voice was rough. 'Stop, unless you want to make love right here, right now.'

She must have communicated her desperation silently because Apollo muttered something unintelligible and let her go briefly to pull down his own shorts and spread the towel on the sand.

He pulled her down alongside him on the towel, shielding her from the rough sand with his body. His hands stroked along every curve of her body, sending her into a frenzy of need. Big hands cupped her buttocks, squeezing, kneading. Her hands moved over the wide muscled plane of his chest, mouth seeking and finding the blunt nub of his nipple, hearing his sucked-in breath when she explored with her tongue and teeth.

He put a hand in her hair, tugging her head back gently. Her vision was blurry.

'Sophy... I want you, now.'

Hearing her name on his lips made her feel absurdly emotional. She ducked her head into his neck. 'I want you too...'

He moved her over his body so that her legs were astride his hips. The centre of her body was embarrassingly hot and damp, but before she could dwell on that her entire being suffused with pleasure when she felt the head of Apollo's erection nudge against where she was so hot and needy.

He looked at her. 'Okay?'

She nodded. He notched the head inside her and she sucked in a breath. He put his hands on her hips. His expression was strained. 'Move up, and back.'

She bit her lip, every part of her being focused on doing as he asked. She came up and felt him under her, power barely leashed…and sank down, taking him inside her. It was the most exquisite agony she'd ever experienced as she felt herself stretch to accommodate his hard length.

She moved experimentally, up and down. Apollo's hands were on her hips, but not controlling her movements, letting her take the lead. It was heady.

A rhythm slowly built and built until Sophy couldn't control it any more. Apollo held her hips then, showing her how much restraint he'd exercised as he pumped powerfully up and into her body. She couldn't stay upright as she convulsed with pleasure, curving over him as he followed her over the edge and into an ocean of total and utter sated bliss.

As the after-shocks pulsed through their entwined limbs, neither one of them was aware of the incoming water lapping around their heated bodies.

Apollo hadn't intended to make love to Sophy. He'd intended to bring her to the island and put some distance between them. Giving himself time to assimilate everything. Absorb the reality that she was who she was. A different person. The same person.

And for about twenty-four hours it had worked out that way. He'd kept his distance—gone to the site, stayed in his study.

But then, this afternoon, he'd seen her far below on the beach. He'd seen her taking her clothes off, her pale body gleaming like a pearl against the azure sky and ocean, like some ethereal being. Not human.

Then she'd looked around, taken her underwear off. Stepped gingerly into the water. Then she'd waded further in, ducking under the waves. Apollo had felt like he was intruding on a very private moment and then he'd realised she was in danger of getting out of her depth. And that she couldn't swim.

When he'd reached her his insides had been in a knot and he'd hauled her up out of the water, her slim body far too light and puny against the might of the sea. He'd been angry.

Scared.

He'd also noticed that her eyes were red and he didn't think it was from the water. She'd been crying. Mourning.

He hadn't intended making love to her there and then. But she'd blasted through any resolve to resist her just by looking at him. Never mind being naked, her skin wet from the sea. Red hair in long silken skeins over her shoulders. Like a water nymph sent to tempt him. Or a mermaid.

The more he had of her the more he wanted. It made his skin prickle with a sense of panic. Exposure. The same kind of exposure he'd felt when he'd realised she had been a virgin, because he'd wanted her too much to look for the signs of innocence, and in hindsight they'd been there. He'd just ignored them.

Today had just proved her effect on him.

Dangerous.

He said, 'We didn't use protection today.'

Sophy's hand tightened on the stem of the wine glass. Heat suffused her body again to think of how carnal she'd been on the beach earlier. She barely remembered Apollo putting the dress over her head afterwards, dressing her. Leading her up the steps. Putting her to bed. She'd woken in her room, alone, as the sun had been setting outside.

She'd taken a shower and come out to find Apollo sitting in the dining area, clean-shaven, hair damp, as Olympia had laid the table for dinner. For a moment she'd almost been afraid she'd dreamt up the beach, but the storm he'd mentioned was lashing at the windows now.

They hadn't used protection. Because she'd all but begged him to make love to her.

She fought the rising tide of heat under her skin. Apollo looked at her and shook his head. 'It's amazing that you can still blush…'

That only made her blush even harder. 'It's okay… I'm at a safe place in my cycle.'

Apollo saw the worried look on Sophy's face. She couldn't hide her expressions. He had to acknowledge uncomfortably that he trusted her word.

'It won't happen again.'

Her face was still pink. Her hair was down around her shoulders. She'd appeared for dinner in long loose trousers and a loose silk top. It kept slipping off one shoulder.

The pink leached a little from her cheeks. She said, 'I think you're right, it's not a good idea.'

Apollo dragged his gaze up from where her pale shoulder was bared. He frowned. 'What are you talking about?'

'Making lo—' She stopped. 'Sex. It's probably not a good idea. Considering everything…'

A visceral rejection of what she'd said rose up from somewhere deep and primal inside Apollo. He might have come here intending to keep his distance but after this afternoon that was an impossibility.

He shook his head and reached out a hand, finding Sophy's across the table and tugging her up out of her chair and over to him. He pulled her down and she landed on his lap, sliding into place like a missing jigsaw piece.

It's just desire, repeated Apollo like a mantra in his head. He said, 'That's not what I meant.'

Sophy hated the way her heart leapt. 'What did you mean?'

'I meant that I won't be careless again, but we will be making love again. I don't see why we can't make the most of this. The chemistry between us is more powerful than anything I've ever experienced. It's unprecedented for me. But it will burn out. It always does.'

It will burn out. Sophy felt something inside her rebel at that assertion. This feeling that she'd never get enough of him…she couldn't imagine it ever fading away.

As if he could read her mind, he said carefully, 'Sophy, nothing has changed. I am not in the market for a relationship or family. It's not something I ever want to experience. If anything, believing that I might become a father has only confirmed my vow not to have a family. I had a family and I lost them, I won't put myself through that again.'

Sophy's heart constricted. His words, painful as they were, actually helped to clarify how differently her very similar experience had shaped her. 'I lost my family too… but I know I won't feel whole again until I have a family of my own.'

Apollo tensed under her body and she held her breath. But then he said in a voice devoid of emotion, 'And I'm sure you'll have that one day. With someone else. What I'm offering is very transient. A couple of weeks to explore this insane chemistry before we part ways and get on with our separate lives. Once and for all.'

Sophy knew that she should stand up and step away. Tell Apollo that she wasn't interested in a transient affair. She wanted more. She'd always wanted more. It was why she'd still been a virgin long after her sister had lost her innocence.

But Apollo wanted her for now. Maybe that was enough. Maybe she would wake up one morning and not feel this insatiable need. Maybe she would be able to move on. Could she stand up and step back…from *this*? This energy pulsing between them even now?

She knew the answer. *No way.* Memories might be cold bedfellows in the future but she knew she didn't have the strength to walk away. Not yet. He'd been her only constant for the last few turbulent weeks. She needed to feel anchored again. Rooted. Even if it was only temporary.

She slid her arms around his neck. 'Okay, then.'

Apollo smiled and it was a smile of pure male satisfaction as he drew her head down to his and took her mouth in a searing kiss. A promise of what was to come, what he was offering, and she, like a miser, would take it.

CHAPTER TEN

A COUPLE OF days later, Sophy was lying face down in Apollo's bed. The morning sun was streaming in, warm on her bare back. A breeze chased the warmth across her skin.

Her whole body ached pleasurably. Since the other stormy evening, the days and nights had melded into one another, punctuated by moments of carnal pleasure—like last night. Apollo had returned from the site in the early evening. He'd taken Sophy down to the beach and given her another swimming lesson in the sea. They hadn't worn swimsuits, and they'd re-created the other day, except this time with protection.

Then Apollo had taken her back up to the villa and after a leisurely and very thorough shower, they'd eaten and gone to bed. But not to sleep. To discover new heights of pleasure and passion.

Sophy had been so crazed last night, so desperate for Apollo to release her from the sensual torture that she could remember her voice breaking as she'd begged him.

She buried her face in the pillow now and groaned softly, so she didn't hear when Apollo entered the room. But she felt the bed dip and tensed. A tension that quickly dissolved when a finger trailed down her spine to the top of her buttocks.

She turned her head to meet a cool green gaze. *This* was what kept her from tumbling into fantasy land, this reserve that Apollo showed when he wasn't breaking her apart. The reserve that reminded her that he had rejected her after making love to her the first time. That reminded her that he'd only married Sasha out of a sense of duty and responsibility because he'd believed she was pregnant. That reminded her of his words to her that he didn't *do* relationships.

So, no matter what this was…it wasn't going anywhere. And she had to remember that.

'*Kalimera.*'

'*Kalimera.*'

She felt shy. Which was ridiculous. She turned and pulled the sheet up, covering her body. Apollo's mouth quirked as if mocking her attempt to be modest. She wanted to scowl at him.

'You mentioned before that you'd like to visit the site… would you still like to?'

That felt like an age ago now. She nodded. 'Yes, I'd like that.' Then she thought of something. 'Will it be okay for me to be seen here with you?'

'We won't be bothered here. It's entirely private. We'll leave in half an hour.'

Later that morning, Apollo looked to where Sophy was nodding studiously as his foreman showed her around the site. She was wearing those yellow capri pants and the white shirt that tied above her midriff. Wedge shoes. A hard hat was perched on her head and a plait dissected her shoulder blades.

She could have passed for sixteen if it wasn't for the X-rated memories of how she'd taken him into her body last night, meeting him thrust for thrust, begging, pleading… sending them both over the edge and into a crashing, burning orgasm so intense— *Theos.*

She might have agreed to this transitory affair but he'd seen something in her eyes the other night that had caught at him deep inside. The same place that had been triggered when he'd believed he was to become a father, and when he'd realised that he wasn't as averse to the thought of a family as he'd believed himself to be.

In the aftermath of Sasha's lies, that weakness had been pushed down. Not allowed room to breathe again. Until he'd heard himself telling Sophy the other night that she would have a family one day. With someone else. Not him. He'd said the words and they'd felt like ash in his mouth.

He told himself it was sheer possessiveness of a lover. Nothing more. He didn't want more. Even with Sophy. Especially Sophy.

Apollo saw his foreman put a hand to Sophy's back to guide her over some uneven ground. That sense of possessiveness surged. He closed the distance between them in a couple of long strides, and took Sophy's hand. 'I'll take this from here, Milos, thank you.'

He was aware of Sophy looking up at him and his foreman's bemused expression. He ignored both and led her up to an open piece of ground at the top of a hill. She was panting slightly when they reached it. He let her hand go, and gestured around them. 'This is going to be the site for the solar panels. The resort will be entirely self-sufficient for energy.'

She was turning around, hand up to shield her eyes from the sun. She said, 'Does it have to be just for solar panels? This would be a beautiful spot for an exclusive suite. It would have three-hundred-and-sixty-degree views of the island and surrounding sea. Sunrise and sunset views.'

Apollo looked around and realised she was right. He followed her gaze, which took in the sea and hazy shapes of islands in the distance. The sky was so blue it hurt. Not a cloud in sight. All around them insects and birds chirruped and called. The scent of wild herbs infused the air.

He shook his head, his mouth quirking. 'I've had one of

the best firms working on this for a couple of years now and no one came up with that idea.'

'Oh.' Sophy flushed, a dangerous warmth infusing her insides. 'Well, it might be a silly idea. I'm sure it was thought of and discarded for some reason.'

'We'll look at it.'

'Why did you decide to buy an island?' Sophy asked then, taking him off guard a little. Apollo looked out over the sea. 'When we were small, my brother was fascinated by the Greek myths and legends. My mother used to tell them to us at night as our bedtime stories.'

His mouth quirked. 'I found them boring. I was more interested in how things worked. He was the dreamer—he took after our mother. I took after our father. After our parents died and we were shuttled from foster home to foster home, he used to tell me that he couldn't wait to be old enough to leave Athens. Get on a boat and go to all the islands, see the places of the myths and legends. Athens was too harsh for him. He was too sensitive. He fell in with a gang, as much to survive as anything else. Once he started taking drugs…that was it. He was lost.'

Sophy's heart felt sore for Apollo and his brother. 'Why didn't you end up going the same way?'

Apollo shrugged, his eyes hidden behind dark shades. 'I guess I was born more cynical than Achilles. I was more street smart too. I stayed out of the gang's way. He was more susceptible. My father had always encouraged me to study hard, telling me that's how I'd make a life for myself. I put my head down and when I looked up, it was too late.'

The self-recrimination in his voice was palpable.

'You were kids. Your brother was older than you. It wasn't your responsibility to care for him. The adults around you should have been doing that.'

Apollo made a derisory sound. 'Our foster parents were

just interested in the money they got from the state to take us in.'

Sophy looked away and out to the horizon again, a little embarrassed at the emotion she was feeling. The fact that he'd done this to honour his brother was beyond touching. The whole site for the resort had touched her—everything was going to be sustainable and designed to make the most of the island's natural resources, which in turn would help grow the local economy.

The resort was going to be seriously impressive and seriously luxurious. Private suites with their own pools, terraces and stunning views would be dotted around a central area where there would be several restaurants, a spa, a gym and shops, showcasing local produce and crafts.

In the main area there would be more rooms, and an infinity pool. Apollo also had plans for self-contained cottages where artists could come and stay in residence for a time—writers, painters, poets. They could apply for sponsorship through the resort and it only just impacted on Sophy now that he must have been thinking of his brother when he'd done that.

'Come,' he said, 'I'll take you to the town. I have a short meeting to attend with the town's council and you can get a coffee and look around.'

She noticed he didn't take her hand this time but she felt his fingers touch bare skin above the waistband of her trousers and it burned hotter than the sun.

Apollo was treated like a visiting celebrity when they reached the small harbour town a short while later. Old men came up to shake his hand, women smiled shyly, bouncing babies on their hips.

He seemed to be embarrassed by the attention, smiling tightly. He took Sophy's hand again, leading her to a shaded leafy square, with little *tavernas* that had seats and tables outside. She was glad of the shade as she was starting to wilt in the hot early afternoon sun.

He spoke to the owner, who answered him effusively, gesturing to Sophy to come and sit down. 'What did you say to him?' she asked, amused by the attention.

'Just to give you whatever you want until I come back. I won't be long.'

She watched him walk off. He was wearing faded jeans and a white polo shirt. The denim did little to hide the firm contours of his buttocks and when the owner came back with a menu, she was blushing.

He gestured towards where Apollo was disappearing around a corner and said something in Greek that Sophy couldn't understand, but she could see the emotion on the man's face and imagined that he was telling her how grateful they were that Apollo had single-handedly breathed life back into this little island. Just because he wanted to honour his brother's memory.

Sophy smiled and put a hand to her chest to indicate that she understood. The man smiled and said in heavily accented English, 'What would you like?'

She asked for a coffee, having developed a taste for the strong tart drink. She noticed that there was bunting up around the pretty square and women were decorating every visible area with flowers.

When they came over to the *taverna*, Sophy jumped up to help them string a garland of flowers over the front of the door. They spoke no English, she spoke no Greek but they laughed and smiled and for the first time in a long time, in spite of her grief, she felt light.

She was dying to know what the flowers were for but her attempts to ask the ladies made them laugh at her mimes. Then she saw them all go brick red and stop talking. They practically bowed down. Sophy had to stop herself from rolling her eyes at their reaction. She didn't have to look to know who was behind her. She could *feel* him.

She might roll her eyes at his effect on the locals but, really, she was no better. He came up alongside her. 'You're helping them prepare for the wedding?'

Sophy looked at him in surprise. 'It's a wedding?'

He nodded. 'The first wedding they've had on the island for a couple of years. It's a big deal…and we've been invited.'

'Oh…' Sophy's heartstrings tugged. She'd love to see a Greek wedding but she didn't expect Apollo would want to bring her with him, as if they were a couple. 'That's okay, they don't know about our…arrangement. You should go, it'll be expected.'

He looked at her and she felt herself flush. Was she being gauche?

'They invited both of us. It's no big deal. Greek weddings are pretty informal in places like this, everyone is invited.'

Now she did feel gauche. 'Oh… Okay, then. That would be nice.'

'I'll show you around.'

Sophy waved goodbye to the ladies and the *taverna* owner and when Apollo took her hand she tried to ignore the hitch in her heart. This was just a fleeting affair. No matter how much she might be falling in love with this lazy, idyllic island.

No matter how much she might be falling deeper in love with the man.

Her feet missed a step and she stumbled. Apollo put his arm around her to steady her. 'Okay?'

She forced a smile. 'Fine.'

Liar.

She couldn't ever afford to forget that she was only here because her sister had gone to this man and told a heinous lie, trapping him into a marriage. He never would have gone after Sophy. She never would have seen him again. She welcomed the dart of pain because this would be nothing compared to the pain she'd feel if she entertained fantasies.

The town comprised of a few artisan shops and a beautiful old Greek orthodox church that was being prepared for the wedding. There was a growing air of excitement.

Apollo led her down another side street and they passed a boutique. Sophy's feet stopped in their tracks. It was a simple boutique but there was a dress in the window that caught her attention. Caught her heart.

It was light blue broderie anglaise. Off the shoulder. The bodice was fitted and it fell in soft folds to below the knees. It was simple and unsophisticated. *Not* the kind of thing Sasha would have chosen in a million years. But she wasn't Sasha. She was Sophy and she wasn't sophisticated.

'You like that dress?'

Embarrassed, Sophy started to walk off. 'No, no, it just caught my eye.'

But Apollo didn't budge. 'It would suit you. Try it on.'

Sophy tried to desist but Apollo was tugging her towards the shop. The saleswoman had seen them too and was opening the door. Too late to turn back. She was obviously delighted that the saviour of the island was frequenting her humble establishment.

They went in and before Sophy could object, she was being whisked off to a changing area.

Apollo paced the floor of the shop. This was something he didn't usually indulge in—dressing his lovers. It would give the wrong impression. But right now he didn't really care. He just wanted to see Sophy in that dress.

He heard a noise behind him and turned. For a moment he felt like he couldn't breathe. He almost reached to his neck to loosen his tie but realised he wasn't wearing one.

He'd seen women in some of the skimpiest and most

expensive haute couture but none of them had had this effect on him. The dress shouldn't be having this effect on him. But it wasn't the dress, it was the woman in the dress. She epitomised simple fresh-faced beauty. No adornment.

The bodice hugged her torso, around her high firm breasts and then fell in soft folds to below her knees. Her feet were bare. Her hair was pulled back, highlighting her slim shoulders and neck. He could see where the sun had turned her skin a light gold. She had more freckles.

His voice felt strangled when he said, 'We'll buy it.'

Sophy immediately started protesting but he just signalled to the owner that they'd take it and she whisked Sophy back to the changing area.

When Sophy emerged again Apollo was paying for the dress and accepting it in a bag. She felt conflicted—thrilled to have the dress but weird because he'd paid for it. Sasha had always favoured boyfriends with money who would buy her things and the sheer volume of clothes here and in Athens was testament to how much she'd squeezed out of Apollo.

When they walked out of the shop into the street Sophy said stiffly, 'I really didn't expect you to buy the dress.'

'It looks good on you, wear it this evening at the wedding festivities.'

He was putting his shades on again, oblivious to Sophy's turmoil. She didn't move. 'I want to pay you back for the dress.' She realised she had nothing, and not only that, she would have most certainly lost her job. There was only a meagre balance in her bank account back in England because she'd loaned Sasha money not long before she'd disappeared to Greece with Apollo. The knowledge that she'd most likely funded Sasha's trip to betray her made her feel even more prickly. 'I mean, when I can. I insist.'

Apollo looked at her. 'Fine. Whatever you want. I can get your people to liaise with my people and set up an electronic transfer for the princely sum of thirty euros.' His mouth quirked.

'Don't laugh at me.'

His mouth straightened. He put his hands on her hips and pulled her to him. 'I know you're not your sister, Sophy. You're nothing like her, believe me.'

'You couldn't tell us apart after the accident.'

Apollo arched a brow over his shades. 'Couldn't I? I never wanted her the way I want you.'

He kissed her there in the street, with people passing by. Sophy was aware of whispers and giggles and she couldn't stop her silly heart soaring.

When they returned to the town early that evening, Sophy felt self-conscious in the dress. She'd dressed it up a bit by pulling her hair into a bun on the top of her head and choosing a pair of Sasha's strappy silver sandals.

Apollo was wearing a dark suit and white shirt, open at the neck. He led her down to the smaller square where the church was located and the couple was just emerging from the entrance to loud cheers and clapping. Musicians played traditional Greek music.

Apollo and Sophy stood on the end of what looked like a receiving line of guests to either side of the couple, who passed down, accepting congratulations and good wishes. The bride was beautiful, with dark laughing eyes and long hair. Her husband was tall and handsome. They looked incandescently happy.

When they'd passed down the line, they walked through the town towards the bigger square. Apollo and Sophy followed them. The place had been transformed since earlier that day. Flowers festooned every available surface and fairy lights were strung across the square. Candles flickered on tables.

It was simple, rustic, humble and beautiful. Sophy knew Sasha would have hated it. She loved it.

Apollo was greeted and feted like a VIP. They were seated at a table for dinner near the bride and groom's table. A steady stream of people came up to converse with Apollo. Sophy was happy to let the occasion wash over her, enjoying the people-watching and lively Greek bonhomie and music.

When dinner had been cleared away, the music stopped suddenly and a line of men got up to dance, including the groom. Everyone turned to look at them. At the last minute they gestured to Apollo to get up and join them. He signalled *no*, but one of the men came over and pulled him up, amidst cheers and applause.

The music started slow and mesmeric, a familiar Greek song, a traditional dance. Apollo was near the middle, near the groom. The men started dancing, slowly, in time to the music, arms around each other's shoulders.

Apollo did the slow deliberate steps with perfect precision, a smile on his face. He looked younger all of a sudden. Less intense. It made Sophy's heart swell, thinking of what he'd told her about his parents dancing. Maybe his father had taught him and his brother this dance?

The music got faster and the steps more intricate, Apollo's torso and hips twisting. He was so dynamic and handsome that Sophy didn't have to look around her to know that every gaze was trained on him. Probably even the bride's.

By the time the music built to a crescendo everyone was on their feet clapping and cheering. The men bowed. Then it was the women's turn, led out to dance by the bride.

One of the women grabbed Sophy's hand and pulled her up. She was shaking her head, laughing, but they ignored her. She caught Apollo's eye and shrugged helplessly.

Apollo watched Sophy being pulled away to dance. Her face was shining and she was laughing, trying to do her best to keep up with the steps of the dance. She stood out with her red-gold hair and blue eyes. Pale skin. She'd kicked off the high-heeled sandals and was in her bare feet.

Physical desire was like a tight knot inside Apollo, winding tighter and tighter. But along with the physical desire was something else, something far more disturbing. A sense of yearning…a need to replace the hollow ache in his chest. An ache he'd ignored for a long time. An ache he couldn't keep ignoring around *her*.

With her questions that struck at the heart of him: *Why did you buy an island?*

A sense of desperation gripped him now. This was just about *sex*. Nothing more. By the time Sophy had picked up her shoes and come off the dance floor Apollo was standing up to meet her.

He took her hand. 'Ready to go?'

She must have seen something of the urgency he was feeling because her eyes darkened and she nodded wordlessly.

Apollo paid his respects to the bride and groom and drove them back to his villa. All was quiet and hushed on this side of the island, only the faintest sounds of the revelry carrying on the light breeze. Sophy's feet were still bare.

They got out of the car and Apollo held out his hand for her. Sophy didn't hesitate. She took Apollo's hand and let him lead her into the villa, dropping her shoes on the way. The need to replace feelings he didn't welcome with the physical reminder of what was between them was overwhelming.

Sophy let Apollo lead her to his room. It was illuminated by moonlight. Standing in front of him, the lingering tipsiness from the wine made her bold. She moved forward and pushed Apollo's jacket off. It fell to the floor.

Then he undid his buttons and opened his shirt, pushing it off his broad shoulders. His chest was wide and powerful. She couldn't resist touching him, running her hands over his skin. His muscles tensed under her fingers and she felt powerful.

He reached for her hair and undid her bun, letting her hair fall down around her bare shoulders. She shivered at the sensation.

He caught her face in his hands and tilted it up to him. His features were stark with need and her insides clenched in reaction. There was something else there, some indefinable emotion. Instinctively Sophy touched his jaw with her hand. 'Apollo? Are you okay?'

Something expressive crossed his face for a second and then it was gone. Replaced by pure unadulterated *need*. 'I'm fine. I just want you. Now.'

She hesitated for a moment, because she sensed that there was some sort of internal battle being fought, but the clamour of her own blood drowned out the need to know. She turned around and pulled her hair over one shoulder, offering him her back. His hands came to the zip at the top of the dress and pulled it down, knuckles grazing the bare skin of her back.

The dress loosened from around her breasts and then fell to her waist. She pushed it off over her hips and it fell at her feet. Now she wore only her underwear.

Apollo came close behind her and she sucked in a breath when she realised that he was totally naked. His arms came around her, hands finding and closing over her breasts. Massaging them, teasing her tight nipples.

Instinctively she moved against him, and she heard an almost feral-sounding growl. Apollo turned her to face him and the electricity crackled between them. Urgency spiked.

He led her over to the bed and she lay down. He reached for her underwear, pulling them down and off. He came over her, all rippling muscles and sleek olive-toned skin. She opened her legs to him, and he settled between them as if they'd done this dance down through lifetimes and not just in this one.

Sophy lifted her hips towards him, her small hand seeking to wrap around his rigid flesh, bringing his head close to where her body ached for him. For an infinitesimal moment he was poised there on the brink and then he took her hand away and joined their bodies with one powerful thrust.

She was so ready for him. She could feel her inner muscles clamping around him in a pre-orgasmic rush of sensation.

There was no time for slow lovemaking. It was fast and furious, both racing for the pinnacle and reaching it at the same incandescent moment, bodies entwined and locked together in an explosion of pleasure that went on and on. Sophy wasn't even aware of Apollo extricating himself from her embrace or of the way he stood up from the bed and looked at her for a long moment.

A week later, Apollo looked at Sophy across the dinner table that had been set on the terrace of the villa. She was talking to Olympia and the older woman's face was wreathed in smiles as she showed Sophy pictures on her phone of her newest grandchild.

Apollo marvelled at how he had been so blinkered by Sasha's deviousness that he hadn't noticed how different *this* woman was.

People responded to Sophy because she was open and kind. Polite. She was also sexy and utterly addictive. During the past week, Apollo had effectively shut out the world to gorge himself on this woman. But her appeal wasn't waning at all, or burning out. It was burning hotter. Becoming stronger.

He'd been ignoring calls from his office in Athens, to the point where his executive assistant had turned up on Krisakis today to speak to him personally. A visit that had broken him out of the haze of desire, shattering the illusion that he didn't have to engage with the outside world.

An image inserted itself into his mind—Sophy laughing and dancing with the other women at the wedding. The way seeing her like that had opened a great gaping chasm of yearning inside him. A yearning he'd had to eclipse by making love to her like a starving man. A yearning that lingered and caught at him under his skin. Chafing. Unwelcome.

A yearning that had made him careless. For a second time. Something he'd effectively blocked out all week. He was losing control, letting her in too deep.

Olympia was walking away with their plates now and Sophy looked at Apollo, her smile fading at the expression on his face. 'What is it?'

A stone weight made his chest feel tight. But he ignored it. 'We need to talk.'

CHAPTER ELEVEN

SOPHY FOLLOWED APOLLO into his study, her insides in a knot. He'd been distracted since his assistant had visited earlier. There was a spectacular view of the ocean and vast sky, which was currently a glorious pink and lavender colour. But that faded into insignificance behind the man dominating the space.

Apollo rested on the edge of his desk, hands by his hips. Hips that Sophy could remember holding only a few short hours before as he'd—

She blurted out a question to try and distract herself from memories of a week spent indulging in the pursuit of sensual oblivion. 'What is it, Apollo?'

But she already knew. It skated across her skin like a cold breeze. In fact, she'd been aware of it all week, even if she hadn't acknowledged it. The real world was waiting, just in the wings.

Even so, she wasn't prepared when he said tightly, 'When we made love...after the wedding, I didn't use protection that night. I told you I wouldn't be careless again but I was.'

Sophy's insides went into freefall. She hadn't even noticed, hadn't even thought about it afterwards.

Faintly she said, 'It wasn't just your fault. I should have been careful too.' It had been the last thing on her mind during that conflagration. Or during this week, when it had felt like their world had been reduced to this villa, this island. Apollo's bed.

You didn't want to think about anything that would burst the bubble.

No, she hadn't. She'd deliberately shied away from thinking about anything that might break the idyll. She'd let the fantasy become her reality. And now she would pay.

She almost put a hand on her belly but closed it into a fist. She said, 'It's okay. I'm at a safe place in my cycle. I'm sure of it.'

Apollo seemed to absorb that, and then he said, 'My assistant brought your personal things today, including your passport. And Sasha's body is ready for repatriation. My office will arrange everything for her funeral if you just give them the necessary information of where you want her buried.'

The cold breeze turned to ice in Sophy's belly. 'That won't be necessary, I can do all that.'

'I insist. She was my wife, after all. You won't have to worry about costs.'

Sophy swallowed. 'When do we leave?'

'Leander, my assistant, is still on the island, staying in the town. He will come for you in the morning and you will travel back to Athens with him, and then on to London with your sister. You'll be met by an assistant from my London office on the other side, they'll help you make further arrangements.'

Sophy searched for a hint of anything on Apollo's face or in his eyes, but he'd retreated somewhere she couldn't reach. She'd noticed it when he'd arrived for dinner—when he'd avoided her eye. He'd been shut up in his office with his assistant for most of the afternoon.

'You won't be coming back to Athens?'

'Not just yet. I have some meetings here on the island to do with the construction and I'll travel back the following day.'

A sharp pain lanced her insides.

Her heart.

And also a sense of panic.

As if reading her every passing emotion, Apollo said, 'My assistant in London will make sure you're looked after, Sophy. You won't be left alone.'

If there was one thing Sophy wouldn't be able to bear, it was Apollo's pity or that she was a responsibility to be dealt with. 'That really won't be necessary. I can go back to the flat I shared with Sasha. I'll...be fine.'

Apollo stood up. 'Leander will be here before ten a.m.'

Sophy looked at him, in shock at the speed and efficiency with which he was apparently willing to dispatch her.

'So that's it, then?'

His face tightened. 'I think it's for the best. There's no point in prolonging something that we both know is at an end.'

Sophy felt emotion swelling inside her. If she'd known the last time she'd made love to Apollo was to be the last time, she would have imprinted every second onto her memory. 'You mean, something that never should have started.'

'Sophy...' he said warningly.

But a volatile mix of hurt, anger and fear made her say, 'The truth is that something happened between us that first night, we had a connection, and I think you used my virginity as an excuse to kick me out. To deny it.'

'You were inexperienced. Naive. I wasn't prepared to let you believe it would ever become something more than just sex.'

'Well, I think it was about you just as much as it might have been about me.'

'What's that supposed to mean?'

'I think you're an emotional coward, Apollo. I understand why it's hard for you to trust again. But I've lost my family too and I don't want to shut my emotions up for ever.'

A muscle pulsed in Apollo's jaw. 'Which is why I said to you that you'll go on to meet someone and have a family some day. You want more, Sophy. I don't.'

Sophy felt something inside her crack and break. 'I think you're a liar, Apollo. I think you do want more, but you're too scared to admit it.'

Or maybe he just doesn't want more with you.

Her insides curdled at that thought. Maybe Apollo would trust his heart again some day. When he met someone he couldn't walk away from, or shut out.

He opened his mouth but Sophy held up her hand, terrified to hear Apollo spell out that it just wasn't *her* who could crack the ice around his heart.

Now who's the coward? mocked a voice.

Sophy pushed it down.

'It's fine, Apollo.' She lowered her hand. 'It wasn't as if you weren't clear about what this was. I'll be ready for Leander in the morning.'

Apollo watched Sophy turn to walk out of his study. At the last moment he blurted out her name. She turned around.

She said nothing. Her face was expressionless. Perversely, Apollo wanted to provoke a reaction.

'You'll let me know if there are any consequences?'

Her face leached of colour. 'You mean a baby?'

Now that he'd got the reaction he just felt hollow. He nodded.

Her mouth was tight. 'I told you, there won't be. I'm sure of it.'

She turned and this time left the room.

Apollo had nothing more to say.

To stop her from leaving.

He was so rigid with tension that he thought he might

crack if he moved. *Theos.* Did he want there to be consequences? After everything that had happened?

Her words reverberated in his head, a mocking jeer.

*'I think you're a liar, Apollo... I think you do want
more...'*

He turned around and stared blindly at the view. She
was wrong. He didn't want more. He had decided a long
time ago what kind of life he wanted and he wasn't about
to let one woman change that.

One woman was no match for the demons that haunted
him, reminding him of a loss and pain so great he thought
he'd have preferred to die with them all.

All he felt for Sophy was physical lust. Nothing more.
And that would fade. No matter how much it still burnt
him up inside.

As Sophy's flight from Athens descended through stormy
summer skies into London, she took in the unseasonably
grey clouds. They mirrored her mood. Volatile.

She was angry with herself for having fallen for Apollo.
For having revealed herself so much during that last ex-
change in his study.

The anger was good—it was insulating her from the
sheer terror of stepping back out into a fast-paced world
after living in a cocoon for these past few weeks. She knew
that not far under the anger her shell was very brittle and
fragile.

She had a sister to grieve and a life to re-start. A job
to find because, as expected, when she'd rung them from
Athens the day before, she'd found out that her position
had been filled once she'd disappeared. The fact that they'd
been so wholly unconcerned about her disappearance only
compounded her sense of isolation now. Sophy shook her
head, trying to dislodge that sense of isolation.

She put a hand on her flat belly. She'd not even noticed

that they hadn't used protection that night a week ago. But Apollo had. She *was* sure there wouldn't be a baby and she hated herself for the hollow ache that thought precipitated.

Did she really want history to repeat itself, except this time with a real baby?

The plane had touched down. She lifted her hand from her belly. It was time to mourn and bury her sister and try to get on with her life and forget she'd ever met Apollo Vasilis.

Two weeks later, just outside London

'Let us go now in peace.'

Sophy stood by the grave for a moment. She was the only mourner at her sister's funeral. She'd told a few of Sasha's friends but they'd said they were too busy to come.

Sophy was sad, and a little angry—for her sister, in spite of her faults, had deserved better.

She had only barest sensation of prickling on the back of her neck before she heard the priest say, 'Welcome, sir. We've just finished the prayers.'

Sophy looked up and at first she thought she was hallucinating. Apollo looked taller and darker than she'd ever seen him. In a dark grey suit, white shirt and steel-grey tie. Dark shades hid his eyes.

Faintly, she said, 'Apollo...'

He dipped his head. 'Sophy.' He looked at the priest. 'Father.'

The priest came and took Sophy's arm. 'My dear, I'm so sorry. If you ever need to talk, you know where I am.'

Sophy tried to control her suddenly thundering heart. 'Thank you, Father.'

The priest walked away, leaving them alone by the grave. Sophy said, 'I wasn't expecting to see you here.'

Apollo's jaw tightened. 'I had always intended coming

but I got delayed. She was my wife...however that came about.'

Sophy clamped down on the dangerous spurt of gratitude and something far more dangerous.

Hope.

'Thank you for your help in organising this.'

'It was nothing. I'll leave you for a moment.'

Apollo walked away and Sophy could see her own funeral limousine and then Apollo's blacked-out SUV. The drivers were talking. Apollo was standing at a respectable distance to give her some time. A gesture that made her feel surprisingly emotional.

She turned her back on him and said a few silent words to Sasha. The last few weeks she'd had to think about a lot of things and her relationship with her sister had been one of them. There was a certain sense of liberation now, but as much as that made Sophy feel guilty, she was also sad that it had had to come at the cost of her sister's life.

Her parents were buried in the same graveyard and Sophy walked the short distance to where they rested in their own plot, laying a flower on their grave.

Then she steeled herself to face Apollo. She turned around, aware of her sober black suit. It was actually the same skirt and shirt she'd been wearing the night she'd met him, and a black jacket. She'd put her hair up in a bun. She felt plain and unvarnished next to his effortless good looks when she walked towards him, where he stood under a tree.

She couldn't see his eyes but she could feel them on her and her skin prickled. She stopped a couple of feet away. He straightened up from the tree.

'Was the other grave your parents'?'

She nodded.

Then he said, 'Can we go somewhere to talk?'

The thought of being alone with him when she felt so raw made her blurt out, 'We can talk here.'

Apollo shuddered visibly. 'If it's okay with you, I've seen enough of graveyards to last me a lifetime.'

She felt a pang in her heart; so had she, come to think of it. She feigned nonchalance. 'Fine…where were you thinking?'

'My apartment in London, it's private.'

Where she'd gone with him the night they'd made love. A penthouse apartment at the top of a glittering exclusive building. The last place she should go with him, but suddenly the lure of seeing him again, however briefly, was too seductive.

'Okay.'

He stepped back and put out a hand for her to precede him to his car. He spoke with the other driver, who left. Sophy got into the SUV.

The journey into town was taken in silence, apart from a couple of phone calls Apollo made. Presumably to do with work. She wondered about Krisakis, how the resort was shaping up. A place she'd never see again.

They pulled up outside Apollo's apartment building and Sophy recognised it. It was bitter-sweet to have her memory back.

The driver opened her door and Sophy got out. Apollo was already standing on the pavement. Tall and gorgeous. Drawing appreciative glances from passers-by. Men and women.

Before, Sophy would have looked at Apollo and compared herself as someone who would fade into the background but she knew she had to stop taking on that role. The one she'd played with Sasha, allowing Sasha to be the noticeable one.

She was never going to set the world alight but she could own her own space in a way she had never done before.

She walked ahead of Apollo into the building, through the door opened by the doorman. She could remember being here the first time, feeling so awed and excited. Tingling all over. Nervous. She felt as if she'd grown an age since that wide-eyed girl.

Virgin.

The lift took a few seconds and then they were stepping out into the grandeur that Sophy remembered. Lots of glass and plush carpets. Oriental rugs. Massive paintings on the walls. Sleek coffee tables with hardback tomes showing beautiful pictures of Greece and house interiors.

Of course, it had been dark outside the first time she'd been here and now it was bright daylight. And, in fairness, she'd only been interested in looking at one thing. Apollo.

He turned to her now. He'd already shrugged off his jacket and was loosening his tie. 'Can I get you tea, or coffee?'

Sophy held her bag in front of her. 'Just some water, please.'

He disappeared and came back a few minutes later holding a glass of water for her and a small cup of coffee for himself. He gestured around them. 'Please, make yourself comfortable.'

Sophy put down her bag and walked over to one of the windows, which took in the lush green gardens of Kensington Palace nearby. Truly this was a billionaire's address.

He said from behind her in a slightly gruff voice, 'You remind me of the night we met.'

Sophy fought to keep the blush down. She turned around. 'That's because I was wearing these same clothes. Pretty much.' The same clothes she'd put on with shaking hands and with tears blurring her vision after Apollo had summarily dismissed her. For being a virgin.

'How are you doing?'

Sophy's hand gripped the glass. 'I'm okay. I'm starting a new job as a receptionist in a central dentist's office in a couple of weeks.'

Apollo's blood thrummed with heat. A heat that hadn't cooled in Sophy's absence, much to his sense of frustration and a kind of futility.

'Apollo...what is it you want?'

He might have smiled at that loaded question, but it would be a bleak smile. He put the coffee cup down. 'I need to be sure...there are no consequences? After that night?'

His gaze dropped to her waist and he couldn't help but imagine it thickening and growing with his child. Before he could control it, that awfully familiar sense of yearning caught at his guts. *No.* Not what he was here for. Never that. Not even now.

Sophy blinked. He was so terrified of the thought of a baby that he'd come all the way here to check...again? She read his body language and something inside her curled up. *Yes.* He was that terrified.

She got out, 'No. I've had my period since I returned to London. I told you it would be okay.'

There was no discernible expression on Apollo's face and Sophy was almost sorry now that she hadn't had another answer. To crack that facade.

'Okay...that's good, then.'

Except he sounded almost...disappointed. Sophy shook herself mentally. She was dreaming. She put down the glass in her hand and straightened up again. 'Was that it, Apollo? Because I really should be going now.'

She walked towards him and Apollo caught her hand as she was about to pass him. 'Wait.'

She stopped. She was so close she could smell his distinctive scent and she had to battle the memories threatening to overwhelm her. For a bleak moment she almost wished she could lose her memory again.

'Look at me, Sophy.'

Sophy really didn't want to look at Apollo. She was too full of volatile emotions. He'd only come to make sure she wasn't pregnant. But he wasn't letting her hand go. Reluctantly, Sophy looked up. Her pulse quickened in helpless answer to what she saw in his eyes. Desire.

He said, 'I still want you.'

A sense of desperation and anger that he still had an effect on her made her say, 'Well, I don't want you.'

She tried to pull her hand away but he held on tighter. He tugged her towards him, shaking his head. 'Don't lie, Sophy. Sasha was the liar, not you.'

'How do you know? You barely know me.'

'Don't I? I got to know you when you were your most genuine self. With no memory to inform you, you couldn't be anyone *but* yourself.'

She had never thought of it like that. She was so close their bodies were almost touching. Apollo finally let her hand go. She could have stepped back now but his scent was winding around her, keeping her there like invisible silken bindings.

He brought a hand to her jaw, cupping it. She wanted to turn her face into it, purr like a kitten. She could feel her will to resist Apollo draining away. She'd missed him.

So when he tipped her face up and lowered his head, she let him prove her words wrong. The kiss started out chaste, a touch to the lips, before coming back, firmer, more insistent. Encouraging her to open up to him. After a moment of hesitation she did, unable not to. Apollo swept inside and then she was lost, drowning in a whirlpool of memories and desires she'd tried to ignore and bury in the past month.

She could feel his hands roving over her back, cupping her buttocks. Just before she lost herself entirely, she pulled back, mouth throbbing. 'Apollo…what are we doing… It's over… You never wanted to see me again.'

'This isn't over.'

She pushed herself out of his arms, immediately feeling bereft. She shook her head. 'What are you saying?'

'Why does this have to end when we both still want each other?'

For a wild moment Sophy's heart soared. 'How would that work?'

He said, 'You could move in here, if you like. You said you're working in central London. I'll be in London regularly over the coming months as I've got a project starting up and I need to be on hand.'

Her heart dipped. 'You mean…this is just a temporary thing.'

'Well, for as long as we want each other.'

Her disappointment was so acute that Sophy nearly doubled over. Nothing had changed. He was just looking for an extension of their affair.

Sophy turned and walked back over to the window, not wanting Apollo to see the effect of his words on her. She spoke to the glass. 'So what you're talking about is essentially making me your mistress?'

Apollo looked at Sophy's slender back. He still had the taste of her on his tongue. The feel of her body under his hands.

'You can call it what you like, I'm talking about continuing this relationship.'

She turned around. 'But just the physical side of it. And once that's fizzled out then we get on with our lives?'

Frustration bit into Apollo. 'Can you walk away from what's between us?'

She came closer and to his shock he saw moisture in her eyes. It was like a punch to the gut.

She said, 'No, I can't walk away. But I'll have to. You see, I want more than that, Apollo. Much more. And, unlike you, I'm not prepared to settle for less.'

Panic gripped Apollo. He felt like he was slipping down a cliff-edge with nothing to hold onto. He said, 'How much do you want?'

She looked at him, an expression of shock and then disgust crossing her face. '*No.* I'm not talking about money. I'm talking about *love.* Family. Emotions. All the things you don't want.'

As if money could buy a woman like Sophy. He felt ashamed. A great yawning chasm was opening inside Apollo—the place where he'd almost lost himself after Achilles had died. When he'd felt so terrified and alone. Abandoned. Sophy was looking at him with those huge eyes, asking him to step into that place.

He shook his head, stepped back. 'I've told you, I can't give you that.'

Sophy felt her heart crack. 'Can't…or won't?'

She wasn't expecting an answer, so she stepped around Apollo and walked towards the corridor leading to the elevator to take her back down to reality.

But she couldn't go without telling him… She turned back and he was looking after her, jaw tight.

She said, 'I love you, Apollo. I fell for you the night we met. I'm so sorry for what my sister put you through, but I'm glad that her actions brought us together because I might never have seen you again.'

She turned and walked out, hoping stupidly that she'd hear her voice or feel his hand on her arm. But there was nothing. She got into the elevator and the doors closed. It descended. She got out and walked forward and out of the building like an automaton.

She went down into the nearest tube station and followed the crowd through the turnstile, not even sure where she was going. She was numb. But she welcomed the numbness, which was protecting her from incredible pain.

You could have stayed…become his mistress.

She shut the voice out. It would have killed her in the end.

She walked towards the signs for the Bakerloo Line,

which would take her back to south London. At the top of the escalator, though, she heard a call.

'Sophy!'

No. It was her stupid mind playing tricks. She was about to step onto the escalator and it came again, urgent.

'Sophy, wait. Please!'

She heard a girl near her say, '*I'll* be Sophy if he wants. He's *gorgeous*.'

Sophy turned around. Apollo was standing on the other side of the turnstiles with his hands braced on the sides—as if ready to vault over. Sophy walked towards him, trying not to let a flame of hope spring to life.

He looked wild. She could feel the electric pull between them, even here.

She came closer. 'I won't be your mistress, Apollo. I'm not mistress material.'

He said, 'I don't want you to be my mistress, Sophy... just come back over here, please?'

Sophy was aware of a crowd gathering. People whispering. Slowly, she walked over to the exit turnstiles and came back through. Apollo had tracked her progress from the other side, his eyes never leaving hers. He was waiting for her. Big, solid.

Sophy knew if he asked her again she wouldn't have the strength to say no. She knew she was weak enough to clutch at any more time he would give her to be with him.

She stopped in front of him and he put his hands on her arms. 'I'm sorry,' he said.

'For what?'

'For disrespecting you. And for the ten seconds too long that it took me to remove my head from my—'

A public announcement blared at that moment, blocking out Apollo's words, but Sophy could guess what he'd said.

She was too full of trepidation to let the bubble of euphoria she felt rise up inside her. 'What are you saying, Apollo?'

'I'm saying that it's too late. Any hope I might have had of protecting myself against the pain of losing you—letting you go in Athens, trying to make you my temporary lover—is well and truly shattered. Because I would prefer to spend one more perfect day with you, if that's all we have, than a lifetime of regret because I was too much of a coward to admit my fears and open my heart.'

Sophy heard someone sigh near them, but Apollo filled her vision. And her rapidly swelling heart. 'Are you saying…?'

'That I love you. Deeply, irrevocably. Infinitely. I fell for you the moment you looked at me for the first time but I didn't know it at the time. All I knew was that I had to have you.'

He tugged her towards him. 'Please…don't walk away from me. Give me a chance.'

Sophy shook her head. Suddenly she was the one who was scared. She whispered, 'I can't do this, Apollo. It'll kill me if you're just saying this to get me back in your bed.'

He kissed her then. In the middle of the concourse of one of London's busiest Tube stations. A deep kiss, full of remorse and pain and…love. A promise.

They broke apart and Apollo looked at her. They were oblivious to the crowd that had formed around them, phones raised.

'All I can do is ask you to trust me. I *do* want more. You've made me want more, and I've denied it to myself, or tried to, but I can't any longer. I want you, Sophy, and I want to spend the rest of my life with you. Will you give me a chance to prove that to you?'

A voice nearby said loudly, 'If you won't, love, I will!'

A giggle of pure emotion burst up from Sophy's belly.

Along with hope…a hope that she couldn't push back down. She smiled a wobbly smile. 'One chance.'

His eyes burned like dark emeralds. He took her hand and raised it to his lips. 'One chance is all I need.' He took her hand and led her back up, out of the dark underground and into the light. The sunlight made everything shimmer. It felt like a benediction. A new start. And Sophy took a deep breath and let herself trust.

Sophy looked out over the sight of the city waking up to a brand-new day under a pink dawn. She was wrapped in a voluminous robe and her body felt pleasantly lethargic and sated. She'd left a sleeping Apollo on the bed, his brow smooth in sleep.

She was still trying to absorb what had happened and she couldn't help but feel slightly fearful that it had all been a dream. Or had she projected her love onto Apollo so much that she'd heard what she'd wanted to—and he hadn't actually made those declarations…

'Here you are.'

She tensed against his inevitable effect on her, but it was useless when his arms slid around her waist and he brought his body flush with hers. He said into her ear, 'When I woke up just now, and I was alone in the bed, I thought I'd dreamed it all up. That you were gone.'

Sophy turned around in Apollo's arms and looked up at him. 'I was just afraid of the same thing, that I'd imagined it all…that you hadn't said—'

'That I love you?'

She nodded her head, biting her lip.

'Well, I did. And I do. I love you, Sophy Jones. And if it's all right with you, I'd like us to marry as soon as possible.'

Her heart skipped a beat. 'Was that a proposal?'

He looked worried. 'I can make it more romantic if you like…'

She shook her head and smiled. 'No, that'll do just fine. And, yes, I accept your proposal.'

But then she sobered again. Apollo tipped her chin up. 'What is it?'

She put her hands on his bare chest. He'd pulled on sweats but she had to not let his physicality distract her.

'What I said about a family... I meant that. I do want a family. Children. When you reminded me that we hadn't used protection...for a moment, even though it would have been the wrong thing, I wanted there to be a baby.'

He cupped her face. 'I told myself I didn't want there to be a baby and that's why I was so concerned about *consequences*, but actually I think deep down I was hoping that you might have got pregnant. I had to come to terms with the thought of a baby when I thought Sasha was pregnant and what surprised me was how much I wanted it. In spite of everything I'd been telling myself for years. Except, in that situation, I compartmentalised the baby very separately from its mother.'

'But now...with you... I want it all too. The baby, *you*. Us, together. Making a life. It scared me for so long, the thought of losing someone I love, so I blocked it out. That's why I was so harsh with you after we slept together that first night. I knew you'd got to me more than any other woman ever had. So I used your virginity as an excuse to get you to leave. But I never forgot about you...and I think eventually the memory of you would have driven me so mad that I would have come to find you.

'But then your sister turned up...and I was relieved I hadn't had to be the one to make a move. Until I realised I no longer wanted you. And then Sasha dropped her bombshell. I told myself I was glad I didn't desire you, because then it meant what we'd shared couldn't have been as amazing as I remembered...but then that all got blown out of the water...'

Sophy looked at him, finally believing and trusting. But he said, 'Need more convincing?'

She nodded and started moving her hands down to his waist. His body hardened against hers. 'Maybe a little more…just to make sure we're on the same page.'

Apollo scooped her up and carried her back into the bedroom and put her down on her feet by the bed. He undid the belt of the robe and tugged it off her body. His green gaze glittered with barely banked heat as it swept up and down her body. He muttered, 'I will never get tired of looking at you, little flame. Or wanting you.'

He kissed her then and she arched into him, pouring all of her love into the kiss. His sweats got discarded and they landed on the bed in a tangle of limbs. When Apollo was poised to enter her, Sophy put her hands on his hips. He wasn't wearing protection. She said huskily, 'Are you sure…it's not too soon?'

He bent down and pressed his lips to hers and then he said, 'It's not soon enough, *agapi mou.*'

And Sophy knew, as Apollo joined his body to hers, that he meant every word, and that today was the start of a new life. For them and for ever.

EPILOGUE

Three and a half years later, Krisakis

'MAMA, LOOK! I'M SWIMMING!'

Sophy stood up from the lounger with a slight huff of effort. She smiled and waved at her two-and-a-half-year-old son Ajax, who admittedly looked as if he was splashing more than swimming, being tugged along in armbands by his father.

She plonked a sunhat on her head and went over to the edge of the pool, which was just one of the luxurious features of the Achilles Villa in the Krisakis Resort, which had opened a couple of years ago. This was the villa Sophy had suggested building at the top of the resort and it was the most sought-after for its views and privacy.

As Sophy had predicted, they were inundated with visitors looking to escape the far busier islands around them, and Krisakis was thriving and growing all the time.

Sometimes they themselves needed to escape, and they went out on the yacht that Apollo had bought at the auction those few years ago. He'd named it *Little Flame*, much to Sophy's delight.

She went down on her haunches. 'You are doing so well, my love. Papa is a good teacher, isn't he? He taught me how to swim too.'

Ajax, dark-haired and a handful, as only a child of Apollo could be, broke into giggles. 'Papa teaching Mama to swim—that's silly! You're a grown-up!'

Sophy saw Apollo's smirk and splashed some water at him. He said warningly, 'You'll pay for that, Kyria Vasilis.'

She was Kyria Vasilis again. Except officially this time. They'd got married here on Krisakis in the small Greek Orthodox church. The inevitable media interest in Apollo marrying his widow's twin sister had been handled well by his PR team and it had quickly faded from the news pages.

Sophy stood up now and undid the wraparound kaftan, dropping it to the ground. She saw the way Apollo's eyes narrowed on her and the inevitable flame in their depths.

Her own body—so attuned to his—tingled and fizzed with anticipation. Lord knew, she shouldn't be feeling sexy. She was eight months pregnant and the size of a small hippo but nothing was capable of diminishing their desire. Even Ajax's arrival had been precipitated by Apollo's very sensual brand of trying to 'hurry him along' when she'd been overdue with him.

She went over to the steps that led down into the pool and sat down, relishing the feel of the water cooling her sun-warmed skin. Apollo left Ajax splashing happily in the shallow end and came over to where she was, sliding his arms around her and stealing a kiss. Something they never got away with for long in front of their son.

He pulled back and sat beside her, putting a hand over her belly. The baby kicked. It was a girl. But they were keeping it a secret from Ajax. She put her hand over her husband's and they looked at each other, a wealth of emotion flowing between them.

They'd already been tested by grief when Sophy had lost their second baby at about four months to a miscarriage, almost a year ago now. But that experience had only made their bond even stronger.

Ajax's voice suddenly piped up with an imperious, 'Mama, come here! I want to show you something.'

Sophy smiled wryly at Apollo and moved into the water,

swimming lazily over to her son, the way her husband had taught her.

Apollo looked at his wife and son playing and his heart was so full he didn't know how it didn't burst. But it didn't. It just grew and expanded every day. And in another month or so it would expand a lot more.

And what he'd found, thanks to his love for his wife and his family, was that it was always infinitely better to make love the goal. And not self-protection. Because the thought of not experiencing this beauty and love and joy... Well, that was more terrifying than anything.

* * * * *

A HIDDEN HEIR
TO REDEEM HIM

DANI COLLINS

In May of 2012 my editor Megan Haslam
phoned with an offer for my first sale to
Mills & Boon. Eight years later, this is my thirty-fifth
title. The longer I do this, the more I appreciate the
entire team at Mills & Boon—particularly Megan.
Thank you for this career, Megan.
I absolutely couldn't have done it without you.

CHAPTER ONE

VALENTINO CASALE HAD long ago hardened himself against useless things like feelings, but he found himself irritated by the congested streets of Athens.

Traffic was his driver's problem, not his, but he shifted restlessly, acknowledging the real pea beneath his mattress. Returning to Greece grated on him. Being sent here as a child had always felt like a punishment and still did. And to be thrust into the space between his father's money and his mother's grappling for it? That was the equivalent of being thrown into a cage with a hungry tiger.

So no, he was not pleased to be here.

This will be the last time, he assured himself with a grim look at the bustling midmorning streets. At least his father wasn't here. *There* was a silver lining.

If he had feelings, Val supposed he would be experiencing grief or what some called "closure." Since receiving the news that Nikolai Mylonas had died two days ago, however, he had experienced no emotions at all, not even relief. His father would be cremated and his ashes interred on his island property. In lieu of a service that no one would attend, Nikolai's two sons and their mothers were requested to appear in person at the reading of his will.

Val had rejected any share in his father's wealth two decades ago. He'd built his own fortune off his own oiled back, *grazie*. He had even supplied his mother with a healthy allowance in hopes she would quit lusting after Niko's money, not that it had worked.

She had continued to take Niko's occasional checks and remained convinced that her son was entitled to *all* of his father's fortune. If she absolutely had to, she would settle for his receiving exactly 50 percent.

Val still didn't want it, as he had reiterated to his father's lawyer when the man had called to set up this meeting. Whatever he stood to inherit could be signed over to his mother if it couldn't be refused.

There were stipulations, he had been informed, that demanded the presence of all parties before anything could proceed.

The king was dead, but his legacy of manipulation lived on.

And yes, Val's mother was mentioned, the lawyer had hurried to state, so it was in Val's interest to show up and keep the wheels turning.

Who *cared* where the money went?

Evelina Casale, that was who. She cared about Niko's money above all things. She most especially cared how much she would receive as compared to Niko's ex-wife, Paloma. If the other woman was bequeathed so much as one euro more, well, Val supposed he would finally meet his half brother with pistols at dawn.

Another silver lining—

"Stop," he commanded, lifting his head off the back

of his seat as his gaze caught the frontage of an art gallery. "Let me out here."

As he stepped from the car, his phone dinged with another text from his mother, informing him she had arrived in the lobby.

She could wait. They all could.

He shoved his phone back into his pocket and crossed the street. Habit propelled him. For three years he had been entering every gallery he glimpsed, no matter what else was on his agenda. No matter if he'd been in the same shop days before.

Perversely, he was forever on the hunt for his own naked form and was always disappointed not to find it.

It didn't escape him that if he had wanted to embarrass his father with public nudes, he could have taken a photo down his drawers and posted it online years ago. Hell, in his heyday Val had modeled underwear so sheer and tight he might as well have been bare-assed, so any barb in such an act was long lost. At this point an unknown artist capitalizing on his notoriety by circulating a "classy" rendition of his junk was pure, pretentious vanity—which he was probably guilty of along with a multitude of other sins.

Alas, today was one more fruitless search.

He smirked at his own joke, but his humor was quickly overshadowed by aggravation. He ought to be pleased when he failed to find himself. Everyone used him to whatever extent they could. In this case he had blatantly given his permission to be exploited, but this one struggling artist hadn't done so.

Why not? It could have been the break she needed. As three years passed, however, and he failed to glimpse anything like her work again, a niggling concern had begun roiling in him that something had happened to her.

Why *that* might bother him, he couldn't fathom. His own father had died, and he had continued with the tennis game his mother's call with the news had interrupted.

There had been something about that young artist, though. She'd been both mature and self-reliant, yet naive. Charmingly open with her opinions and genuinely curious of his, unafraid to challenge his assumptions or have her own views picked apart. She hadn't taken anything from him, either. Not even the money he'd left for the sketch he'd ripped from her book and tucked into his briefcase so he wouldn't lose or crumple it.

His phone buzzed again. His mother was worried she might run into Paloma and Javiero before Val arrived.

As if Val would allow *them* to hurry him along. He didn't respond, only moved leisurely through the gallery, skimming his gaze across landscapes and abstracts, cats and fruit bowls and a view through a window that bore only the vaguest resemblance to the framed sketch hanging in his bedroom. The execution on this one wasn't nearly as skilled, and the signature was not the KO he sought.

One of these days he would go to Ireland and poke around their galleries, see if he was hanging out there.

He smirked again at his double entendre, but his glimmer of amusement fell away as he walked the final few blocks through blistering heat into the ninth circle of hell, otherwise known as the Mylonas office tower. He hadn't been here since, well, it must have been right before he'd flown to Venice three years ago, acting on a social media post that his father's rival was vacationing there.

Val wondered yet again whether he might have backed out of his ill-fated marriage if he'd come back to his hotel room after that initial meeting and found his unassuming artist still in his bed, rather than finding all the cash he'd had in his wallet still in its tidy stack on the night table, her and her sketchbook gone.

She'd been guileless and refreshingly oblivious to his position and money. He'd been utterly relaxed as she sketched him. It seemed ridiculous to say he had felt "safe." He was a powerful man with strength and position and money, rarely at a disadvantage, but it had been a surprising relief that he hadn't felt a need to keep his guard up with her.

He hadn't fully appreciated that until much later and to this day, he was annoyed with himself that he'd left her that morning, giving her a chance to disappear without a trace. He hadn't caught her last name and, with his father's ultimatum still ringing in his ears, he'd gone through with his plan to firmly divest of the old man once and for all.

That ruthless move had been the last time he'd allowed emotion to drive him. The "marry in haste" cliché had its roots in truth. He'd found no satisfaction in his marriage, only a sexless existence with a woman whose interests were not his own. At least their divorce was finalized, and he could turn the page on that chapter in his encyclopedic collection of sordid mistakes.

"Take your time," his mother said as he came through the revolving doors. She gave him a dismayed once-over. "Would a suit have killed you?"

"A suit would have implied this meeting was important to me."

She *tsked* and moved toward him from the waiting area, almost as tall as he was and still catwalk-thin at fifty-eight—though she would slay anyone who tried to claim she was a day over fifty-one. Of course, that would have made her pregnant at eighteen, when she'd been gracing the cover of swimsuit issues, but she reserved her math skills for counting calories and money.

"Good afternoon, Mr. Casale. I'm Nigel," one of his father's minions said. "May I escort you to the meeting room?" He waved them toward the bank of elevators.

Val turned and a megajolt of electricity shot through him as he was smacked in the eyes by the large oil behind the security desk.

"Where did that come from?" he demanded.

It hadn't been there three years ago. He had never seen it before in his life. The seascape framed by a window was unfamiliar, although the view itself had to be Greece. The blend of colors was new to his eyes, but they were gloriously understated while providing infinite texture and depth. Something in the composition was deeply familiar to him, too. The waft of the curtain in the breeze was reminiscent of the drape of a charcoal shirt over the back of a chair.

The painting was so bizarrely evocative of *her*, she might as well have stood next to him, whispering in his ear, telling him that she felt safe in here, but the wildness beyond called to her. This painting was a threshold of sorts, as she contemplated moving into a new world filled with uncertainty, but also with vast and glorious new experiences.

"You can't come back here, sir."

He brushed past the security guard and examined the signature. Not the KO on his own sketch, but *Kiara*. His skin tightened all over his body.

"Where did you get this? I want to speak to this artist." He didn't ask himself why, but when the security guard only gave a baffled shrug, Val wanted to punch him.

"Um, sir?" Nigel the minion offered a perplexed look. "Miss O'Neill is upstairs. She arrived for your meeting ten minutes ago."

"For the reading of my father's will?" His scalp prickled. The sensation kept going, lifting a sharp tingle along the sides of his neck and running the length of his spine. His gut knotted and his groin twitched. His skin felt too tight for the heat that was suddenly pressurizing inside him, crystalizing the carbon in his body tissue to diamond hardness.

"Who is she?" his mother asked at a distance.

Val barely heard her over his harsh laugh of outraged, gallows humor.

"Someone who worked for Dad." How had he missed that? Blinded by his own libido, he supposed. Cursing himself, he said, "Yes. By all means. Take me to her. I. Can't. Wait."

Kiara O'Neill could tell that Niko's lawyer, Davin, was trying to put her at ease with his incessant small talk, but it wasn't working. Maybe he thought he was charming her? They'd met several times in the past three years and he had invited her to dinner more than once, but her priorities were always her daughter and her art, in that order. If she squeezed in an evening of wine and a rom-com with her best friend, Scarlett, she considered her life complete.

Trying to fit a man into her narrow world would only complicate her to-do list. Besides, the last time she'd gone on a date, she'd wound up pregnant.

And the man in question would enter this boardroom any second.

Her whole body was soaked in a clammy sweat, her mind incapable of holding a sensible thought, let alone a conversation. Her belted dress and flowing kimono jacket, chosen so carefully to be unobtrusive and comfortable while offering an impression of quiet confidence, felt constrictive. Her unsettled stomach was full of snakes, and the feminist inside her who had happily told men to talk to her hand for three years was wringing said hands like an adolescent girl when the grad ball was announced. The cute boy was coming down the corridor and she didn't know if she wanted him to notice her or not.

She kept thinking she should have done something different with her hair. Straightened it, maybe. She should have worn more makeup, to disguise her apprehension. Or maybe not so much, so she didn't look so…polished. Niko had liked her to look and sound and act a certain way and she'd gone along with it because, ugh, *reasons*, but this wasn't who she was.

Deep down she was still a mixed race orphan from Cork's dodgiest neighborhood. Scarlett would point out she was actually a mother and an artist, but Kiara was faking her way through both of those things so she wasn't sure they counted.

Val Casale had seemed like a smart man. She suspected he would see straight through to the fraud she was, no matter how she presented herself.

Although, he had seemed to think her work had genuine merit. When she had demurred, he'd said, "You really don't know who I am, do you?"

She hadn't. Not until much later.

It was all coming home to roost now, though.

She concentrated on not licking the lipstick off her mouth. Her throat was dry, making it impossible to swallow. All morning her heart rate had been picking up to a panicked speed, then petering out in a cold flush, leaving her light-headed and vaguely exhausted. She worried she would faint any second and reminded herself yet again to *breathe*. She didn't want to be stroked out on the floor when Val walked in.

She wanted to text Scarlett to hurry back from the ladies' room, but she had already set her phone to silent and tucked it into her clutch. Pulling it out midconversation would be rude.

With a stiff smile she fought to keep in place, she waited for Davin to pause in his rattling on, planning to say something about checking on Scarlett. Scarlett was heavily pregnant. It wasn't strange that she pretty much lived in the ladies' room these days, but she was taking a long time. Had she bumped into some of their guests? Was today's meeting taking place out there without her?

Had Val already heard the news and walked away, before he'd laid eyes on her or offered her a chance to explain? Given everything she'd heard about him since, that was probably for the best, but her heart twisted in anguish on behalf of—

The door opened and the air changed in a subtle

rush. A thrust of tense energy came in with the three people who entered.

"*Signor* and *Signora* Casale," Nigel announced, glancing at his tablet as it dinged. "The other party has arrived. I'll return with them shortly." He melted away, closing the door.

"Davin." Val's mother, Evelina, sounded as frosty and cultured as she had the one time Kiara had spoken to her three years ago. In person, Evelina was the epitome of what fashion magazines deemed sexy and attractive, nearly six foot and wispy. She had ivory skin and lustrous brunette hair that shimmered as she floated down the far side of the table. Her clothes were designer, her neck and ears and fingers bedecked in glittering jewels. She greeted Davin with perfunctory air kisses.

"Evelina. Lovely to see you again," Davin said politely before introducing Kiara. "This is Kiara O'Neill."

Evelina's gaze skimmed past her with a dismissive, "Water will do for now."

Kiara might have been amused—or insulted—but a millennium's worth of fireworks were going off inside her at the sight of Valentino Casale. Every emotion possible whistled and burst in her ears while sparks and flashes of color exploded in her vision.

He hadn't bothered with a suit. He wore ripped jeans and a black shirt open at the throat. They clung to a frame that was every bit as athletically lean and flawless as it had been three years ago. His hair was still tousled, his jaw still in need of a shave.

His gaze was exactly as piercing and unsettling. His silvery irises—endearingly familiar—pinned onto her, unwavering and fierce.

Adrenaline urged her to run for her life, but the sting

was laced with a bizarre excitement. An urge to run *to* him. Between those imperatives sat a mixture of more complex emotions. Cavernous guilt and angry resentment and something like painful relief.

She had dreaded and anticipated this day from the moment she had agreed to Niko's offer to live with him. She would finally confront Val about their daughter. She had braced for whatever consequences that might produce, but she hadn't braced for the effect Val still had on her.

Profound attraction accosted her. She shouldn't be surprised. The first time she'd seen him, he'd caused a stab of irresistible fascination in her. Time had stopped and her blood had sizzled as she had begun caressing the lines of his face in velvety shades of charcoal.

That same sensual yank took hold of her today, but stronger. It was deeper, immediate and sexual. Not simply a compulsion to study and re-create him on a page, but a gut-deep desire to close the distance and touch him. She wanted to feel him with her entire body and bask in the fire he lit inside her. She wanted to feel the sweep of his hands down her naked back and his strong grip on her hips.

Her body heated and tingled and grew aroused simply by standing in a room with him because she knew what making love with him felt like. She knew how he could make her feel—animalistic and alluring and *good*.

She hadn't calculated the effect of their connection through their child, either. She had spent over two years living with his father and his daughter. She knew so much more about Val Casale now, yet she still didn't know *him*. Her brief crush and the memory of a sweet encounter had become a spellbinding enthrallment with someone who had had a profound effect on her life.

Despite the things she'd been told about him, however, and despite the fact he'd ultimately slighted and discarded her, everything within her wanted to reach out and rediscover the sexy, hedonistic man she'd glimpsed that night.

The indulgent smile of her lover was gone, though. His cynicism and contempt were palpable in the polished chrome of his gaze.

Did he know that she'd had their baby? Was that why he was throwing accusation at her like bolts of lightning with his bitter look?

His antagonism was obvious. Her stomach bottomed out as she recalled one of the first things Niko had told her about his son.

Val is a bastard, Miss O'Neill. He takes pride in the distinction and seizes every opportunity to live down to the label.

At different times Niko had used all manner of unsavory descriptors—disrespectful, rebellious, confrontational, reprehensible, *vengeful.*

He hadn't been a man one contradicted, even though his view of Val hadn't sounded like the man she'd met. Regardless, anger with his father had prompted Val to turn his back on a fortune and marry a woman he didn't love. That made him a man no sensible woman would cross.

And Niko might have offered her protection from Val while he'd been alive, but Niko was gone. Kiara was on her own.

Davin broke the thick silence by setting down the jug

of water with a clunk. He held out the glass to Evelina, who ignored it as she stared between them.

"Do you know each other?" Evelina asked.

Kiara's arteries stung with a fresh release of fight or flight. She looked to the door, willing Scarlett to appear.

"What are you doing here, Kiara?" Val's voice, for all its lethal sharpness, was still deep enough to invoke a sense of curling into a soft bed under a thick quilt.

She glanced at Davin.

"When all mentioned parties are present, we'll discuss the particulars of dispersal," Davin said with a twitch of a smile that died on contact under Evelina's death-ray glare.

"Do not tell me this…*person*…is entitled to some portion of Niko's estate?" Evelina's outraged gaze went down Kiara's ample curves in pale yellow and summer-sky blue. Her lip curled with distaste.

"Not exactly," Kiara croaked, snatching up her own glass of ice water and dampening her throat. "I should check on Scarlett." Perhaps they could hide together in the ladies' room until this blew over.

Before she could take a step toward the door, however, it flung open.

"Very sorry," Nigel stammered. "There's been a development. Miss Walker has gone to the hospital."

"What? Why? What happened?" In her shock, Kiara misjudged the height of the table. Her glass tipped as she set it down on her way to the door. The puddle of water streaked out alongside her as the glass rolled toward Val on the other side of the table. He caught it before it fell and shattered.

"She's in labor," Nigel said. "*Señor* Rodriguez has taken her. His mother has chosen not to stay. The, uh, central message of this meeting was, um, conveyed by Miss Walker and…" Nigel glanced uncomfortably toward Evelina then swung his attention back to Kiara. "She said to tell you to finish your business here and call her when you're able."

Of course she had. Scarlett never thought of herself.

"I'll leave you to it," Nigel said, drawing the door closed on his exit.

"Do *not*—" Evelina flung around with ominous warning toward Davin "—tell me that some gold digger is having Paloma's grandchild and all of Niko's money is going to *them*." Tears of rage glittered in her eyes.

Val, on the other hand, gave an ironic snort. A dent of acrid humor twitched one corner of his mouth. "Touché, Javiero," he drawled.

"Not…um…all of it." Davin hurried to mollify Evelina. He flashed a cautious glance at Kiara. "Perhaps we should sit?"

"I'll stand." Kiara grasped the back of a chair to steady herself while the world spun off its axis around her. Her mind was splintering with concern for her best friend while her heart hammered as the moment of truth arrived like a cliff before her. Her toes curled to keep her from tumbling over it, but she was going to fall regardless.

Her eyes clung to the punishing contact in Valentino's unrelenting stare. She watched comprehension dawn the way clouds parted and the sun suddenly pierced through in a shaft of brilliant, searing hot light.

A whooshing sensation tipped her past the point of no return. She couldn't speak, but she didn't have to.

"Calm down, Mother." His tone descended to a grim, deadly rasp. "This gold digger has also had a child."

* * *

"Sir," the lawyer admonished, but Val didn't let the man's disapproval impact him. He was suffering too—a sharp sting of betrayal.

Kiara had presented herself as a sensual, self-deprecating, penniless artist with a heart that he now realized had been iron pyrite.

And he was the fool who'd believed in her.

He'd thought they'd enjoyed a chance encounter, one where he hadn't needed to deflect or overpower the situation in order to keep control of it. He had thought they had shared, if not secrets, a lack of lies.

She had haunted him.

And she'd been working for his father the whole time.

She had been more than Eve with an apple; she'd been the snake, slithering her way into his periphery, seemingly harmless then turning on him when he least suspected it. How was he surprised? *How?* And *of course* his father had played the long con. Of course he had.

But how had they managed it? Had she already been working for his father when they met? Had Niko hired her to lure Val into bed and get her pregnant?

Nice work if you can get it. And lucky shot to make it happen in one go and only because one of the condoms broke.

"You have a child?" His mother clawed a pale hand at the diamonds around her throat.

"Yes." Kiara's knuckles stood out like brass bullets where her brown hands clutched the back of a chair.

Her hair was longer, parted on one side. Light played through the brown-gold mass of springs that were so fine and narrow, each strand looked as though it had been wound around a pencil or something smaller. The coils piled upon themselves in wild abandon around her oval face, accentuating her high cheekbones.

Her big eyes were pools of espresso, her mouth a round pout painted in brick red. Had she had elocution lessons? Or had the broad Irish accent she'd used that night been a put-on to trick him into believing she was the harmless backpacker she'd pretended to be?

Her teeth had been straightened, but the rest of her was still mouthwateringly curvaceous, draped in clothes of a much higher quality than the last time he'd seen her. She wore heels so she seemed taller than he remembered. A wide belt at her waist emphasized the thrust of her breasts and the generous flare of her round hips and bottom.

A very carnal memory threatened to take hold and dull his wits all over again. Sex was only sex, he reminded himself. It was a pleasant pastime to be enjoyed like dessert or sailing on a hot day, not something that should be used against others the way she had clearly used it against him—on his father's behalf—*damn her to hell*.

"Since things have taken such a sharp turn, I'll come straight to the point," Davin said, fingering through the papers before him. "Given that both of Nikolai's sons have renounced their claim to his fortune, he has bequeathed the bulk of his estate in equal parts to his grandchildren. Obviously, we're wishing everything goes well with Miss Walker's delivery. With that happy event, to the best of our knowledge, there will be two heirs who will share equally in the assets. Evelina and Paloma have been allotted a one-time, one-million-euro payment." Davin slid a cashier's check toward Val's mother. "Each."

"One— That's not enough!" she cried.

"Sounds like you'll have to be nicer to Kiara," Val said, drinking deeply of that satire. "Don't assume she's only here to fetch your beverages, for instance."

"This can't be right." His mother hurried to Davin's side and demanded to read it with her own eyes.

Val met Kiara at the end of the table.

"You understand what this means?" he asked, jerking his head to indicate his mother. "She will never let you rest. I thought you were on the pill," he recalled.

Kiara's shoulders twitched, but any guilt was short-lived. Her gaze sparked with affront as she met his.

"We're doing that here? Now?" Her cheeks darkened with a blush. "It was a low dose to regulate my cycle. When I spent the night with you, I missed one. Apparently, it was enough to disrupt the effectiveness. There's no such thing as a perfect contraceptive, you know."

"My father didn't pay you to spend the night with me and get pregnant?"

"And break the condom? No." She rocked back a step, scowling as if insulted.

"If you knew him well enough to pry half his assets out of him, you know he would be capable of something like that." Look at the disregard Niko was showing toward the mothers of both his sons right now, throwing them a token settlement while he enriched the women who gave him grandchildren. Niko had been unswayed by sentiment. Ruthless. "Did you sleep with him?"

"*No*. That's a disgusting suggestion."

"Says the woman using a baby to get her hands on a fortune."

Her chin came up in a tiny signal of challenge.

Challenge accepted, *tesoro*.

Why? He didn't care.

He shouldn't care, at any rate.

But he discovered that he did. Deeply. Emotions he couldn't name were churning in his gut.

"You pretended you didn't know who I was that night," he accused.

She had seemed charmingly unaware when he had told her his name, but at the time he'd been weighing the idea of marriage to a stranger. Obviously, she'd taken advantage of his distraction.

"You skipped the pill on purpose, in hopes of winning the jackpot? Such tactics have been tried in the past, with limited success." He sent a mocking wave down his front. "You'll come to regret this."

"Having my daughter?" she asked with another lofty notch of her chin. "I doubt it. She has a name, by the way. Would you like to hear it?"

"No." He could have exited on that. The man he had cultivated himself into nearly always stole the last word and tossed a match over his shoulder as he walked away.

Something kept him rooted, however, listening for the name. Waiting for Kiara to take another shot at him. He didn't know why, but he wanted both. He wanted to stay right here, feeling the streaking pinball of incendiary energy continue to heat as it bounced between them.

How could she still hold such a spell over him when he now knew her to be mercenary and devious.

"I told him to give you the money you needed to take care of it," Evelina spat from the other side of the room. "He said you *did*."

Val had been in enough scraps to duck any punch, but that one suckered him. His abs belatedly clenched as he snapped a look at his mother. "You *knew* about this?"

"You didn't?" Kiara's gaze flashed back to his with wary confusion.

"I knew she was claiming to be pregnant with your child. I didn't know she *had* it." Evelina glared censure at Kiara.

Kiara's lashes swept down again, and her mouth firmed as she pronounced with dignity, "Niko *has* given me money to take care of her."

Evelina caught her breath as she realized how badly she had misplayed her hand.

Val should have found that hilarious, but learning of his mother's involvement had taken him by the throat and shaken him.

"You knew she was pregnant? And you didn't tell me?" he demanded of her.

"You were on your honeymoon." His mother's voice dropped to the syrupy, conciliatory tone that wheedled for him to take her side. "You didn't need an ugly scandal."

"Like the one I grew up in?" When had he last bothered to be angry? Truly furious? Maybe his last visit to this tower? Maybe it was the air in here that stoked his rage. The fetid stench of manipulation and jealousy and profound selfishness. "You live for making a scene. Blaming Niko for my shortcomings is your bread and butter. You could have used the baby for leverage all this time if you had— Oh, my God."

Val hooked his hands on his hips and laughed drily

toward the ceiling as he realized why she had preferred his baby be erased from existence.

"This is a new low for you, Mother." He was uncharacteristically, profoundly astounded. And sickened. "Or should I say… Nonna?"

"Do *not*…" she warned in shaken outrage.

"Oh, I will. Because your precious vanity sent *her* to *him*." He pointed at Kiara then the folder representing the fortune that had been the reason for, and the bane of, his very existence.

This situation was abhorrently reminiscent of his childhood, when something clean and precious and *his* would be sullied and used as leverage and snapped apart in the struggle between his parents and his half brother and his father's ex-wife, Paloma. Val's wants and needs had never been part of any conversation. If they had, they'd been dismissed as irrelevant.

And Kiara had played along with all of that.

"Why did you tell her instead of me?" he demanded of Kiara.

Whatever culpability flickered into Kiara's face was quickly schooled into something more facetious. "I guess I could have left a message with your *wife*?"

It was a darling effort at shaming him, but, "I've been divorced a year. You've had time."

"There were circumstances." She shifted uncomfortably. "Niko was ill and needed us there."

"You've been *living* with him? This whole time?"

If Val believed people were capable of true remorse, he might have thought the way Kiara bit her lip might have signaled regret.

He had played this game too long to believe she felt anything but glee, however, at claiming the pot of gold.

Walk away, he thought. *Just. Walk. Away.*

"He thought if you knew Aurelia existed, you would pressure me to leave the island instead of staying with him."

Aurelia. It was the name of the villa in Venice where they'd spent their night together. The site of their love-making and, apparently, the conception of their daughter.

Every morning, when he gazed on Kiara's sketch, he was back there on the bed with her, seated behind her in the rumpled sheets, teasing her into continuing with her study of the open balcony doors while he sampled the scent in her neck and tasted the smoothness of her shoulders and felt her breast rise and fall in growing excitement against his palm.

He swallowed, trying to dismiss any profundity in her bestowing that villa's name on their child. He didn't buckle to sentiment. It was a manipulation tactic. Everything was.

Even so, he couldn't take his eyes off her as she turned her attention to his mother, showing no fear as she said baldly, "Niko didn't want you or Paloma to know about her or about Scarlett's pregnancy. He thought it would create more conflict than he could deal with in his weakened condition. Since he was terminal, we respected his wishes."

It was so poetic, it bordered on sappy, but to keep the knowledge of his daughter from him for *three years*? He would never forgive any of them for this.

"We'll wait for a DNA test before we continue this discussion." Evelina took care to tuck her cashier's check into her clutch. "Niko can't overlook his son in favor of a child we've never seen. We'll fight this."

"You'll be wasting your money," Davin said. "There's already a DNA test that proves Aurelia is Niko's descendant. Her sample was correlated with the DNA test that proved Mr. Casale's paternity. Niko was of sound mind. Further tests won't change anything."

Val didn't need a test. He wasn't so gullible as to take Kiara's word, but his father had always been diligent about such fine points.

He didn't care anyway, he assured himself. Not beyond how galling it was that Niko had gotten the last laugh, but so what? Val had never wanted offspring—one of the reasons his marriage had tanked—and he hadn't wanted his father's money, either. He had no desire to take responsibility for the child in possession of that fortune— Oh, wait. The girl was only entrusted with half. That meant any involvement he had with her would mean dealing with Javiero on some level, as well.

And all the while, his mother would continue to claw at him for her piece of the pie.

Definitely time to exit stage right. He certainly could. Kiara was financially equipped to meet the needs of his child. Nothing in his life had to change. In fact, his mother would become Kiara's problem. The solution was elegantly simple and utterly freeing.

Yet, he remained where he was, coldly enraged. His insides were gripped by a wrath that swelled his chest with the pressure of a primal yell he couldn't release.

He could hardly pick apart why this provoked such a volcanic rise of fury in him. It had something to do with the grotesque replay of history. While he'd been married to Tina, Kiara had been having his child, sentencing an innocent to the label he'd worn like a dead albatross until he was old enough to make damn sure he deserved the slur.

No. He might not have crafted himself into the most upstanding of men, but he was decent enough to pluck a child out of a toxic spill before she was lethally poisoned and scarred forever.

"Refuse that money," he told Kiara. "My daughter will inherit *my* fortune, not his."

"A minute ago you didn't even want to know her name."

"She can have *mine*," he shot back. "You're going to marry me. *Today*."

CHAPTER TWO

"VAL. DON'T BE RASH." The whites of Evelina's eyes showed. "We'll fight this—"

"Take your money and go home, Mother. I'll call when I'm ready to speak to you again."

Evelina wasn't rattled, but Val's tone had Kiara shaking in her designer heels. She was doing her best to channel Scarlett, who never ruffled, but Kiara regularly lost battles against her two-year-old. She had folded like a cheap tent when Niko had dragged her into this arrangement, hadn't she? She was no match for Val.

And marriage? Of all the reactions she had tried to anticipate… No, she wouldn't let herself process that. She was still absorbing the fact he hadn't known she had been pregnant. That seriously undermined her ability to resent him and take the high ground.

"Kiara can't refuse the money," Davin said. "It's Aurelia's. When she takes full control at twenty-five, Aurelia can do what she likes. Until then, the money remains in trust for her. A reasonable allowance is allocated to Miss O'Neill so she can provide Aurelia a stable home and upbringing. There's also a provision for a financial manger's salary. Miss Walker was intending to act in that capacity—"

"The Miss Walker currently birthing my half brother's heir? Hell, no," Val stated.

"Scarlett *is* in labor." Kiara's brain had been splintering with worry for her best friend this whole time. "And I'm her birth coach. I need to go to the hospital."

She would take her friend's place in the stirrups if it would grant her an escape from the malevolence coming off Val in waves.

"Hell, no again," he said, tone implacable. "The last time you disappeared, you had my child and conspired with my parents to hide her from me for *three years*."

Kiara had one decent coping strategy for confrontation—sarcasm.

"Did we have sex today? I didn't notice." She blinked. "You do move fast, I recall, but I think we're safe this time."

Val set his hands on the table, pushing a force field over and around her, trapping her with his dangerous mood inside an airless bubble.

"Shall I recite everything *I* remember from our night together?"

A fluttering swirl of erotic memory accosted the pit of her belly. Heat flowed into secretive spaces and her nipples pinched. Why had she thought silk was a good choice? He could probably see the effect his words had on her. He was a practiced seducer, after all.

One who was, perhaps, entitled to his outrage. She had been hurt by his cavalier treatment, but keeping Aurelia's birth a secret from him had never felt right. From the moment she had known she was pregnant she had wanted to tell him about their daughter. So far, his reaction wasn't very encouraging. It wasn't very *per-*

sonal, but she had always cherished a small dream that he would ultimately fall in love with their daughter.

Why? Because of her own fatherless upbringing? Ugh. Daddy issues were so clichéd.

"Replays won't be necessary," she mumbled as she gathered her clutch and looked for the bag she usually carried, the one bulked with art supplies and baby wipes, snacks and clean clothes. She was traveling light today, having planned for a brief meeting and a quick bolt back to the island.

"I have to make some calls," she said, realizing she would have her first night away from her daughter while Scarlett brought her own infant into the world. "I'll leave you to wrap up?"

Davin nodded and Evelina turned with umbrage toward him, but Val met Kiara at the door.

"Thank you," she murmured as he held it for her.

He followed her through it and sparks condensed in the air between them as he paced her down the hall to the elevator.

"Um…" She started to ask him what he was doing, but it was obvious he was leaving.

He took out his phone to make a call as they waited for the elevator.

She took out her own phone and saw Scarlett's texts. She read them as they stepped into the elevator.

My water broke. Help!

That one must have been sent from the ladies' room. Kiara could have kicked herself for silencing her phone when she had entered the boardroom.

Javiero's mother just came in. What do I do?

Then:

Javiero is taking me to hosp. Call me when you can.

Kiara bit back a groan of contrition and dialed.

Beside her, Val told someone, "I want to get married. No, not here. Italy."

As her jaw dropped, and the elevator hit the bottom floor, rocking her on her heels, Scarlett answered in her ear.

"Are you okay?" Kiara asked her dumbly, watching Val tuck his phone into his pocket.

His gaze held hers as he leaned on the door to brace it open, trapping her where she stood.

"I'm in labor, what do you think?" Scarlett groaned. "Oh, my *Gawd*, how did you do this?"

"I'm on my way," Kiara promised, forced to brush against Val's intimidating frame as she stepped from the elevator. Another shower of tingles washed over her. "Leaving the office now."

"Wait." Scarlett made a helpless noise. "Javiero wants to stay with me."

"Okay." Kiara halted in the middle of the lobby. "What do *you* want?"

"I don't *know*! I had to tell him everything and now he thinks you shouldn't be here." A small hesitation, then, "Because of Val."

Val paused to loom beside her, probably able to hear every word.

Until today, she had understood there was animosity between the men, but after Evelina's resentful reaction, and the grate in his words as he'd pronounced "my half brother's spawn," she had a clearer picture of how much genuine dislike existed between them.

"Listen." Kiara gentled her tone as she spoke to Scarlett, reminding herself that her friend's delivery wasn't about her. "If you want Javiero there, that's fine. I completely understand. If my coming to the hospital will cause you more stress than comfort, I'll go to a hotel and stand by. If you decide you want me, call. It doesn't matter if it's the middle of the night. I'll come. Sound good?"

"Thank you," Scarlett said on a little sob. "I'm a wreck and— Oh, here comes another one." She sucked in a breath. A male voice said something, and she replied with a petulant, "I *am* breathing. What do you know about it? Oh, my God, I *hate* you for doing this to me."

The call ended, presumably cut off by Javiero taking the phone from Scarlett.

Kiara frowned with concern as she tucked away her phone.

"It takes two weeks," Val said.

"Labor? Mine was fourteen hours."

"Marriage." He narrowed his eyes at her remark, but continued, "We can do it faster elsewhere, like here in Greece, but I want to marry in Italy."

"Or not at all," she suggested with a falsely bright smile, even though a weight of anger that had been sitting on her lungs for three years had shifted and angled deeper into her heart, leaving a painful ache.

She avoided the flash in his eyes by striding across to the security desk.

"I need my car and a reservation at a hotel near the hospital."

"My driver is here." Val nodded at the black sedan that halted against the curb beyond the glass front of the building.

Kiara opened her mouth to protest, but he said darkly, "We're not finished, Kiara. We haven't even started."

She swallowed a groan of resignation and went with him.

Beside him, Kiara was telling someone that Scarlett had gone into labor. "A little early, yes, but only a week or so. I'll stay the night here in case she needs me. Is Aurelia napping? Call me when she's up. I'll text you when I have news. Thank you."

"Where is she?" Val asked, barely processing that he had a child, still blinded by the conspiracy of lies and secrecy that had kept her hidden from him.

"The island. That was one of her nannies."

"One of," he repeated. "Does she even know who 'Mama' is?" He skimmed his glance over tailored silk and pearl buttons, a vintage handbag and a contemporary Italian designer's shoe that featured a gold wristwatch as an ankle band. "I know couture when I see it. And I know guilt when I see it, too," he remarked as her expression tightened.

"A mother is automatically issued a stone's worth of guilt for every ounce of child." Her chin notched up as she looked forward. "Especially if she works. You get double if working isn't necessary for survival. And if the job you do is creative and doesn't pay by the hour? I need a freight train to carry it all."

Val's mother had never been burdened with such inconvenient emotions as guilt, but Evelina was in a constant battle against excess weight of any kind.

Kiara didn't diet herself skeletal. Her body was luscious and ripe.

He had thought his reaction to her three years ago had been more about burning off the tension of the decision he'd made to marry a stranger, but sitting next to her, detecting her scent beneath the light fragrance of her cosmetics, was affecting him. He had to shift to make room behind his fly, which aggravated him. He didn't lust after any woman. He enjoyed sex, but desire was one more feeling that could be used to manipulate. He preferred free will and he sure as hell wasn't letting this woman have any advantages over him again.

Even so, his gaze snagged on her knee and he recalled vividly the softness of her skin, the way it warmed under his caress and tasted rose petal-soft against his lips. The pull in his groin sharpened.

Kiara flicked at the hem of her dress to cover her knee. Her gaze swept up to see if he had noticed and clashed into his.

Yes, he was aware of the woman beneath the clothes, he conveyed. Sex was never a power game for him, but she had started this one. And if anyone knew how to weaponize sex and win that game, it was a man who'd sold everything from fragrance to tuxedos with a bared chest and a libidinous pout.

He let his eyelids drop to a sultry half-mast and touched his tongue to his bottom lip. The muscles in his face were as well exercised and disciplined as those in his chest and abs and thighs. He softened his expression into admiration. Approval. Come hither, my beauty.

"Feel guilty for letting my father dress you," he said

of the muted yellow dress that had Niko's stamp of conservative authority all over it. "I'll find you more flattering colors and styles." He indulged himself with a thorough study of her unabashed curves.

Her breasts rose in a shaken catch of breath, and the way her nipples stood up against the silk caused a responding stiffening in his pants.

She didn't notice his reaction. Her eyes had gone so wide as she looked into his face, he could practically count each of her thickened lashes. Color darkened her cheekbones. She looked away and swallowed loud enough that he heard it.

That swift, exquisitely sensual response was exactly what had ensnared him the first time. The way she had caught her lip in a soft bite after the graze of their fingertips as they discussed her sketches. The longing in her eyes as she had traversed his nude form with her gaze, transferring what she saw to the page.

Had that reaction been real or was it something in her playbook? She was averting her eyes so he couldn't be sure.

"Niko insisted I needed a proper wardrobe," she stammered with an ingenue's waver of uncertainty cracking her voice. "Since I've been going back and forth to Paris, we shopped there. We always take Aurelia, though."

"We?" His naturally possessive nature rose to a new level with that tiny word.

"Scarlett and I," she clarified with a wary flick of her glance.

"She's really having that SOB's kid? She does go above and beyond, doesn't she?"

"Scarlett is having Javiero's baby, yes." Her spine

straightened, thrusting her breasts out. "She's also my friend so I would appreciate if you spoke more kindly about her."

He snorted. "How did it come about? Aside from the obvious. Did Dad pay *her* to get knocked up?"

"*No.* Where do you get the idea women run around getting pregnant for money?"

"Not all women perhaps, but in this family, it's all too common. I am the embodiment of such a tactic, and Paloma married my father and had Javiero because her family was broke."

"Well I took precautions that failed and Scarlett can speak for herself on that topic if she so chooses. I won't gossip about her, but try to have some empathy. These last weeks have been very difficult. Her pregnancy wasn't the easiest, Niko was in his final days, and you know that Javiero just got out of the hospital?"

"I saw the headlines."

Val wasn't pleased that his half brother had nearly been killed by a jaguar. Javiero had lost an eye if reports were accurate. Sounded damned hellish, but caring in any way about what happened on that side of his father's gene pool was a recipe for madness so Val hadn't let himself dwell on it.

They arrived at his hotel and, moments later, he watched her get her bearings much as she had three years ago, when he had brought her into his suite in Venice. She moved through the grand space with every indication she was absorbing minute details. She touched the tassel on the corner of a cushion, lifted her gaze to ornate plaster at the top of the walls, tipped her head into a floral arrangement and moved the curtain, watching where the light fell.

She removed her kimono jacket and went to stand at the window, tilting her head as she studied the Acropolis. He hung back and let his gaze wander her soft shoulders and the tuck of her waist and that glorious bottom pressing against silk that was weightless as a cobweb against her curves.

His palms twitched and so did hers.

She glanced around, gave a muted sigh.

"Is that why you did it?" he asked, instinctively knowing she was looking for her sketch pad. Her compulsion to capture an image was as strong as her ability to do so. He'd learned that much about her in their short acquaintance. "My father supported your art? I saw the painting in the lobby."

Her lips parted and culpability flexed across her expression.

"*I* gave you a stepladder," he reminded through gritted teeth.

"And I may have resorted to selling those sketches if your father hadn't offered to support me, but he did." She rolled her bottom lip inward and chewed it without mercy.

"When? Were you working for him when we met?"

"*No,*" she insisted, but he would reserve judgment on how much truth her words held. "And I didn't mean to get pregnant. I honestly thought I was protected. By the time I found out, you were on your honeymoon."

"So you called my mother and told her you planned to terminate."

"Are you judging me for that?"

"I'm judging you for telling everyone *but* me that you were pregnant with my child."

"Your mother was the only person I told," she muttered, looking at her short, unpainted fingernails. "And I only called her because I felt quite desperate, financially and emotionally." She frowned. "I didn't have any family or even a network of friends. I had no idea what sort of mother I might turn into since it had never been my plan to become one. I had put Venice on my credit card and had other debts. I'm not proud of that, but I'm not ashamed, either. Until I turned up pregnant, art was all that mattered to me. I took whatever job bought me a meat pie and colored pencils, not necessarily in that order. I didn't have a flat, just a room with a shared kitchen and bath. That standard of living was fine for me, but I knew I couldn't bring a child into it. I didn't have the education to get a better job, though. I can barely type and even graphic designers need computer skills. Putting 'currently pregnant' on your CV doesn't get you a lot of job offers. I would have had to rely on benefits from the state for years to get on my feet. I'd already spent most of my childhood on government assistance. I had to explore all my options, no matter how hard that sounds, so I called your mother. I thought that, since she'd been in a similar situation, she might have some empathy, perhaps offer other solutions."

"Well, aren't you charmingly naive?" Val's mother had been Nikolai Mylonas's long-suffering mistress right up until the day Niko had married Paloma. Val didn't know if she had poked holes in condoms or if his father had misjudged her desire to preserve her figure, but Evelina had turned up pregnant about the time Nikolai's bride had conceived. Val had been a deliberate effort on Evelina's part to stake a claim on Niko's fortune, but Niko had had two sons by two different women two days apart.

The war over rights of succession had raged ever since.

"Your mother said that my having your baby would ruin your life as well as my own and that I should never contact her again," Kiara said somberly. "But she must have called Niko because Scarlett called me a few hours later and turned up the next day. She talked me into coming to Greece to meet him."

Ah, Scarlett. His father's infinitely polite and pathologically single-minded enforcer.

"Niko was in treatment and said both his sons had turned his back on him. He wanted an heir and said your child would do nicely. He offered to build me a studio. It was an offer I didn't want to resist, but the most compelling reason I stayed was simply that he was Aurelia's family. I wanted to give her that. I won't say he was doting or openly loving, but he was proud of her in his way. It seemed like the right thing to do."

"You thought it was morally correct to let him into her life even though he kept you from telling *me*. Her *father*."

"For all I knew, you knew and didn't care!" she said with a spark of temper. "The way you've reacted so far has only reinforced that Niko was right. You would have pressured me to take sides."

"You did take a side. His."

"I see it as taking turns." Her strident tone came down a few notches. "Niko's time was finite. Having Aurelia in his life brought him a sense of peace in his last days."

"How nice for him."

"You knew he was sick! You could have come at any time and would have learned you had a daughter."

"Is that his oversimplified rationalization or yours? Dad knew I wouldn't come and so did Scarlett. That logic doesn't wash."

"Why did you hate him so much?" she asked with bafflement.

He might have withstood the comparisons to his brother, the harsh punishments and the constant demands for good, better, best. What Val could never forgive was Niko overriding the complaint Val had made against the school's administration. Niko had had the entire thing dismissed as 'troublemaking' on Val's part so it was swept under the rug.

Val had never felt so helpless and furious in his life. So abandoned. Out of sheer desperation, he'd begun a campaign of unrelenting fighting and pranks and drinking until the school had had to throw him out for good.

"Why the hell did you *like* him? Why did you think he deserved time with my daughter more than I did?" It incensed him to imagine his father basking in the satisfaction of stealing those moments and milestones from Val.

"He was *dying*." Her voice softened to a plea. "He was diagnosed right before… Venice. I know he didn't tell you that at the time. When I met him, though, he was quite sick. Weak and scared. I didn't plan to stay in Greece, but I couldn't leave."

"I'm sure it was a difficult choice."

"It wasn't *greed*," she cried.

"Oh, I don't blame you for taking whatever incentives he offered," he assured her. "If he hadn't gotten you with the honey of money, he would have moved on to more aggressive and oppressive methods." He moved behind the bar to select a bottle of whiskey. "That's the sort of man I remember and I know he was. Controlling. Demanding."

If you leave, you're taking your mother with you. I won't support her. That will be up to you so button your lip and appreciate the education you're being given.

"I rejected his fortune, so I didn't have to bow to him the way you have. You think I don't see him in all of this?" He drew a circle around the conservative ensemble and the way she was justifying actions that were unjustifiable. "He kept you on the island like a goat in a petting zoo."

"That's not the way it was!"

From a man who had compared his sons—and women!—the way a horse breeder spoke of stallions?

"It was. It's adorable you think his interest was his grandchild, but he was getting back at me for marrying Tina against his wishes. Any 'peace' he was exhibiting in his last days was the gloating knowledge of the kick in the shorts he would deliver to me today."

"How is this a kick in the shorts? You didn't want his money."

"I don't." Val's best day ever had been his final one at boarding school, when suspension had finally turned to expulsion. He had told his father to stuff his fortune and had sought out Javiero for a final, *Have it all. You need it more than I do.*

Javiero *had* needed it. His mother's family had been in dire straits, and resolving their issues had fallen on Javiero's young shoulders. But Javiero possessed his own set of faults and one of them was pride. Val had known it would grate on his brother to win by default.

It would soil any sense of achievement for him that Val had forfeited.

True to form, Javiero hadn't been able to stand it. He had subsequently rejected Niko's support and clawed his way to the top under his own steam, proving some point that escaped Val, but he had never expended much energy trying to work out what it could be.

"Niko told me once that he regretted how he handled things with your mothers," Kiara said in a conciliatory tone. "He wished he had fought harder for a better relationship with you both."

The top of his head nearly came off, but Val ignored the fresh knife into an old wound.

"If he had wanted a better relationship with us, he shouldn't have used his last act to set us at odds yet again." In the absence of being able to express his disgust at a dead man, he pointed accusingly at Kiara. "And *you* shouldn't have stood by him and kept me in the dark all this time."

"What do you want? An apology? You were *married*. As far as I can tell, you left me in your bed to go propose to your future wife." Her hand flung out with agitation.

"I spoke to her father." He dismissed that with a roll of his shoulder.

"Either way, it was clear you and I didn't have a future." Angry hurt flashed into her expression. "Being paid for my services didn't make me think, *Gee, I bet he can't wait to raise a child with me. I'd better tell him straightaway.* Your mother—"

"Wait. Stop." He held up a hand. "I left you money for the sketch I took."

"Sure. All right." Her jaw was clenched, but offset.

She turned away to hide what might have been a frown of insult. Humiliation?

A lurching sensation in his chest pulled a sickening roil from the bottom of his stomach. His conscience was so small he barely wore it at all anymore, but there were some lines he didn't cross. Sex was very much a freely-given-or-not-at-all thing for him.

"You knew I wanted that sketch," he reminded her harshly. "How did my leaving money for it turn into you thinking I was paying you for sex?"

Her face darkened as she flung around to confront him. "I told you I usually got thirty or forty euros. You left me *five hundred*." Her eyes glittered with shame. "For something you probably threw away a week later."

"That's why you didn't take the money? You didn't think you were worth that much?"

He was talking about her work, but a flash of stark vulnerability seemed to hollow out her soul before she crossed her arms and turned back to the window.

"Obviously, I came to regret that," she muttered.

When? Before or after she had become beholden to his father?

He poured the whiskey he'd mostly forgotten, moodily trying to assimilate this new information.

"How much are you getting these days? For your artwork," he clarified when she stiffened.

Silence, then a reluctant, "A few hundred, but they're fully finished oils. The one in the lobby was nearly two thousand, but that was nepotism on Niko's part. Most haven't sold yet. They've gone to my agent for my show."

"At a gallery? Where?"

"Paris. In three weeks." She mentioned the name,

watching him for a reaction as he approached with the drinks. "My agent booked it ages ago," she added as she took the glass he offered. "When we thought Niko had more time and before Scarlett— Right." She shifted to set aside her glass. "I can't drink. Scarlett might need me. In fact, I should keep my phone out so I don't miss another call."

Kiara used the search for her phone as an excuse to put distance between her and Val, still taking in that he hadn't paid her for sex. It was yet another brick in her wall of defenses that had crumbled to powder, leaving her feeling in the wrong, but what choices had been *right* back then?

Her phone was annoyingly empty of notifications, not that she typically had many. On Niko's request, she had closed her social media accounts when she had moved to Greece. Aside from emails from her agent, she typically only exchanged a few texts with Scarlett or the nannies and only when she was too lazy to walk from her studio back into the villa.

"That's a good gallery." Val poured her rejected drink into his own before he took up her spot by the window. "Who's your agent?"

She told him and told herself she was only gazing on his male form as an artist, but seriously, the way his jeans hugged his butt was sublime.

"Dad really came through for you," Val said derisively as he sipped.

She squirmed internally. Niko had, and his leg up contributed to her feeling like a fraud, not that she wanted to hand that weapon to Val.

She looked at the shoes Niko had bought her. She

hadn't liked taking all these things. She hadn't felt entitled to live like royalty and had been aware that doing so put her in a beholden state to Niko's implacable wishes.

The studio and agent and standard of living had all been cherries, though. The real draw had been the connection to her child's family. Val had been out of reach and his mother hadn't wanted her grandchild to exist, but Niko had wanted his granddaughter to be part of his life.

Kiara hadn't been able to turn her back on that request, not when she'd spent almost her whole life without any blood ties of her own.

As for Aurelia...

"Sit on your high horse if you like, Val, but when Niko learned I was pregnant, his first reaction was to offer support. Yours was to call me a gold digger and say you didn't want to hear your own child's name. Do you *want* to be a father?" She brought her head up, never comfortable in confrontation, but she refused to be cast as a villain. "Or do you just want to judge me for the choices I've made as a mother? Does all this anger you're spewing have anything to do with me and Aurelia? Or is it actually unresolved issues with a man who is dead?"

Val might have stiffened, but a dark smile of warning crept across his face. "Do you really want to psychoanalyze me, Kiara? You'll be swimming with sea monsters."

"I really want to know." She picked up a cushion and hugged it, running her fingers over the silky tassels, dimly aware of the betraying body language in using it as a shield, hugging it the way Aurelia hugged her bear, but she needed something to bolster her. "Would you like me better if I'd relied on *your* money all this time instead of your father's? Should I have scraped by in low-end jobs to prove that I'm, what? Above needing help? Would noble suffering on my part neutralize your disgust in me?"

"It would be a start." *So* disparaging and sanctimonious.

"Do you know what disgusts me?" She threw the cushion back onto the leather sofa. "That you had the *luxury* of rejecting your father and his money and *did*. Is your mother difficult to live with? Mine's dead. Try hearing *that* at nine years old."

She hadn't meant to reveal that. It was her own very deep, very private anguish, but she refused to be slotted into his pigeonhole of "greedy sycophant."

"I was given a bed in a room with three other girls and a single drawer to hold what I'd been allowed to take from my home. For the rest of my childhood, I wore used clothes from a box that arrived four times a year. I wasn't good in school and I'm terrible at sports. I'm not outgoing, I don't sing well and I didn't put out. The few friends I made were as miserable as I was and moved on as soon as they could, distancing themselves from everything about that life, including me."

He wasn't moving, not even drinking, only watching her as though weighing every word, turning each one over, inspecting it for lies.

"But I had my art." Her voice shook with the emotion she couldn't suppress. "Charcoal doesn't care if you stink like a deep-fat fryer. I worked awful jobs for awful people and lived in squalor and it never mattered because my sketch pad was my door to a better world.

When you left me that money, I stared at it for a full thirty minutes before I decided it was a line I couldn't uncross."

"It was for the sketch," he reiterated, swirling his drink before he took a gulp.

"When I found out I was pregnant, I didn't care what you had paid me for," she admitted. "I just wished I'd taken it." She hugged herself as she recalled those bleak days as she had tried to figure out a future that wouldn't result in being labeled an unfit mother. "My life had always been hard. I knew I would plod along one way or another, maybe see what I could get for those sketches I had of you, but your father made me an offer that meant I could give Aurelia the kind of future that would never include bedbugs and pervy landlords. If *I* died, she would always have *something*. Doesn't your daughter deserve to live comfortably? Am I really a villain for giving her the very best start in life that was available to me?"

She was shaking and he was only staring at her with that cynical curl of disdain at the corner of his mouth.

"If you knew how many sob stories and rationalizations I've heard out of my mother in my lifetime," Val drawled, throwing a healthy sting of whiskey into the back of his throat. He was trying to keep himself from swallowing all that she'd said. "The bit about wanting what's best for your child? I've seen that episode more times than I can count."

Kiara sucked in a pained breath as if he had physically struck her. She blinked. Rapidly. She had already been looking shaken enough to make it seem as though relaying the story of her deprived childhood had been difficult. And real. Now her eyes welled.

"I need the ladies' room," she choked.

Val frowned as she rushed away.

Tears were meant to be displayed, to sell him on how hurtful he'd been with his scathing dismissal so he would believe she'd been pouring real heartache onto the floor. That's what his mother would have done.

Something wobbled in his chest as he watched her go, especially when she didn't add an enticing roll of her hips, as some women might, to cloud his head.

He tried to loosen his tie only to discover he wasn't wearing one.

Don't fall for it, he warned himself. She was the enemy. Exactly like the rest of the people he called "family."

Then why had she left the money that night?

He kept coming back to that, especially in light of what she'd said a few minutes ago.

At the time, he'd seen her leaving the money as a charming gesture, as though she had gifted him with the memory of their night by letting him have the sketch without payment.

Of course, he had fully expected her to be compensated once she sold his nudes, but as far as he could tell, she never had. Not even to support their child— although that would likely have revealed to the public her child was his, so he could see why she might have balked.

But that would have allowed her to soak him for support.

I stared at it for a full thirty minutes before I decided it was a line I couldn't uncross.

If she was as mercenary as his mother, and as cold-bloodedly intent on advancing her own interests as his father, why hadn't she taken the money he'd left and why hadn't she come back for more?

She *had* taken money, of course. Later. From his father.

After trying to reach him.

She hadn't reached out to his father. His mother had brought about that alliance.

Why did it bother him so much that she had let herself become reliant on Niko? *Was* he obsessed with gaining the upper hand over a man who was already dead?

If Niko and his fortune had never existed, neither would Val. Maybe the old man's footprints weren't the pair he wished had never trod this earth, Val thought darkly. Maybe he wished his own hadn't.

Kiara came back, not looking at him as she found her clutch. She had washed the makeup off her face. Her hair was damp at her hairline and there were a few water spots on the front of her dress.

"Delightful as this reunion has been," she said in a voice that still held a quaver, "I'll ask the registration desk to find me another hotel." Her hand trembled as she picked up her phone, voice hardening as she added, "And the fact my daughter will have the same ability to walk out on a man trying to cut her down is the reason I will *never* regret taking your father's money."

She leveled him a look that cut past his shields to punch into his gut. It would have been an exit worthy of him if she'd managed it. Her phone buzzed in her hand, though.

Tremendous vulnerability overcame her at whatever

she saw on the screen. He instinctively leaped on it as an extraordinary weakness he could exploit.

She arranged a smile on her discomfited face as she swiped. "Hi, baby."

The most joyous, dollish voice he had ever heard said a very exuberant, "Mummy!"

"Are you having fun with Nanny?" Kiara sank onto the sofa, disappearing into the screen the way he'd seen her do once before, when she had opened her sketch pad.

Fascinating.

The voice babbled about "bubberflies" in the garden.

"Did you see Kitty?" Kiara asked.

He couldn't resist. He crossed toward Kiara and she lifted a gaze that held real fear. Her hand tightened on the phone and her whole body tensed.

He stayed out of the camera angle but took in the small oval face on the screen. She had a slightly lighter shade of her mother's brown skin and Kiara's lips. Her corkscrew hair stood around her face like dandelion fluff with sun-tipped ends. She was pointing off screen, telling a story that made no sense, but he could have listened to her earnest chatter for hours.

When she looked back at the screen, he saw pale, silvery eyes, familiar as his own in the mirror. Something heavy landed in his chest. He wanted to apologize to her for tainting her with any shred of himself. She was so damned natural and unbroken and pure.

And even though he knew he had no business soiling her existence with his own, all he could think was, *Give me that child.*

Why? He had never liked children even when he'd been one. They were mean and whiny and most of them were vanity projects on the part of parents who shouldn't have been granted the license to duplicate themselves. He'd been a small adult in the workforce before he'd understood that it wasn't normal to let people take your picture for money.

This child, though? He wanted to reach through the screen and *take* her. Where? And do what? He didn't know, only that he wanted to hold her. Curl his arms around her and ensure nothing impacted the sweetness she wore so artlessly.

"Oh, no, lovey, I'm not in my studio," Kiara said as a joggled vision of grass appeared. "Remember? I went in the helicopter with Auntie Scarlett. I have to stay here with her. She's having her baby."

The image stopped and righted. Aurelia's face appeared again. "Can I see?"

"Not yet. Soon."

Kiara's smile was so tender, Val found himself rubbing the heel of his hand against his breastbone, trying to ease the sensation of the hard shell around his heart being pried open, leaving breezy cracks and raw spots. Wind whistling into chasms. He had to remind himself to breathe.

"I'll be back in the morning. One more sleep," Kiara assured her.

"No, Mummy." The little girl frowned with dismay. Maybe even distress. "I want you now."

"Oh, baby." Kiara's eyes welled and her smile wobbled.

The nanny stepped in to distract the girl and they quickly said their goodbyes, promising to talk to Mummy at bedtime.

The call ended and Kiara pressed the phone between her breasts, drawing a breath to gather her composure.

"See?" she said with a falsely cheerful smile. She stood and wiggled the phone. "I don't need any guilt trips from you. I'm on a permanent self-inflicted one, thanks." She threw the phone into her handbag and started for the door.

"Kiara."

Do you want to be a father?

He didn't know what he wanted beyond, "I want my daughter."

CHAPTER THREE

THOSE WORDS WERE her kryptonite. Perhaps she'd given that away when she had mentioned having no family.

She was still shaken by his callous dismissal of the poverty she'd endured most of her life. A poverty both material and emotional.

She shouldn't have been surprised by his behavior. Niko had warned her that Val was contemptuous and judgmental and had learned the fine art of manipulation at the knee of his mother. Even Scarlett had called him "challenging" and "intentionally difficult."

That hadn't been her experience the night she met him, though. He'd been arrogant, yes, demanding she show him the sketches she'd made of him, but he'd then praised her talent and sat for more. Part of her had wondered if he was flattering her to get her into bed, but he'd offered constructive critique and positioned himself in better lighting, sitting patiently while she worked. He had very generously encouraged her to use his notoriety to make a name for herself.

It wasn't until he was married and his mother was so dismissive that she had begun to worry she'd misread him. Then Niko's and Scarlett's reports had further helped her rationalize going along with Niko's wish that she keep Aurelia a secret.

Val had a right to his anger over that, but, "Are you saying you intend to challenge me for her?"

Her heart pulsed as a lump in her throat. She would fight to the death to keep her daughter, but didn't want to put any of them through it.

"I told you, I want to marry you. I want her in my life." He spoke firmly, but his shoulders were tense, his gaze guarded.

"Are you certain?" She wasn't an outwardly tough person. She had the strength of perseverance, not push-back. When it came to her daughter, however, she was pure mama bear. "Because I would do nearly anything to give Aurelia a good father. And I will do everything in my power to avoid giving her a bad one."

Meeting Val's gaze was such an act of courage every time she tried it. She wasn't nearly as brave as she was pretending to be, but her statement wasn't bravado or warning. It was a heartfelt vow.

Something she couldn't interpret flickered in his silvery-blue eyes. Her daughter had those same steely, piercing irises. She tried not to let the glimpse of her beloved girl in this ruthless man sway her. He already affected her merely by being in the same room.

His cynicism had nearly cut her in two a few minutes ago, but even when he was denigrating her choices and mistrusting her motives, she couldn't stop looking at him. She wanted to sketch him again. Talk in the meandering way they had that night. Like equals. She wanted to touch him and lie with him and feel his powerful body thrusting into hers.

As that unbidden image entered her mind, a prickling sting climbed from her breasts to her cheeks.

Heat came into his eyes as though he read her mind. A faint smile touched his smooth lips. "Anything?" he mocked softly.

Her heart caught the hiccups and her knees went weak. She yanked her gaze away.

"I—I'm open to letting you meet her," she said, scrambling to recall things she had prepared herself to say when she had believed this conversation would play out in a boardroom where Scarlett and Davin would smoothly step in if she stumbled. "But you have to be sure about your commitment level. I won't bring you into her life only to have you disappear if things don't work out."

"Has that happened?" His tone dropped like an ax. "With other men?"

"Like Niko?" she shot back. "Yes. She wasn't seeing much of him the past few weeks. He was rarely conscious. She's confused and keeps asking when he's coming back."

Kiara was still struggling with the loss herself. Niko had been in so much pain, it had been a merciful relief when he had finally let go, but everything had changed with his passing.

"You know I mean lovers," Val growled.

She offered him the blithe smile she was learning from him. "I don't feel we're at the stage in our relationship where we can ask about each other's lovers."

"*We* are lovers." The velvety timbre in his voice caressed her ears, swirling heat through her with nothing more than a careless reference to the memories they shared.

"Were," she said in a strangled voice.

"I am a seer of all things, Kiara. Especially human nature." He knocked back the last of his drink and set it aside, then used his gaze to stoke the desire taking hold in her. "You want back into my bed."

Tendrils of culpable desire curled in her abdomen, but she managed to choke, "There's that arrogance I've heard so much about."

Her words were smoke and mirrors, no substance to back up her bravado.

All shreds of humor fell from his expression.

"I see through lies as clearly as you see pictures on a blank page. Look me in the eye and tell me you don't want to have sex with me."

She tried, but she couldn't. Her throat seized up and her gaze dropped to his shoulder then strayed across to the open button where a few fine chest hairs were visible. Her artist's eye began cataloging shades and angles, the strain of fabric on his biceps and the flat bones of his bare wrist. The time-worn softness in his jeans. The missing rivet at his pocket and the ripple of his fly. Denim hugged hard thighs, and swarthy skin peeked through exposed threads above his knee.

She watched his black boots walk toward her until the toe of one halted between her painted toenails. The other caged the side of her right foot.

Heat radiated off him. The embers inside her glowed red-hot. Sparks seemed to rise around them as if bellows fanned her latent desire into a conflagration.

Her gaze snagged on the sardonic indentation at the corner of his mouth.

"You would prefer a platonic marriage?" His voice

had gone sensually rough the way it'd gone when they'd been in bed.

Her mouth pursed to form her answer, but she dimly realized that saying no would be an agreement to marry. He was a very dangerous, crafty man. Infinitely seductive and infinitely sly.

"Hmm?" he prompted. His warm hand cupped her neck.

Her pulse was already thudding. The pressure of his hand against her artery made her heartbeat reverberate in her head.

She couldn't see what was in his eyes. All she saw was his mouth. She could sketch it in her sleep, that full, squared-off bottom lip and the well-defined peaks of the upper lip. Photographs didn't do justice to the smoothness of them. To the way they darkened and sheened when his tongue dampened them.

She wanted that mouth on hers. Ached with three years' worth of yearning to taste him again.

His mouth hardened with savage satisfaction right before he crashed it onto hers.

His lips arrived in one hot sweep that tasted of whiskey and triumph. He pressed and angled in a lazy, confident demand for full possession, taking her simmering desire to an explosive, rolling boil.

She rocked weakly into him, thrust into the depths of passion, the kind she'd only experienced once, and that time there'd been a gradual buildup to get here. The suddenness of pure want that speared into her made her light-headed. Maybe she wasn't even breathing. She didn't care. Thought abandoned her and she opened her mouth wider to welcome his ravaging. To deepen their kiss and greedily take everything he offered, slaking an arid thirst.

His arms closed around her, deliciously hard as he dragged her body into his, sending her mind spinning even more as he squeezed her against his strength. She wanted more. More heat. More sensations of firm muscle ironed to her front, strong hands molding her back, his sharp scent hitting her brain like a drug.

She ravenously thrust her fingers into the silky strands of his hair. Her other hand went around his neck as she lifted on tiptoe, trying to increase the pressure of their kiss to the point of pain, needing a more acute sensation to appease the depth of longing in her. Needing all of him. Faster.

His tongue sought hers and that wicked intrusion stole the air from her lungs and tightened every inch of her skin. Her nipples hurt and heat rushed so sharply into her loins she groaned at the ache.

With a growl, he slowly ran his big hands from her hips to beneath her butt cheeks and pulled her higher, almost off her feet so the steely shape of him, fully aroused, ground against her mound while his entire body strained tautly against hers.

She hung against him, drowning in sensations, only startled back to awareness when he blatantly sucked on her bottom lip, teeth raking the sensitive inner tissues as he released her and lifted his head.

Now she saw his eyes, narrowed in mockery, but with a feral light that called to her. Taunted but urged. Lie back. Open for me.

With her pulse hammering low and hard in the aching place between her thighs, she nearly did. Instead, she protectively folded her top lip over her bottom one, aware now of the tender sting his teeth had left there. Her muscles were weak, her skin sensitized, her libido well and truly returned from whatever maternity leave it had taken.

She dropped her hands to his chest and he very slowly eased his grip on her backside so she could settle onto her unsteady heels. She had to hold his forearms to keep herself upright, still breathless and dizzy. And mortified.

Look me in the eye and tell me you don't want to have sex with me.

She couldn't. Not now. She could fairly smell the grim satisfaction wafting off him and had no way to deny how she'd reacted. She was appalled to realize that if he hadn't called a halt, she might have been on her way to another unexpected pregnancy.

"There are different levels of want," she managed to say. She dropped her hands from his arms and moved away, feeling as though each unsteady step only found dunes of sand.

When she was beyond arm's reach, she turned and pushed her gaze to meet his. It was like thrusting herself into the center of a fire gone silver-white with heat. Her eyes stung and her lungs strained for air, yet she wanted to walk straight back into that inferno.

"Of course I'm attracted to you. Point me to the woman who isn't." Did he think she *liked* being one more in a line he could choose from at random? "I don't *want* to be attracted, though. I don't *want* to act carelessly when I need to forge a mature relationship with the father of my daughter. You look *me* in the eye and tell me I would be your lover in the truest sense of the word. Then we'll talk about whether we'll have sex. Or marry."

She watched his mental retreat as clearly as if he took several steps back himself. The unmistakable rejection stung, but at least she knew exactly what this had been—a lesson. Not reunion or nostalgia or, in her case, indulgence of a lingering crush on a man who had accidentally given her nearly everything she had ever wanted.

She fiddled with her clutch, trying not to betray how skinless his rebuff left her.

"Which hotel is your mother at? I don't want to accidentally bump into her. Actually, I'll sit at the hospital until there's news."

"You'll stay here with me," Val said on reflex.

"No. I won't." Kiara spoke with a quiet dignity that held an underpinning of wariness, maybe hurt. Whatever it was, he understood it to be a concern that he would pressure her for sex.

"There are two bedrooms." As he said it, his libido howled against his efforts to bank it. *That kiss.* He hadn't felt so alive in three years. He wanted more. *Now.*

The fine tremble in her fingers revealed the wild depth of desire still lurking beneath her efforts to pull her composure back into place.

That passion had intrigued him from the first time they met. She came across as a wide-eyed observer on the sidelines of life, but it only took one kiss to tap into the absolute essence of life that teemed within her.

Both then and now, everything had fallen away when she had yanked him into her world of pure, unbridled sensuality. He'd never experienced anything like it with anyone else. It disturbed him.

It seemed to outright terrify her.

While her demand to *tell me I would be your lover in the truest sense of the word* unsettled him.

There were some lines even his pathetic standards of behavior wouldn't cross. He didn't pay for sex, didn't force it and he didn't lie to get it. In fact, his brutal honesty was the core of his reputation as a complete waste of unblemished skin.

While Kiara's brand of truth telling kept jabbing holes into his thick hide.

"It's too early to go for dinner," he noted. "Let's buy you some art supplies." He checked for his wallet and headed to the door.

"Why?" She stayed where she was, frowning with suspicion.

"I'm afraid you'll compromise my virtue if we stay here," he said, not entirely being facetious.

Her flush and the way she tucked her elbows into her sides as though a shiver of excitement accosted her nearly undid him, but he had fallen into bed with her once before and look where they were.

No, he would set the ground rules before they went any further. Did she really believe in love? Because he had hard proof it was a lie sold to children like Santa Claus and the tooth fairy. But they shared a child and they *would* share her.

"I could simply leave. We can take this up another time," she suggested.

She wished.

"You said your sketch pad is your way of coping.

You'll relax if you have one in your hands." Perhaps be less inclined to plot or lie.

"Why would you want that? Oh, is this like when a colonel offers a nice meal as a switch-up from torture to get the interrogation victim to trust him?"

"You see straight through me."

"I can't be won over with a sable brush and a pre-stretched canvas."

"Would you prefer to stay here and hammer out the terms of our marriage?" His phrasing was deliberate, and the way she caught her breath was deeply gratifying.

"I'm getting the feeling my preferences don't matter."

"Smart woman. Shall I look up some shops or—"

"I know where I'm going."

"I thought you might."

The shop owner greeted Kiara like a long-lost daughter, asking if she was on the hunt for something in particular.

"I happened to be in the city and came to browse." She spoke Greek, a language Val could speak fluently, but he preferred his mother tongue of Italian.

The owner urged her to take her time and she began poking through the shelves.

Val wandered behind her, content to observe as she weighed long-handled brushes across her fingers and opened drawers in a supply stand and smelled pastel sticks.

"I lied," she said with a sheepish upward glance through her lashes. "I can be bought with cheap crayons and a paper bag. I am a child in a candy store here and will likely throw a tantrum when you insist it's time to leave."

"Tell me about your show. More important, will I be in it?"

She paused in studying a pane of glass, setting it back with careful attention to its sharp edges. "I've never shared your sketches with anyone."

"No?" The paradox of Kiara was that she seemed truthful but behaved in ways that went directly against the way he expected. That left him wanting to doubt her, but she hadn't seemed to spin or prevaricate her reasons for accepting his father's support. Why would she lie about something else that was quite small in comparison? "Why not?"

She flicked him a glance that snagged a barbed hook into his chest and hauled him three years back in time to the moment she had straddled his naked thighs. The soft cotton of her skirt had bunched against him as he had dragged her deeper into his lap. Beneath the faint scent of charcoal dust on her hands had been a more earthy fragrance on her skin. Something reminiscent of savory herbs and the damp history imbued on the air of Venice itself. She had smelled of his own country while she tasted of the chocolate and strawberries and wine they had sampled along with an elemental flavor he couldn't name, but had instantly found addictive.

He didn't hide the lascivious memory expanding in his mind. He vividly recalled every caress and moan and pleasured cry they had shared that night. It was a highlight reel he tapped into far more often than all the other kinky fantasies in his self-pleasure vault combined.

A deep flush rose on her cheeks as she met his gaze. He half expected her to turn away, but even though self-consciousness and vulnerability flickered across her expression, she only said, "Niko didn't want our connection made public until after his death. And please don't knock me for this, but…" Her brow crinkled and she tickled her lips with the hairs of a fan brush. "Niko may have provided my supplies, but I did the work. When I sell something, I want people to buy what I've created, not try to acquire the object I've rendered, in this case *you*."

"That was kind of the point. You didn't lack talent, Kiara, only visibility and resources. That's why I told you to use me."

You'd be the one getting exposure, she'd said with a blushing smile when he'd told her to sell his images.

Today she chewed pensively at the corner of her mouth and dropped the brush into the basket he held for her. "I wasn't sure *I* wanted our connection made public. I mean, if I sold them so I could raise your baby, someone likely would have figured out she was yours. And since those images were all I had of her father, was it right to sell them? It was a quandary."

"You preserved my nude images as a memento for our daughter? I *am* flattered."

"I'm saying there were a lot of complicated factors to consider. Every action had serious repercussions." Her shoulder rolled self-consciously. "Also, our night together was private."

"I don't even know what that word means." His illegitimate birth had been headline news, and the start-up capital of his personal fortune had been earned in his underwear. His bad-boy reputation had been as valuable as his startlingly piercing eyes and perfectly proportioned physique. Even as they spoke, he could tell the shop owner had recognized him and was working up the courage to ask him for a selfie so he could post it and gain some publicity for his store.

Kiara's reaction didn't make sense. She sounded protective of their affair, which suggested their night was special to her in some way. Or shameful?

The back of his throat went gritty and dry at the thought.

"I've tried to paint off them a few times," she murmured absently. "In oil and watercolor. Even tried acrylic and pastels. Nothing has ever turned out right. I haven't figured out why." She frowned. "I've had success working off other sketches. I'm pleased with Aurelia's."

She took out her phone, swiped and handed it to him. "Go left and you'll see the rough work. My agent is framing them up and displaying them with the finished painting as a representation of my process."

Even the small image of the painting brimmed with the girl's irrepressible spirit. A half dozen charcoal sketches followed from different angles, all showing her blowing bubbles through a wand. He went back to the oil and expanded the image to see Kiara had caught prisms of light in the soap bubble and the gleam of delight in Aurelia's eyes.

More viscerally, he could sense the pride and joy Kiara felt toward the girl.

"I want all of these." He flicked back to the first sketch of the girl.

The anxious desire for approval in Kiara's expression fell away. She primly took back her phone. "They're not for sale. I won't let anyone acquire *her*, either."

* * *

Two hours later they were shown to the best table on a rooftop restaurant overlooking the Acropolis.

The sun wouldn't set for a few hours, but an overhang shaded them and a light breeze came across from the sea in the distance. The city sprawled along that sparkling backdrop and the Parthenon stood in ancient glory against it.

Kiara had been on the verge of panic after their kiss but had relaxed once she'd spent time amongst her most steadfast friends. Strangely, she hadn't felt pressured by Val's presence as she shopped. Aside from the odd, "How do you use that?" he'd allowed her to wander the aisles at her own speed. Talk about a gift!

One that came with a catch. She had tried to put her supplies on her own account, but he had been adamant about covering what had mostly been impulse buys. Now she felt indebted, which had likely been his intention.

Her nerves were creeping back, too, as they moved from her world back into his. She ought to be used to wealth after living with Niko, but despite the fine dining and even finer linens, she hadn't experienced a lot of this lifestyle. She didn't socialize or jet-set or dance at night clubs or sail between islands. She still felt like a guest at Niko's villa, a welcome one, but nothing was hers.

She would be a guest in her daughter's home now, she realized. Or would she?

She glanced uncertainly at Val, and her stomach swooped. He was watching her from beneath hooded eyes. The light threw shadows into his face, accenting his hawkish bone structure.

"You should have brought some of your new toys."

She had left her purchases in the car. "I would only get my hands dirty and not be able to eat. Thank you for indulging me, though." She offered a faltering smile. "Between being a new mother and building my portfolio, then preparing for my show and Niko's declining health, I haven't had an unscheduled moment in forever."

In fact, she was feeling very much at loose ends. She glanced at her phone as she set it next to her plate. "Still nothing from Scarlett."

"Why are we waiting around like this?" he asked tersely. "She's a grown woman in the hospital doing something quite natural. Let's get Aurelia and go to Italy."

She blinked in shock. "Are you joking?"

"I'm not saying childbirth sounds easy or fun, but pretty much every female goes through it. There doesn't seem much that anyone else can do while she does."

"Wow. I'm glad I had Scarlett with me rather than you when I delivered. Now I'm genuinely worried she's only got your brother." Was Javiero as absent of compassion as Val?

Her words seemed to arrest him. "Did you *want* me there?"

Oops. "Um..." She tried to shrug it off. "A little, I guess."

"Why?" He seemed genuinely astounded.

"Exactly what I'm asking myself right now," she retorted, sipping the water that arrived.

Val declined the wine list and ordered a mixed platter of appetizers.

"Tell me," he commanded when they were alone. "I

thought sentiment or morbid curiosity drove a man into the delivery room. What possible use is anyone but a medical professional?"

"Are you kidding me?" Her accent slipped back into Cork, but she could see he was dead serious. "Fine, I'll play." She folded her arms on the edge of the table. "Have you ever been really sick or had a broken bone or been helpless in some way? In a way that made you physically want to step out of your body, but you couldn't?"

Silence crashed down like an iron curtain between them. The frostbite in his gaze jumped so far down her throat, a jolting thud rocked her in her chair. He pinned her with that arctic stare for interminable seconds, impaling her while a panicked tightness clamped around her throat. The oxygen around them evaporated so fast the air sizzled with electric warning, as though a lightning bolt could strike at any second. Her pulse began to pummel her inner ears.

Kiara pushed herself into the back of her chair while she searched his face, trying to discern what she had said to make him that angry, that fast.

His inexplicable rage vanished as swiftly as it had manifested. He transferred his attention to the view, profile inscrutable. "What good would I have been, if that's how you were feeling?"

She took another hasty sip of water, trying to gather her thoughts after that disturbing interchange.

"Well, um, it's terrifying to feel that way," she pointed out and waited to see if he would agree.

Nothing. He was made of granite now, faceless and toneless and immovable.

When she didn't continue, he finally looked at her

again, all his emotions banked behind an impenetrable expression. "I couldn't have changed what you were going through."

"No. But… Well, Scarlett held my hand and spoke for me when I couldn't. That meant a lot. The whole process is incredibly undignified. She was a sport about it, but I think a woman who's physically intimate with her partner probably feels less awkward in the moment. When you need an ice chip or a towel, it wouldn't feel so much like you're prevailing. Your partner is as invested in the baby as you are, so I imagine labor feels a little more of a team effort."

She let herself travel inward to those intense hours.

"Scarlett was concerned for Aurelia, of course, but not the way I was. I felt very alone. I couldn't help thinking the only other person who would be as worried for her safe delivery would be her father."

His gaze was unwavering now, not so much holding hers as caught in it. He was hanging on her every word, which perturbed her, making everything she was saying feel even more personal and profound.

"It feels as though it lasts forever and just when I thought I couldn't do it anymore and had to give up, she arrived. They put her on my chest, and she was this ridiculous little tree frog making croaking noises." Her eyes teared up so the sun reflecting off a glass at the end of the rooftop splintered rainbows through her vision.

"Scarlett was thrilled for me, of course, but I thought you might be happy *with* me. Everything I've ever made has been a solo effort, and I've never been more proud of anything in my life, but I needed you to make her happen, and I wanted to show her to you and say, *See what we did*?" She swiped her napkin beneath her damp eyes and warned with a sniff, "If you say something withering or dismissive right now, I will get up and walk away and you will never see her in my lifetime."

He said nothing and she didn't look at him.

Their meze platter arrived, offering her a chance to gather herself back under control while the server spoke to them as though they were tourists. He identified the spanakopita and dolmades, the lamb meatballs and grilled octopus and described the types of cheese and olives and ramekins of tzatziki and hummus and tapenade.

She and Val scooped a few items onto smaller plates.

"*That's* why I'm concerned about Scarlett," Kiara summed up in a voice that still held strains of emotion. "If Javiero isn't giving her the support she needs then I want to."

Val made a noise of disparagement that she took to be an indictment of his brother's ability to be of use to anyone.

"Is that prejudice or should I be worried?" She set down her fork.

"Javiero loves to play the hero. He'll step up."

His cynical statement was hardly reassuring, but Kiara was fairly confident Scarlett would call her if she needed her.

"Are you upset that she's having his baby?" She was curious about the rift between the brothers. How had it gotten so deep? So irrevocable?

"I'm not wishing tragedy on them, if that's what you're asking."

"I didn't think that." Much. "Scarlett likes *your* baby, if that means anything."

"It doesn't," he said flatly. "My feelings toward Scarlett are ambivalent. She did her job for a man I hated. That often meant she was persistent when I wanted her to go away, but better to talk to her than him. I'm not happy she's frightened or in pain, but nor will I experience any happiness when her child arrives. As for Javiero, he does not have the power to affect me in any way. Not anymore."

"Why *did* you hate him? Niko, I mean. And Javiero, I guess."

Val's pensive gaze traversed the horizon, much as it had that afternoon in Venice when he'd appeared in her frame as she made a study of a bridge. She'd been unable to resist sketching him. He ticked all the boxes on classic standards of male beauty, ageless and virile and emanating strength. His skin was smooth over incredible bone structure made up of even, well-defined lines. His strong brow and jaw spoke of power and confidence while his mouth was pure sex and sensuality. His penetrating gaze was observant and intelligent while his stubble and rumpled hair and irreverent remarks ensured the world knew he gave no damns for anyone or anything.

Valentino Casale was very much a man in possession of himself, compelling yet untouchable.

"My father waited until the last possible minute to cut things off with my mother. Granted, a woman with an ounce of pride would have walked away when he told her he was engaged to someone else, but she continued throwing herself at him and he let her."

"Niko told me that she gave up birth control without telling him, hoping to get pregnant before he married Paloma so he would marry her instead. Did she love him?"

"No," he scoffed. "She wanted his money. He wanted a biddable, respectable wife who didn't make public scenes and came with an appropriate pedigree and portfolio of assets. By the time Mother had a positive test to show him, however, he'd applied his best efforts toward making an heir with Paloma. Her pregnancy was confirmed days after they returned from their honeymoon."

"She divorced him when she learned your mother was pregnant, didn't she? Did Niko not consider marrying your mother at that point?"

"Mother expected him to. That's why she went through with having me. But he knew she would lord that advantage over Paloma. No, he decided to recognize us both as his heirs and treat us 'equally.'" He air quoted the word. "He gave my mother exactly what he gave Paloma, a house and an income to support us, which put Paloma's nose out of joint since she would have been entitled to much more if she'd stayed married. How could she, though, amidst such a massive public humiliation?"

"Do you wish Niko had married your mother?"

"I wish he had cut her off cold when he told her he was engaged, rather than continuing to sleep with her. I wish he had paid her off once instead of naming me as Javiero's equal and dangling the promise of any of his money coming to me. I wish he had kept me apart from Javiero instead of sending us to the same boarding school where the legitimate son was placed on a pedestal and the bastard one kicked around like garbage by administration and other children alike. My father should have *picked* Javiero instead of letting our mothers battle incessantly over which one of us was more deserving of his fortune. Javiero was legitimate, but I'm older by two days. Neither woman ever lets the other forget those completely irrelevant details."

Kiara was baffled. "The half that Aurelia stands to inherit is an obscene amount. What on earth is the point in fighting for *all* of it?"

"They were fighting over *him*, Kiara. And he *liked* it. His ego ate up my mother's jealousy and seductions while he was engaged. The squabbles and catfights through his divorce and afterward fed his ego even more. He worked us like fiddles, too, loving those early years when our mothers prodded us to vie to be his favorite. He sent us to school together to prove he was treating us the same, but he compared us all the time. He berated Javiero if I bested him in math. He heckled me if Javiero won the blue ribbon in track and I came second by a hair. I had a sore stomach for three solid years, trying to become what he wanted without knowing what that was. It was hell."

That didn't sound like the Niko she knew, but he'd only had the one grandchild and had thought the sun shone straight out of her.

He'd still seemed angry that his sons had called his bluff and forced him to disinherit them, though. Her impression had been that Niko hadn't known how to bridge the divide, but when she gave it real thought, she recalled his idea of taking responsibility for their rift had always been to say he had allowed Evelina and Paloma too much influence. Kiara had never heard him own up to any particular failures as a father—which, as a parent herself, she knew came with the territory. Her mistakes were pretty much a daily occurrence.

Surely recognizing his own stumbles would have

been a first step? Acknowledgment and remorse might have gone a long way with his sons.

"I judged you as spoiled," she admitted. "Earlier, when I said you had the luxury of turning your back on him. That wasn't fair, was it?"

"I gave up on *fair* when I realized what a perverted version of it I was living."

"Is that why you began to rebel?"

"Yes." Cruel satisfaction laced his tone. "My mother had been renting me out to modeling gigs from birth. One day I threw a tantrum. I'd seen her do it a thousand times and I had genuine, pent-up anger. At thirteen, who doesn't? Mostly, I was emulating her, though. It was still an incredible feeling. By acting as though I had lost control, I gained it. Everyone began promising me all sorts of things. I refused to work again until the money I earned went into my own account, not my mother's. She nearly disowned me. Went to my father, of course."

"What did Niko do?"

"He said if I wanted to work, I should work for him. Javiero and I had been dragged into the office every school break for years. That experience taught me the importance of hiring a decent manager and paying attention to what people did with my money, so it wasn't wasted, I suppose. But having my own money allowed me to tell Niko to go to hell. I said the same thing every time we spoke until the night before I met you in Venice."

At which point he had married into the family of Niko's business rivals, firmly building a wall between himself and his father that had never been dismantled.

Kiara knew Scarlett had been in touch with Val a

handful of times in the past year, letting him know Niko's health was failing. Val had rebuffed every invitation to visit Niko.

"You don't have any regret that you didn't reconcile with him?" she asked gently.

"None," he confirmed flatly.

"Even though he was not fully to blame? Your mother… I'm sorry, but she seems like she bears some responsibility. How did you maintain a relationship with her all this time, but not him?"

He took a moment to consider his reply, which left her suspecting his answer was incomplete.

"Until today, she believed I was still her golden ticket to at least half of my father's fortune. That kept her on her best behavior. All bets are off now, though, especially once you and I marry. She will become our worst nightmare."

"*And* I could share my daughter with a stranger whom I barely trust? Gosh, how can I resist?"

"You can't. We both speak sarcasm. We're practically soul mates."

His remark was pure mockery, but her heart *thunked* in her chest and sat there reverberating at the thought of finding The One. She took a fresh helping from the platter to hide any secretive yearnings he might glimpse in her eyes. She did sometimes wish for a true, intimate connection with someone, even though—

"Marriage has never been a particular goal of mine," she stated truthfully. "Growing up, I watched the pretty, bubbly girls get attention from boys and wondered what that was like, but the few times I went on a date, I was always waiting for it to be over so I could get back to my sketch pad. That made me realize I wasn't cut out for serious, intimate relationships."

"Is that how you're feeling right now?" he asked drily.

"Is this a date?" A funny tingle curled through her, as if this was the sort of banter a couple might share on a date. A good one.

"If you have to ask, I'll have to try harder." The rakish sweep of his gaze as it struck her lips and throat and breasts was pure, carnal invitation.

She couldn't match his level of nonchalance. Her heart was skipping again so she settled on telling the truth.

"I'm a certified workaholic," she admitted. "I always feel compelled to be making progress with my art if I'm not with Aurelia, but she is my highest priority. That makes this conversation a priority." She swirled a toasted pita bite through some dip. "So this isn't a date. It's a working lunch." Afternoon tea, given the hour, but whatever.

"We're getting married. That usually starts with a date."

And ends with…

She had to fight to swallow her bite of pita.

"I didn't expect you to propose," she said in a small sidestep, rather than confronting his assertion head-on.

"How did you expect me to react?"

"Angry about the money," she admitted honestly. "I thought you'd want to fight for it. It's a lot of money," she added when his expression twisted with annoyed aversion. "Or I thought you would be angry that I'd had her after all and would tell us to have a nice life."

"I am angry. There will be no more keeping secrets

from me once we're married. Anything you need, I will provide. My father's money can be dumped in the sea for all I care. This is a clean break from him. Understand?"

So implacable. She didn't dare point out she'd heard an eerily similar command in Niko's tone as he'd extracted her promise to keep Aurelia's existence from Val.

With her eyes on her plate, she said, "Look, it means a lot to me that you want to meet her, but marriage—"

"Kiara," he cut in. "I am the last man to buckle to convention. Marriage is an idiotic social construct that serves no sensible purpose that I can fathom. But it means something to the rest of the world. Being illegitimate was not fun for me. There were people who made sure I suffered for something that was not my fault. I won't sentence my own child to that experience when it's such an easy fix. Claiming Aurelia as my heir is not enough. You and I have to marry."

Her heart somersaulted. She understood his motives better now. In fact, she felt even guiltier for not telling him about Aurelia sooner. But marriage?

"Is it enough for *you* that she merely knows who I am?" Val challenged softly. "Where was your father when your mother died? Why were you orphaned?"

And here it came. Intellectually, she knew everyone was equal and he was hardly in a place to judge, but that didn't stop others from judging. It didn't stop her from feeling the hollowness of absence.

"I don't know anything about my father," she admitted, locking down her insides so she betrayed no emotion. This was purely a fact about her personal history, she reminded herself. "Maybe my mother would have talked about him once I got older, but she only said he was someone she loved and thought would come back but didn't. After I lost her, I told people I was an orphan so I didn't have to reveal that they hadn't been married. I was never persecuted for it, though."

No, people had expressed pity or maybe puzzlement that it was possible for a person to exist with absolutely *no one* in their life. She'd felt her father's nonexistence in other, subtler ways, though. At times she had thought that at least if she had carried his name, it would have been something. Some tiny connection.

"I could see my way to marrying as a formality, for Aurelia's sake," she allowed carefully. "Perhaps divorce after a year or so?"

"No," he rejected swiftly, cheeks hollow. "I already have one divorce behind me. I didn't think it would bother me, but the stench of failure is intolerable. More important, I don't want to repeat history. I don't want Aurelia torn between warring houses. I won't give you the chance to pit her against me."

"The fact you think I would do that is reason enough we shouldn't marry," she said, spine stiffening. "I don't want to live with someone who doesn't trust or respect me." She let a beat pass, then batted her lashes. "Do you?"

His mouth twitched. He looked off into the distance, faint humor lingering in his profile. "You're entertaining, at least."

"I'm actually very boring. Reclusive. I don't bother with current events or pop culture. I don't care what's trending. If I read, it's romance—not your top pick, I'm guessing. Same goes for movies. My ability to hold court at a dinner party is limited to describing my process, which I hate talking about for fear I'll jinx it. In fact, if you're serious about marriage, brace yourself for two topics of conversation: if the weather supports my plein air aspirations, and how you're coming along with Aurelia's homework, because I had enough trouble at school that I'm calling it right now as your bailiwick."

"Dinner parties are overrated." He lounged easily in his chair, unruffled by her outburst. "Homework I can handle. The talk will be you. I'd suggest anywhere except the dinner table, but I'll leave that up to you. See? Progress. I travel a lot. I assume that appeals. You went to Venice to fill the creative well, didn't you?"

He remembered her saying that? She had been shocked he'd even remembered her name today, let alone the things they'd talked about.

"If my showing goes well, I'll need fresh inspiration," she said, tentatively letting herself consider what marriage to him might look like. "I suppose we could travel with you until Aurelia starts school."

"What difference will that make? She'll be at boarding school."

"You're adorable when you're wrong." She stabbed a meatball, but paused to see how he reacted, prepared to fight to the death on this one. "Aurelia will attend day school. I haven't decided where."

"You're sexy when you're aggressive." He stole her fork and ate the meatball off the tines, chewed and swallowed. "Which I like. And you know that."

Ride me. Kiara had known how sex worked in a theoretical sense, but she hadn't realized she could take charge of the act and revel in having all the control.

A rush of sensual heat arrived with the memory of

undulating on him while the bed creaked. They had already made love twice by then and her body had been tender, but her growing confidence had had her nipping at him. Squeezing him. Pleading, *Once more*, until he'd dragged her atop him.

Ride me, he had urged. *So I don't hurt you.*

She had nearly killed both of them, determined to wring every last ounce of pleasure from the experience. When she had come down from the profound fulfillment that had swept over both of them, she'd been sprawled weakly across him, their heartbeats—

"What's on your mind, darling?" he asked in a tone of exaggerated intimacy.

He knew exactly where her thoughts had gone. He'd sent her there on purpose, probably to disarm her after she'd asserted herself.

Her flush of sensual tingles turned to a stinging heat of mortification.

"Why was I even there that night?" The question had haunted her for three years. "Online it says you hated modeling and quit as soon as you had capital to pursue other things." Green energy and tech initially, but these days he had fingers in pies from hotels to broadcasting. "Why did you offer to sit for me?"

"I wanted you to come to my room," he said as if that was obvious.

"But *why*? Because even when I thought you'd paid me for sex, it didn't make sense that you would ask *me*. There were far more experienced professionals if that's what you wanted, and fine." She held up a hand. "That's not what it was, but the sort of women you're usually seen with are CEOs and socialites, not impoverished art students with zero sophistication and a stone's worth of excess weight."

"Which one of us are you insulting?" He angled his head in forewarning.

"I know what I am, Val. I didn't like being an ugly duckling as a child, but I'm fine with turning into a plain duck as a woman, not a graceful swan—which *is* your usual type. There were women flirting with you in the restaurant that night so why take *me* back to your room? Was it the thrill of picking up a virgin?"

"What?" The crack of his voice was loud enough to turn heads at the tables that had begun filling up. He gave an annoyed glance around, then asked her more quietly, but with equal intensity, "How the hell was I supposed to know that?"

"I thought it was dead obvious." Granted, the act hadn't really hurt. She'd been incredibly aroused, and the sting of penetration had been more a moment of heightened stimulation than anything else.

"You were on the pill," he reminded under his breath. "That led me to believe— Are you being straight with me right now?"

She shrugged. "Why would I lie?"

"I don't *know*," he growled and rose to throw down some bills. "We're not continuing this discussion here."

"Can we go to the hospital?"

"So Javiero and I can compare notes on how we wound up in the same situation? *No.*"

"There's a park next to it. It's nice this time of day. Quiet. I really want to check in on Scarlett."

He relented and ten minutes later his driver let them out to walk through wrought iron gates into a small sanctuary where families could wheel relatives for a breath of fresh air.

The area was abandoned at the moment since the shadow of the building had moved, but there were still a few patches of shade beneath some trees, and a light breeze picked up the mist off the fountain, offering respite from the heat of the sinking sun.

Kiara had come here at different times with Niko but didn't have a tiny hand clinging to her fingers today while little feet walked the rim of the pool. She felt bereft without her girl and gave a sigh of melancholy as she watched water overflow the center vase and fall in a curtain around it.

"Did you—" he began, then ran his hand down his face. His voice tightened as he tried again. "When I invited you to my room and made it clear I would undress, I interpreted that to mean you were up for more than modeling. I said we would see where the rest of the night took us."

"I knew what I was signing up for." She ducked her head with awkward shyness. "I wasn't *that* inexperienced."

"But you let me seduce you, even though you'd never made love before. Why?" He was back to suspicion, not that she'd imagined she had won him over in any way, but the wall of hostility had returned to his expression and made her heart dip.

"I was flattered," she admitted baldly. "I don't get attention from handsome, sexy men and—"

"Stop talking about yourself like you're not attractive."

She closed her eyes. "*Please* don't think I'm fishing for reassurance. I am genuinely happy with looking average and normal. I like food and see no point in sweating at the gym when I'd rather be painting. The life of a supermodel seems vastly overrated."

"It is," he said flatly. "Most thin people I know have eating disorders. My mother is a raving lunatic because she's in a constant low blood sugar psychosis."

"And you?" She opened her eyes wide with false innocence. "Is this charm you exhibit natural or is there a similar underlying issue?"

He dipped his chin and glowered a silent warning.

This was why she used a canvas as a shield against life. Even when she did try to stand up for herself, she wound up getting knocked into the dirt with a wordless glance.

"I do hate modeling," he stated. "When I realized you were sketching me, I assumed you knew who I was and almost walked away, but your intensity made me curious. I wanted to see how it turned out, so I asked you to dinner."

Actually, after standing motionless for twenty minutes, he had walked over and said, *Models are entitled to compensation. Buy me dinner.*

He had wound up paying, thankfully, because he had chosen one of those expensive outdoor cafés where they charged more for the table than the food.

His gaze drifted over her features the way it had that night, in a way that made things shift inside her, so she felt very feminine and shy. Pretty and aware. *Sexy.*

"You should have told me you'd never made love."

"Would you still have wanted to?"

"Yes." His response was so unapologetic, she choked on a laugh. "But not *three times*. Did I hurt you?"

Childbirth hadn't exactly been a picnic, but that wasn't what he meant.

"A little. I mean…" She wrinkled her nose and looked toward the fountain, cheeks stinging with self-consciousness. "Can we settle on, it was a perfectly nice experience until I thought you had paid me for it?"

"Perfectly nice," he drawled. "Two words that have never been applied to me."

This was the man who had made her laugh and feel talented and more exciting than she had ever aspired to be. He stole her breath, this gleaming god of a man, tall and wide-shouldered, virile and angular and watching her with a knowing smirk.

"This, Kiara." His voice became graveled and intimate, swirling a buzzing heat through her like the richest red wine. For one second she felt as though they were perfectly aligned. Equal and opposite. Yin and yang. "*This* is why I asked you to my room that night."

"What is it?" she asked with bewilderment. *Soul mates*, she wondered with a depth of yearning so sharp it stole her breath.

"Chemistry," he said, snapping their connection as he frowned. "Have you had other lovers?" His tone suggested he already knew the answer and didn't like it.

She folded her arms and lined her toes up with a seam in the paving stones beneath her feet. "I haven't had time to set up my online dating profile."

Thunderstruck silence followed, then, "So me. That night. That's all the experience you have. And today you kissed me like—" He waved off in the direction of his hotel then took two steps away and turned his back on her. One hand hung off his hip, the other squeezed the back of his neck. "A decent man would not take advantage of you by seducing you again. I am not a decent man, Kiara. You know that, don't you? I will use this attraction to get you into my bed, put a ring on it and that will be the end of it."

He sounded like one of those cartoon villains who revealed his dastardly plan so the hero was forewarned and forearmed, but there was a part of Kiara that didn't want to fight him. The primal female in her was darkly excited by the threat of being dragged to a cave by the male who claimed her.

That ancient imperative to submit had a purpose, however; one that was as clear today as it had been then.

"Can I ask you a related question?"

He looked over his shoulder.

"Do you want more children?"

"No."

It was such a swift punch; she caught her breath.

He turned and frowned. "You do?"

She nodded jerkily. "I hated being an only child."

"Siblings aren't all they're cracked up to be."

"You were poisoned from an early age against one another." She took a step forward, anxious to persuade. "Have you even given Javiero a chance lately?"

"No," he scoffed. "And I won't."

She shook her head in bafflement while her heart felt pulled and strained between him and Aurelia, the past and the future, her own will and his.

"That sort of hatred is not what I want Aurelia to learn."

His jaw tightened. "That is why I won't have another one," he shot back with a forceful point of his finger. "You're already using her to manipulate me."

"Into doing what?" she cried. "Reconciling with your

brother? That's between you and him. Do it or don't.
I don't care. But my job as a parent is to teach Aurelia
how to be a decent human being. To model behavior like
kindness and forgiveness. If you're only going to show
her how to hate, then no. You don't get to be her parent."

A muscle in his cheek ticked.

Remorse gripped her. She felt as though she was
kicking a dog for being a dog.

"Do you understand that being a father is more than
giving her a name and a bedroom and three square
meals?" she asked more gently. Maybe she even spoke
with tendrils of pity because her life might have been
a lonely struggle, but his had clearly been a Siberian
wasteland.

"This isn't an ultimatum, Val. It's a *choice*. One *you*
have to make. If you want me to marry you, you have to
also want a relationship with Aurelia. You can't let her
form an emotional attachment that isn't reciprocated.
That's cruel. *You know that*. She needs all the compassion and respect and affection you can pour over her.
You'll have to listen and compromise. That's what was
lacking between you and Niko, wasn't it? That's why
you're so bitter and malevolent. Do you really expect
me to set her up to become just like you?"

CHAPTER FOUR

WALK AWAY, VAL THOUGHT.

But Kiara did it first, saying, "I'm going to check on Scarlett."

He had instructed his driver to park at the hospital, which was the direction she took, but he stayed where he was, staring at one of the handful of shiny coins in the bottom of the fountain.

Did he feel manipulated? Yes. Aurelia had already become a pressure point and he hated giving anyone leverage over him. He'd been weak and manipulated and exploited as a child. Objectified and controlled, lied to and lied *about*. He'd been abandoned by Niko when he had most needed him to stand up for him.

So yes, he was bitter and malevolent. Mostly, he compartmentalized and got on with life, but he had made a habit of caring very little about anything. The minute he cared for more than money or his immediate comfort, he opened himself up to being used and cornered and crushed.

But he already cared about his daughter. He didn't understand the powerful force that had risen in him at the sound of her voice, but something instinctive within him wanted to protect his child in every possible way, most especially from the bullies and predators he'd experienced in his own youth.

Of course, his mere presence in her life would expose her to the tainted world he came from so the best way to protect her was to *walk away*.

His feet refused to budge.

Why not? Kiara had the means to take excellent care of Aurelia. She was proving fierce enough to stand up to him, wasn't she? A savage excitement swelled in him, witnessing how glorious she was in her desire to slay dragons for their daughter.

Then there was their kiss. Their sexual compatibility hadn't faded one iota. Her fire and simple truth drew him as inexorably as the night they'd met.

Do you really expect me to set her up to become just like you?

He pushed the heels of his hands into his eye sockets, convinced he was too far gone to become the better man his daughter deserved.

But he couldn't bring himself to walk away.

Prepared to wait, Kiara detoured to the car to collect a pad and some graphite pencils.

After a brief inquiry with the main desk clerk who promised to make a call to the maternity ward, she settled into a corner of the waiting room and looked for something benign to draw. There were a handful of people here, an elderly couple and a woman with a child absorbed in screen time. There was a potted plant in the corner and a small courtyard beyond the window, but nothing inspired her.

Her mind was brimming with Val and all the fresh angles and expressions he had revealed in the hours she'd been with him. His blade-like cheekbones and the inimical set of his jaw, the sensual sweep of his mouth and the spiky lashes around his pale, steely eyes.

Her own eyes were damp, her throat tight.

She felt so stupid for hoping. No. Robbed. Somehow, deep down, she had convinced herself Niko and Scarlett were wrong. It wasn't as if Val went around murdering people or committing high treason. Sure, he was given to making scathing remarks and pulling ruthless business moves, but he wasn't a bad person. Was he?

She wanted—needed—to believe he possessed a heart and was capable of offering it to his daughter and yes, she was chagrined to admit, to her, too.

She understood now, though. He was broken. He was all ropy scar tissue, no flexible tendons or muscles capable of stretch. He was contemptuous of humanity and lacking in compassion. It was sad. What the man needed was some unconditional love and if she didn't have Aurelia's trusting heart to protect, she might have taken a chance on him.

But she had to put Aurelia first.

Oh, shoot. Her pencil had absently begun blocking in his naked shoulders, about to re-create the moment when he had turned his head and asked with throaty seduction, *Would you like to make love?*

Her heart had flipped over. She had already been doing so in her mind. The compulsion to caress him with more than her eyes had been impossible to resist.

Her defenses were still as easily breached by him. Was it purely her inexperience? Or that chemistry he'd alluded to? She hadn't known what to think of that. He was a highly sexed man; that wasn't up for debate. She was not a highly sexed woman. Unless she was around him, apparently, because he turned her into some kind of nymphomaniac.

Cheeks stinging, she glanced around as she surreptitiously flipped her page to hide what she'd begun to sketch.

The sound of the entrance doors sliding open lifted her head.

Val entered. His gaze found her, and her heart leaped at the sight of him.

Don't hope, she cautioned herself, but what did his arrival mean? What did that grave expression mean?

Into the charged silence, the distant ding of an elevator sounded.

Before he even looked in that direction, Val stiffened like an animal going on alert.

Footsteps approached. She couldn't see who it was, but Val turned his head, his expression hardening to iron. He was bristling like a wolf and it made all the fine hairs on her body stand up with trepidation.

Instinct had her rising against a cloud of such dark animosity; the elderly couple sensed it and frowned with concern as she moved past them.

Javiero. She'd seen photos of his rugged features before the attack, but her heart bottomed out when she saw him in person. He was a little taller and broader than Val and wore a black eye patch. Savage red lines stood livid on his face and across his throat. His haggard expression was as rigid as Val's.

They held an unblinking stare, a pair of territorial beasts primed to rip out each other's throats at one false move from the other.

She made herself ignore Javiero's disfigurement and forced a friendly smile.

"Javiero. It's nice to meet you. I'm Kiara."

She tried to put out her hand to shake, but Val swept his arm in front of her, catching her wrist and wrangling her behind him, all without breaking eye contact with his brother.

"For heaven's sake," she muttered, struggling against his tense hold. "He's not going to eat me."

"No comment?" Javiero taunted Val, completely ignoring Kiara. "Not going to say you like what I've done with my hair or something equally banal?"

Antagonism simmered off Val in waves. She fairly tasted it. How could she not? He had his arm bent to wrap around her and she could hear his teeth grinding together.

She gave up trying to twist away and peered around his shoulder. "How is Scarlett?"

"Sleeping."

"She delivered? Boy or girl?" she asked with excitement.

"Boy." Javiero was still holding a macho staring contest with Val.

"How lovely! Congratulations." She pinched Val, trying to get him to ease his grip on her. "Everything went well? No complications?"

"None."

These men! She leaned into Val, trying to nudge him off balance to break their stare, but he was a concrete wall. "Have you chosen a name?"

"No."

"I'd love to see him," she said wistfully.

"No." Javiero seemed to enjoy rounding out the word. His brows lifted ever so slightly in a signal that he was refusing purely out of spite toward Val.

Somehow Val grew harder and larger, his muscles seeming to gather for attack, threatening to tear through the constraints of his shirt, but all he said was a gritty-voiced, "I'll stay here. Let her up."

"No." The satisfaction that dripped from Javiero's tongue should have left a puddle on the floor.

Val's body bunched further.

Kiara wrapped her arms fully around him and squeezed with all her might.

"It's fine," she declared firmly. Strenuously. Even though Javiero's refusal fractured her heart. "It's late." It wasn't, but she would defuse this any way she could. "I'm sure you all want to rest. Please give Scarlett and your son my love. Tell her to call me when she's up for a chat," she babbled.

Javiero didn't promise to relay any messages. He pivoted and stalked away.

The press of Kiara's curves against him eased, but Val had to consciously tell himself to release her. His heart was slamming in his chest, adrenaline leaving an ache in his muscles.

She expelled a hissing breath of pent-up tension. "I'll get my things."

He watched her return to her seat and collect her pad and pencils and followed her out.

He should have walked away instead of coming after her. What had he thought to accomplish? He had only known he was still determined to marry her, not expecting an immediate test of his resolve.

For all his claims that Javiero had no effect on him, the sight of his half brother had clashed old anger through him—after the unsightly, stitched-up tears in

Javiero's face had briefly taken him aback. The damage was more extensive than reported, but Val knew better than to pity Javiero. He was still the arrogant hard-ass Val preferred not to know.

And after all the times Val had knocked over Javiero's attempts to claim authority over him, today he'd had to stand there and suffer it. Javiero's refusal to let Kiara see his baby had been pure malice. It had been an attempt to dig at Val and it had *worked*.

Val was incensed to learn he had a crack in his armor, one that Kiara had caused and that Javiero had found quickly and easily. How? It wasn't as if Val had *wanted* Kiara to go anywhere with him. Javiero had talked more than one ally into changing sides in the past. It was one of the reasons Val rarely trusted anyone anymore.

But Kiara's confession earlier about wanting him with her when she had delivered was still panging uncomfortably in his chest. Given her concern all day for her friend, he understood that reassuring herself Scarlett and the baby had come through the ordeal meant a lot to her.

So there he'd stood, helpless to force Javiero into giving him something he didn't even want. This was why he hated Greece! There were never any good choices, only lousy and worse.

"What's wrong?" Kiara asked, coming around from stowing her pad with the rest of her supplies. Her brows came together as she noticed Val's tense fist braced on the roof of the car.

"Scarlett doesn't need you. We can leave." He opened the car door.

"But—"

"He won't let you see her, Kiara. We're getting Aurelia, going to Italy and getting married."

"I haven't agreed to that!" Kiara's eyes widened in anxious uncertainty. Her gaze went back and forth between his eyes as she searched for an answer of some kind.

She didn't have to repeat the question. He heard it loud and clear.

Do you really expect me to set her up to become just like you?

"I didn't finish what the jaguar started, did I?" He had nearly bitten clean through his tongue for her sake, even though he'd been provoked. "*I* wasn't the one being petty, refusing to let you see your friend and her baby. I take your point about Aurelia's confusion over losing Niko. I'm completely committed."

Her breath left her, but still she hesitated to duck into the car.

He knew what she was waiting for—his agreement to develop a bond with their daughter. To be a better father than his own. When the bar had been set that low, how hard could it be?

"I will *try*, Kiara," he promised through his teeth while a band tightened around his chest. "That is more compromise than anyone has squeezed out of me in years. Accept it as the triumph it is."

Kiara didn't feel as though she was winning anything. In fact, she was losing what little autonomy she still possessed.

She had known her life would change with Niko's death. She had known Val would be informed and she would have to handle his reaction.

Knowing hadn't prepared her. Maybe she spent too much time hiding from the real world in her art, making the anguish of daily life easier to bear by painting over it with bright colors and clean lines. That tactic left her with few coping strategies when reality crashed in. She wanted to believe she was strong inside, but she wasn't. She leaned on Scarlett *all the time*. And Scarlett wasn't here. Would she see her again? She'd already lost Niko. Now she would lose her home and her best friend?

What was the alternative, though? She could pick a fight with Val and maybe come out on top after a long, bloody battle, but that would serve no one, least of all Aurelia. If Val was willing to make a concession for their daughter, Kiara ought to, as well, right?

Even if it terrified her?

She kept herself together until they returned to the hotel where she took refuge in the guest bedroom to "freshen up." Instead, she threw herself facedown on the bed, trying not to scream with hysteria into a down-filled pillow.

Twice. She had met Val *twice*, and he had completely overturned her life each time, this time even faster and more completely than the first. What did that say about how marriage to him would go? She couldn't do it. Couldn't.

But she wanted to. Which scared the hell out of her.

A knock sounded and Val's rumbling voice had her scrambling to sit up.

"What?" she stammered.

He opened the door. "I said—"

Her turmoil must have been clear in her flushed, disheveled appearance. His steely gaze flicked to every corner. "What's wrong?"

"What's right?" she choked out as she scooted herself to the edge of the bed and grabbed a tissue. Two. Three. She felt like crying if only to release the pressure inside her. "The closest thing I've had to a father died two days ago. My best friend had a baby that I'm not allowed to see. Maybe I'll never get to talk to her again. *You* expect me to move to a strange country as if it's as easy as rolling over in bed. Would I even have a studio? Because the culmination of my lifetime's aspiration is happening in three weeks and I'm not ready!"

If she lost *that*… Cripes. Now the tears were really pressing up against her composure.

"It's a lot to process," she muttered, shoving panic to the edges of her consciousness as she moved to the mirror. Good grief. Her face was ashen, her hair squashed.

"Of course you'll have a studio," he said behind her.

She flung around. "Really? Because it is an absolute deal breaker for me."

He gave her a smirk that could only be described as patronizing. "I don't claim to be an inventive man, Kiara. If my father was able to bribe you with four walls and a roof, why wouldn't I use the same incentive?"

Lord, she was predictable. And easy. "Where?" she asked.

"There's a space on the grounds of my villa that should be big enough. Design whatever you like."

"Really?" She couldn't help a skip of excitement at the idea. She loved her studio on the island, but there were things she would do differently if starting from scratch.

"Of course. I want my wife to be happy."

For some reason, she found that incredibly laughable and she chuckled.

"Why is that funny?" His eyes narrowed.

"I don't know." She sobered. "I appreciate that you want to indulge me, but..." She sighed. "Much as I dream we could become a family for Aurelia's sake, I can't agree to marry you. Not until I have a better sense that you and I will be able to make a proper go of it."

"You make a proper go of it by going all in," he said in a hard voice. "By making a commitment and sticking to it through thick or thin."

"It's just that easy, is it? You're going *all in*? Not going to hold anything back?"

She watched his cheek tick. She wasn't sure why that went straight into her heart like a branding iron, but it did. She gripped her elbows.

"I'm willing to bring Aurelia to Italy and see how it goes. That's as much as I'll give you right now."

His turn to offer a harsh chuckle that scraped along her nerve endings.

"Take as long as you like to think it over," he said in a mild tone belied by his granite posture and ruthless smile. "So long as you've decided to marry me when our wedding date rolls around in fourteen days. I came in to say you should call the villa, tell them I'm sending my pilot to collect Aurelia. He'll come back for us and we'll proceed to Italy from here."

"What? *No*." Her blood zinged with alarm. "I can't leave from here. I have things I need. From my studio."

"Make a list. Someone can pack and forward it."

"No." Her arms shot straight down at her sides. "No one goes into my studio. Not unless I'm there and invite them. No one touches my things." The idea made her

hyperventilate on a good day. Today she was already overwrought and bordering on mania.

With a weary sigh, he said, "Tantrums don't work on me, Kiara."

"I'm not joking!" Her arm flailed. "I get uptight when someone comes in and I'm *there*. People can't go in and touch my *things*."

He caught her wrist and studied the way her fingers were trembling. His touch shifted so he could feel the unsteady race of her pulse.

"They're only things, Kiara," he said quietly.

"They're *my* things and we're going to need a safe word if you're going to make outlandish suggestions like telling me to let others touch them." She pulled away from his touch, embarrassed and trying to turn her reaction into a joke but failing spectacularly. "I know it's not rational." Her eyes were welling with helplessness. "But my studio is where I'm...*me*." Where she allowed herself to be vulnerable. "You don't let strangers walk up and touch everything under your clothes, do you?"

He quirked a brow. "Wrong man to ask. I strip for strangers all the time."

Not all the time. Not anymore. Did he? What would happen if they were married? Would he have other lovers besides her?

She hadn't let herself think about sex. About what she might gain with this marriage—like *him*.

Now her pulse tripped into a different kind of gallop. Still fearful, but anticipatory. He was a force, this man. He would never, ever be easy.

But all he had to do was touch her and she melted.

"*No* has always worked for me." He touched her arm

again, his touch light and the suggestion of invitation that she come closer even lighter. "As a safe word."

She would never be safe with him.

She knew that without a doubt. She might have money, but he would always have the advantage of experience and control and less personal investment. Wasn't that the definition of her life, though? Whether it was Niko's power or her agent's assessment of her talent or simply her daughter's best interest, Kiara was forever giving or forgiving, allowing or enduring.

Except when it came to sex with Val. Tension was crawling across his cheekbones, some of it sexual, some of it dismay. He was reacting as inexorably as she was, and she didn't think there could have been a stronger aphrodisiac. She might be helpless to the way he made her feel, but he suffered a similar reaction.

She was pretty sure.

Her instinct for creative discovery took over, governing her as she stepped forward. It was the same compulsion that gripped her when she was deep in the throes of painting, when something unexpected happened, but wasn't a mistake.

This might be. She saw Val's gaze dip to her mouth, saw the sway in him the way a redwood rocked in the wind, trying to withstand a force that could topple it.

Yearning curled with eagerness in her belly as she waited.

With a soft curse, he dropped his head and covered her lips with his, releasing a pained noise into her mouth as he did it.

A moan left her at the same time, one that was both a signal of welcome and a noise of agony at the intense sensation of lips scraping hers. A damp lick—hers—

and the friction became a glide. Heat expanded down her throat and across her chest, prickling her nipples to life. Her hand found his stubbled cheek and encouraged him even as his arms wrapped around her and locked her into a tight embrace that squeezed the air from her lungs.

His kiss was devastating. His hand cradled the back of her head, fingers massaging through her hair while he worshipped her mouth. He made love to it so blatantly, a flash flood of heat went straight to her loins. Her knees weakened and she clung all the tighter to him, hips tilting forward, seeking the pressure of him where she ached.

He dragged his head up and his unsteady breaths moved his chest against hers as he walked her backward to the bed.

"Are you going to say it?" he growled.

"What?" She stumbled over her own feet, grasping at his arms to keep her balance.

"Our safe word."

Her tongue went to the space behind her front teeth. Realization struck with a pang of helpless humor along with confusion and a rather tender, frightening feeling because as unwise as this was, it felt incredibly *right*. A quivery, joyous sensation had lodged itself somewhere between her heart and her stomach.

"I'm taking everything," he warned. "Unless you say it."

"Me?" she asked, sinking onto the edge of the mattress because her knees wouldn't hold her. Her agonized gaze pinning to the spot in his throat where his carotid artery pulsed, confident and strong. "Why? To prove I can't resist you?"

"To prove I can still make you scream."

A squeaking sob escaped her, and she continued to hold his arm as he slowly began releasing the tiny buttons that closed the front of her dress.

She wanted him to kiss her again, blank out her mind so her surrender wasn't so blatant, but he was giving her every chance to voice that tiny word she couldn't seem to find because now his hand was invading. Sliding with surety into her dress, under the cup of her bra, gathering the abundant swell of her breast and baring it.

Another growling noise escaped him, and he overwhelmed her then, pressing her back as he took her brown nipple into his mouth, wet and hot and ruthless.

He caused such a spear of pleasure into her loins; she bucked her hips against his weight.

He shifted, still pinning her, but drawing up the hem of her dress and dancing abstract patterns across her inner thighs until she was squeezing them together to try to ease the growing ache between them.

"This is happening too fast," she gasped, clasping his head.

"Is it?" His voice sounded drugged and his eyelids were heavy as he raised his head. His hand stilled on her upper thigh. The branding heat of it made her intimate flesh throb. "I can smell how excited you are, Kiara."

The tip of his nose circled hers and his erotic words against her lips sent a shower of tingles through her. The line of his own arousal dug into her hip.

"You don't want my touch here?" His thumb skimmed ever so briefly against the line of her panties, causing a fresh release of dampening readiness into her aching folds. "My mouth?"

He grazed his lips against hers, teasing, not giving her the kiss her parted mouth craved, only the flick of the tip of his tongue.

"Tell me what you want," he said with dark command. "Say it and I will give it to you. I promise. I won't make you beg. This time," he added with a carnal smile.

Heaven help her, she did. She said something earthy and flagrant. He revealed his teeth in a wolfish, predatory smile, but in the next second smothered her with a kiss. Then he did as she'd asked, giving her his mouth all over her body, working his way down, exposing her other breast and lifting her skirt high enough to lick into her navel. Then he peeled away her panties and kissed the flesh he'd exposed.

He made her scream.

Then he said, "Louder," and did it again.

"What are you doing?" Kiara's voice was heavy with lassitude as he picked her up.

"I need a condom." If he didn't get inside her in the next sixty seconds he was going to go out of his mind.

"I'm too heavy."

"Don't insult me." He shouldered into his own room and set her on his bed, rather enamored with the way her disheveled clothing exposed a shoulder and a breast. Her skirt rode up and the wrinkled silk told its own story. Her crushed hair and swollen eyelids made him want to push her knees apart and feast on her all over again.

He wrenched his shirt off then slowed as her gaze heated with lust. He popped the button on his jeans and lowered the zipper with care since he was aroused and, as always, commando.

She drew in a breath as he revealed that fact, gaze pinned to the flesh that was aching to thrust into the heat he'd tasted.

When she licked her lips and stared at him with unabashed craving, he had to squeeze himself to keep from losing control. A pang of pleasure-pain throbbed into the tip, warning him how close he was, but he couldn't resist asking, "Want this?"

She swallowed and her eyes came up to his, her gaze full of vulnerability as she nodded.

This woman would be his undoing, he feared, but he moved closer and let her take him in her too-gentle grip. She was as tentative as she'd been that first night, but the caress of her tongue and the close of her lips and the light suction she applied was pure paradise.

He withstood it as long as he could, fists gripped onto her shoulders, weight pushing into his toes while his abs pulled into his spine.

Everything in him wanted to capitulate to her delicate torment, but he made himself press her back. *He* was in charge. Wasn't he?

"*Grazie, bella*, but take off your clothes," he said, barely recognizing his own voice, coming from such a deep place inside him. "I want all of you."

He helped, skimming his fingers across her soft shoulders, bringing her to her feet again so her dress fell off her hips and onto the floor. She released her bra and it dropped away, too.

He feasted his gaze on every inch of her brown curves. The musky scent of sex was all around them and he started to reach for her, then remembered he needed a condom. He picked up his jeans for his wallet.

"I'm, um, still on the pill," she said very softly. "A

proper kind. But it's okay if you want to use one," she said as she watched him apply the latex. "To be sure."

He did want to be sure, but as he pressed her onto the mattress beneath him, he wasn't sure of anything anymore.

CHAPTER FIVE

THIS WAS HOW it had been that other time, Kiara thought distantly. The thrust of his body into hers stung, but she gloried in the sensation. In the sheer possessiveness of his action. In the power of his undulating form beneath her hands as they roamed over his back and hips and flexing butt.

Her senses were overloaded, but she loved it. And the pleasure, the abject joy that filled her as they writhed in the throes of lovemaking, was incomparable. It was raw and intimate and her defenses were nonexistent, but she had never felt more free. She released all the constraints within her, at one with him in a way she had never experienced with anyone in any other way except like this, with him.

Orgasm peaked sudden and sharp in her, pushing a cry of surprise from her throat.

He laughed and speared his hand into her hair, not pausing his rhythm as he nipped at her jaw.

"We can do better than that. I want you to *weep*, it's so good." He dragged her hands over her head and stretched her helpless beneath him while his busy mouth traversed dips and curves, finding all her erogenous zones, making her groan under the onslaught of pleasure.

Climax rose again, stronger. The next one was stronger still.

She said things then, things that were pleas for mercy and entreaties for more. She forgot everything she was. The only thing that mattered was the man who commanded her here, in this bed. She was his, utterly and completely his.

It should have terrified her.

And it did, later, when she came back to herself and realized how much power he had over her. But for now, she exulted in it.

"I hate the island," Val said forcefully, hours later, when they had emerged from his room, sleepy and famished, to order room service and circle back to the discussion that had preceded Kiara's forging herself onto him like iron filings to a magnet.

Kiara looked up from folding back the sleeve on her robe, shocked by the vehemence in his tone.

"*Hate* it," he reiterated. "I didn't go back when my own father was dying there. What makes you think I'll go back tomorrow?"

"Your daughter?"

"My daughter can come to me. *You* want to go back. Why? Your studio?" He made it sound like a very lame excuse.

"Yes." A deep quavering accosted her as she watched his eyes narrow the way a cat's did when a bird landed nearby. If he'd had a tail, it would have flicked with predatory anticipation. "I can go alone," she said, scooping saffron-flavored rice into her mouth.

"I'm not afraid, *bella*."

Her heart skipped at the endearment even though he pronounced it with such lethal warning. "Then come with me," she dared.

He snorted at her audacity and reached across to cup the side of her neck. The possessive action was enough to heat her blood afresh.

She understood then that she had placed herself in the palm of his hand. The sense of obligation Niko had held over her was nothing compared to the casual dominance Val could exert with a smoky look at her mouth or the sensual caress of his fingertip against her nape.

"You understand that you're mine now? I respect the delicate artist within you, so I will give you this gift, but you will only bring what is truly yours. Nothing of that man will enter my house."

Tears came into her eyes. She didn't understand it, but its roots might have been in shame. Her allegiance was shifting—had shifted—to Val, whether he deserved her devotion or not. The hours of entrusting him with her body had left her feeling exactly as he'd said. His. And his hatred of Niko was so palpable, she felt disloyal for the years she'd spent with him.

"Say thank you."

"Grazie," she whispered, tentative with his language.

"I like hearing Italian from your swollen lips. And you're very pretty with your limpid eyes and whiskerburned chin but come here and say it properly." He pushed his chair back and his robe parted, exposing his chest and stomach and the thickening flesh between his powerful thighs.

She went.

* * *

Val's heart iced over as the enormous villa came into view and continued to harden as the helicopter landed on the pad behind it, exactly as it had four times a year when he'd been a child.

Run up to the green chair. Whoever gets there first can have cake.

Let them fight. Boys will be boys.

Why are you making trouble? That's a good school. Be grateful for the lesson.

He kept his mirrored aviators on as they disembarked, but the blinding white walls of the villa still hurt his eyes. His first breath of island air propelled him back in time, provoking an old, sick tension in his gut that warned him he would disappoint no matter what he did or how hard he tried.

The sprawling, three-story building had been kept well, but looked smaller than he remembered. Had there always been only six steps up to the back door? Why had it always felt like a full flight to the gallows?

"Ready?" Kiara asked beside him.

He had bought her a new dress and yes, it had been a means of stamping his possession on her, but he had wanted to see her in a brighter color. The chartreuse green accentuated her dark eyes and made her skin glow.

Maybe it was all the sex. Few women matched his appetite, but after they'd exhausted each other into a deep sleep, she had turned to him early this morning, hands sliding without hesitation beneath the sheets to wake him.

"Don't gloat," she had pleaded.

His mouth had quickly been too busy for that and he

was too irritated with himself for giving in and coming here to do anything of the kind now.

"Being here doesn't require plucking up courage," he said flatly. "It's more about suppressing the urge to vomit."

"That's not what I meant. Are you ready for—"

The door opened and a woman with a toddler in her arms said, "We heard the helicopter."

"Mummy!" Aurelia launched herself at Kiara. "I mitt you!"

"Oh, lovey." Kiara caught the sprite and hugged her tight, swiveling back and forth as she did. "I missed you, too."

Val wasn't ready. Seeing Aurelia on screen hadn't prepared him for the aura of sheer joy that seemed to radiate off her as she pulled back, tiny arms and legs clinging to Kiara while they exchanged a peck.

"I'll keep her with me," Kiara said to the woman Val realized was the nanny. "You can finish packing."

The young woman nodded and disappeared.

"Where did you go?" Aurelia asked, still on Kiara's hip.

"Remember I said Auntie Scarlett was having her baby? He's called Locke."

"I want to see him."

"She said she would send me a picture later. Right now I want you to meet someone else. This is—"

Her mouth hung open as they both seemed to realize that they hadn't discussed how she would introduce him to their daughter.

"Papà," Val said, feeling as though the ground shifted beneath him.

Kiara's smile took a split second to cement itself, but then she said, "We're going with Papà to his house."

Aurelia looked at him, one arm still firmly curled around her mother's neck as she decided what she thought of him.

For his part, Val was absorbing an instinctual sense of *mine*. Not ownership, but a primordial recognition he'd never experienced before. It was probably what he should have felt toward his father or mother—a sense of kinship or being alike. He had never experienced it so strongly with them, but when he looked at Aurelia, for the first time in his life, he knew she was a part of some abstract collective they both belonged to. She was *his*.

"I have to pack some things from my studio," Kiara said to Aurelia. "Would you like to show Papà your slide?"

Aurelia nodded and they went through the house to the side door. Kiara disappeared into the old guest bungalow, leaving the door open. Val took note of Aurelia's climbing gym and empty wading pool, the miniature picnic table and the cat that appeared and rubbed against his leg.

Niko hadn't provided anything like this for him and Javiero. Val's earliest memories involved kicking a ball at each other or learning to swim in the cold waves of the sea because learning in a pool was "soft." They'd had chores in the vineyard, raking and gathering twigs, and had listened to endless droning lectures on how they would inherit all of this and needed to know how to manage it from the bottom up.

Every conversation with Niko had been one way and about one topic—the future and what he expected of them. There had been no sense of them being good enough as they were. Niko hadn't even been mindful of the fact they were children. He hadn't been present in a meaningful way—

Neither was he, Val realized with a snap of his head. The climbing gym was empty. Aurelia was gone.

"Aurelia. No!"

The barreling shout was so loud and imperious, it arrested Kiara's heart. She dropped what she was doing and ran out to see Val running toward the pool.

The gate was open and Aurelia stood there paralyzed. When she saw Kiara, she let out a wail and lifted her arms, running toward her and tripping onto the grass as she came off the paving stones.

Kiara hurried forward and picked up her screaming toddler while Aurelia clung to her with all her wee might.

"You're fine. Settle down," Kiara murmured, rubbing her back. "You know you're not allowed in the pool without a grown-up." Kiara's own heart was pounding. As far as she'd known, Aurelia still couldn't reach the latch. She'd either grown in the past two days or the pool boy had been sloppy about closing it properly.

"I took my eyes off her for *one second*," Val muttered as he came up to them, emanating umbrage.

Kiara tried to calm Aurelia, but it took effort to keep her agitation from her voice. "Listen, baby. Papà thought you were going to get hurt. He didn't mean to scare you." She sent him a pointed glance.

"That went both ways," he retorted sharply.

"Fair enough, but maybe dial back the volume to an age-appropriate two. You scared *me*, yelling like that."

His mouth flattened as he looked at Aurelia, who was

keeping her face firmly turned from his, still bawling her heart out, tiny body quivering. Remorse creased his expression along with lingering concern. "My heart completely stopped."

"Welcome to being a parent."

He jolted at that and watched her continue rubbing Aurelia's back as she wound down to sniffles.

"We're working on our apology skills," Kiara told Val and tucked her chin to address her daughter. "Would you like to tell Papà you're sorry for giving him a fright?"

"No, Mummy." She began to sob again, this time more pitifully.

"Aurelia, I'm sorry," Val said quietly and sincerely. His hand came up as though he wanted to touch her, but he hesitated at the last second and let it drop back to his side. "I shouldn't have yelled. I was afraid you were going to fall in the water. I may yell again if I'm afraid for you, but I'm not angry. I promise I will never, *ever* hurt you. Please don't be afraid of me."

Kiara was pretty sure Val had never apologized to anyone. Ever. She melted from the inside out, limbs going so weak she could barely hold on to her daughter.

"Do you have something you want to say to Papà?" She prodded Aurelia in a husky voice.

"I'm torry," Aurelia said, lifting her heartbroken, tear-tracked face.

As naturally as if she'd been doing it from the moment she had arrived on this earth, she tipped out of Kiara's arms and went to her father for a make-up cuddle.

He caught her with an audible inhale of surprise and then released a shaken exhale.

Kiara's defenses crumbled to nothing then, as she

watched the impact of Aurelia's freely offered love hit Val like a meteorite. The glimmer of something flashed and shattered in his eyes before he closed them, yet he failed to hide his emotions as he cradled her tiny form against his chest. He hung his head over her, and his brow pulled with torment, as though he had indeed rescued Aurelia from the bottom of the pool.

Or she had rescued him.

Kiara pressed a hand to her chest, trying to keep her heart from breaking through her rib cage, while Aurelia let her head settle on Val's shoulder and stuck two fingers in her mouth. Tears still stood on her cheeks as she blinked at her mother, but her trust in her father had been secured.

Eight hours later Val removed Kiara's charcoal sketch from where it hung between the pair of tall, double doors that led onto the master suite's balcony. He didn't glance out at his nonstop view of Lake Como or down to where the architect and his team were discussing retaining walls and rooflines.

His palms briefly felt the dig of the sleek chrome edges as his hands tightened on the frame, but he didn't allow himself to get lost in reminiscence. He moved it to a high shelf in his walk-in closet and brushed his hands together, angry with himself for feeling compelled to hide that he'd not only kept her sketch, he'd also had it matted, framed and mounted in his bedroom.

It seemed a greater weakness to let Kiara see it, though. And he was already reeling under the punch that had been Aurelia. He'd overreacted on the island, he knew that, but in the moment of realizing she'd slipped away into the pool area, he'd been utterly terrified. Convinced he wouldn't reach her before she drowned.

She might have been gone before he'd felt the weight of her head on his shoulder. Before he'd allowed her to crawl on him like a kitten as they traveled, showing him her handful of books and favorite toys. She would have been gone before she'd clung to his finger as she jumped the stepping stones down to the lower terrace so Kiara could approve the site for her new studio. Gone before he'd known that she was bright and curious and stubborn and had a giggle that filled his heart with joy.

He had known she could become a vulnerability for him, but he hadn't *known*.

She wasn't an exposed flank; she was an offered throat. He couldn't bear it. He most especially resented that Kiara knew what was happening to him. A dewy smile appeared on her face every time Aurelia said *Papà* in her high, musical voice.

"Oh...um—" Kiara walked in and came up short as she saw him hovering in the middle of the room. "I was looking for my things. The maid said this was my room."

A mad craving leaped in his blood at the sight of her. It was another weakness, born in a single night of losing himself with her, and it further undermined his sense of self and autonomy.

"This is our room. Our bed," he acknowledged with a nod toward the wide mattress, liking the flush of awareness that stained her cheeks. He needed the surge of power that filled him as he saw he could turn her on with a careless few words the same way she could light his fires just by appearing in front of him.

"It's not a his and hers...?" She warily looked for a

connecting door in the expansive room, but there was only the door into the bathroom and the one into the closet. Presently, the room had a cozy sitting area and a desk, but he expected there would be some changes to balance the masculine decor with some feminine touches.

"I bought this villa after the divorce and didn't expect to marry again," he explained.

Her little frown of consternation eased slightly. Perhaps she'd been bothered by the idea of sleeping in his ex-wife's bed.

"Well, I just came to get changed." She plucked at the shoulder of her dress where Aurelia looked to have cried herself to sleep.

He waved at the closet.

Kiara hesitated, then closed the bedroom door and stayed near it.

"I'm sorry about the meltdown." She released an exasperated breath that lifted a corkscrew of hair out of her eyes. "Tantrums are fairly normal at her age, but she doesn't usually go nuclear like that. I think it was a combination of missing me last night and all the new faces today." Aurelia had screamed bloody murder when Kiara had tried to hand her off to the nanny for her nap. "She'll probably be out of sorts until we find our routine here."

She eyed him warily, perhaps expecting an indictment on her inability to discipline their daughter, but the kickup hadn't fazed him.

"I've seen far worse displays from my mother over far less."

Kiara gave a short laugh, but he was completely serious. She sobered.

"Well, I'm glad you don't think less of her for it. She's only little and still figuring things out." And there was that starry look again, lips curving into an emotive smile.

She wanted another glimpse of the man whose armor had been breached and he refused to give it to her, hardening against her melting look.

Her gaze lowered and her lashes fluttered with brief confusion.

"I'm a little out of sorts myself," she confessed, clutching her elbows, flashing him an upward look. "This must feel like an invasion of your space."

He shrugged it off. "As a child, I had a lot of surprises thrust upon me. I learned to adapt very quickly."

"Witness the installation of your child and her mother in your home barely twenty-four hours after learning about her."

Plus, two nannies and a *cat*.

"I prefer to act, not react," he said truthfully, even though he was reacting to her against his will as she moved cautiously into the room, trailing her fingers across the smooth polish on the desk and picking up a stray bottle of his sandalwood cologne for a sniff.

"I don't know what I expected, but your home is very beautiful." She glanced at the filmy dark blue of the curtain clasped back with a silver cuff. "Airy and full of textures and light."

"Mother likes a project. Of her many faults, taste is not one of them."

"I'll be sure to compliment her when I see her."

"You won't," he assured her. "I'm leaving her in time-out until she's learned her lesson about keeping things from me."

Kiara's expression grew somber. She set the bottle back on its shelf.

"And me? Am I to be punished for keeping Aurelia from you?"

"Our marriage is very much two birds with one stone." He discovered he wasn't joking about that, either. He resented her for doing this to him. Not so much the hiding of his child, but the giving him one. He could stand that his life was changing. He couldn't stand that *he* was changing. That wasn't Aurelia's fault, but Kiara knew what she was doing to him, provoking things in him. *Feelings.*

A brief wrinkle of hurt pinched her brow and he braced himself for the inevitable refusal to marry him.

She surprised him by asking with quiet dignity, "Do you know what I find striking about you and me? That we're both determined to be the thing we hate most about ourselves. After my mother died, I didn't matter to anyone. I tried to fit in, but I was a square peg in every cliquey circle. The subtle rejections became too much for me. I decided friends were overrated and took introversion to its furthest degree. It was lonely, but it was safe. So there's a part of me that prefers you to hate me and block me out. Then I can tell myself that trying to have a relationship with you is futile. I can refuse to marry you and retreat behind my walls. While you want me to believe that tying myself to you is a life sentence because you're such a terrible man."

"I'm not a good one," he scoffed.

"Why not?" She cocked her head. "I mean, I understand that other people told you that you weren't. And that you were angry with Niko and did whatever you thought you had to, to cut ties with him. But why is bitter misery such a comfortable place for either of us? I have to believe you have redeeming qualities, Val, otherwise, why am I here? And you have to believe I feel genuine remorse and forgive me for keeping Aurelia a secret. Otherwise, we have no hope, and a life without hope is a very dark place."

Blows and insults and disparagement he could take. Her incisive honesty, however, peeled layers off him, leaving him raw and exposed. He couldn't bear it and reached for the quickest, easiest means of turning the tables on her.

"I warned you against swimming with sea monsters."

He ambled across to her, watching her eyes widen as he did. The glimmer of misplaced faith in her gaze dimmed to apprehension. Some distant, misguided part of himself wanted to preserve that hopeful gleam as badly as he wanted to dispel it.

He cupped the side of her throat and felt her swallow.

"I will be gentle with our daughter because she is a child, but whatever tenderness you think is inside me is imaginary. I never forgive people who wrong me." He scraped his thumb across her bottom lip to pull it free from the wary catch of her teeth. "I never trust them again."

"So you'll—what? Get revenge by making hate to me, not love?" she asked shakily, color rising in reaction to his touch.

"That would imply I have strong feelings for you." He would squelch such things before they sprouted. "No, you matter to me only insofar as it gives me incredible pleasure to watch you surrender to passion. So I'll exact that sort of compensation from you again and again, because I like it. But I will never offer you a piece of my soul."

"And if I say no to that?" Beneath his palm, her carotid artery was a rapid tattoo.

"Can you?" he chided, allowing his gaze to travel down to where her breasts were quivering as she panted in growing arousal.

He needed that. Needed to see that she was powerless against this force of lust between them because its grip on him was so inexorable, he could hardly breathe.

He brought his free hand up and rippled his knuckles across the point of her nipple where it strained against the cup of her bra and the fabric of her dress. Lightly, lightly, so the only sound was the faint brush of skin on linen. A straining silence that stretched and stretched as he moved his fingers back and forth, until she made a small noise and clasped his wrist, stopping his teasing caress.

"That's—" A small sob escaped her.

"Too much?" he asked, dropping his hand to weigh heavily on her hip. "Or not enough?"

She clenched her eyes shut in sensual struggle.

"Come here, little mermaid," he coaxed mockingly. "Let the monster take a bite."

With a choke of capitulation, she moved forward to press against him.

He did bite her. He gently grazed his smiling teeth against the side of her neck until she trembled and arched and sighed. Then he showed her *exactly* how much penance he could wring out of her.

As retribution went, his was all the more powerful for its thrilling, torturous highs and her soaring abandonment of self. Val kissed her until she could barely stand, then he made her stand there before him anyway, skirt bunched around her waist, wrists pinned in one of his strong hands behind her back while he lowered her panties only enough to taste her until she whimpered.

Then he knelt her on the sofa cushions and stood behind her, thrusting lazily into her while she grasped at the slippery, striped silk. He brought her to such a peak, she didn't care if people heard her pleasured cries across the lake.

He took her to the bed, stripped her and licked every inch of her, until she was nothing but one throbbing nerve ending, then he entered her again, made her come again, strong arms tucked behind her knees. Still, he wasn't finished. He tumbled her across the bed until he was sitting on the edge and she was in his lap.

Oh, he pretended to love her then. He soothed and caressed and teased and incited until she was writhing. And all the while, the stiff thickness of him filled her. Each twist and arch of her body was stifled by strong arms as he fought his own release while provoking her to the very limits of her endurance of pleasure.

Only when she was running mindless fingers through his hair moaning, "Please, Val, please," through swollen lips that clung to his did he shift her onto her back again and thrust steadily into her, keeping her on that acute point of unbearable arousal.

"Soon, *bella*," he crooned, body shaking with exertion and the strain of maintaining his control. "When I say. Not before."

"I can't, I can't," she moaned, so close she was dying. She wanted so badly to let climax overtake her, but she fought it. For him. Because he wished it.

"Now," he growled with a plunge of his hips.

The world went supernova. Her vision turned white, her scream silent, her only thought *yes* as orgasm exploded through her. Shock wave after shock wave of intense pleasure was made all the more exquisite for the pulsing heat within her and the ragged call of her name in Val's triumphant voice.

Kiara slipped out of bed and into the shower while Val was dozing, half expecting him to join her. She wanted him to, even though he had pretty much destroyed her.

He left her to shower alone, however, and she heard his voice when she was drying off. She used the adjoining door from the bathroom into the closet and discovered clothing in her size, but none of it was familiar. Still wearing the black robe that smelled of him, she crept out to find him on the balcony sharing cheese and fruit with Aurelia, teaching her the Italian names for grape and orange and peach.

"See? I told you she would join us," he said as Kiara appeared.

"Hello, lovey," she greeted her daughter warmly, then held up the clothes in her hand and said to Val, "These aren't mine."

"They are," he confirmed.

Kiara looked at the sky blue top and the indigo skirt that were super cute, but a bolder statement than she usually made. "Where are the clothes I brought?"

"I told you how I felt about his things coming into my house." He avoided using Niko's name, glancing at Aurelia as though sensitive to how she might react if he mentioned the old man. "I won't ask Mousy here to give up her attachments. She'll grow out of most of them quickly enough, but *you* will wear what *I* provide."

If their daughter's tiny, listening ears and wide, curious eyes hadn't been trained on her, Kiara might have reacted more reflexively—and heatedly—but Aurelia's presence forced her to take a breath and mentally count to ten.

She pinned a smile on her face and used a light tone but made sarcastic use of his own words. "I wanted to give you the gift of abiding by your wishes."

He narrowed his eyes.

"That's why I only brought clothes I'd bought with my own money," she continued with false cheer. "I have a little income from a handful of prints and other early works. It's not extravagant, but neither are my tastes. Which means I don't have to rely on anyone's support. Not even yours."

"But I want you to rely on me," he said, adopting a similar tone of friendly conversation to hide the fact they were engaged in an epic power struggle.

"I know what you want."

To consume her.

That had been obvious in the way he'd made love to her. She could withstand that in bed, barely, but she wouldn't let him take every shred of independence she possessed. It had been too hard won.

"I am a fashion mogul, Kiara," he said as though explaining it to a child. "That means I am under constant scrutiny for the way I look. My wife must be as much a brand ambassador as I am." He wore a plain white T-shirt over a pair of wrinkled, linen pants, casually elegant in a way she never could be.

Her stomach tightened.

"You do realize the industry will lose its collective mind if we marry? I said *if*!" she added quickly when a slow smile began to form on his lips. "I am the opposite of iconic. You couldn't have picked a worse person if your reputation is important to you."

"I think I've made it abundantly clear that I never do as I'm told. If I want my wife to have curves, then curves she shall have. The fashion world will adjust accordingly."

Dear God, if she could have a tenth of his confidence. She looked at the clothes she held.

"Klaus is my lead designer. A genius. I had him drop everything and I want to see how he did with the little direction I gave him. He's sending a team to measure you properly, by the way."

"And I promise to be ever so polite when I explain things like this aren't *me*."

"How do you know if you haven't even tried them on? I'm surprised at you, Kiara. How would you feel if people dismissed your paintings without even looking at them?" Humor made his silver eyes gleam like chrome. He had her with that one and knew it.

She pressed her lips together, annoyed in the extreme as she flung around and went back to the closet, determined to hate this outfit.

Curse him and his designer. The cut somehow balanced her figure, so she looked taller and more evenly proportioned. There was something crisp and eye-catching in the color palette, too. Feminine without being frilly. Confident in her curves, authoritative, yet sensual.

There would be no fading into the wallpaper in clothes like this, though. She wasn't sure how she felt about that.

She returned to the balcony and Aurelia gasped. "Oh, Mummy, you're pretty!"

"Thank you, baby," she murmured, but Val's was the judgment she waited with held breath to hear.

She was doing it again, she realized as his critical eye traveled over her. She was trying to fit in, be something she wasn't, longing to earn acceptance that wouldn't come.

She hated herself then for being so needy. Still an orphan at her deepest level, yearning for a place. For love.

"I'll have Klaus remove this button." Val fingered the slit in the skirt, not even touching her, but setting her alight all the same. "It distracts from an otherwise perfect vision. Do you like it?"

His gaze came up to hers, absent of mockery, only lit with such admiration she could have fallen into his gaze like dropping through a looking glass into another world.

She tried for blasé, saying, "I wouldn't paint in it," but she did like it. Nothing felt constraining and the textures were nice. She liked that it made her feel pretty. She liked that he liked it.

Somehow, she would have to pull herself back from the brink of this chasm. Otherwise, she might allow him to take her over completely, the way he clearly intended to.

But she still obeyed his crooked finger and bent to touch her mouth to his, saying a husky *"Grazie..."* against his lips.

His taste swept through her, as irresistible as the man himself.

CHAPTER SIX

KIARA HAD KNOWN this period after Niko passed would be disruptive and she might not have as much time in her studio as she normally liked. But she hadn't counted on trying to turn a guest cottage into a makeshift studio between meetings with architects and clothing designers, decorators, and stoic lawyers who were drawing up a *marriage* contract.

She kept telling Val she wasn't ready to commit while he kept saying, "I'll be ready when you are."

Then he inevitably made love to her, showing her exactly what she would gain by becoming his wife.

She was desperately trying to retain her autonomy, trying to envision the place she would have in this world of his, but it was hard.

Her studio was usually the space that restored her. It was her sanctuary and the place where she meditated on her problems and made herself whole. The new one would take time to build, however, and Val insisted she go ahead with meetings about layout and materials and breaking ground even though she hadn't agreed to marry him.

What if she didn't? she kept wondering.

Wasted money didn't seem to faze him. He was having Klaus design her a wedding gown, too.

Perhaps Val thought if she was invested enough in her new studio, she would be unable to resist marrying him. What he didn't realize was that all of these meetings were getting between her and a return to painting. The fact she wasn't painting was putting her on edge in a way she hadn't experienced in years, not since right after Aurelia had been born and she'd been overwhelmed by her new responsibilities.

At least today Val had gone into Milan on errands. She had a feeling he was finalizing wedding arrangements, but she gratefully seized the opportunity to properly organize the bungalow into a space she could use. Then she was going to use it. She would spend a few hours with brushes and a canvas on her easel and finally decide whether to stay here with him or go back to the villa.

Oh, part of her longed to go back to the island where life was simple!

But she couldn't.

The way Aurelia was bonding with her father was everything Kiara had ever wanted for her. And Val was so patient with her, so gentle. He claimed to have no tenderness in him, but his hard features softened every time he saw her. He was turning into an amazing parent, learning the fine art of misdirection to avoid an outburst and watching their tot like a hawk while giving her space to roam and explore.

All of that was turning Kiara's heart inside out. She could see there was a good man inside him, but he only offered glimpses of him, refusing to let him fully reveal himself. She wanted to hate him for that guard of his, but she was too enthralled by the side of him he did let her see—the virile, generous lover. Being locked with him in sensual ecstasy gave her the sense of closeness and unity she'd longed for all her life. As though she'd found her match. The place she belonged.

But it was demoralizing to be so defenseless when he was always in control of everything from their love-making to the cadence of their days. He never seemed as rent from the world as she was by their physical encounters. He withdrew afterward without words of affection or fondness. He might compliment her and hold chairs and make endless requests of the staff on her behalf, but she was certain he would have done that for any woman who shared his bed.

Given the way he was withholding his heart, she knew she couldn't offer hers. It would only be trampled and destroyed, but it was a struggle every hour of every day. One she didn't know if she could withstand for a lifetime.

"Scusami..." A timid maid knocked on the open sliding door.

Kiara bit back a scream. She had expressly asked that she not be disturbed and realized that she would have to train the staff that when she said that, she meant it.

"Signora Casale has arrived to see you," the maid said.

Kiara's heart lurched. At least Aurelia was firmly ensconced upstairs. They'd had a lively morning in the pool, and she was pooped out, watching a show and having a snack with the nanny.

Kiara hadn't bothered with a shower, too anxious to get to work. She had ruthlessly sleeked her hair back into a ponytail, but the ends ballooned out in a cloud of frizz behind her head. She wore painting clothes of jeans chopped at the knee and a loose T-shirt.

She had an urge to run up and put on a decent day dress but decided against it. She doubted it was coincidence that Evelina had shown up the moment Val was out of the house. Kiara refused to give Evelina the impression she was intimidated—even though she absolutely was.

"What a lovely surprise," she lied as she entered the lounge to find Evelina hovering with a sour look on her face. "Shall we have tea on the terrace?"

Her potential mother-in-law wore six-inch heels, a pencil skirt and an air of malicious intent. She towered over Kiara as they walked outside.

"The house is beautiful. Your influence, Val tells me," Kiara said, trying on a compliment as they settled into an outdoor lounge around an unlit gas fire.

"Yes. I have so many excellent contacts eager to assist me at any time. Many of them are in Paris." Evelina crossed one graceful leg over the other. "I understand you have a little art show there next week."

The implication was obvious and it made Kiara's stomach turn over.

Kiara realized then how often she had ducked behind Niko or Scarlett in the past. *Tell me what to say*, she would often implore, even when she only faced a friendly business conversation with her agent. She was tempted to invoke Val's name as a shield but being used as a weapon was the reason Val was as cynical as he was. Besides, much as she wanted to believe he would have her back, she didn't know that for sure.

"I do. Shall I ask my agent to send you an invite?" She played dumb, as though she wasn't clear that she was being threatened in the most effective way. As if her palms weren't clammy and her throat wasn't aching with a stifled scream.

"That won't be necessary. I'm so well-known in those circles, I'm welcome wherever I wish to go. Many would say my appearance can make or break the success of a given evening. I'm prepared to speak to critics about you. It would be such a *shame* if they found your work wanting. Or failed to attend at all."

Kiara's throat closed and the backs of her eyes stung with angry, helpless tears. She fought the sensation. Hysteria wasn't an option. She racked her brain, barely able to form words, her jaw was clenched so hard.

"I wouldn't want you to feel a need to interfere." She saw a maid coming with the tea service and waved her away. "I presume this is about Niko's will. Please understand I had nothing to do with how he structured it."

"I'm not a stupid woman. I've been on my own since I was fifteen. I understand that a woman has to look out for herself and this—" she twirled a finger in the air "—was a very nice try. I'm impressed. But I have spoken to my lawyer and he agrees that Val is entitled to Niko's fortune. If you would like to relinquish all claim to it, I will see my way clear to ensuring your little show is well received."

Kiara was having trouble keeping down what little she'd eaten this morning. She knew for a fact that Evelina had a very shaky leg to stand on in making any claims against Niko's fortune, but the last thing she needed was to have her lifetime dream trampled by a battle royal.

"Val doesn't want Niko's money," she reminded quietly.

"Val doesn't know what he wants," Evelina threw back. "It most certainly isn't *you*. You're not marrying him."

"I haven't agreed to," Kiara said, adding tartly, "He brings a lot of baggage."

"You—" Evelina gathered herself the way a lightning strike might gather ions, preparing to crack the earth open. "I will *destroy* you."

Angry emotion was driving color into the skin beneath the powder of Evelina's makeup. Kiara could read it as clearly as she knew when Aurelia was building toward a tantrum.

Aurelia lost her self-control when she had no control. When Mummy said no to something she wanted.

Kiara's mind was racing through all of her options, catching on the fact that she wasn't without resources or options. She actually had something Evelina wanted that she could give up. It would cost her, but...

"I may have a solution." Kiara held up a shaking hand. "Val doesn't want me to accept the allowance I've been granted from Niko's estate. He wants to support us himself. I had a mind to put that money into real estate as an investment for Aurelia. I could be persuaded to let you choose that property and occupy the house at no cost to you. It's quite a generous amount." She told her how much.

Evelina's eyes were still flashing with acrimony, but her mouth trembled as she pinned it closed, trying to calculate how to play this.

"That's *if* I marry him. I haven't agreed," Kiara said quickly. "I can leave here and live on that myself. You and I can argue over Niko's money until the cows come home. It will be expensive and, frankly, I would think you must be tired of that fight by now."

"You underestimate me," Evelina assured her.

"Well, make up your mind however it suits you, but

my offer stands. Of course, if I marry Val and our marriage falls apart—" Kiara licked her dry lips "—I will be forced to evict you so I could live there with Aurelia."

"You're buying my support of your marriage," Evelina stated bluntly. "Bribing me to keep my nose out of it."

"I see it as a smart investment in my daughter's future." She was shaking inside, skin running hot and cold.

"You *have* learned well at Niko's knee. Are you going to tell Val about this arrangement?"

"Yes." She couldn't imagine keeping something like this from him. "If you're worried he'll cut off the allowance he gives you, I'll do my best to persuade him to continue it."

Evelina didn't know whether to trust her; Kiara could see it. She wanted to sigh with futility. These people were *so* broken. Instead, she smiled as gently as she would at Aurelia when she was at her most truculent.

"You are my daughter's only grandparent. She wouldn't exist if you and Niko hadn't made Val. I think it's right and fair that you live comfortably. Perhaps, when the time is right, you'll introduce Aurelia to the best boutiques in Paris, since that is definitely not my forte. What do you say? Do we have a deal?"

Val was waiting to announce the existence of his daughter until he and Kiara were married—and they would marry. Aurelia's future and well-being were too important to risk. Any misgivings Kiara had could be worked out after the fact.

Her hesitation was bothering him, though. Especially because it was accompanied by a withdrawal that shouldn't have gotten under his skin but did.

At night she was wholly his, completely abandoned to the pleasure they gave each other. Then she would spend the day pulling back in little ways. If she happened to be laughing or playing with Aurelia, her mood would dampen when he entered the room. Over a meal, she would grow animated as she spoke, then cool unexpectedly, as though regretting she had allowed herself to warm to him. She was forever switching the focus of a conversation from herself to their daughter, avoiding his attempts to learn more about her.

Outright challenge he could handle, but she went along with most of his dictates unless they concerned Aurelia. Then she would put forth an argument with calm logic. He would only realize she'd been on the defensive when her shoulders fell after winning him over to her way of thinking.

He didn't like a quiet enemy that kept him guessing.

He didn't want to think of her as an enemy at all. He was too enthralled with her.

He dragged her physically close every chance he got. Stripped her naked so there were no barriers between them, insatiable for her and their particular brand of madness. *Connection.* This thing between them was reaching the point of addiction, and he'd finally left her sleeping this morning just to prove he could.

He drove to Milan, determined to be his old self and put in a long day—despite the fact he would ensure the first of the banns were posted. After that, news of his engagement would begin making headlines across the usual gossip sites, drawing out the paparazzi.

It was a dirty move, putting that kind of pressure

on her. It was exactly the sort of ruthless tactic he was known for, so he wasn't sure why it ruffled his conscience. This was who he *was*.

He was a cutthroat corporate raider completely lacking in empathy or compassion. That was why he was browsing for toys himself, wandering store aisles, picking up dolls that annoyed him because they were so sexualized. He gathered crafts instead, and puzzles, and building blocks, and a child-safe baby drill with plastic pieces that would hurt like hell to step on, but gender expectations could go to hell. Aurelia could be whoever she wanted to be.

He never gave gifts, not thoughtful ones, only corporate nonsense. As for receiving them, aside from the warehouses of free samples that arrived daily, with pleas for him to feature them in one of his many magazines, he had only received one real gift in his lifetime—and he'd basically stolen it. Kiara's sketch.

The blank space on his bedroom wall was only obvious to him, but it made him uneasy each time he looked for the sketch and didn't see it. It was similar to looking for the laughing woman who'd drawn it and finding only the subdued, unreadable expression on Kiara's beautiful face.

Maybe he was being too hard on her, he thought as he drove home—early, hoping to catch her while Aurelia was down for her afternoon nap. Maybe Kiara was right. Maybe he did have to forgive her for colluding with his father. Maybe then she wouldn't be so apprehensive about marrying him.

Then he heard that she'd entertained a visitor while he'd been out. The identity of that visitor was like blood in the water to a shark.

* * *

Kiara was still shaken, still questioning whether she'd made the right choice.

She had. For Aurelia. She knew that much. But this situation was testing her more severely than anything else in her life. Her own needs were being pitted against her daughter's, and Kiara still wasn't sure whether she was winning, losing or falling for a con.

Because she was still here in Italy, not on a plane back to Greece and, after that conversation with Evelina, she had pretty much thrown away her chance to make an escape.

She didn't even *like* confrontation, let alone playing hardball with a pro. Her hands were still shaking as she finally set up her easel.

These trembles were promising a very poor result when she got a brush in her hand, but she was fixated now. If she could just paint something—not even with serious intent, more like journaling—she would find her equilibrium and be okay. She would be able to face this new life she had accidentally embarked upon.

"You met with my mother today?"

The growl of Val's voice was so unexpected and lethal, she almost knocked over her easel.

"You're home," she said dumbly, whirling to the open door.

"Surprised?" He strode in, flicking the sliding door closed behind him with a thud that held such aggression she frowned. "Oh, don't even *think* of locking *me* out of your studio."

Her heart was skinned and overworked from all the conflicts and hard conversations and massive changes she'd suffered since the doctor had pronounced Niko "gone." Now it flip-flopped and shrank and quavered at the way he loomed over her.

This was the man she had backed herself into marrying?

"I didn't know what to do except offer her tea," she said stiffly, moving to find a prepared canvas.

"Tea," he scoffed.

"Was I supposed to slam the door in her face?"

"Yes."

"I wish I had," she blurted, managing to set the canvas and pry her tense fingers off it without throwing it across the room. "It wasn't exactly a 'welcome to the family' visit." More like a viper popping out of a harmless-looking hatbox.

"Did she see Aurelia?" His tone crackled with danger.

"No." Kiara crossed her arms defensively, but shot her shoulders back, willing to die on the hill of making that decision, not that Evelina had *asked* to meet her granddaughter.

A fraction of Val's enmity receded, but he still glowered with accusation. "What did you two cook up, then? Because she's not here. That means she got what she wanted. Don't even try to tell me you're leaving," he warned.

Kiara's stomach was still full of gravel over the entire thing, but now her blood hit full boil at the way he was treating her like she was some sort of criminal. Like she'd orchestrated the meeting. She'd been the victim. Ambushed!

"She *wanted* to destroy my show." Her voice cracked as she relived hearing that threat. Her whole body was plunged back into the fight or flight that had gripped her while she had talked herself out of a hostage situation.

"You know I will undo any damage she attempts," Val said on a growl.

"No, I don't know that!" she cried on a choke of humorless laughter. "Every time I turn around, you're looking for a new way to punish me for relying on your father. Losing my show would be the ultimate revenge and probably make you very happy. So no, Val. I fixed it myself. Thanks anyway."

His head went back, and he narrowed his eyes. "How?"

"I bought her off with Niko's money, of course! I told her you didn't want me to touch my living allowance, but I thought it should be invested for Aurelia's future. I said that if she found a suitable property that would appreciate over time, I would direct those funds into purchasing a home for her and she could have the use of it for her lifetime."

His eyebrows climbed into his hairline.

"Then I told her that if our marriage broke down for any reason, like an interfering mother-in-law, I'd have to evict her so Aurelia and I could use it, so she had better think long and hard in the future about which battles are important to her." Her throat was still scorched by all the adrenaline that had coursed through her. It was still there, searing her limbs and making her heart run so fast she was exhausted.

Val swore. Snorted and spoke with what sounded like reluctant admiration. "You're a quick study. Well-done."

She had been fighting for her very existence, but okay. Sure. *Scoff away.*

She turned to find her smock.

Val was still bristling that his mother had had the gall to show up uninvited and that Kiara had let her in.

Even more infuriating was the fact she had caught Kiara alone. That told him he had a mole in his home. Heads would roll over that, but he wasn't finished with Kiara.

Losing my show would be the ultimate revenge.

He preferred to be angry with her. It was easier to hold her at a distance when he had that resentment between them, but surely she knew he would shield her against real harm of any kind? If she didn't believe that, it made her still being here a profound statement, given the vile threat his mother had used to try running her off.

That surprising show of loyalty sawed holes in his defenses against her.

"Come here," he coaxed, wanting the feel of her to erase the gnawing ache in his chest.

"I thought I'd finally get some painting in." The enticing fit of her cutoff jeans over her round bottom and shapely thighs disappeared as she shrugged into what looked like an old lab coat bedecked in years of paint smears. She didn't look at him as she began to button it.

He crossed to still her hands.

"Come on, *bella*. Let's kiss and make up. I'll make it worth your while," he coaxed, stroking his thumbs across the backs of her hands, smiling at the way they trembled.

"Are we fighting? I thought this was our normal, where you blame me for your parents' actions and I put your daughter's needs ahead of my own." She pulled her hands from his and opened the buttons she'd closed, voice quavering as she continued. "But if you want to have sex, by all means, let's have sex. Why did I even engage in hand-to-hand combat with your mother if not to keep having sex with you?"

An anvil hit the pit of his gut. "If you don't want to have sex—"

"I always want to have sex!" she cried, throwing down her coat. "But I *need* to paint, Val. I haven't held a brush since before Niko died and it's killing me!"

"You're in here every day." Usually after Aurelia had gone to bed, before they sat down for their own dinner. "What have you been doing?" He glanced around at the cleared space where furniture had been removed, the stacks of blank canvases against the wall and the shelf where tins and trays of brushes and other supplies were arranged.

"Everything but painting," she said in a voice that was still strident. Her arms flailed helplessly. "I've been unpacking and organizing. Scrambling out sketches of how my paintings should be displayed at the show, answering emails about it. Do you know I had to write descriptions for each one? And that I have *revisions*? My artist's statement wasn't good enough, so I have to rewrite *that*. I paint because I don't know *how* to express myself in words."

She was shaking, eyes brimming with fresh tears.

"Kiara," he said soothingly.

"Don't you dare tell me to calm down," she warned with a raised finger. "This is not a tantrum. This is a breakdown." Her mouth was wobbling, and she used the inside of her wrist to wipe the tears off her cheeks. "I used to paint when Aurelia slept, but now it's all you. Sex and *this*." She circled her palm through the air. "The blame. The contempt for the choices I've made. The demand that I completely change my life while the one thing *I* want gets further away."

She clutched her chest as she sucked in a breath that

shuddered. Her wild gaze swung around the room as though she didn't know where she was.

"If this is what you want, if your punishment is to push me to the point of breaking, you're there, Val. I am going to snap in half if I can't paint. Then I won't be me anymore. I'll be like you and your mother. A damaged human being incapable of love. Sorry, Aurelia, but Mummy is one more casualty of Niko's war."

Her last words struck like a sledgehammer, reverberating through him.

He did want to tell her to calm down. He wanted to take her by the arms and remind her he was building her a studio, wasn't he? Of course he wanted her to paint. He wasn't *a damaged human being*. He was matured by experience to an enlightened one.

"Why are you still dressed?" she added caustically, lashes damp. "Work your magic. Make me forget I ever wanted this," she choked.

He consciously fought the jerky reflex trying to lift his arms to reach for her. Everything in him wanted to coil his arms around her and hold her tight until her shaking stopped. To kiss away those tears that tracked down her face. Until this grim darkness that had taken hold of her eased back into the warm light he hadn't appreciated until it had been eclipsed.

He wanted to blame his mother for this. A visit with her left anyone full of poison and spewing venom, but this wasn't all Evelina. This was him trying so hard to control what was happening between them, he was crushing the spirit out of Kiara.

He knew what he had to do, and it went against everything in him. He *never* walked away from a fight.

But if he didn't leave her now, he would make love to her until she was too weak to lift a finger.

And she wouldn't forgive him for it. He knew that in his soul. Something would be damaged between them that would never be repaired.

"I'll eat with Aurelia and put her to bed this evening. Stay in here as long as you like."

Walking out and closing the door on her stunned expression was the hardest thing he'd done in a long, long while. The angry bastard in him balked, told him to get back in there and assert his will.

But something else flickered inside him, an ember of heat he couldn't name, it was so old and forgotten. Hope? Caring? It retained some heat, whatever it was. Just enough to ease the frigid cold that encased his heart.

It was after midnight when Kiara slid into bed.

She was exhausted, but alert. Buzzing with excitement. *Revived.*

She had steeped herself in the scent of her linen canvas and the wood stretchers and the nutty smell of the oil paints. She had danced her brush into color, conducted a symphony, tapped it into solvent, then swirled and done it again. She had dazzled herself with colors and lost herself in a world where hurtful people couldn't touch her. Where her emotions ran free, rather than trying to fit into ever-shrinking boxes.

She couldn't recall when she'd last painted like that, in a flurry from blank canvas to completion. Not that the finished product was anything worth showing off, but it would forever be a favorite for its claiming of this new world and thus the reclaiming of herself.

And now she was overwhelmed with gratitude toward Val for giving her that. Each time she had come up for air and thought of Aurelia, she had remembered she was with her father. Leaving her in his care was different than leaving her to the nannies. Giving Val and Aurelia time to bond was as important as the time she spent alone with their daughter.

He had even sent over a tray of finger foods that she'd picked at while she painted.

Was he awake? She slithered closer, heart off center as she remembered her eruption of fury. He could have dismissed her or tried to make her talk out her frustrations and hurts and anxiety, but he hadn't. He'd let her work through it in her own way. In the way that made sense to her.

She found warm naked skin. His abdomen tightened as she smoothed her hand across the firm muscles and the light trail of hair. His breath hissed.

He didn't say anything, though, and neither did she. She only stretched herself alongside him with a sigh of homecoming. She was as naked as he was, her nightgown never lasting long, but tonight she was the instigator. She brushed her mouth across his once as she pressed over him, then skated her parted lips down his throat and across his shoulders.

His strong hands clasped her and pulled her fully onto him. His legs parted for hers and she lifted slightly to allow his thickening flesh room to grow against her stomach. She used her whole body to caress him, loving the feel of his strength, the scent on his skin, the possessive, inciting roam of his hands over her back and butt and the sides of her breasts.

Desire ran like honey in her and she poured it over

him. Poured herself over him along with all the uplifting, invigorating energy she had soaked up while creating.

Down, down she went, dislodging the sheet as she found the steely shape that thrilled her. Here was the essence of him, salty and musky and fierce. She anointed and played her tongue across his erotic shape, took him into her mouth and pulled, bobbing her head in the rhythm she knew he liked.

He snarled and spread his legs, tangled his fingers in her hair, pulling her away when he was about to lose control. Dragging her up, he kissed her and rolled her beneath his weight, thrust his straining flesh into her.

They groaned and gasped and hissed and writhed. It was so good she thought she might die, but it was different. He was with her in this place where reality ceased to exist. This was how it had been that night in Venice—two lost souls finding one another in the dark and celebrating the end to solitude.

She closed her ankles behind his back, and his fingers bit so hard into her bottom, he would leave bruises on her cheeks. She didn't care. She only needed him deeper. Within her. Part of her, the way she was becoming a part of him.

Culmination hit them at the same time, anguish and ecstasy, loss and discovery. An ending, but also a beginning.

Val held her all night, a fact Kiara only became aware of when he carefully extricated from her as morning light sliced through the blinds.

She blinked in confusion as he walked out of the closet seconds after he'd walked in, still naked, but with something in his hands. It was the size of a sofa cushion, but flat and shiny. He walked across to hang it on the wall, his movements sure in the half light.

She rolled over to watch, puzzled. There was no need for a hook to be screwed into the wall. He was replacing something.

She came up on an elbow, then sat up and blinked harder. She pinched her arm to ensure she wasn't dreaming.

"Don't say a word," he said quietly, touching a corner to straighten it. "Not one word."

She had to bite her lips because how? *Why?*

She stared at it like an old friend, one that filled her with a rush of nostalgic joy. She was staring so hard at it, lost in the memory of that night, she didn't realize Val had moved until he was sitting beside her on the bed, showing her a velvet box.

"I was supposed to do this over dinner last night."

Oh, God.

She started to shrink into her shoulders, but he made a dismissive noise.

"That's not a scold. I've worked with enough creatives to appreciate their temperament and know their value. I want to preserve the artist in you, Kiara," he said sincerely. "Your ability to make beauty out of nothing, to find it where none exists, is a gift." He smoothed his hand over what had to be wild hair and cupped her cheek, caressing her skin briefly with his thumb. "And after last night, I see there are advantages to giving you time to find yourself."

The dry remark was rife with self-deprecation, but teasing, too, reminding her how greedy and assertive she'd been when she'd come to bed.

She sat there boiling in self-consciousness while he leaned forward and stole a lingering kiss that relit barely banked flames between them.

Before they let passion take over, however, he drew back and opened the velvet box.

"Oh, my God."

"Val is fine," he corrected with such obscene arrogance, she would have laughed, but she was too spellbound by the three rings.

The engagement ring was a huge princess-cut diamond that picked up the narrow rays of golden sunlight. The platinum band was set with smaller diamonds interspersed with—

"Onyx?" she guessed.

"Black diamonds. Hard and dark as my heart."

He had certainly done his best to convince her of that, but he had also revealed that particular organ had flecks of gold.

She plucked out the bigger band and let it swallow her finger. "You'll wear this?"

"If you'll marry me, yes. Will you, Kiara?"

She went into a kind of free fall.

Maybe he even knew what he was doing, this wicked, crafty man. He had been trying to convince her she didn't have a choice, that she had to marry him for Aurelia's sake. She had believed it, too. But she did have a choice. And she had a suspicion it was as important to him that she *choose* him as it was for her to make this decision of her own free will.

She considered that they had a child together and an intimate relationship that showed no signs of wearing off. He respected her art and *he had kept her sketch*. He had had the charcoal fixed and framed with all the care given to the work of an Old World master.

Most important, she realized with a sharp pang in her chest as if her heart ached with yearning, she was falling for him. He might yet disappoint her. In fact, she was sure he would break her heart, probably more than once.

But that foolish heart of hers longed to go to him anyway, regardless of what her head told it.

"I will," she said huskily.

Triumph flashed in his gaze before his mouth came down on hers. She thought she heard the little box hit the floor beside the bed. The larger ring definitely fell off her finger into the sheets, but he was pressing her into the mattress and she was melting in welcome beneath him.

A faint ding pulled his head up.

She twisted a look to the night table where she left her phone each night.

"Aurelia is probably asking for you," he said.

"How was she last night?" She left her hands twined around his neck, caressing the hint of stubble she found in the hollow at the base of his skull.

"If I say fine will you dismiss the bribery charges?" He looked to his own night table. "That reminds me, I have to find a zoo with elephants. We have a date today."

To say Val softened in the ensuing days would be an overstatement, but the thorns in his personality weren't quite as pointed and sharp, at least where Kiara was concerned. He did ruthlessly fire the chef who had tipped off his mother that Kiara was alone that day.

The rest of the staff was still walking on eggshells a week later.

But someone named Consuela had appeared when they returned from the zoo. She helped Kiara rewrite her statement and descriptions. She also brought a photographer to their wedding, to witness the event and prepare their press release.

"We can organize a proper wedding for later in the year if you want one," Val said as they were waiting at the courthouse.

"Goodness, no. The fact I'm having my picture taken today is giving me anxiety." But maybe it was marrying this man.

Val wore a suit for the first time since they'd been together and dear God he ought to need a warning as a dangerous substance. Aside from his tie, which had shots of silver in it, he wore all black, tailored scrupulously to his frame. The jacket was tuxedo in style with satin lapels, but had a subtle pattern embossed into it, like a smoking jacket. It should have looked affected, but it was as carelessly stylish as he always was.

He'd *shaved* and oozed so much sex appeal, Kiara's knees were weak.

She had put her faith in Klaus, who had assured her he wouldn't be working for Val if he didn't have a better eye than his boss for texture, color, line and form.

Her dress was the height of simplicity, knee-length with drop shoulders in silk colored with the barest hint of lemon yellow. The color made her skin seem luminous and the diaphanous overskirt was generous enough to gather on her arm. It fluttered and trailed with her movements, making her feel like a princess.

When Val saw her, he didn't say anything for a long

moment. She thought he might have swallowed. Then he picked up her hand and slowly twirled her, saying, "Here she is. I knew she was in there." His smooth, freshly shaved cheek had brushed hers so he didn't ruin her makeup with a kiss.

It would have been a perfect day except for one thing—Scarlett wasn't here. She had gone directly to Spain with Javiero when she'd checked out of the hospital.

Kiara was trying not to take it personally that she was hearing so little from her friend. A new baby kept a mother busy. She knew that. And she didn't want to rock boats with Val by flaunting that particular friendship under his nose. She completely understood Scarlett's reluctance to do the same with Javiero, but she missed her.

She sent a photo of Aurelia in her flower girl dress and got back a photo of a sleeping Locke, wearing a onesie imprinted to look like a tuxedo.

Scarlett had texted.

We're there in spirit, which made her smile wistfully.

In every other way, her wedding was perfect. Brief, but intimate. The vows weren't sentimental, but when she spoke them, and heard Val's steady tone repeat them, Kiara felt the promise in them. She had thought the weight of his ring on her finger would feel heavy, but it was more of a touch point. A reassuring symbol of their linked lives that would be with her even when he wasn't.

When he bent his head to kiss her, a shower of sparkling light went through her, all the way to the soles of her feet. This was a real chance, a real beginning.

She hoped.

* * *

In lieu of a honeymoon, they flew to Paris a few days early. It was the opposite of romantic, despite being one of the most beautiful cities in the world. Kiara took meetings and was a bundle of nerves the whole time, only sleeping because she was exhausted by Val's attentive lovemaking.

Now that their marriage had been announced, the paparazzi was in full force. Their determination to get a photo of Aurelia bordered on criminal, and if one more person asked her about Val and how they'd met, Kiara thought she would scream.

The media interviews were pure hell, but Consuela, the goddess, had prepared her well for the most idiotic questions.

"Will your daughter follow her father and grandmother into modeling?"

"When she's old enough, she can decide for herself," Kiara murmured by rote.

Val would have said, *Over my dead body*, and Kiara felt the same, but boring answers to stupid questions helped bring the focus back to the more important ones, or so Consuela had assured her.

"Where did you learn to paint?"

"It's been a lifelong passion. I was studying art in Venice when I met Val three years ago." Kiara had been stumbling through the streets, drawing on impulse, visiting whichever museum or gallery had a free or discounted entrance fee, but Consuela had assured her no one needed to know that.

"That sounds romantic."

"It was," Kiara confirmed. Keep it simple. Tell them how to feel about it.

After the day his mother had visited, Val had been in contact with Kiara's agent. They'd restructured her show into a much more exclusive event. Most of her interviews had been conducted before a single painting had been shown to anyone. Today, hours before the official opening, her work had finally been unveiled for critics. Photographers were confined to a single room. Her more intimate portraits of Aurelia and a pregnant Scarlett remained hidden from view.

It was still a struggle to concentrate, especially because her new husband was among the handful of people wandering with slow, hollow steps through the gallery before the throngs—please let there be throngs—arrived. Or not. Maybe it would be safer if no one came. If the critics and collectors decided they hated her work, she wanted as few people as possible to witness her humiliation.

Her stomach was nothing but snakes and butterflies as they sat in the backseat of his car, returning to the hotel to get ready for tonight.

"You're folding in on yourself again, *bella*. I don't like it," he said quietly.

She shot him a look. "I'm nervous as hell."

"Why?"

"Why?" She choked out a humorless laugh. "What if they don't like it? All that work, all those years of *kidding* myself—"

He reached across and squeezed her hand, frowning when he felt how clammy and cold it was.

"You weren't kidding yourself. Do you want to know what I was thinking as I saw everything for the first time?"

"No," she lied in an anxious whisper, squeezing

his hand so hard, her nails were probably cutting into his skin.

"I was thinking that you made the right decision. I don't like it. I will always see it as a deal with the devil, but I've pulled some cold-blooded moves in my time for results that were far less meaningful. Your work is profound. Standing in front of each painting, I felt what you felt when you were painting it. Curiosity, frustration, joy. The one of Aurelia...?" He brought her hand to his mouth and kissed her knuckles, leaving her shaking inside. "Your love for her is depthless, isn't it?"

"Do you think everyone is going to experience them like that?" she asked with mounting horror. "Because that makes me feel naked. I don't think I can bear it."

He made a noise of pity. "Come here, then. Let me show you that being naked has its advantages."

And if the car had cooled in the underground parking lot before they climbed out, and she couldn't meet the eyes of the driver smoking a discreet distance away, such was the consequence of being the wife of an incorrigible rake like Val Casale.

CHAPTER SEVEN

VAL WAS IN TROUBLE. He had known it when he had
left Kiara to paint that night. He had known it when
the compulsion to put her sketch back on the wall had
forced him from the comfortable bed and the press of
her warm body to his. He had known it when sliding
his ring onto her finger had made something click inside his chest that locked them together and felt *good*.

He had known it when he had wandered the gallery
earlier and was so awed and moved, he had ceased to
care how she had made it happen; he'd simply been
overwhelmed with pride and admiration that she'd done
it.

And he knew it when a floral arrangement arrived
at their penthouse suite.

He was nursing a drink, waiting for Kiara to finish
dressing, when the courier arrived. He handed Val the
certificate of authenticity and left the packing box for
the vase as he departed.

The hourglass vase was handblown by a Venetian
artist, Val learned from the certificate. The mosaic of
gold that spiraled in a ribbon from lip to base had been
painstakingly applied to the scorching glass through an
ancient technique mastered by few in this modern age.

The fragrant flowers, arranged to resemble fireworks, had been chosen to symbolize luck and success.

Val had not ordered these flowers. He had given his wife a ridiculously expensive diamond necklace with matching earrings to celebrate her achievement.

This had better be from her agent, he decided, as a green haze fogged his vision and curdled his gut. If it came from any other man, he would start by knocking over the vase, then hunt down the interloper and do the same to him.

Was he *jealous*? Jealousy was a symptom of insecurity. He knew that because he'd had a front row seat to that emotion his entire life.

Uncomfortable with that insight, he flipped the card and ran his finger beneath the flap to unseal it, completely disregarding the fact it was addressed to Kiara. It was written in flowing calligraphy, likely by the florist, but the message was personal.

K.
Is break a leg *appropriate in this circumstance?*
I am so sorry to miss your big night. I know you'll knock 'em dead.
Enjoy every second and call me soon to tell me all about it.
I miss you!
Love
Scarlett, Javiero and Locke

The clip of a woman's heel sounded on the parquet floor.

He glanced up and felt the whoosh of a train headed straight toward him.

She wore patent leather boots that went up to her *thighs*. Her bronze coatdress was tailored satin and ended a few inches above the boots. Her hair had been pulled flat to her scalp then the tight curls arranged on the top of her head to resemble an offset beret. Her earrings dangled brightly while her necklace was a subtle glint from her turned-up collar.

She started to roll her lips together uncertainly but seemed to remember at the last second that they were outlined in metallic gold. She swept ridiculously long eyelashes down, revealing the shimmering shades on her lids.

"Is it too much?"

"It is exactly enough of too much," he assured her. "I'm not going to survive the drive to the gallery, let alone the rest of the night." He held out his hand, wanting her to come to him. Wanting her close even though he couldn't touch. "You're a vision."

She came across and ran light fingers down the lapel of his tuxedo. "I thought we were going to my art show, not spying on the Russians in a film noir."

"Well, there are things you don't know about me, aren't there?"

Her smile of amusement was a burst of sunshine in his chest.

He was in so much trouble.

"Are those for me? Val," she scolded, leaning to inhale the blossoms.

"They're not from me." He picked up the card and handed it to her. "Scarlett and company."

"Oh." Her smile turned poignant as she read.

"Have you been talking with her?" He hated the talons of threat that dug into him, forcing the question from him.

"Not much," she murmured with a small, brooding frown. "A few texts, mostly about diaper rash and other baby questions. It's an overwhelming time for her. I wish I could be there more." She set aside the card and lifted a troubled gaze to him. "I wish I understood why you and Javiero are still so completely at odds."

"He knows what he did," Val said flatly, only hearing how his dismissive words had come down like an ax when Kiara flinched.

"I didn't mean to pry," she murmured, gaze bruised.

And that, too, pulled apart things inside him.

"Kiara." He held her before him, the most bizarre impulse to tell her rising in him.

No. That part of his life had been kicked into the farthest corner of a vault, the thick door slammed and welded shut. He had spoken once about it and got nothing for his trouble. He had sworn he would never speak of it again.

And yet the fingers of that darkness were somehow leaking out of the cracks in his vault, willing to be aired out and seen even as the shame that accompanied that bleak memory arose as sharp and painful and throat-locking as it had been twenty years ago.

"Another time we'll talk about him," he lied with an apologetic caress against her jaw. "Tonight is yours. I refuse to spoil it with my messy family history."

A pulse of silence as she absorbed that, then her lashes came up again. The worst of the shadows were replaced with a teasing light.

"A fine aspiration when your mother has threatened to make an appearance."

In support, she had assured him, although Val knew it was also an attempt to catch a glimmer of Kiara's spotlight. Even so, the tightness in his chest eased as the tense moment between them passed.

"I will make that up to you, I swear."

The culmination of what felt like her life's work passed in a blur.

Val's celebrity and his mother's influence had magnified attention onto the event, turning it into a full-out media circus. Kiara walked a red carpet into the gallery, camera bulbs flashing like fireworks around her. Inside, she was introduced to rock stars and countesses and gallery curators from around the world.

Her agent and the gallery owner were beside themselves, glowing under their own brilliance in "discovering" her. The success of the night was a fait accompli.

Lest she be too humble, however, and attribute her success to Niko's patronage and Val and Evelina's notoriety, and the gallery's name, and her agent's ruthless drive, an art critic known to be scathing caught her alone and gave her the best compliment of the night.

"I was convinced this was a stunt," he said in a bored, nasal tone. "Your husband is hardly above using his influence, and neither is his mother. But you're actually good. I'm buying the seascape tryptic. I don't buy art unless I believe it will appreciate. I certainly don't display it in my home unless I genuinely love it, and yours will take pride of place in my den, where I will see it every day."

"Thank you," she murmured, stunned and moved beyond words.

He was pulled away and she stood there a moment surrounded by the din of voices all talking about her, not to her. Feting her accomplishment without truly understanding what it meant to her.

In that second, all of this felt like a tremendously hollow victory. She had never felt more alone in her life and didn't understand why. She had done this. It had been her dream and here she was, living it. She ought to be euphoric.

Across the room, she caught Val's gaze on her. As they held the eye contact, he lifted his glass in a silent toast and she realized she wasn't alone. Her heart soared as she absorbed that he was here with her. Proud and genuinely happy for her.

She loved him for that.

Loved him.

Oh, dear. All of her realigned as the knowledge rippled through her. She loved him. Loved him, loved him, loved him.

That was good, wasn't it? He was her husband. The father of her child. He was enamored with their daughter and had become so very protective and generous toward her. They were making a life together.

But he didn't love her.

And all of a sudden, she was alone again.

She woke to rave reviews and the news from her agent that her show had sold out and there was a clamor for more.

Val congratulated her by pleasuring her past mindless into a soaring climax that shattered her into a million pieces.

"Your sensuality is a glorious thing to behold, *bella*,"

he said huskily as he covered her and thrust into the flesh still singing with joy. "Is it because you're an artist? Or are you an artist because you live life with your whole body?"

"I can't talk when we're like this," she moaned, lost, utterly lost to the slow power of his body moving upon hers. Within her. Her own body responded to ancient signals and matched his rhythm, hips lifting to greet his. The buildup was steady and incredible, doubling and redoubling until she didn't know how she could withstand the tension, but she still wanted more and more and more.

This, she thought as they achieved utter synchronicity. It might not be love, but it was art.

In a swooping move, he hooked one strong arm behind her knee, and everything changed. The angle, the depth, the way his impact struck her nerve endings.

She cried out at the acute slam of pleasure that went through her and opened her eyes to the blinding gleam in his. The show of his clenched teeth.

His knowledge that she was *there* with him. His shoulders tensed and he thrust harder, coming with her as she fell off the cliff and discovered she could fly.

Over the next few weeks Val began to realize the hidden truth in that senseless expression "wedded bliss." He rather expected it was ignorance of the future, but he had to admit such blind contentment was enjoyable while it lasted.

When they were home, he and Kiara had fallen into a comfortable routine whereby he worked from the villa as often as he drove into Milan, and she disappeared into the guest cottage for a few hours every day to paint.

When they traveled, they booked an extra day or two purely for family fun, spoiling Aurelia silly with days at the beach or amusement parks or other local attractions.

He was turning into that most tedious of animals, the domesticated married man. And despite eschewing all things conventional for most of his life, he was ridiculously smug in his role of husband and father.

"Slow down," he teased Kiara when they were eating breakfast the morning after a week in New York. "It will still be there in ten minutes."

Her baleful look made him chuckle.

"I think it's safe to assume your mother will not be joining us for lunch," he said to Aurelia.

"Why?" Aurelia stuffed a bite of crepe over her new favorite word.

"Because her studio is ready and she's excited to work in it. Shall we walk down with her to see it?"

Aurelia nodded and a few minutes later, they ambled through the dewy grass, Val particularly enjoying the way Kiara gasped and halted in her tracks when she saw his surprise.

"You are shameless," she declared of the small replica of her studio that had been placed a suitable distance from her own, far enough that a child's playful cries wouldn't be too distracting, but close enough she could see her daughter from her studio window.

Crouching, she pointed it out to Aurelia. "What is that? Who do you think that is for?"

"Me?" Aurelia took off in her wobbly gallop before she heard the answer.

"I always wanted a playhouse as a girl," Kiara said, looping her arm around his waist as they followed her. "Thank you for being such an indulgent father."

"Thank you for giving me someone to indulge." He kissed the tip of her nose, not sure if he meant his daughter or his wife.

So housebroken and not the least bit regretful, he acknowledged with bemusement.

Of course, his daughter was determined to humble him. She popped out of the little house with a crestfallen expression.

"Where's *my* paint?"

"Wow." Val nodded as he absorbed his own failing. "How did I not see that coming?"

"At least you're leaving room for *me* to be the hero sometimes," Kiara said with a teasing pinch of his side. "I'll order you some, lovey. Special paint for children. What else do you need?"

Kiara started to poke her head in and Aurelia stopped her with grave importance, holding up her palm. "You have to ask."

"Oh. Of course. May I come in?"

"Yes."

"Wonder where she got that from?" Val asked under his breath.

Kiara shot him a doleful look, but they cracked up as she disappeared into the house.

It was the most genuinely carefree moment he'd ever experienced. He wasn't forcing himself not to care, he merely felt all the heavier, darker cares fall away. They weren't important when he had this.

He would give these two females the blood and bones and breath from his body, he realized. There was nothing he could ever deny them.

Which was why he experienced such a schism of sheer agony when Kiara told him she wanted to leave him.

* * *

Kiara knew it was a big ask. More than that, it was a plea for trust. It was a test of this nascent, fragile, beautiful bond that was beginning to form between them.

"Javiero won't be there, just Scarlett and Locke. I'm not sure what's going on between them, but I'm worried about her. Being a new mother is hard and she was there for me—"

She cut herself off as he glanced at her, the dark admonishment still there that she hadn't leaned on *him* when she'd had Aurelia.

They had come a long way and most of her time with Niko was water under the bridge, but Val wouldn't listen to her complain about any struggles she'd had then when she hadn't even tried to reach out to him.

She swallowed. Tried a different tack. "I want to finish packing up my old studio." Hopefully, he would hear that as the permanent shift from her time with Niko to her life here with him that it was.

"You're not taking Aurelia."

She clenched her hands together. "Scarlett is the only auntie she has, Val. I know that doesn't sit well, but I didn't know Scarlett had an intimate relationship with Javiero until she told me she was pregnant, and he was the father."

"And if she keeps that sort of secret from her supposed best friend..." He didn't finish, just left it hanging as a denunciation of Scarlett's character.

"You and I are not the only two people in this world who have painful things in our past," she said in a slightly sharper tone. "I haven't forced you to tell me about yours. Don't judge Scarlett for keeping her own pain to herself."

"What does that mean?" Val's head snapped around. "What did Javiero do to her?"

"Nothing. I mean..." She sighed. "Look, she didn't tell me much about their relationship and I don't like betraying what she did confide, but I guess she saw him occasionally, the same way she turned up to badger you on Niko's behalf. You didn't ever sleep with her, did you?" she blurted with low horror as it occurred to her.

He glared. "That's beneath you."

It was an ironic remark from a man who had prided himself on acting inappropriately, but his mouth twisted as he admitted, "I flirted in the early days, more to test her loyalty than anything. The fact she stuck by Dad so unwaveringly made her less and less attractive to me as time wore on."

"Yes, well, I gather that was the bone of contention between her and your brother. Javiero expected her to leave Niko for him and she refused."

The curl of disgust at the corner of his lips deepened. "Poor Javiero."

"I'm worried about how things have been going between them, Val."

They don't have what you and I do, she wanted to add, but she wasn't sure what they had. She was terrified of making a false move that would somehow damage his regard. "Javiero isn't there. She said they needed a break and I get the feeling he's like you and hates the island."

"Never again assume that he and I are alike in any way," he warned dangerously.

"Fine, but you and he still have a relationship that goes beyond hating one another!" She shot to her feet in agitation. "Javiero is Aurelia's blood relative. Do you realize that? And *you* have a nephew. Locke is your daughter's cousin and I will risk your wrath to give our children a better relationship than you have with your *equally pigheaded* half brother."

"Pigheaded? The man lacks a basic moral compass," he snarled. "He had a chance to do the right thing and he *didn't*."

She halted and let her own ruffled feathers settle to make room for the barbed bristles shooting off him.

"Val, what happened?" she asked with pent-up anguish.

His face filled with the bleak rage she'd seen the day of the will reading, when they had dined on the rooftop in Athens before going to the hospital.

"It doesn't matter," he muttered, surging to his feet. "Go then. Before I change my mind. Be back within the week or I'm coming to get you. And he had better not come anywhere near either of you."

Scarlett burst into tears when Kiara arrived and so did Kiara. When Kiara held sweet-smelling Locke, her ovaries throbbed with longing. Maybe, she thought yearningly, but Val wasn't ready to talk about more children. He was barely talking to her at all.

She and Scarlett didn't have that problem. At first, they couldn't talk fast enough. Scarlett wanted a blow-by-blow on how the gallery showing had gone and where Kiara's career was taking her. She spared no details about her labor and Locke's colicky start and how little sleep she was getting.

But slowly, slowly, as the children were put to bed and they shared a bottle of Niko's best vintage, Scarlett began to cry.

And cry.

She cried so hard Kiara feared she wouldn't stop.

"I think she's suffering postpartum," Kiara told Val over a hushed video chat from her studio a few days later. "I'm trying to convince her to see a doctor and helping with Locke as much as she'll let me, but she's so stubborn, convinced she has to do everything herself. She's pushing herself way too hard."

"How much longer are you staying?"

"I'm not sure," she said apologetically, moving quickly as she spoke, boxing up items without her usual care. "I'm only coming in here when everyone is napping, trying to spend as much time with Scarlett as possible. It sounds like things have been a struggle with Javiero's family. A few more days at least."

He didn't bother hiding his scowl of dismay.

A knock at the door had her glancing up to see a maid waving toward the landline extension on the wall.

"*Señor* Rodriguez is asking for you," the maid said.

"You said he wasn't there!" Val snapped.

"He isn't! He's on the phone," she hurried to clarify, but had to text him a few minutes later or risk his thinking she was hiding things from him.

Javiero is coming by boat in the morning. He won't stay on the island but insists on seeing Scarlett.

She paused, loath to say it, but she had to.

I can't leave her to face him alone.

Val didn't respond.

* * *

"That's him," Scarlett said in an ominous, hollow tone the next morning while they ate their breakfast on the terrace.

A yacht had appeared on the horizon and it was headed straight toward them. Kiara had the sense of panic ancient people must have felt when the enemy ship appeared and there was nowhere to run. They could only wait, hearts in their throats, for feet to reach land.

When Kiara had spoken to Javiero yesterday, she had discovered he and Val had both inherited Niko's streak of unstoppable single-mindedness. He was coming whether Scarlett was ready to see him or not, bringing his own accommodation so he could wait her out if necessary.

"If you don't want to see him, you don't have to," Kiara reminded her, even though she had no serious means of stopping him if he wanted to push past her.

Scarlett seemed to realize that. She made a noise of hysterical amusement and brought Locke to her shoulder, yanking her robe closed as she did.

"I'll burp him. You can shower and put your best face on." Or go back to bed, Kiara wanted to urge, frowning with concern at Scarlett's bruised eyes and translucent skin.

Scarlett hadn't slept last night, worried about this coming confrontation. She wasn't likely to rest now, however, since Javiero was almost here.

"I can do it," Scarlett insisted absently.

"I want to hold him while I have the chance," Kiara said truthfully, but she also knew a gentle guilt trip was about the only way she could persuade Scarlett to give herself a break.

Scarlett was refusing to let the nannies do more than restock the diapers and fold laundry, terrified she wasn't bonding with her son properly. Kiara had a feeling it was Scarlett who was struggling with her feelings, not the contented baby who settled every time he was in his mother's arms.

Scarlett was in a bad way, convinced she was merely tired and upset about an argument she'd had with Paloma. Kiara suspected there was more to it and doubted Javiero would be anything but added stress. She intended to take Scarlett to see her old doctor while they were here.

"I'll put him down if he falls asleep," Kiara promised, holding out her hands.

"Thank you," Scarlett murmured with defeat, handing across the infant and drifting into the house after a last conflicted look at the approaching boat.

Kiara had just finished settling the dozing infant and agreed with the nanny that yes, Aurelia could watch her show for a few minutes, when she heard the unmistakable *rat-a-tat* of an approaching helicopter.

The world stopped. She knew instinctively who it was. Her pulse began to throb in time to the rotors. Both excitement and anticipation of disaster whirled within her.

She hurried to the terrace. The yacht had come as close as it dared. A smaller boat had been launched and was headed to the private pier.

She turned and shaded her eyes. The helicopter was closing in.

It was a slow-motion collision that she couldn't watch. She ran inside to warn Scarlett.

Seconds later Kiara was changing from her yoga

pants and T-shirt into a decent dress when the muffled sound of the landing helicopter rumbled the stone walls of the villa. She hurried to the stairs and exchanged an apprehensive look with Scarlett as they trotted down and out to the terrace.

As they emerged, a sound like snarling wolves filled the air.

"Oh, my God," Kiara murmured as she saw the men.

They had met on the lawn between the stairs to the beach and the path around the house. They were both puffed up, locked in a clash of wills, ready to come to blows.

"Val," Kiara shouted and hurried down the steps toward them.

"Get Aurelia. We're leaving," Val bit out, holding his half brother's gaze in the way she'd seen him do at the hospital. They were practically nose to nose, teeth bared by their curled lips. "If Scarlett can't survive without you, she can come with us."

"Don't even think—" Javiero started to lunge.

Kiara threw herself between them.

"Stop!" she cried, arms out to hold them apart even as Val gripped her by the shoulders and tried to move her aside. "For the sake of your babies, stop acting like children. Bury the hatchet," she insisted.

"Let me just turn around so you can get it in beside your *knife*," Javiero sneered, thumbing over his shoulder.

"Me? I stabbed *you* in the back?" Val asked with outraged astonishment.

"You know you did."

"When?"

"Don't play dumb, Val. She's right about one thing." Javiero stabbed a finger toward Kiara. "We're far too

old for this." Javiero looked old. Tired. Haggard and defeated as he let his attention flicker to the terrace where
Scarlett stood frozen and pale.

"I'm serious," Val muttered. "What the hell did I ever
do to you to deserve what you did to me?"

"I've never done a damned thing to you," Javiero
roared, turning back on him with aggression that sought
a target that wasn't a fragile woman who'd given birth
two short months ago.

"You've never done anything *for* me, either. Have
you?" Val charged, the disillusionment in his face stopping Kiara's heart.

Her hand instinctively tried to soothe by moving
against his chest, but he brushed her hand away.

Javiero faltered. His mouth tightened. "You're blaming me for the bullies at school? I was a child, Val. I
didn't ask for anyone to behave that way and I told them
to stop. They weren't my friends. I didn't pile in. The
administration should have taken steps. You didn't need
to cut my entire family loose over it."

"I cut *myself* loose," Val said with a knock of his fist
into the middle of his own chest. "I told you to take all
of this." He flung out his hand to encompass the island.
"Don't put it on me that you refused it."

"Nice fairy tale you've told yourself. Dad wasn't
about to leave his fortune to the weaker son who *wasn't*
capable of supporting himself. How the hell was I supposed to do that at *thirteen*?" Javiero scoffed. "My family sat on the brink of ruin for a *decade* because of your
precious need to stick it to everyone around you. So
screw you very much for that. Now, get the hell out of
my way because I want to see my son."

"Don't you pin that on me. If you had backed me

up when you had the chance, I might have made other choices, but you didn't. I had every right to walk away. I *had* to," Val bit out in a graveled, bitter tone. "You know I did."

"How the hell was I supposed to—" Javiero's enraged face blanked.

The air changed and Val's emanation of fury seemed to flip on itself, turning into a shield of wariness. All his defenses had come down like a wall, one that slammed his expression blank. One that pushed both of them to some perimeter where they couldn't touch him.

She looked to Javiero for a clue. He had gone ghostly gray beneath his naturally swarthy skin. The fading pink scratches on his face stood out as bright and angry as they'd been the day Kiara had seen him at the hospital.

"That was real?" Javiero asked in a rasp.

If Kiara hadn't been tunneling her way around the door to his vault all these weeks, it wouldn't have snapped open the way it had. Suddenly, there was Javiero, his worst enemy, staring in shock at Val's deepest shame.

Somehow, when Val had believed that Javiero knew the truth all along, and had preferred to beat him with it, he had been able to bear it far more easily than seeing horror and something like compunction dawn on his half brother's face.

The naked boy in him shrank but had nowhere to hide. And when Kiara touched him and said, "Val?" she might as well have branded him. Amputated his arm. Torn him asunder.

Anger at being disbelieved had always been his sword. Without that bitter resentment to deflect the world, he had to snatch up other excuses to lash out, otherwise shame would settle on him and smother him to death.

"You said he wouldn't be here," he said, rounding on Kiara. "If you're not in the helicopter by the time I get there, you're not coming."

"Val!" She trotted after him as he strode away. "Talk to me. Tell me what's going on."

"I don't have to tell you anything. Do you understand that?"

She backed up a step, her fear of him so tangible he tasted its coppery flavor on his tongue.

He hated himself then. Hated the poison in him that festered to this day. Hated what he was and that he hadn't been able to stop turning into this.

"You've made your choice, Kiara," he said with a chuck of his chin toward the villa and Javiero and Niko's haunting presence.

"That's not true," she said, hand coming up, but she stopped short of trying to touch him again. "I choose you, Val. Always. I love you."

He couldn't bear to look at her then. She couldn't love him. *Couldn't*. Not if she knew.

"Love is a lie, Kiara. It's something people say to get what they want. My lawyers will be in touch about visitation."

He walked away.

CHAPTER EIGHT

KIARA WAS GUTTED. *Lawyers?*

Her love wasn't a lie. It was as vast as the horizon. As wide as the sky Val rose into the air seconds later, while she stood there paralyzed by agony, emotions filleted by the punishing blades of the helicopter.

Her love wasn't something he wanted, though. *She* wasn't, either.

A scuff behind her had her flinging around. Javiero was starting toward the terrace and Scarlett was disappearing into the house.

"Javiero," Kiara said through a raw throat. "You have to tell me."

He paused and cast her a glance of angry distraction. She saw the struggle in him as he wanted to follow Scarlett, but at the last second he relented. He ran his hand down his face.

"I don't even know what to make of it." He looked to where the helicopter had become a speck in the sky.

"Of what? I love him. He's hurting. He's been hurting for *decades*. What *happened*?"

He flinched and the weight of guilt seemed to slump his shoulders.

"There was a teacher. A woman. Yes," he said as her

eyes widened. "You have to remember how Val looked at thirteen. The image he projected. That's not blame," he hurried to add, lifting a hand to keep her from interrupting. "I'm just trying to explain how a woman three times his age might have seen a young man, not a boy. Not that it excuses her behavior."

Kiara covered her mouth and shook her head, certain she didn't want to hear the rest, but for Val's sake she had to.

"I don't know much, only rumors. I thought—" Remorse dug deeper lines into his disfigured face. "As a man, I can see how wrong it was. If the roles had been reversed, there would be no question that a man chasing a young girl was utterly disgusting. Deeply unequal. At the time, given our age, our history… I'm ashamed to say I thought that his getting with a teacher sounded like something he would do. He was always very confident, Kiara. I didn't become this obdurate by being pitted against a pushover. Until a minute ago, it didn't fit in my head that something like that would be anything but his choice."

"Well, you were wrong," she said with subdued outrage, heart aching for Val. "Is that what you told Niko? Is that why Val thinks you didn't back him up when he needed you to?"

Javiero made a helpless gesture with his hand.

"Dad asked me whether anything was going on between them. I told him the truth, that I hadn't seen anything, only heard other boys tease him because she flirted openly with him in class."

"What did Niko do? Anything?" she asked desperately.

Javiero drew a deep, pained breath. "He said, 'Well,

I guess your brother is a man now. When will *you* become one?'"

She rocked on her feet. Why did that surprise her after all she'd heard about the old man?

"That's disgusting," she choked. "You're saying he believed it happened, he just didn't believe it was wrong? Did he try to put a stop to it?"

"She continued to teach after Val had been expelled so I don't imagine he said a word to anyone about it."

I had every right to walk away.

"I have to go home," she said, mind skipping over the things she still needed to pack, but all she really needed was to collect their daughter and hurry to Val's side.

No wonder he had struggled to forgive her for relying on his father. She could barely stand herself right now.

Her heart skidded into the dirt as she recalled why she was here, though.

"Javiero, we need to talk about Scarlett."

He paused with one foot on the steps to the terrace and cast her another impatient look.

"She doesn't want to get married, I know," he said through his teeth. "But they're coming home with me."

"It's not about that. She needs a doctor."

Val had no one left to hate. No one left to punish.

Even his mother failed him in his time of need. She called while he was pretending to work in London, where he had told his PA not to disturb him so he could glower broodingly at the pouring rain beyond his skyscraper window.

Evelina, being Evelina, talked the young woman into risking her job and putting the call through.

He wouldn't have picked up, he realized as he heard her voice, but he had expected a different one. Had *wanted* to hear a different one. He longed for Kiara's lilting intonation, even if she was calling to tell him their marriage was over.

"Your wife is wondering where you are," Evelina stated.

"Then give her this number."

"She seems a soft touch where you're concerned. I'm better versed in handling you when you're in one of your moods."

"Mmm, no one could accuse you of possessing an ounce of tenderness, could they?"

"Take your shots, Val. You always will, but are you really going to throw away a marriage that has every chance of long-term success?"

He snorted. "Hang on to Dad's money is what you're saying. And don't kick her out because she'll kick you out."

"I'm saying she's a surprisingly laudable addition to our family. Who knew she possessed such talent?"

"I did. I knew," he couldn't help asserting.

"And she's not forever seeking the front page with a fresh part in her hair the way what's-her-name was given to doing." Read: Kiara posed little threat to Evelina's ability to garner attention.

"What do you want, Mother?" he asked wearily.

"I want you to go home to your wife, of course."

He wanted that, too. It was an ache he couldn't seem to quash, but he didn't know how to face her.

"She's not home. She's on the island."

"She's at your villa," she informed as if he ought to

know that. "Has been for days, awaiting your return like a stalwart shepherd."

"Do *not* refer to her like that again or I will cut you off completely."

"I only meant she is blind to your faults and far more patient with your petty behavior than you deserve."

His chest was tightening as he thought of her in their bed. Something that might have been homesickness washed over him.

"Val, it's time we put the past behind us," Evelina said firmly.

"Ha!" he barked out. "You really just said that? To *me*?"

"You know damned well why I had to fight so hard for everything I have," she said sharply. "What I cannot understand is why you fight so hard to throw *away* all that you have."

You know why, he wanted to shout. But they'd had that conversation once and he hadn't liked her response. It had made him feel all the more powerless and sickened by life.

"Goodbye, Mother."

"Go to her," she insisted.

He hung up, the words *I'll do what I want* unspoken.

Because what he wanted was to follow his mother's directive. He swore at the ceiling, hating that his good, reliable, self-destructive tendencies were no longer as easy to fall back on. There had been a time when going in the opposite direction of wherever he was being sent had been the most satisfying of actions.

It was no longer that simple. No, if he really wanted to burn down his marriage, then he would have to go back to Kiara and do it properly. Show her his soul and let her kick it to the curb once and for all.

* * *

Kiara finally understood why she'd never been able to paint Val. She hadn't known exactly how she felt about him.

She did now. She loved him. So much it engulfed her like a spell, compelling her to make him appear on her canvas. She took days to get her sketches right, working from the Venice ones and a handful of photos on her phone and her myriad store of memories, built over the two months they'd been married.

When she came to render him in oils, she considered the affectionate expression he wore when he gazed at their daughter and the killer seductive gaze he often leveled at her. That one that curled her toes every time and she adored it. She even played with the cynical curve of his mouth when his mood was light and the glower he wore when the world and the people around him failed him in some way.

Ultimately, she settled on a very familiar, austere three-quarter profile. This was the man she knew best. The one who kept his thoughts and feelings well hidden behind his mask of undeniable, classic male beauty.

She knew what that mask hid, though, and those deep hurts made her take great care with her brush strokes, as if she could somehow heal his aches and disappointments and betrayals with each caress of sable to his smooth skin.

"Papà!"

Kiara's heart leaped out of her chest and she almost bobbled her brush into her canvas. She hurried to the door of her studio in time to see Val bend and scoop their daughter off her feet as she ran toward him.

The nanny hovered awkwardly, but Kiara held up a

hand to signal she should stay. She wanted her to take their daughter so she and Val could talk. She would give them time for their reunion first, though.

"I mitt you!" Aurelia told him in a scold, pulling her arms from around his neck and taking his unshaven cheeks into her tiny starfished hands.

"I missed you, too," he said, voice not quite steady as his gaze ate up her little face.

She tilted her head and lifted an imploring shoulder to ask sweetly, "Can we swim? *Per favore*?" She used Italian, the minx, because she had learned that nearly always got her what she wanted out of him.

"Later," he promised with a rueful smile and pecked a kiss onto her button nose. "After your lunch and nap *if* you do both without a fuss." He tucked his chin so his gaze was level with hers. "Deal?"

Aurelia copied his very serious chin tuck, stating firmly, "Deal."

"*Grazie*. Now please go with Nanny. I need to speak with Mummy."

She gave his neck another squeeze, then let him set her on her feet and skipped up to the villa.

When Kiara dragged her eyes off their daughter, she clashed into Val's unreadable gaze. It knocked the breath out of her to see shades of that same greedy hunger he'd exhibited with Aurelia, as though he had been starving for the sight of her as well as his daughter.

"She's been asking for you," she said, not knowing what else to say.

"I got those texts. I thought we agreed we wouldn't use her as emotional blackmail against each other."

She bit her lip, guilty as charged, but, "It was true."

She realized she was still holding her brush and

moved into her studio to drop it into the jar of solvent next to her easel. Her hand was shaking.

He followed her in, uninvited, as was his habit. And, much as she hated for anyone to see her work in process, she had come to trust that his circumspect study of her unfinished work would never be critical or hurtful.

Today was different, though. This portrait was different. *They* were different.

He swore as he saw his own image. Swore and ran his hand down his face and sounded both defeated and... moved? "You've been busy."

He backed up to the sofa he'd had brought in there "so we have a comfortable place to make love." She'd told him he was dreaming, then had blinds installed in her wall of windows.

"What am I supposed to think of that?" he asked in a graveled voice as he continued to stare at his portrait. He braced his elbows on his thighs, fingers clawed into his hair.

She looked at it, thinking it was some of her best work, even though it laid her heart so bare. She had essentially rolled it out onto the floor for him to walk across.

"I missed you and wanted to see you. I—"

"You love me. Yes, I can see that, Kiara."

His harsh words went straight into her chest like an arrow.

"The things you feel are always right there, on every single canvas." He pointed his flat hand at his image in a type of accusation. "I see it and hear it and feel it, but there's no way you can love me. Not that much. Not—" He cut himself off, seeming utterly vanquished as he threw his head into his hands again, tortured by whatever was gripping him.

"I do, Val," she swore gently as she moved to sit beside him. "I love you so much it feels like a bruise inside me, throbbing all the time. And it's okay if you don't feel the same."

Her artist's eye studied him as he looked again at himself and she smiled a little at how perfectly she'd captured that particular mask he wore as he tried to suppress all that was going on inside him.

"I mean, I hope you feel something," she whispered. "But—"

"Kiara," he chided, looking at her now with such agony in his gaze her swollen heart felt pinched in a vise.

She wanted to take his hands, but wasn't sure if he would welcome it, not when they had to go into painful places inside him. Places he had spent a lifetime navigating alone.

She swallowed and spoke tentatively. "I can imagine why love feels like a lie to you when people who were supposed to love you let you down. More than once. I didn't mean to."

"Javiero told you." He closed his eyes, shutting her out.

"Only what he knew, which wasn't much." She didn't want to defend Javiero, but nor did she want to stoke Val's animosity toward him. "He did tell Niko there were rumors, but that was all he knew, Val. I'm so sorry that happened to you. That Niko didn't do anything to stop it. It was wrong and it wasn't your fault."

"Wasn't it? I didn't exactly fight her off." He pushed the heels of his hands into his eye sockets. His sigh was jagged and heavy. Tormented. "I was selling sex to the cameras. I knew I was. Everything around me told me I was supposed to want what she was offering. So I went along with it and felt *sick*."

"You were too young and inexperienced to know how you were supposed to act or feel. That's not your fault. She was the adult, Val. It was her responsibility to see that acting that way was wrong and not do it. *Niko* should have seen that. He should have had her fired. Arrested."

Val made a choking noise and dropped his hands to let them dangle loosely between his knees. "Dad thought I was a damned hero for losing my virginity so young. He was proud."

He wasn't looking at her. His cheeks were stained with disgrace.

"Niko was wrong," she said as firmly as her unsteady voice could manage. "I don't blame you for hating him, Val. Parents are supposed to keep their children safe, not send them to predators." She frowned, prying very gently. "Did your mother know?"

Despair filled his gaze and the noise he made was utterly defeated. "She said, 'How do you think I got where I am? That's how the game is played.'"

"Oh, my God."

"Exactly." He turned his head to look at her with concern. "Have you ever…?"

"I've had my share of difficult experiences. Nothing violent, just the wrong sort of attention. Catcalls." Landlords and employers who said inappropriate things. Teachers who commented on her developing body. *The usual*, she wanted to call it, but sighed instead.

"That's why I support her," Val said broodingly. "Financially. That's why she's still part of my life even though she makes me crazy. I'm fairly certain what I went through was nothing compared to what she faced at different times in her life. There was a stepfather she refuses to talk about, and she moved to Paris alone at fifteen. If she's self-serving and incapable of genuine connection or anything that resembles empathy, I'm sure she has her reasons."

"That's sad," Kiara murmured.

"She pointed out something to me, though." He rubbed his thighs. "While she was busy trying to save my marriage so you wouldn't yank the money you're giving her. That was a dirty move, by the way. Siccing her on me like that. It's the sort of merciless attack I would use to get what I want."

"I was genuinely worried about you." *And* inclined to believe that Evelina would be strongly motivated to interfere in the best possible way. "What did she say?"

"She drew my attention to the fact she had fought long and hard to climb out of being victimized. She has never said it in so many words, but I've had time to realize how badly Dad took advantage of her, exactly like damned near every man she'd ever encountered. She was in her late twenties, worried her career would begin to fade, when Dad said he was breaking things off to marry Paloma. She did the only thing she thought she could to finally have some power and agency. I don't agree with it, but I see why she did it. Then here I was, born into power and money. Influence. And because I felt victimized, I spent years trying to break away from it. That doesn't make sense."

"You were angry. Understandably."

"But I had convinced myself I didn't feel anything.

And that's the thing about emotions. You can't pick and choose what to feel. It's all or nothing. You have to take the bad with the good and when the bad is really bad?"

She nodded, heart sinking. "I understand. You need to protect yourself."

"I want to. But when something feels really good, it's hard to resist letting it happen." He sighed and looked to the ceiling but opened his palm to her. "The way I feel about you… There aren't enough words, Kiara. I wish I could paint. I wish you could see what I see when I look at you. When I touch you."

Oh. She set her hand in his and his warm grip closed over her fingers, injecting a sensation of pure joy up her arm and into her heart.

"It's not fair for me to say that love is a lie. I said that because I had never experienced it so I thought it didn't exist. Then Aurelia—"

His eyes were damp as he met hers, and her own suffered a fresh sting of tears. They exchanged a knowing smile, both so powerfully smitten with their girl that only the other could possibly understand the intensity of love she inspired.

"She's pretty amazing, isn't she?" Kiara choked.

"She is pure magic. And I have to give you credit for that because her brand of pureness did not come from me."

"Please don't talk about yourself like that."

"I've still been a bastard in many ways," he said, bringing her hand to his lips.

"And I still love you. Exactly as you are. So much."

"And I love you, Kiara. I love that you take your own pain and turn it into something beautiful. I love that fighting back is your last resort, not your first, but you'll do it when you have to. I love that you rock my world when we're in bed."

"You rock mine," she countered wryly.

"That's what does it for me," he said throatily, but sobered as he added gravely, "I love that you make our lovemaking feel right. That's precious to me. *You* are precious to me."

Oh. She sniffled, only becoming aware that her eyes were leaking when the tickling sensation brought her hand up to brush her emotive tears from her cheeks. She could hardly bear the pressure in her chest and throat, but she exulted in it at the same time.

"I don't believe in fate, but I do believe you are the only woman who could have brought me out of the darkness like this. I want to be the better man who deserves you. I love you with everything in me and I'm going to stop fighting it. I'm going to embrace what we have."

"I just want you to embrace me—oh!"

He grabbed her onto his lap and tumbled her down into the sofa cushions at the same time, kissing her surprised mouth with his smile.

"I am going to embrace the hell out of you. We have an entire week's worth of lovemaking to make up for." He lifted enough to open the buttons on her smock, glancing at the back of his fingers as he picked up a smear of the cerulean blue she'd mixed with titanium white to match his eyes.

"Remember to save some strength for your swim this afternoon," she teased, filtering her fingers through his thick hair.

His eyes, which she'd gotten exactly right with her shade of icy blue, came up to stare with disgruntlement into hers. "Whose dumb idea was it to promise *that*?"

"I don't know. A man who is far more generous and thoughtful than he would want anyone to believe, I think."

"I do have a brand to protect." He rearranged them so he was between her denim-clad thighs.

"Your chewy caramel center will be our little secret," she whispered, tracing the lips that were making her strain with longing beneath him. "But speaking of keeping secrets…" She arched her neck as his mouth dipped to nibble against her throat.

He brought his head up abruptly, face blanked with shock. "Are you pregnant?"

"What? *No.* I was just going to ask you to close the blinds so people don't see what we're doing in here."

"Oh." The way his expression fell had her clasping his shoulders to keep him atop her as he started to push up.

"Wait. Did you *want* me to be pregnant?" she asked with a dip and roll of her heart.

His tongue ran over his teeth behind his closed lips as he considered.

"I think I did." He nodded slowly. "I'm pretty sure I'm disappointed. But let's save that conversation for when we have more time." He dropped a kiss onto her mouth then rose to drop the blinds. "Right now I only have two short hours before I'm due with a toddler in a swimming pool and I want to make the most of it."

And they did.

EPILOGUE

Two years later...

KIARA BLINKED SLEEPY eyes at him and sounded as petulant as their daughter did when she was resisting bedtime.

"I don't want to sleep. I want to look at him."

"I'll look at him for both of us," Val said, cupping her cheek tenderly and dropping a soft kiss on her pouted mouth before he stole their swaddled and sleeping son from her arms. "You need to rest. That was a lot of work you did."

Watching Kiara deliver Rafael had been the most singularly overwhelming experience of his life, and Val had only witnessed his wife pushing their son into this world. She was the one who had labored long and hard to make it happen. He was so proud of her. So proud of their son. So happy he couldn't describe it, only revel in it.

"You're tired, too," she said on a yawn. "Lie with me." She scooted over a little in the narrow hospital bed.

He *was* tired. Apparently, babies didn't always arrive at a civilized dinner hour the way Locke had. Sometimes they woke you at midnight and made their appearance at dawn.

"I'll hold you until you fall asleep," he promised, settling their son in his bassinet in case he dozed off himself. He had every intention of rising, though. That tiny boy was a magnet pulling his cast-iron heart out of his body.

"I should text Scarlett," Kiara murmured as Val settled beside her. She snuggled her head onto his shoulder.

"I'll do it," Val promised, thinking he understood now why Javiero had been such a jackass that day. The only other person Val could stomach entering their tiny bubble of contentment was the daughter who was probably not even awake yet, but who had impatiently been waiting for her little brother or sister to arrive.

"Val?"

"Yes, my love?" He caressed her upper arm.

"I'm really glad you were here this time."

"Me, too." He turned his head to kiss her brow. "You were incredible."

"You, too."

He snorted and picked up her hand to kiss her fingertips. "You give me too much credit, *bella*, but I shall continue to do my best."

She made a little noise of contentment, arm growing heavy on his waist as she drifted into sleep.

Meanwhile, he drew the bassinet a little closer to the bed so he could see the small miracle they had made together.

* * * * *

COMING SOON!

We really hope you enjoyed reading this book.
If you're looking for more romance, be sure to
head to the shops when new books are
available on

Thursday 28th May

To see which titles are coming soon, please visit

millsandboon.co.uk/nextmonth

MILLS & BOON

MILLS & BOON

Coming next month

BEAUTY AND HER ONE-NIGHT BABY
Dani Collins

Scarlett dropped her phone with a clatter.

She had been trying to call Kiara. Now she was taking in the livid claw marks across Javiero's face, each pocked on either side with the pinpricks of recently removed stitches. His dark brown hair was longer than she'd ever seen it, perhaps gelled back from the widow's peak at some point this morning, but it was mussed and held a jagged part. He wore a black eye patch like a pirate, its narrow band cutting a thin stripe across his temple and into his hair.

Maybe that's why his features looked as though they had been set askew? His mouth was...not right. His upper lip was uneven and the claw marks drew lines through his unkempt stubble all the way down into his neck.

That was dangerously close to his jugular! Dear God, he had nearly been killed.

She grasped at the edge of the sink, trying to stay on her feet while she grew so light-headed at the thought of him dying that she feared she would faint.

The ravages of his attack weren't what made him look so forbidding and grim, though, she computed through her haze of panic and anguish. No. The contemptuous glare in his one eye was for her. For *this*.

He flicked another outraged glance at her middle.

"I thought we were meeting in the boardroom." His voice sounded gravelly. Damaged as well? Or was that simply his true feelings toward her now? Deadly and completely devoid of any of the sensual admiration she'd sometimes heard in his tone.

Not that he'd ever been particularly warm toward her. He'd been aloof, indifferent, irritated, impatient, explosively passionate. Generous in the giving of pleasure. Of compliments. Then cold as she left. Disapproving. Malevolent.

Damningly silent.

And now he was…what? Ignoring that she was as big as a barn?

Her arteries were on fire with straight adrenaline, her heart pounding and her brain spinning with the way she was having to switch gears so fast. Her eyes were hot and her throat tight. Everything in her wanted to scream *Help me*, but she'd been in enough tight spots to know this was all on her. Everything was always on her. She fought to keep her head and get through the next few minutes before she moved on to the next challenge.

Which was just a tiny trial called *childbirth*, but she would worry about that when she got to the hospital.

As the tingle of a fresh contraction began to pang in her lower back, she tightened her grip on the edge of the sink and gritted her teeth, trying to ignore the coming pain and hang on to what dregs of dignity she had left.

"I'm in labor," she said tightly. "It's yours."

Continue reading
BEAUTY AND HER ONE-NIGHT BABY
Dani Collins

Available next month
www.millsandboon.co.uk

LET'S TALK
Romance

For exclusive extracts, competitions
and special offers, find us online:

 facebook.com/millsandboon

@MillsandBoon

@MillsandBoonUK

Get in touch on 01413 063232

For all the latest titles coming soon, visit
millsandboon.co.uk/nextmonth